The Undaunted Debutantes Series

THE UNDAUNTED DEBUTANTES

Three innocent debutantes must work to solve the mysterious death of their childhood friend. With undaunted determination they pledge to not only expose the man responsible for their friend's tragic death on her wedding night, but to also uncover other unscrupulous men of the *ton* who would jeopardize the future of other young women.

The Disappearance of Lady Edith
The Misfortune of Lady Lucianna
The Misadventures of Lady Ophelia

PRAISE FOR CHRISTINA MCKNIGHT'S NOVELS

THE THIEF STEALS HER EARL

"When I started reading this book I could not put it down...it caused another book-hangover for me. I wanted to see how things would go when the truth of Judith came out and how Simon was going to handle it...loved it."-*Sissy's Book Review*

"Jude and Cart's story is such a delight! So refreshing to see the hero shy, socially awkward and not super wealthy. I love it...This was definitely one of the best books I've read this summer." -*Reviews from a Thrifty Mom*

FORGOTTEN NO MORE

"This author has made me love historical romance again."
-*TwinsieTalk Book Reviews*

HIDDEN NO MORE

"The storyline was really good, the writing was great. So smooth and engaging, I was able to zip right through the story, it flowed so well. I love finding new to me authors and with this wonderfully written story by Ms. McKnight I've found a new historical romance author."-*Bound by Books*

CHRISTMAS EVER MORE

"*Christmas Ever More* was a wonderfully written festive novella full of hope, renewal, love, and new beginnings. If you're a fan of Christina's Lady Forsaken series, this is a must. Even if you aren't caught up, this stands well enough on its own to be a lovely addition to your holiday reading list."-*Literal Addiction*

BOOKS BY CHRISTINA MCKNIGHT

The Undaunted Debutantes Series
The Disappearance of Lady Edith
The Misfortune of Lady Lucianna
The Misadventures of Lady Ophelia

Lady Archer's Creed Series
Written with Amanda Mariel
Theodora
Georgina
Adeline
Josephine

Craven House Series
The Thief Steals Her Earl
The Mistress Enchants Her Marquis
The Madame Catches Her Duke
The Gambler Wagers Her Baron

A Lady Forsaken Series
Shunned No More
Forgotten No More
Scorned Ever More
Christmas Ever More
Hidden No More

Standalone Titles
The Siege of Lady Aloria, A de Wolfe Pack Novella
A Kiss At Christmastide
For The Love Of A Widow
Bedded Under the Christmastide Moon
Bound by the Christmastide Moon

ACKNOWLEDGMENTS

There are several people I'd like to thank for staying with me through the hectic journey of writing these books.

To Marc, my amazing boyfriend—thank you for always being *you*!

To Lauren Stewart, my critique partner and best friend, you pushed me to explore new avenues of thought that I never dreamed possible. If we were in a true relationship, it would be one based on co-dependency, but in a good way. My writing would not be what it is without your comments, criticism, suggestions, and guidance.

I'd also like to thank the wonderful women who've supported me in both my writing career and life, including (but not limited to): Erica Monroe, Amanda Mariel, Debbie Haston, Angie Stanton, Theresa Baer, Ava Stone, Roxanne Stellmacher, Laura Cummings, Dawn Borbon, Suzi Parker, Jennifer Vella, Brandi Johnson, and Latisha Kahn. I know I'm forgetting people…You have all been very patient and wonderfully supportive of my eccentric ways.

A very special thank you to my editor, Chelle Olson with Literally Addicted to Detail, your skill and professionalism surpass all that I expected. Chelle Olson can be contracted by email at literallyaddictedtodetail@yahoo.com.

Also, a special thank you to historical and developmental editor, Scott Moreland.

And to my proofreader, Anja, thank you for embarking on yet another journey with me.

Cover design by The Midnight Muse.

Wraparound cover design credit to Sweet 'N Spicy Designs.

Finally, thank *you* for supporting indie authors!

THE Disappearance OF Lady Edith

THE UNDAUNTED DEBUTANTES
Book 1

CHRISTINA McKNIGHT

DEDICATION

To Marc
Thank you for your unwavering support and love!

PROLOGUE

Devonshire, England
December 1813

As it sounded its final gong, Lady Edith Pelton glanced at the towering, mahogany clock nestled between two bay windows overlooking the dark gardens below. The fire in the hearth had long been reduced to nothing but glowing embers.

However, the chill that had settled on the room hadn't been noticed.

"I truly must return to my chambers before His Grace suspects I have slipped out...before our marriage was so much as consummated." Lady Tilda Abercorn, formally Miss Tilda Guthton—the lowly daughter of a mere baronet—leapt to her feet from the lounge she shared with her dearest companions. That very morning, she'd wed the Duke of Abercorn, becoming a duchess.

And the envy of her three bosom friends.

Edith laughed along with the other two women, Lady Ophelia and Lady Lucianna, as they stood, all prepared to send Tilda off to her waiting marriage bed, her new husband, and the delights certain to await her.

Not that Edith or her friends knew anything about

what awaited Tilda behind those closed doors; however, this hadn't stopped them from gossiping about it for the past hour.

They likely would have remained ensconced in the salon had the tall clock not chimed twelve...it was even now five minutes past midnight.

Tilda was rightfully anxious; innocent and demure, much like Edith and their two other friends. She'd asked them to meet her after everyone else retired, not because she was avoiding her marriage bed—certainly not. She'd simply needed to draw a measure of confidence from those who cared most for her.

The hour was scandalously late; however, it meant all the other guests had retired to their beds. As such, it would be much easier for Edith and her friends to go unnoticed as they made their ways to their own rooms. The darkened household gave them the perfect opportunity for a few private moments with Tilda before she departed to France for her bridal tour with her new husband. It was unlikely the couple would return before the end of the Season.

"You will tell us everything on the morrow? At breakfast, and not a moment later. I truly must know if everything is as I've been told." Lady Lucianna raised one brow suggestively. Her green eyes sparkled with mischief as she wrapped Tilda in a tight embrace before withdrawing and taking in her appearance from head to stocking-covered toes. "You look breathtakingly innocent."

Edith noted a flash of unease when Tilda's soft, brown eyes widened.

Tilda, for all her bravado, was petrified.

Edith stepped forward and wrapped her arms around Tilda, much as Luci had a moment before, pushing from her mind the revelation that the girl's shoulders shook with nerves. "You are beautiful. You are smart. And today was a perfect way to start your married life. I only hope that Ophelia, Luci, and I are blessed with such generous husbands," Edith whispered to her friend.

"Thank you, Edith. You have always been a great friend." Tilda melted into Edith's embrace before pulling back. "I must hurry. It will not do for my *husband* to arrive and find I have fled. He said he would arrive by half past midnight, after attending to a few business matters."

Luci slipped her arm through Tilda's, while Ophelia grabbed the book she'd been reading and held it to her chest as she followed the women toward the door.

"Now remember that thing we spoke about. That thing with your tong…" Luci's whispers trailed off when the women moved out of hearing.

"I will extinguish the candles," Edith called to their retreating backs.

"Always the responsible one," Luci said over her shoulder with a smirk.

Ophelia paused at the threshold, her long, auburn locks mussed as usual. "I will help you."

"No, hurry along," Edith said, waving the woman off. "I know you are eager to return to your book. It will take but a few moments. I will meet you in our room as soon as I am done."

"If you insist." Ophelia smiled. With the corridor light at her back, she appeared an angel with her tousled hair and pale complexion. "I am eager to see how the fair Lady Daniella escapes the rogue pirate, Xavier."

Edith laughed softly. "Well, do get back to their story."

The woman didn't wait a moment longer, she flipped her book open and began reading as she turned to follow Tilda and Luci through the door.

Edith hurried about the room with the candlesnuffer, and before long, the salon was cast in shadows. The only remaining light came from a single lit candle—and the sconce in the hallway.

Grabbing the candleholder, Edith made certain that

the room was as they'd found it—tidy, without a thing out of place—and turned to pull the door closed behind her, her friends nowhere in sight.

A scream tore apart the stillness of the sleeping manor, echoing down every hallway and bouncing off closed doors.

The hair on the back of Edith's neck stood on end, and goose pimples spread across her bare arms as the shriek cut off, followed by the *thump, thump, thump* of something.

"Edith!" Lucianna shouted. "Ophelia!"

With her empty hand, Edith took hold of her skirts and ran toward the foyer, unconcerned that candle wax splattered on her exposed hand and the floor in her rush.

Edith turned the corner...and halted dead in her tracks, her heart pounding clear out of her chest.

A sob escaped Ophelia as her book slipped from her grasp and hit the polished floor.

Edith took a few steps until she stood at Ophelia's side. Luci was crouched on the bottom landing of the stairs, her long, raven locks blocking Edith's view of what she knelt over.

"Luci." Edith took a step forward as her friend stood. "What is it—"

But there was no need to go on. A trail of soft brown hair lay across the bottom stair, spilling onto the foyer floor.

"No, no, no," Edith sobbed as she hurried forward. "This cannot be—"

"He did this." The venom in Luci's tone had Edith looking away from the prone body of Tilda to where Luci stood, pointing toward the top of the stairs.

Following her friend's indicated direction, Edith narrowed her eyes on the darkened landing above them but could make out nothing—no person, no movement, no noise.

"Who?" Ophelia squeaked behind her.

"That is not important at this moment," Edith scolded, hurrying to Tilda's side. "We must wake her up, make sure she is all right and call for the duke—and a physician."

"There is no point." Luci knelt next to Edith, sweeping Tilda's hair from her face. "She is gone."

Vacant, chestnut-brown eyes stared back at her.

Tilda's doe eyes, always seeing to the heart of a matter, were empty of life. Tilda's carefree demeanor and the positive outlook she so desperately adored would never guide Edith again. Never again would Edith and her wonderful friend giggle behind their fans at some London dandy, cloaked in all the colors of a peacock's feathers, nor amble in the park, speaking of matters much more delicate—their fears, their passions, and their hopes for the future.

In the blink of an eye, it was all gone; as if the last sixteen years of friendship had never been.

A candle extinguished at the end of a long day.

"They argued," Luci insisted, grasping Edith's arm to halt her from touching Tilda. "He was up there, and he pushed her. I swear it."

Edith was helpless to take her eyes off Tilda, still unmoving at the bottom of the stairs. Even if her eyes hadn't been open, staring at the chandelier above, Edith would have known something was not right. Tilda's head was cocked at an odd angle, and one arm was tucked behind her back under her prone frame. Her demure, white nightshift was tangled between her legs, exposing her stocking-clad calves.

Tilda's innocent yet intense light was gone. It did not fade over time as it should, but was cast out without warning.

"Wha-wha-what should we do?" Ophelia wailed.

"We will rouse the house and tell them what the duke has done!" Lucianna shot to her feet once more. "Someone must have heard the commotion."

Edith glanced around the foyer, deserted except for

Luci, Ophelia, Edith, and, of course, Tilda. "You are correct. I heard her scream, and then the thump"— Edith cringed at her choice of word—"as she fell down."

"She did *not* fall." Lucianna's tone reached hysterics as she narrowed her glare on Edith. "She was *push*ed by Abercorn!"

The trio stood, staring at one another. Tears overflowed and fell down Ophelia's reddened face, while Luci appeared far more in control. Her widened green eyes held no hint of the waterworks Ophelia had been reduced to. Edith was oddly in between—neither overtaken by grief nor completely in command of her faculties. Edith reached out toward Luci, but the woman ignored her hand.

"How could this happen?" Ophelia asked, stooping to collect her book as she dashed the tears away.

Luci's long, onyx hair swung over her shoulder as she turned to Ophelia. "That is a question for him. You saw him, right, Ophelia?"

The color drained from the girl's face, making her pale complexion turn almost green.

"Tell her what you saw." Luci took an intimidating step toward Ophelia. "You were standing right here."

"I—I—I was reading." Ophelia turned to Edith, her book held tightly against her bosom. "I swear it, Edith, I did not see anything. I was reading about Xavier and—"

"What is going on here?" Townsend, the Abercorn butler, bustled into the foyer, his hair askew as if the noise had pulled him from slumber. "Your Grace!" His eyes widened and fastened on Tilda as he rushed across the room to where she lay. His hand moved to her wrist and settled. "No pulse. She has no pulse!"

The servant shuffled to his feet, teetering for a moment at the shock of seeing his new mistress dead at the bottom of the grand staircase—on her wedding night.

"Petunia, Petunia!" Townsend shouted as he flapped his arms to and fro, rushing toward the kitchens. "Petunia! We must summon His Grace. Petunia, where in all that is holy are you, woman?"

Doors opened, and voices sounded above from the guests' wing as Townsend continued calling for Petunia.

Edith hadn't the faintest notion whom Petunia was, but she was obviously very important.

"Oh, Your Grace!" Townsend said, staring toward the top of the stairs. "Please, do not look. This is not for your eyes."

Scanning the landing above, Edith noted the duke, still garbed in his wedding day finery, his once blond hair now shot through with grey, starting down the stairs with a tumbler in hand. His leisurely pace and unhurried movements spoke volumes. Either he'd had no hand in the matter of Tilda's fall, or he knew damn well what had happened and could care less. He took a measured swallow from his tumbler, and his eyes narrowed as he scrutinized the scene below.

Abercorn had not yet set eyes upon his bride— lying prone below him, a trickle of blood now escaping her parted lips.

Or perhaps he knew exactly how Tilda lay, haphazardly broken. From the stiff set of his shoulders and his cold, unaffected stare toward the gathering in his foyer, Edith did not know.

Out of the corner of her eye, Edith watched Luci's hands ball into fists at her sides, and her face redden in fury.

Could the duke have pushed his new bride down the stairs as Lucianna claimed? If so, what did he gain by doing so? The thought that a wealthy lord, with everything within his grasp, would take a young, beautiful woman as his bride only to push her to her death before the marriage had even been consummated made absolutely no sense.

And how could the man look so unaffected by it

all?

CHAPTER 1

It is hereby stated that this writer has born firsthand witness to the 7ᵗʰ Duke of Montrose, scandalously alone with a golden-haired nymph in his private opera box, all whilst betrothed to the widow, Lady Cavendish.

As this writer can also attest, Lady Cavendish's hair is pure night, compared to the observed doxy's crown of light. Let this article stand as proof that Lady Cavendish would do well to find herself another eligible lord to take as husband.

-Mayfair Confidential, London Daily Gazette

St. James Place, London
January 1815

TRISTON NEVILLE, VISCOUNT Torrington, glared at his father, forcing himself to breathe in deeply and hold the stale air, heavy with cigar smoke, in his lungs to avoid it exiting in a rush of rage.

The Marquis of Downshire couldn't possibly fathom what he was asking of his son. Triston doubted his father understood the ludicrous nature of his demands, masked as simple fatherly requests.

"Did you hear me, Triston?" His father's nostrils flared, and the tiny vein that ran up his forehead pulsed…once, twice, three times. The man's frown deepened, and Triston was uncertain if the marquis was annoyed at his son's antics or only mildly agitated.

To be fair, Triston had been aiming for annoyance.

He straightened his shoulders, holding in his sigh once again, but responded before his father fainted from holding his breath. "Yes, Father. I heard you and will keep all you've said in mind."

"You will accompany your sisters during their Season?"

"Yes."

"You will endeavor to not draw attention to yourself and, therefore, away from your sisters?"

Triston looked up at the study ceiling, attempting to suppress his irritation. "I have never sought the *ton*'s notice, if you will remember."

Downshire stood, pushing his chair back. He placed his hand flat upon the desk separating the men and leaned forward. "That is neither here nor there."

In his younger days, Triston would have needed to steel himself from quaking in terror at his father's imposing stance and razor-edged words. However, those days passed when Triston grew several inches taller than the marquis, and his shoulders spread far wider than his sire's. Though both men towered over six feet in height and had matching golden-brown hair, Triston was larger on every scale that mattered—including intellect, which he hadn't vocalized since leaving the schoolroom for Eton.

"Father, I will do my best to make certain Lady Dow—" A movement over his father's shoulder, out the study window, caught Triston's notice. A flash of white was visible in the tree between the Downshire townhouse and their neighbor's. "I will make sure Esmee is not inconvenienced in any way."

Normally, his stepmother's name would have stuck in his throat, clawing to get free as he attempted to keep it unsaid. At present, he was determined not to allow the woman to overshadow his day; it was enough Triston would be forced to accompany the dreadful woman on social outings whenever she chose to attend.

His father nodded, apparently accepting Triston's pledge to see his sisters, Prudence and Chastity, safely wed before the year was out. To do that, the girls needed proper gowns with all the trimmings, and then needs must be presented to society to have the opportunity to meet eligible lords—all without their raven-haired stepmother criticizing their every move.

Triston leaned forward slightly to gain a better view out his father's study window. There was certainly something going on; however, alerting the marquis to it would not be wise and only lengthen their meeting. Blond hair hung down the back of a petite, female frame, the flash of her white petticoats being what had drawn his attention in the first place.

"Very well, Triston, I believe…" His father's brow scrunched, his eyes narrowing on his only son. "Are you even listening to me?"

"Of course." Triston took his eyes on the figure nestled in the tree. "It is only I have a prior engagement I am tardy for."

"A prior engagement, you say?" the marquis asked. His father's face reddened once more when Triston nodded. "You knew full well we meet each week at this precise time and place."

"Unfortunately, this could not be avoided." Triston shook his head as if he were loath to depart his father's home. "I surely must take my leave."

"If you must—"

Triston didn't wait for him to finish before turning and stalking toward the open study door.

His father's words echoed in his wake. "Impertinent, always were and always will be. Shut my door!"

Triston pulled the door closed, the thud reverberating through his entire body, though in a satisfying way.

He'd bought himself another week. Seven full days until he would be summoned again to his father's study to discuss trivial matters to keep up the appearance that the men were not at extreme odds with one another.

Triston only hoped that society had bought the ruse they'd been carrying on with since the marquis married his third and latest wife. If not, the *ton* would take great exception to his return to society, even with his two young sisters on his arms.

The hall window afforded a view similar to the study.

Triston took the few steps necessary and stood framed in the arched panes, gazing out as the afternoon sun warmed him through the glass. Sure enough, there was a woman perched in a Downshire tree, hunched over and staring at Lord Abercorn's upper window. A thick limb prodding her back prevented her from sitting completely upright.

It appeared his father requesting he accompany his sisters during their debut Season was only one of the peculiar occurrences he would witness during his day. Triston was hard-pressed to determine which was more alarming: his need to return to society, or a woman perched precariously in a plum tree.

Certainly, one did not regularly see a person, a woman especially, balanced on a thin tree limb at least six feet off the ground.

He tapped the window to gain her attention.

No response.

Triston looked up at the window she stared at, but the sun only reflected a glare off the glass, preventing him from seeing what held her attention.

Turning his focus toward the front drive and then back toward the gardens, Triston searched for the Downshire's groundskeeper. Frederick was usually tending the roses lining the drive during Triston's weekly visits to his father's home, but today he seemed to be absent.

He watched as the woman slipped something into her skirts, rubbing her hands together and looking about.

Was she not concerned someone would question why she was in a tree?

Triston shook his head. If the groundskeeper were nowhere in sight, it was his responsibility to inquire as to why the woman was trespassing on Downshire property.

That and assist her down from her perilous post.

LADY EDITH PELTON sat perched in a tree, her head bent low, and a branch poking into her backside. She was filthy, she was sore, and she hadn't managed to learn anything from the last several hours. The only thing she'd witnessed was the duke moving from his office on the first floor to the second floor—after a particularly buxom woman with midnight locks had joined him. They hadn't entered any of the rooms facing her direction, nor had they returned below. That had been nearly an hour ago, and Edith had yet to note any other movement on the second floor, besides the occasional servant attending to their chores.

If she returned yet again with no new information on the Duke of Abercorn, nothing that condemned him for his wrongdoings—nor absolved him of his accused crimes—Lucianna would be irate. She'd likely demand to investigate the man herself, or worse yet, instruct Ophelia to write the article for the *Gazette*, attacking Abercorn, regardless of his culpability in Tilda's death.

Edith would not allow that to happen, could not permit her dear friend to ruin a man's life with no proof of his misconducts. Lucianna had agreed to wait until sufficient evidence existed, but with each passing day—and more articles submitted to the *Gazette*—her friend grew impatient.

Suddenly, a drapery on the second story toward the back of the townhouse was pulled aside, revealing a quite naked, raven-haired woman, her long tresses the only thing covering her exposed bosom.

It was impossible for Edith to take her eyes off the sight before her as the duke, fully clothed, stepped up behind the woman, wrapping his arms around her tightly as he fondled her breasts. The large window framed the couple perfectly. The woman began to sway before Abercorn, her backside still flush with his front.

Edith's face flamed red with embarrassment at the scandalous spectacle.

The duke whipped the woman around until her naked breasts were pressed against his chest, and the woman's rounded derriere pressed solidly against the windowpane. Abercorn slowly moved his lips to the woman's neck and traced his mouth along her shoulder before suddenly straightening and throwing his head back in a silent chuckle.

She wondered what the raven-haired beauty had said to gain such a reaction from the cold, stoic duke.

Edith's stare narrowed on the pair as the woman reached up and began to undo Abercorn's cravat.

Before Edith even suspected what was happening, the duke's eyes scanned the landscape outside his townhouse, his glare seeming to find Edith perched in the tree bordering his property. Abruptly, Edith ducked her head and slipped her journal into the secret pocket she'd sewn into each of her gowns for exactly this purpose before easing from the branch she sat on to scurry down the tree.

I cannot be caught, I cannot be caught, I cannot be caught, she chanted, placing her booted feet on another branch before dipping low to take hold of it and swing down to the ground below.

Almost there. Edith's hands were mere inches from grasping the thick limb to lower herself…only six feet from escape.

"You, there!" a deep voice sounded behind her. "What are you doing up there?"

"Eeep!" The sudden exclamation took her mind off the limb she reached for, and Edith's boot caught on her skirt, causing her to miss the branch completely. She stiffened her body as she fell, bracing for the impact she knew was to come as the air rushed by her.

The seconds slowed.

Giving her ample time to contemplate what she'd done in her life to end up falling from a tree in the fashionable St. James area of London, her arms pinwheeling as she hoped to ease her landing.

Thump.

Everything went dark, and Edith feared she'd landed on her head, doing irreparable damage.

She blinked several times and willed her mind to command her fingers to wiggle and her toes to curl in her boots.

Everything worked.

She said a silent prayer to whoever was looking out for her.

"I asked what you are doing on my property!" the man huffed.

Edith blinked again—still complete darkness. Maybe she *had* hit her head on the way down, but would it not ache?

"Do stop this ridiculousness and remove your garments from your head."

She moved silently, rolling to her side, a resounding pain in her backside cluing her in to exactly how she'd landed.

Lifting her hands, Edith pushed at whatever covered her sight, only to see a pair of Hessians solidly placed beside her. Lowering the material farther, she noted thick, muscular calves leading to tree trunk-sized thighs clad in tightly tailored breeches.

Edith cringed, allowing the material to fall back

into place, blocking out all view of the man once more.

"I would suggest righting your skirts, as your derriere is exposed to all and sundry who happen to pass by on the street," the man commanded sternly.

From the dampness seeping from the ground beneath her hip and into her exposed knickers, Edith suspected she'd landed in a particularly well-tended and watered part of foliage.

The mention of her derriere brought back images of the raven-haired beauty's bare buttocks pressed firmly to the window of Abercorn's townhouse. Her face heated immediately, and Edith longed for nothing more than to stay hidden.

She wished a carriage would come along and put her out of her misery, as it were.

It was difficult to decide which was more embarrassing: her fall from the tree, her skirts being cast over her head, or that whoever the man standing above her was had witnessed it all.

"If I remain as such, will you go away and act as if this never happened?" Edith asked.

"What sort of gentleman would I be if I did not verify a damsel in distress was uninjured after a fall such as this?" His Hessians crunched dry, fallen leaves as he moved before her. "Besides, you are still trespassing, and I cannot allow that to go unresolved."

Suddenly, her skirts were pulled away, and Edith looked up, the bright sun momentarily blinding her, causing spots of colors to cross her vision. She closed her eyes tightly and rubbed at her face.

"I am going nowhere, so it's best if you remove your hands from your face and permit me to help you regain your feet."

"What if I simply roll myself into the street and allow the next carriage or man on horseback to resolve this dilemma for us?" she said into the palms of her gloved hands.

"I would say that is a mess I would not relish

cleaning up." His stern tone had lessened, taking on an almost jovial quality.

Edith allowed her hands to fall from her face, and the man's outstretched hand appeared before her. She took a moment to ponder his offer, knowing if she raised her eyes to his, she'd be far more exposed than her backside had been only a moment before.

"Come now, I do not bite—unless commanded to," he said with a chuckle.

She couldn't avoid the man any longer. He was not going away, nor did he appear the type to allow questions to go unanswered.

But blast it all, Edith did not need to accept his assistance to gain her footing.

Her backside and pride were already bruised; she had no intentions of accepting his hand.

With a huff, Edith placed her gloved palms upon the dirt on either side of her, preparing to push herself to her feet—without his help.

But with the action, her gaze traveled from the man's offered hand and back to his thick thighs. The male could be a Highlander of old with such a foundation. Edith was helpless to stop her eyes from straying farther upward. His muscular legs gave way to a solid midsection that had her halting at his expansive chest. She need not allow her mind to wander far to know that under his linen shirt lay a chest of pure muscle, capped off by broad, sinewy shoulders certainly capable of lifting a fallen tree. Or a damsel in distress, as he'd dubbed her.

Edith swallowed, gulping down her purr of pleasure. What had overtaken her? He was only a man—a very *strong* man, his frame proving he exerted himself vigorously with regularity. It would not surprise her if he spent each day undertaking pursuits of manual labor, carrying carriage wheels as if they weighed no more than a bowl of orange marmalade.

He cleared his throat. "It is improper to stare,

miss."

Edith's eyes widened in alarm. She *was* staring, and with no sense of regret. Whatever had come over her?

The moment she pushed on her palms to try and raise herself, a shot of pain traveled to her elbow. "Mayhap it is more than my backside that is bruised," she mumbled.

"I am here to assist," he repeated.

"You would like that much, I am certain, Lord—" Edith's words ended abruptly. She hadn't any notion if the man before her *was* a lord. He could be no more than a common gentleman. "I can stand without help, but thank you nonetheless."

"Torrington."

"Pardon?" Her eyes snapped to his face—another colossal mistake as her mouth gaped at the Adonis before her, the noonday sun highlighting his umber brown hair, chiseled jawline, and decidedly aristocratic nose. He was what the great poets of old wrote about in their sonnets. He was the image every artist struggled to achieve in oils. He was what sculptors in Roman times worked a lifetime to create.

And he was standing before her…flesh and blood.

His eyes seemingly capable of seeing to her very soul.

"My name, miss. Lord Torrington—Triston if you prefer, as I feel we are now adequately acquainted." He smirked at his jest and shook his hand before her face once more.

"Lord Torrington, it is," Edith said, relenting and taking his hand.

"Come, miss, we can do away with formalities. After all, I know the fabric of your knickers." His arrogant, amused grin grew, softening the hard line of his jaw—if it were possible.

At her gasp, he chuckled, hoisting her to her feet with one swift tug of her arm.

CHAPTER 2

WHEN SHE'D REGAINED her feet, the golden-haired siren pulled her hand from Triston's quickly, as if his touch had scorched her palm through her sullied glove.

He raised a brow in question.

As a gentleman, he should inquire as to any injuries obtained in her fall. Yet, the memory of the sight of her pristine linen drawers, her skirts and cloak flung haphazardly over her head, took up his every available thought, making it impossible to organize his words in any semblance of order.

Her copper-colored eyes widened on him and then narrowed.

"How dare you—" she stammered.

"How dare I?" He took a step closer, causing her to stumble back. "It is you whom I found lurking in a tree—on the property of a home where you do not belong."

Triston did his best to keep his tone stern and his stance intimidating, though the urge to laugh nearly overtook him. Truly, he didn't care what the woman was doing in the tree. However, he would be lying to himself if he didn't admit that her motives intrigued him, especially as it took his mind off his *meeting* with his sire, the Marquis of Downshire.

It was more of a summons than an optional invitation to meet with his father to discuss the upcoming Season and his younger sisters' presentation to the *ton*.

Yes, Triston would much rather focus his mind…and imagination as it were, on the jumbled woman before him.

Her brow scrunched, and her lips pressed together. "How do you assume to know if I belong here or not, my lord?" Her hands landed on her hips, her tone challenging.

"I assure you, I would know if you belonged on Downshire property." He crossed his arms, refusing to advance any farther but also unwilling to back down. He'd had quite enough of women thinking they could order him about and instruct him on what is what. He was a bloody viscount, after all, heir to a marquis. The slip of a woman before him hadn't any notion whom she dealt with.

Instead of holding her tongue, however, the hellion laughed—at him. A sweet, melodic sound that echoed down the row of townhouses along St. James.

"What, may I inquire, is so comical?" Triston demanded.

She sobered enough to reply, "You, thinking you know where I do and do not belong—or even whose property we are standing upon."

Maybe he should have thought twice before approaching the woman. She seemed a bit peculiar, to say the least—and possibly utterly insane at worst. And this was exactly the type of situation his father demanded he refrain from being involved in until after Prudence and Chastity were safely, legally, and indisputably betrothed.

Yet, could an angel of such captivating beauty be absolutely unhinged?

It would be the ultimate paradox.

However, it would be little different from his own dear sisters, Pru and Chastity, who were also a complete contradiction. They were not beauties, but their wit, grace, and agreeableness would make them the perfect brides for any man—if one could only look past their plain, wallflowerish exteriors.

"Why are you looking at me as though I've sprouted horns and will gallop away at any moment?" she asked.

"I was contemplating the possibility that you are stark raving mad." Honesty was good—forthright responses were always what Triston fell back on when confronted with a question he'd rather not answer.

"Why, I never…" She jammed her gloved hands into her pockets as her voice faltered, her face a perfectly composed mask of rage. "That…well…certainly…"

Her angry expression told Triston this was another occurrence his father was determined to avoid during the upcoming Season. A public confrontation between his wife and son would draw unwelcome attention to them all, casting Pru and Chastity in a negative light.

Her shoulders straightened, and her chin notched up several degrees. "I assure you I am not mad—neither insane nor angry."

He would beg to differ as she'd just been caught perched in a tree, then had fallen from said tree—which was irrefutable even to those who hadn't seen, as she had leaves stuck to her cloak and a stick protruding from her hair. "I am pleased to hear this, but you still have not told me what you are doing on my property, nor your name."

She glanced over her shoulder and up at Lord Abercorn's townhouse before turning back to him. "There really is no need for all of this. I am uninjured, as you can see." To prove her point, she flapped her arms, shrugged her shoulders, and bent over, touching her toes before straightening with a confident smile.

A lock of pure-spun golden hair came loose from her updo and fell across her face, the stick coming with it.

Unaware of his intentions, Triston reached out and pulled the stick free, then presented it to her before tossing it into a nearby shrub.

"Thank you, my lord." She pushed the wayward lock of hair from her face. "I will be going now."

"How will you arrive home?" He looked up and down St. James. No waiting carriage and no horse were in sight—besides his stallion, Blitz, being led around from his father's stables. "I cannot, in good conscience, allow you to leave unchaperoned without proper conveyance."

Her eyes darted down the drive bordering the foliage where they stood when she heard his stallion's hooves on the cobblestone.

"Not so fast." Triston made to grab her arm before she fled, but the woman flinched, freezing to her spot as if too terrified to move. "I only seek your name and the reason for you being on my property. That is all."

"I am not on your property, and you have no right to demand my name."

THE MAN WAS swiftly turning from an Adonis to Dolon—demanding, arrogant, and forthright. She much preferred admiring him when he kept his mouth closed. Edith hadn't thought her schooling in Greek and Roman mythology would ever be of use, yet, here she was, dredging from memory the attributes of legends long past.

Lord Torrington, or whatever the man claimed his name to be, was incorrigible. Unlike any gentleman she'd ever met.

Not to touch on the matter of his handsomeness…which did not matter to Edith in the slightest, yet was undeniable.

"My name is none of your concern because I am not, in fact, on your property." There, she'd spoken her mind—and the world hadn't crumbled around her, nor had the Adonis before her disappeared into the mist. "And I would thank you not to concern yourself with my travel arrangements."

"Whose property do you assume we are standing on?" His brow rose, and the corner of his lip turned up in a smirk.

"Lord Abercorn's," she stated simply.

Torrington pointed to a line of stones, barely noticeable but still a definite line between her and the Abercorn townhouse property. "As you can see, the tree you climbed is securely on Downshire property. And I have every right to demand your reason for being on the marquis' land—and more to the fact, summon the magistrate."

She'd assumed being caught by Abercorn, or the woman he currently shared his chambers with, was as dire as her afternoon could get. Yet, the lord before her seemed determined to have the information he sought. But what would he do with it? If he took her name to Abercorn, she and her friends could be in serious peril; and if he insisted on calling the authorities, her parents would be notified.

Edith would not allow that to happen. "Wait a moment, did you not say your name is Torrington?"

"I did," he confirmed with a nod.

"And we stand on the Marquis of Downshire's property?"

"Correct once more." He said the words slowly as if she were daft.

Yet, it was Edith's turn to smirk. "Well, as I see it, you have no authority here if you are not the marquis." Maybe, just maybe, she'd be able to escape without Abercorn or her parents finding out. It would only leave her to inform Luci and Ophelia they were no closer to proving Lord Abercorn's culpability in Tilda's death.

The positive side was that she would be free to continue searching for evidence that Abercorn had pushed his new bride down the stairs of his country manor on the night of his wedding.

Edith slipped her hand into her pocket to make sure her journal hadn't fallen from its place. When her fingers touched the familiar leather binding, Edith's assuredness returned, and she pivoted to depart.

"Where are you going?" The lord's feet sounded behind her as she picked her way through the shrubs on her way to the street. "Stop."

Edith glanced over her shoulder, determined to keep out of Lord Torrington's reach until she made it to Pall Mall and the nearest hackney she could wave down. "Good day, my lord."

CHAPTER 3

TRISTON GLANCED ABOUT the crowded ballroom, or at least as much of the room as he could see from his current location. "Do we plan to hide behind these potted palms all evening?"

His question gained him a scathing look from his two sisters, six and seven years his junior, before they turned their stares back to the ballroom in unison.

"For at least another set," Pru hissed, her pastel green gown blending in exquisitely with the foliage bordering the dance floor. He wished he could say the dress complimented her just as exquisitely, except the shade clashed with her pale complexion, and the gown was far too tight by any person's standards. "Now hush, or we will be noticed."

"We are at a ball, Prudence, we are supposed to be seen." He shook his head at this sister's reprimand.

"We are not ready to be seen as yet, brother," Chastity chimed in, her dull brown curls bouncing as she shook her head. "If we are discovered, that will mean we must speak with someone."

"Which we are certainly not ready to do."

The pair shared an exasperated look, leading Triston to think that something was going on he was not privy to, which would not surprise him.

It was going to be a long Season if this was how it was to start. Triston glanced at his sisters on either side of him. Many mistook the pair for twins, though they were born ten months apart. Their hair was always styled in a similar fashion, their gowns always the same cut, and they rarely left one another's side.

A pang of jealousy hit him, something he'd endured far more often in his younger days. Not that he was ancient, by any means, but at twenty and three, Triston was securely the older, odd-man-out sibling. Certainly, he adored his sisters, doted on them even, but they shared a bond that Triston could never hope to be a part of.

"I know I am going to regret inquiring, but *why* are you not ready to do that?" he asked, as the musicians concluded another set, and the dancers departed the floor.

"Because, dear brother…" Chastity spoke slowly, as if uncertain he understood her words. "If we are noticed, that would mean we need speak with someone, likely a horde of eligible men seeking a dance partner, and we are not ready for such a commitment."

"And because, dear brother," Pru said, picking up when Chastity sighed, "we have many things we seek to see before becoming entangled with a gentleman who might offer for our hands."

Both girls' heads bobbed, but they did not take their eyes off the dance floor when the musicians signaled another set was about to start.

Triston couldn't help his open-mouthed stare. Commitment? Eligible men? And offers of marriage? He wondered if his sisters had a looking glass in their bedchamber—or if their eyesight was good enough to afford them an adequate view of the other women in the room.

Not that his sisters would not find suitable matches, maybe even highly sought after lords with the dowries his father had settled on each girl; however, they were not diamonds of the first water. They took much more after their father and Triston than their mother. Both debutantes more firmly weighted on the side of stout rather than lithe. They were built in a similar fashion to Triston: broad of shoulder and thick of waist, with legs more suitably constructed for scaling tall mountains than graceful waltzes.

For a man, the attributes were looked upon favorably by the fairer sex.

While for women, men usually gazed upon his sisters as if they were reckoning the value of a brood mare.

Which only made Triston seek to put his fist through the unlucky bastards' faces.

They were his baby sisters, after all—they were delicate *bloody* flowers.

Innocent, intelligent, and great conversationalists.

And any man who sought one of their hands in marriage—or even a dance—should best well understand that.

This was exactly the reason Triston had argued with his father a few days prior. He was not qualified to escort his siblings about London. It was not safe—for his sisters, himself, or any sorry gent who thought themselves worthy of one of the Downshire sisters.

Maybe Triston's doting ways had given the pair an incorrect estimation of their visual appeal, leaving him to tidy up the mess that would be made when they either hid behind these palms all Season or turned down every man who asked to put their name upon Pru's or Chastity's dance cards.

"I am in need of refreshments, ladies." Triston stepped around his sisters and turned, blocking their view of the room. "It would be best if the pair of you accompany me."

He held out both arms, and his sisters eyed his offer with matching skeptical expressions before slipping their arms through his.

"Very wise, dear sisters," Triston whispered. "I think you both are in need of a glass of sherry."

"Heavens no," they gasped in unison.

"Stepmother would never allow it," Chastity said.

"Yes, Lady Downshire is adamantly against women of fine breeding consuming any type of spirits," Prudence agreed, keeping true to her name.

"Well, the good Lady Downshire is not here to witness anything," Triston argued. "What she does not see will not hurt her, as the saying goes."

Pru's eyes widened. "But she will find out."

"She always finds out," Chastity said, her head shaking. "And then we will be made to do without."

Triston weaved through the crowd gathered around the edges of the ballroom, careful to not make eye contact with anyone, lest they approach him for conversation.

However, he could not disagree with his sisters' fears in regards to Esmee Neville, the latest Marchioness of Downshire. She was a spiteful woman with a tendency to enact retribution on anyone who disobeyed her commands. She was a raven-haired beauty, who captured a man's heart before crushing it between her elegant, pale hands; watching the pieces crumble to the ground before stepping on them.

Not that Triston could blame his father for falling in love with such a beautiful creature—he only wished the marquis would have heeded his son's warning about the sharpness of the woman's talons.

"Do not allow the beast to crush your spirits, my dear sisters." They stepped into the line for refreshments. "She will shortly attain what she wants, a babe of her own, and then she will leave the three of us to our own devices. I am certain of it."

The current marchioness was only a year younger than Triston and had yet to start her own family. But he assumed she would soon, as she did not consider the marquis' previous children up to her required standards, nor would her position be solidified if something were to happen to her husband without a child born of the union. And so, she'd set out to provide Downshire with a spare heir, should something untoward happen to Triston.

The girls looked to one another before Pru responded. "We will have one sherry—"

"Wonderful!"

"To split between us," Chastity finished. "And we shall endeavor to hurry to our rooms when we arrive home to avoid the marchioness catching the scent of spirits on our persons."

"Whatever you must do," Triston said with a chuckle. "I am happy I no longer have to put up with the ice queen's edicts."

Both girls pouted at his mention of no longer residing with them at their father's townhouse. "We do not understand why we could not go with you," Chastity whined.

"Yes, Esmee would not mind, so long as we were no longer underfoot."

Triston took in their downcast expressions and, not for the first time, he sensed they felt as if he'd abandoned them. "You both know living in a boarding house is not proper for two young women, especially ones seeking to find elevated matches."

"We are not looking to wed!" they protested as one.

He'd known the comment would distract them from thoughts of Triston's recent departure from their family home; however, he could not reside under his father's roof a moment longer, especially if it meant he remained under Esmee's control.

However, the girls' insistence that they were not looking to wed was preposterous. Every young debutante was taking part in the elaborate fiasco that was the Marriage Market for the eventual outcome of…marriage. He could not see Esmee taking kindly to

Pru and Chastity spending money on a Season when neither was actually inclined to wed.

As the marquis' third wife—Triston's mother having passed from influenza when he was only a toddler, and Pru and Chastity's mother having died giving birth to Chastity—the woman was set on vanquishing all memories of those who'd come before her, even Downshire's previous children.

And that meant marrying off Triston's two young sisters.

A voice cleared behind them, and both women stiffened on his arms, making no move to turn to see who sought their attention.

"Good evening, my lord." The deep, throaty voice sparked a familiar memory. "Lady Prudence, Lady Chastity. You are both the height of composure this evening."

Abercorn.

Their father's neighbor—and friend. And a man Triston was barely acquainted with beyond their two bordering townhomes. In fact, it was odd to have the blonde vixen mention Abercorn followed by the man appearing.

"Good evening, Your Grace," Triston greeted the elderly man as he turned. "Lovely to see you."

"And you, as well, Torrington." Abercorn's evening attire was tailored to fit his frame perfectly—and Triston suspected outfitting a man as tall and rail-thin as Abercorn was no easy feat. "Your father said you'd be in attendance tonight, and I must claim a dance from both Lady Prudence and Lady Chastity."

A shiver went through both of his sisters at the man's lecherous stare.

He wondered if his sisters knew things he did not.

How his father stood the company of the duke was beyond Triston's comprehension; however, Pru and Chastity dipped into graceful curtseys before holding out their wrists with their dance cards.

Abercorn hastily scribbled his name on Pru's card, but only glanced at Chastity's blank slip. "A set is about to begin. May I have this dance, Lady Chastity?"

Triston wanted to deny the gentleman's request, but was left without reason. The duke was his father's friend—and even if the girls despised the marchioness, they adored their father and always sought to please him, even if that meant dancing with a man old enough to be their father—or an uncle.

"Chastity would be honored," Triston answered when his sister's gloved hand squeezed his arm. He handed his sister off and watched as the pair made their way to the dance floor. "That man is an odd one."

Pru giggled, highly improperly, before ending it on a snort. "Chastity feels sorry for him."

"Sorry, why?"

She turned a stern look on him. "Dear brother, do you not follow societal gossip at all?"

"No." And he was surprised his sisters did. "Why in heavens name would I want to know what Lord so-and-so does after he deposits his wife following a ball? Or who the widow, Lady Palmer, has sunken her claws into this time." Mainly, his lack of interest was because he'd been the topic of hurtful, slanderous gossip, and he took zero stock in any of it.

Hell, his family was likely still a topic of conversation in most drawing rooms.

When a man's betrothed leaves him to marry his father, the *ton* does not forget.

Even now, Triston noticed a woman avert her stare when his eyes landed on her.

Yes, he was commissioned to see his sisters safely about London proper—not hoard all the attention for himself.

Thankfully, they'd reached the front of the refreshment line, and he selected two flutes of sherry. Handing one to Pru, Triston downed the other and held it out for a refill before they moved on.

"I hope you do not plan to slip deep into your cups this evening," Pru commented, her eyes wide with astonishment, her own glass forgotten in her hand.

He certainly would not disagree with a tumbler or two of scotch, but at best, he had watered-down sherry. "It would take an entire trough of this sherry to see even a hint of drunken behavior. Worry not, dear sister."

They resumed their place on the fringes of the dance floor and turned to watch Abercorn and Chastity swirl about with the other pairs—a bit slower than the other dancers, and less coordinated. Triston supposed age did that to a person.

His eyes settled on a trio of women standing on the far edge of the ballroom, across from Triston and Pru. The group also watched the duke and Chastity as they whirled in time to the beat.

An auburn-haired woman tried to hide her interest in the couple, while her two companions, a towering, midnight-haired beauty, and a woman with hair the color of spun gold, glared openly at Abercorn and Chastity. Triston could only gain a side profile of the group, but they were most definitely watching Chastity.

"Do you know those women?" he asked Pru, nodding in the group's direction.

Prudence took to her tiptoes to see over the dancing crowd. "Oh, yes. I do."

"Who are they?" Just then, the blonde woman turned in his direction, and his mind stopped short. It was the woman from outside his father's townhouse. Her hair was respectably coiffed, and her evening gown was expertly crafted to fit her short frame. He'd need ask after her seamstress, as she'd likely create a miracle for Pru and Chastity's wardrobe. "I do not think I have made their acquaintance."

Pru shook her head dejectedly. "It is unlikely you have. They were presented last Season, but quickly retreated after that unfortunate night."

"What unfortunate night?" he asked.

"And this is why you should take greater note of the gossip rags," Pru sighed. "They are Ladies Lucianna, Edith, and Ophelia. They were the talk of their Season, with their friend, Miss Tilda Guthton."

The last name was vaguely familiar; however, Triston was unsure from where he knew it. "What happened? Why would they retreat?"

Pru dropped his arm and turned to face him, bewilderment clouding her features. "How are you so unaware, Triston?" When he remained silent, she continued. "Miss Tilda became the Duchess of Abercorn only a few short weeks into last Season."

"Abercorn isn't wed," Triston challenged.

"He isn't wed *now*." Pru folded her arms across her chest and then quickly uncrossed them, running her hands down the front of her satin gown. "Miss Tilda…Lady Abercorn, died on the night of their wedding. Fell—or was pushed—down the main staircase, depending on who's account you believe."

Triston narrowed his eyes on the trio of women, suddenly making sense of why the blonde woman had perched herself in a Downshire tree to watch Abercorn's townhome. "And her friends believe she was pushed?"

Why in heaven's name would a duke take a wife only to see her gone on their wedding night? Besides, Triston found it hard to believe Abercorn capable of such an act.

"Mayhap." Pru shrugged and turned back toward the women. The dancers had moved, enabling his sister to gain a decent view across the dance floor. "The black-haired woman is stunning, is she not?"

Triston took his stare off the blonde to take in the sight of the tall, willowy, raven-haired beauty; however, his appeal for the darker variety of women had been snubbed long ago. Though it made sense for his sister to assume he would be taken with her.

"She is certainly alluring. What do you know of them and their families?" he asked in way of steering the conversation—hoping Pru didn't catch on to his true intentions.

"Lady Lucianna Constantine is the black-haired beauty. Lady Ophelia Fletcher is the one with the downcast eyes—a terrible introvert, they say. And the petite blonde woman is Lady Edith Pelton."

Lady Edith.

He allowed the name to roll about in his mind. He'd never heard of her before; which, from his sister's explanation, made ample sense. Triston had avoided society after his broken betrothal forced him into the unwanted spotlight of every gossip-minded matron in London. He glanced about the room at the mere thought, but found no one staring at him. It had taken two years, but finally, the scandal sheets had moved on to other topics of fodder.

"The trio only just arrived for the Season a few weeks ago, their mourning period having ended; however, it is said that not a single gentleman has dared ask them to dance or for a turn in the park." Pru lifted her chin as if she were impressed by the women's skill at keeping men at bay. "Chastity and I have been trying to gain an introduction since seeing them at the Crofton's garden party a fortnight ago, but the women do not often socialize, and quickly depart societal events after a brief appearance."

Most likely because the trio was spying on Abercorn.

Triston watched Lady Edith as she leaned close and whispered something to Lady Lucianna before nudging the auburn-haired chit to gain her attention, as well.

Their glares still intensely observed Abercorn's every movement. Did they wait for the man to strike again—in the middle of a crowded ballroom?

If Abercorn were able to get away with killing his

young bride, he would not be so foolish as to cause a scene before all of society.

Suddenly, Lady Edith's stare scanned the room—landing on him.

Prudence tugged at his arm and hissed, "They are watching us, brother. Mayhap they will talk to me."

The excitement in his sister's tone was evident; though Triston also sought to speak with the women, or more accurately, *one* of the women.

Lady Edith owed him answers, and Triston was determined to gain them, even if that meant confronting her in a crowded ballroom.

CHAPTER 4

EDITH SCRUTINIZED LORD Torrington across the crowded ballroom as the Duke of Abercorn returned his dance partner to the viscount's left side before taking the gloved hand of the woman on Torrington's right and returning to the dance floor.

The women held a striking resemblance to Torrington and must be a close relation—sisters, perhaps?

That would make the young women neighbors of Abercorn's—and likely friends. The woman now in the duke's arms seemed a bit too stiff and only spoke in answer to Abercorn's unheard words. She did not look the blushing debutante, thrilled to be dancing with a wealthy, eligible lord.

But, Torrington and the young women were positively acquainted with the duke. How close their relationship was, Edith could not guess.

However, she was vastly relieved she'd fled when she did, or Abercorn would have been informed of her presence outside his townhouse. If the neighbors were known to one another well enough to associate at a ball, then there was little doubt Torrington might share news of Edith's presence outside the Abercorn townhouse.

"Do you know the man?" Ophelia asked, leaning

close but managing to keep her eyes trained on the polished floor nonetheless.

The woman was perceptive, always had been, noting things that both Edith and Luci continually missed.

"Yes." Edith needed to distract her friends before other guests noticed the way the trio kept a close watch on Abercorn. "He caught me outside Abercorn's townhouse a few days ago."

"The day you fell out of the tree and bruised your backside?" Luci asked with a throaty chuckle, never taking her attention off Torrington. "He is certainly a handsome—"

Edith crossed her arms and cut Luci short. "That is him—all arrogant, incorrigible, and…"

"Massive," Ophelia sighed, her eyes moving from the floor to the hulking man across the room. "He looks as if he could drive a hansom cab…without the horses."

Edith took in Torrington's sheer size. His shoulders appeared far broader in a crowded ballroom, and his tight pants gave an optimal view of his muscular legs.

"It is likely the man must turn sideways to enter a door," Luci continued, prolonging the jest. "Those thighs could crush a boulder—imagine the fate of a woman between them."

"Lucianna," Ophelia hissed, her cheeks flaming with embarrassment as she glanced to both sides to make certain no one had heard what was spoken. "That is a highly improper topic for a ballroom."

"Yes, however, it does appease my imagination," Luci retorted with a sniff. "Do not be such a prude."

"I…well…I most certainly am not—"

"Did your mind instantly visualize the man, complete with bridle and reins, sans a stitch of clothing, pulling a hackney?" At Luci's question, Ophelia's eyes widened and quickly returned to the floor. "I thought not. Prude."

Edith cocked her head and examined Torrington once more. Her mind hadn't conjured Luci's visual either, but now she thought of little else. She averted her stare to stop her own flush and scanned the ballroom. Highlighted in shades of gold and blue sheer bolt fabrics, the chandeliers above cast a glow that sparkled off the polished silver pots holding tall palms in several spots around the room. Gentlemen and fashionably adorned ladies swirled about the dance floor while many wandered the room and out onto the terrace beyond.

She'd spotted Lord Torrington as he stood close to the refreshment table as the Duke of Abercorn had made his way toward them.

Where he'd come from, Edith didn't know. One moment, she and her friends were keeping watch on Abercorn's movements while avoiding any gentlemen who might ask one of them to dance; and the next, Lord Torrington stood with two demurely gowned brunettes on his arms. Not that she and her friends had been observing anyone but the duke; however, Edith had been shocked to see Torrington.

The man who currently observed her and her friends, just as they watched him.

"What is his name?" Luci purred, not verbalizing the one thing Edith heard loud and clear from her tone: what is the *handsome man's* name?

"Torrington. Lord Torrington." Edith watched him chuckle at something the woman on his arm said as he avoided eye contact with Edith. Pain shot through her jaw when she realized she clenched it tightly, her teeth grinding into one another. "He is certainly hiding something."

"Oh, I'd much enjoy seeing what his trousers are hiding." Luci's jest had Ophelia choking on her breath.

Irritation caused Edith's muscles to tense before she shrugged half-heartedly. "Likely nothing but an enlarged ego and unveiled arrogance."

"Why are you so overly critical of him?" Ophelia

asked. "Has he done something to displease you?"

"I would think his mere association with Abercorn should displease us all," Edith retorted. "I will admit the man is hiding something."

"Hiding something more elaborate than Abercorn?" Luci asked, intrigued.

"Possibly." Or Lord Torrington was nothing more than a lord born and bred to be the arrogant gentleman. He appeared the Goliath rather than the Adonis from their previous meeting. "I think it best I keep watch on him. If he is hiding something, I will find it—and Ophelia will use the information in her next *Mayfair Confidential* piece."

"Are you suggesting we stop our surveillance of Abercorn?" Lucianna set her long, gracefully gloved hands on her hips.

"You know we cannot jeopardize our true intentions and plans by reporting on Abercorn until we have solid proof of his culpability in Tilda's death," Edith argued, keeping her voice low. "If we write about him too soon, everyone in London will know who is behind the *Mayfair Confidential* articles in the *Gazette*."

Luci's eyes flared with anger. "Are you saying I did not see what I have told you I saw?"

"Come now, Lucianna," Ophelia soothed. "You know *we* believe you, but that accomplishes nothing if we cannot prove anything to the magistrate or Tilda's parents."

But Edith was uncertain she believed Luci's accounting from the night Tilda fell to her death. She wanted nothing more than to believe her friend and prove her accusation true, but until that happened, she refused to be party to a story that would ruin a man's life—more than they'd already ruined him.

They'd agreed to have Ophelia write a story on Abercorn only when they had irrefutable evidence and did not fear any backlash if they were discovered as the people behind the *Mayfair Confidential* pieces. But they were all in agreement on the importance of warning other debutantes against men with unsavory pasts, the tendency to drink heavily, or an inclination toward violence. So, each week on Thursday, the *London Daily Gazette* published a column called *Mayfair Confidential* that highlighted gentlemen with distasteful habits. As of now, no one suspected who was responsible for the pieces—but the instant Abercorn was mentioned, with Luci's firsthand account of the incident, there would be no doubt as to whom was supplying the information.

Edith was uncertain she was prepared for the repercussions once London—and the many men they worked to expose—knew they were responsible.

"Do not look now, Edith, but he is looking this way, and he does not appear happy to see you," Lucianna said with a laugh. For reasons unknown to Edith, Luci always acted untouchable and invincible, as if no person could harm her; however, the stark reality of the matter was they were all as susceptible to injury as Tilda had been. And they all knew where their dear friend was now after her hasty betrothal and marriage to a man over twice her age.

Edith notched her chin high and turned her narrowed stare in Torrington's direction. If the man thought to intimidate her, he vastly underestimated the woman he was dealing with.

CHAPTER 5

"TRISTON!" A VENOM-DIPPED voice, which many mistook for a honey-coated melody, called to him as he attempted to escape his father's townhouse without being waylaid after their weekly meeting. "Torry, stop, I am calling you."

He despised the pet name—always had—which was likely why his latest stepmother, Esmee, insisted on using it. The mere sound of her voice, and her quick steps behind him, had Triston longing to flee and never return.

His teeth clenched tight, and his jaw ached.

However, he knew enough to know that if he angered the woman by ignoring her and departing, she'd only take her wrath out on Pru and Chastity. Again, something he had little control over, and it irked him to no end.

"Yes, Esmee?" Triston pulled his lips into a smile, but judging from the way the woman shrank back in horror, it was more of a snarl. "What can I assist you with today?"

Meaning: in what way could she complicate his life?

She hurried down the hall after him and flipped her fan, connecting with his elbow. "You know I prefer you to call me Mother," she scolded. At his continued frown, she said, "But that is not why I stopped you. Your sisters and I are in need of your accompaniment to Hyde Park today."

The raven-haired, ice-blue-eyed snake was a year *younger* than Triston. Hell would freeze over and implode before he *ever* addressed the vile woman as "Mother."

Huffing, she tapped her slippered toes on the rug covering the floor and pushed her bottom lip out into a pout. "Well?"

Once upon a time, it would have worked on Triston—the innocent-maiden-in-need-of-help charade, but not in over a year. *And never again*, he'd vowed the night he'd caught his father in bed with his betrothed.

He'd like to say it was Esmee's betrayal that had wounded him so deeply he never sought to tie himself to another woman, favoring a life of uncomplicated relationships with no lasting attachments instead.

Mother…it was almost incestuous to think.

She set her hand on his sleeve and gently caressed his arm, sending a shiver of revulsion through him.

"I will accompany my sisters…under one condition." He paused, waiting for her to acquiesce to his demand. When she only smiled as if she'd won some battle he hadn't been aware they were fighting, he continued. "I will bring my own horse." There was absolutely no way he'd willingly share a carriage with Esmee—or anything else for that matter. Though punishing his sisters and diminishing their chances of making suitable matches was not something Triston would carry on his shoulders.

Her smile faltered slightly, but Esmee nodded in agreement. "We shall meet you in the drive." With a flip of her hair, as black as her heart no doubt, she pivoted, calling, "Prudence. Chastity." She punctuated each name with a clap of her hands. "To the carriage with all due haste. Do not be so rude as to keep Triston waiting."

He would wait for eternity if it made Pru and

Chastity happy…what he would *not* do was inconvenience himself to appease Esmee.

This was about his sisters' futures, not pleasing the wolf in sheep's clothing who'd almost duped him into marriage.

He stalked from the townhouse, calling for the butler to have his horse brought round. He would be ready and mounted by the time the women arrived—making further idle chit-chat impossible. To the park, a turn or two down the trail, and he would be on his way.

Blast it all, but he'd managed almost a fortnight without coming into contact with Esmee, and his temper hadn't flared once. Now, with only a moment of conversation his blood boiled again.

A Downshire livery brought round his horse at the same time his sisters' carriage ambled down the alley leading to the stable house.

He swung up into the saddle at the precise moment Pru and Chastity exited the front door, each beaming at seeing him in the drive.

And Triston could not help but return their looks of joy with his own grin.

They wore matching puce-colored gowns with walking boots, cloaks, and each had a fur muff to keep their hands warm. Their curls were pinned back in tight coiffures and garnished with strands of black beads. For not the first time in the last week, Triston wondered how the pair had grown from annoying girls in short dresses with pleats to the women who stood before him. Damn it all, but he wished he still resided at his father's townhouse and could enjoy a bit more time with his sisters before they selected husbands and left home to start their own families—their time for their roguish ancient brother gone.

And he had no doubt, despite their claims to the contrary, that they would marry. They need only find the right men—those who stole their hearts and saw beneath their outward appearances.

Triston was determined to make certain they had enough time in London to do just that.

"We are so pleased you will be accompanying us." Pru accepted the footman's assistance into the open carriage. "We have so missed you the last couple of days."

Triston chuckled. "Drop the demure, proper miss act, Prudence."

Both women looked back at the door, their stepmother still safely out of sight and earshot. Chastity sighed. "We are so grateful you've agreed to come—to save us from an afternoon of lectures on proper decorum during our ride in the park."

"Or another scolding on the proper way to address this lord or that lord."

"Bloody hell, Triston," Pru continued. "The foolish woman thinks to betroth us to men older than Father. Did you hear that? *Older than Father!*"

"And only half as wealthy," Chastity retorted. "She seeks us to be wed and bedded by any old, poor lord who will have us."

"Father will not allow this to happen, I assure you." Triston's words were meant to soothe his sisters' unease; however, even he was uncertain whether their father would be able to put his foot down and stop his newest wife from marrying off Pru and Chastity to unsuitable men. "And if need be, I will step in and rescue you both."

"Rescue them from what, precisely?" Esmee's shrill voice sounded behind them.

His horse paced anxiously as he turned to see the woman, wearing white from her hat all the way to her boots as she made her way down the front steps and to the waiting carriage.

"We were discussing the news that a wild bear has escaped from a traveling sideshow and is said to be roaming Hyde Park."

Both women nodded in unison as if to confirm

Triston's fib.

"Ah, well, it may well be a foot race if that happens." Esmee eyed the pair when the servant handed her up into the conveyance. "And I fear the pair of you would never make it far on foot."

All happiness and excitement drained from both women at their stepmother's cruel comment directed at their ample size.

He cringed as Pru's and Chastity's gazes fell to their laps. "Yes, my lady."

Bloody hell, but he would remove them from the abyss that was their home if he had the power—and the resources.

"Shall we be off?" Lady Downshire signaled for the driver to put the horses in motion as she sat back in her cascade of white. The color represented purity, innocence, and goodness. The woman was none of those things, not now, and not on the fateful day Triston had met her.

Thankfully, he was about to ride ahead of the carriage, cutting off the sight of her and giving him time to diminish his anger. He was here for Pru and Chastity. It was their future that a turn in Hyde Park would improve. He was only here for them, regardless of what anyone thought.

If his presence kept Esmee's spiteful tongue from lashing out at his sisters, then his discomfiture was worth it. It was suspicious he did not notice the woman's many flaws during their brief courtship—he was too overcome by his lust to see that Esmee was not the graceful, adventurous lady he'd thought, but a cunning, manipulative viper.

Triston saw that now—it was all he saw when he looked at the woman.

When they arrived at the most fashionable time to be seen, the park was near to bursting with carriages, horses, vendors, and people walking along the paths. The shouts from orange vendors ripped through the air at the park's gates, and the sound of carriage wheels created a din that echoed through Triston's head.

A bit of his sisters' joy returned as they waved to a friend and then greeted a gentleman who sidled up on his horse. Both girls tittered into their muffs when the lord complimented their upswept hair. However, Esmee cut their conversation short and pushed the carriage onward and away from the lord, who only gave notice to Pru and Chastity.

Triston slowed his horse and fell in line behind the carriage, wanting to keep watch over the girls, but not draw untoward attention to himself. People still openly gawked when he and his stepmother found themselves in the same room—as if the *ton* thought they'd fall back into one another's arms even though his father, the marquis, had solidly won her hand in marriage.

Either that or they thought the Marquis of Downshire would seek to avenge his wife's honor by challenging his son.

Triston would admit to anyone who would listen that his father had done him a grand favor—a boon of epic proportions—by stealing Esmee as he had. If anything, Triston now held a measure of pity for his father to be tied to the she-devil.

The *beau monde* were just as senseless as Lady Downshire if they thought Triston still held a candle of hope for the one he'd once thought himself in love with.

Betrayal had a way of clearing one's muddled eyesight.

And so, Triston tried to remain unnoticed and yet fulfill his obligations to his siblings.

Lady Downshire waved to a cluster of gentlemen standing alongside the carriage path and called to her driver to halt. The gathering of men slowly made their way over to the Downshire carriage, each offering a greeting to Esmee before turning to be introduced to Pru and Chastity. He recognized three of the men, friends of his father, and all as old as his sire.

What was the woman up to? She was supposed to be securing favorable matches for the girls, but she only seemed interested in settling them with older men who were not up to snuff.

The gentlemen said their farewells when Pru and Chastity refused to converse with them, and the carriage started off once more.

Triston kicked his horse into action and rode up alongside the carriage. He was exhausted, he was bored to tears, and this ride in the park had nothing to do with making certain his siblings met men of high caliber. No, this was another performance for Esmee—a way to show all of London how far she'd risen, and that she would never allow Pru or Chastity to wed above her.

"Lord Gaston may only be a baron, but let me be frank, girls, you will likely not do any better," Esmee lectured. "And it would be in your best interest to take your Season seriously. Once I am with child, I will be unable to flit about London with the pair of you, and your father has agreed some time in the country will suit us all until the little lord is born."

The woman's prattling on and on about giving the marquis another child had grown tiresome over the last few months, and Triston could not trust himself to steel a disparaging retort for much longer.

Triston caught Pru's eye and shook his head. "Ladies, I fear the day has gotten away from me, and I have another engagement to attend to. I bid you all good afternoon."

"It was lovely to see you, brother," Pru called with a wave.

"Thank you for accompanying us," Chastity said.

"I will be around again soon." He winked at his sisters, hoping they understood he'd never allow them to be married off to an impoverished baron, nor be relegated to a future confined to their father's country manor. "Enjoy the rest of your ride."

When Pru nodded, Triston knew he was cleared to depart. His siblings understood the restraint it took for him to be around Esmee for any length of time, and they did not take offense to his less than regular attendance.

CHAPTER 6

THE WIND CASCADED across her face, a welcome respite helping to banish the negativity that had come to fill her life of late. She pushed her filly to a trot as the fresh breeze lifted her loose, golden locks. The wind tangled in her tresses, tossing them to and fro, but Edith could care less about the knots she'd have to endure later when her lady's maid put a brush to them.

If it wasn't Luci demanding they more diligently pursue Abercorn to expose his misdeed, then it was Ophelia reminding Edith they only had two days before another article was due. If they did not keep up with their pieces, the *Gazette* would find another gossip columnist to take the place of *Mayfair Confidential*—and that would mean dire consequences for many young, unsuspecting women who thought themselves smitten with a nobleman, only to learn far too late he kept secrets.

Edith slowed her horse's pace, allowing her mother and father to gain some distance as she surveyed them. They rode close, their horses almost rubbing against one another, keeping their hands clasped between them the entire time.

They were in love.

Held a deep, undying commitment to one another.

Shared a life unrestricted by lies, secrets, and betrayal.

They told one another everything, traveled everywhere together, and the only thing they cherished more than Edith was each other—and their mutual adoration.

It was something Luci refused to admit existed, and Ophelia was openly skeptical of.

It was the sole reason Edith would not circulate or back a piece not rooted in solid fact.

Edith could not deny what had been in front of her, her entire life.

Love existed. Commitment was not an elusive trait. And with continued communication and openness, a relationship could flourish and last a lifetime.

Her parents, the Earl and Countess of Shaftesbury, were solid, irrefutable proof.

They gave her hope that one day she, too, would meet a gentleman worthy of her affection and trust. Yet, she hadn't been able to convince Lucianna or Ophelia that every lord was not a cruel, vile man with vices and secrets. If they dedicated a fraction of their time to finding honorable men, then maybe there was hope for all of them.

In the end, Edith was uncertain of Abercorn's role in Tilda's death. Until she was certain, either way, she would continue to help her friends find the answers they sought.

The answers, Edith grudgingly admitted, they all desperately needed.

If she turned her back on their mission, she would not only be turning away from her friends, but she'd also be casting shame on Tilda's memory. They owed it to the girl to find out what had happened to her.

Wherever the facts should lead.

Her head ached at the daunting undertaking she'd agreed to assist Luci and Ophelia with. Her heart hurt for what Luci claimed to have seen; however, her senses demanded they make certain before ruining a man's life. Tilda dying was tragedy enough. There was no need to further compound things by shouting Abercorn's name to all who would listen.

Edith followed her parents as the trail they traveled ended, depositing them back on the main carriage path, still cluttered with fancily garbed men and women in pursuit of social endeavors.

A group of finely dressed men in riding boots galloped across the far grass and around the pond toward Kensington Gardens. And a pair of women hopped out of the way in surprise as the men nodded but continued on. On the trail before her, Edith's parents chatted and laughed, drawing their horses apart to avoid colliding with another horseman. No matter how many times another got in their way, they always drew close once more, their legs almost touching as they rode side by side. They continued on, passing carriage after carriage, but Lord and Lady Shaftesbury never paused to speak with anyone.

Up ahead, a familiar set of brown curls came into view, ensconced in a luxurious open-air carriage with forest green material covering the interior. Edith moved her mare a bit to the right to gain a better view of the conveyance and its occupants.

Why she cared she did not know, but she nudged her horse to quicken her pace as the carriage neared. The broad shoulders and chiseled jawline she'd expected to see across from the two women was not present; instead, Edith was greeted with the back of a midnight-haired woman with a white hat on her head. Over the rear of the carriage, she noted the woman's cloak was also white—a clear contrast to the brown jackets over puce gowns of the women nestled on the seat across from her. The woman in white looked one way, but the other females were focused on something in the opposite direction.

Edith followed their stares, her eyes settling on the

figure she'd hoped—did she truly long to see the man again?—to see in the carriage. He sat tall upon his horse with his chin raised in confidence. He was certainly a horseman with the way he deftly held the reins.

Her stomach fluttered. If she'd been standing, and not astride, her knees would have crumbled beneath her.

Lord Torrington's shoulders were every bit as wide as his horse's hindquarters. It seemed impossible a horse as large as the man existed, yet, Edith could not deny they were a perfectly matched set. The mount was eighteen hands tall if he were one.

If she'd thought Torrington dashing and powerful in evening garb, he was pure strength and dominance astride in riding attire. It was easy to picture the man and his horse charging into battle to fight off opposing soldiers, never pulling back in fear or hesitation.

With a quick wink to the women, Torrington tugged the reins and spurred his mount into a gallop toward the park exit with nary a look for the raven-haired woman.

Edith glanced toward her parents and back at Torrington's retreating frame.

She'd promised her friends a new story—which meant Edith needed to *find* that new story.

Lord Torrington was most certainly the man to give her one. She had no doubt he kept a secret…and she would uncover it.

He was dashingly handsome, obviously wealthy, and born into the grandest circle of society; yet he was unwed. Why was that?

Edith suspected this was where his secret began—and possibly ended.

"Mother!" she shouted above the noise of slow-moving carriage wheels and horse clopping. When her parents turned toward her, Edith continued, "Lady Ophelia and Lucianna have arrived." She pointed to a cluster of horses, carriages, and people all fighting for entrance and departure from the park. "May I continue on with them? They will see me home after."

Edith had never made a habit of lying to her parents—in fact, they rarely gave her an excuse to have to lie.

Her father glanced toward the exit, trying to spot his daughter's friends.

"Please, Father?" she begged. "If I hurry, I can catch them."

She could catch *him*. Lord Torrington was nearly at the gate. If he managed to slip past the crowd and out into London traffic, she'd never find him.

"Edward." Her mother smiled, setting her free hand on her husband's arm. "Allow her to go. It is only a ride in the park, not a night at the opera."

When her father nodded in agreement, Edith called her thanks before sharply pulling her reins and spurring her mare into a fast trot. Glancing over her shoulder, she saw her parents had continued their ride, their attention safely on one another. Edith kicked her mount into a gallop until she reached the exit, desperately trying to keep Torrington's brown hair in sight. It proved rather easy as his mount stood taller than most carriages—and with his added height, the man was in no way inconspicuous. However, Edith needed to be far more subtle in her pursuit if she hoped to follow him unnoticed.

The man would not reveal his secrets if he suspected he was being followed.

As she navigated the crowd, Edith felt for her journal and nub, both securely in the pocket of her gown. Today would be the day she gained some truly worthwhile information to share with Ophelia and Lucianna. It had been nearly a week since she'd discovered the clandestine meeting between the duke, Montrose, and his fair-haired nymph alone in his opera box. It did not appear so scandalous upon first glance until one noticed the woman's bosom was exposed—

and Montrose was set to wed Lady Cavendish in a short three weeks.

She only hoped anything she could find about Torrington was enough to keep her friends occupied and away from Abercorn.

EDITH CONTINUED TO follow Torrington down endless London streets. Her only moment of hesitation was when he crossed the river toward Vauxhall—and ventured into an area known for its crime, poverty, and unsavory entertainments. The notion of turning around and admitting yet another failure was not an option.

As she expected him to keep going—maybe he suspected he was being followed, taking them both on a wild chase—Lord Torrington turned down a narrow lane and slowed his horse to a walk as he maneuvered around a cart loaded with textiles ready for market.

She paused at the end of the lane. There was no conceivable way she could follow him down the narrow path without him noticing her. He must be close to his final destination because it did not appear the lane, truly no more than an alley, led anywhere beyond.

Torrington dismounted his horse about half a block down and flipped the reins to a waiting footman. Why would a servant be waiting outside a building in this part of town?

Once he entered, Edith determined it safe to journey into the alley.

A sign painted on the front of the building Lord Torrington had entered gave the name of the establishment as *Langworth Inn*. The exterior was well kept, the entrance cleared of filth and rubbish. Windows lining the second and third floor were polished clean with their draperies pulled tight. It was in stark contrast to the neighboring buildings, one with not a solid windowpane and another missing its door. The livery who'd taken Torrington's horse had disappeared down an even narrower alley to the side of the inn.

"Ye lost, miss?" A woman pulling a cart of textiles looked up at Edith, her brow furrowed in concern. "I don't be think'n this be the place for ye."

Edith looked back to the inn Torrington had entered—she certainly did not belong here. It only begged the question: what was Lord Torrington, a viscount, doing in this part of London?

He might very well be inside for an afternoon tryst, maybe with a ladybird from Vauxhall. She'd learned recently gentlemen of all ages enjoyed an afternoon with a lovely woman. Imagines of Abercorn and the dark-haired woman sprang to mind, the way her bare rump had been pressed to the windowpane, the devious smile upon her lips, and the laughter she saw brim from the duke. Was that what Torrington was doing at this very moment, enjoying a few brief hours wrapped in a woman's arms? Her heartbeat thrashed in her ears, and her vision clouded for an instant. Edith filled with the urge to kick something.

It was also possible his presence here had nothing to do with a woman and everything to do with business, more accurately, a sham business dealing.

From the appearance of the building, the owner did not lack funds for upkeep, but how could an inn this deep into London remain a profitable endeavor? The lane did not see a heavy flow of traffic, nor was it close to the docks. Could it be the house of an opium den? She'd never seen one, but the *Gazette* had published a story about the insurgence of opiates and those who found pleasure in smoking the nefarious substance. Torrington didn't appear a gentleman who partook in anything stronger than a tumbler of scotch or a pint of ale.

However, there was only one way to find out…she would follow him into the inn.

But first, Edith had to decide if she truly wanted to

know Torrington's secrets.

With a nod, she glanced back at the woman with the cart, still paused before her. "I am not lost, but thank you all the same for your kindness in asking." She gave the woman a reassuring smile. "I am waiting for the servant to take my horse, and then I will be going into the Langworth Inn."

Edith wasn't sure if the words were meant to convince her nothing untoward would happen to her if she dared dismount her horse, or if it was to appease the woman's curiosity.

"Very well, miss," she replied before taking hold of the cart handles. "Ye be careful."

"Thank you." Edith watched the woman pull the heavy cart down the lane before dismounting and peering about. The servant hadn't returned, and she doubted she would be inside long. The street was deserted except for the woman headed to the market.

Edith quickly dismounted her mare and tied the reins to the post outside the inn, knowing full well she could be without a horse when she returned, but she'd promised her friends new information for Ophelia to write about—and she was desperately close to getting it.

There was no turning back now.

The entrance of the inn was as deserted as the street outside. No proprietor waited to greet new customers. No sounds traveled toward Edith from deeper inside the inn. The place certainly was not seeking people looking for accommodations. Highly odd for a place labeled an inn.

A bark of laughter came from the door bordering the stairwell leading to the floors above. Edith inched toward the partially open door, careful to keep her footfalls quiet, and then she peeked into the room. Circular tables were arranged about the space with four stools at each. On the far side was a long bar with an assortment of clear decanters behind it.

A taproom. Edith had never seen an actual

taproom before, let alone entered one.

And today was not the day to explore—she was here for a purpose, and neither of the two men in the room were her objective. One was an older gentleman with his sleeves rolled past his elbows as he poured a pint of ale for a lanky, blond young man who sat on a stool at the long bar.

Neither was Lord Torrington.

She crept a bit closer to make sure she could scan the entire space before stepping back.

A door closed above, and Edith pressed herself against the wall, waiting to be discovered when whomever it was above came down the stairs. She held her breath, fearing she'd be caught and questioned. Turned over to a magistrate and hauled off to a holding house long before she knew what was happening.

Edith hadn't been successful in playing the detective outside Abercorn's townhouse, and she didn't understand why she thought she'd do any better in an inn. On a positive note, there was no chance of her falling from a tree.

When no footsteps sounded on the stairs, Edith sighed in relief.

The cold, rough wall bit into her back even through her many layers of clothing.

She was discovering nothing here, and only risking being caught if either of the men wandered from the taproom.

Hurrying up the stairs, attempting to make as little noise as possible, Edith rushed down the single corridor on the second floor. Room after empty room—a parlor, a library, and a dining room stood open for her scrutiny. The farthest three doors on the floor were solidly closed. She pressed her ear to each, heard nothing, and tried each respective lever. The first two opened easily on well-oiled hinges to reveal empty sleeping quarters. The third was tightly locked.

There was little chance Torrington was on this

floor.

Edith hurried back down the hall and up to the third floor. The hallway looked exactly as the last had: several doors opened to a receiving room, an office, a dining area, and four closed doors at the far end. All entirely uninhabited.

He must be in one of the closed rooms. There was no other place he could be hiding, unless he'd entered the inn and departed out the back. Blast it, but Edith hadn't even thought of that possibility.

No, Edith needed to have faith that Torrington hadn't seen her trailing him, and that he was unaware she was searching for him at this very moment.

She tiptoed down the hall, once again placing her ear to one of the closed doors. Nothing.

She moved on to the next. Silence.

The third, however, proved fruitful. She heard male mumbling from the far side, and something solid hit the floor—a boot, perhaps? The sound was followed by yet another thud.

Images of Torrington undressing surged into her mind, followed quickly by visions of him bare-chested and pulling a carriage with his brute strength. She swallowed, suppressing the need to fan her heated face. She didn't know what she wanted more, to giggle or scold Luci for introducing the foolish fantasy to her mind.

She pressed her ear more firmly to the door, trying her best to decipher his mumbling—or if another occupied the room with him. Damnation, she wasn't even certain it *was* Torrington in the room.

Worse still, Edith couldn't understand what was being said on the far side of the door, although she was fairly certain it was only one voice she heard. Her shoulders sagged with an unexpected release of tension. She'd truly thought to find him here—with a woman.

It was ludicrous she was concerned with what Torrington did or whom he did it with.

He was a stranger—an arrogant, demanding stranger.

Yet, still an Adonis among men.

She shook her head at the thought.

Edith was here to learn what dastardly secrets the man kept, not to spend her afternoon woolgathering over the man's prowess—which she had little doubt was great.

Lucianna would be proud to know that at least Edith wasn't a prude as her mind swirled around images of a certain lord's bare chest.

The squeak of bed ropes sounded as the room's occupant most likely either sat or laid on the bed. And now, Edith was thinking of Torrington's massive frame strewn haphazardly across *her* bed as a pool of heat settled in her most private area. Dash it all, but she was not attracted to the man. And she knew she should not be attracted to him in any way.

She was here to explore his misdeeds, not his body.

"May I help you, miss?" a gentle voice sounded from behind Edith.

CHAPTER 7

TRISTON ALLOWED HIS head to fall into his hands, and he scrubbed away the tension of the day. This was his safe place, where he could just be Triston—not Lord Torrington, not the marquis' son, not the responsible brother of two hoyden sisters, and not a man marred by scandal. No one looked at him with question when he entered this inn. No one inquired as to his hardships. No one demanded anything of him. The place was quiet, and he went undisturbed and unknown to everyone—except his father and his man of business.

It was for this specific reason Triston had chosen the boarding house—and leased the entire third floor—when he could not stand living under his father's roof a moment longer.

Here, he answered to no one.

And, in turn, the inn's other occupants paid him little mind.

As long as no one ventured into his area—except the servants—Triston remained happy with his accommodations. That he did not reside in the most elite area of London only added to the Langworth Inn's appeal. Coming and going, he crossed no one's path unless it was his intention to do so.

A screech sounded outside his door, followed by

the sloshing of water and a tin hitting the wooden floor.

Triston shot to his feet and started for the door.

Water cascaded under his door and reached his bare feet, the lukewarm liquid surely intended for the bath he'd summoned be brought to his room.

He hoped no one was injured.

Pulling the door open, his eyes widened at the spectacle in the hall. Molly, the upstairs maid, scattered to collect the tin she'd dropped, while also attempting to stop the water from traveling farther down the corridor and into other rooms. On her knees, Lady Edith Pelton used her skirts to halt the bathwater from flooding into his room.

The scene would have been highly entertaining if Triston weren't shirtless and barefooted with his trouser flap hanging open in preparation for his bath.

He was indecent, and Edith was so distracted helping Molly, she didn't realize her derriere was positioned perfectly for a pinch as it wagged back and forth as she soaked up the water.

The urge to reach out toward her was strong—as was the need to laugh—but he kept silent and unmoving. Triston relished the opportunity to see how this would play out before him.

"I am dreadfully sorry," Edith gushed. "My friends always speak to my clumsy nature. They will find much enjoyment once again, knowing they have been proven—"

Her voice cut off as Molly stood and stared past her, finally noting Triston's presence.

The time to put the debacle to an end had arrived, accompanied by the stirring in his pants.

"Thank you, Molly," he said with a smile. "I can get this tidied up. You may return to your other chores."

"What—what—what—" she stammered, wringing her hands. "What about your bath, my lord?"

"I am certain it will take some time to heat more water. I can wait." He kept his eyes trained on the servant, hoping she too did not focus on Lady Edith, still on her hands and knees, outside his bedchamber door. "Hurry along."

"Are you certain, my lord?" The maid blinked rapidly, clutching the basin to her chest. What little water remained, dripped down the front of her uniform and pooled at her feet.

He waved her off with a nod. "I am certain, Molly."

With one last glance at Lady Edith, the servant curtseyed and fled back toward the landing.

When Molly had disappeared down the stairs, Triston extended his arm to Edith. "Lady Edith, may I assist you to rise?"

Her shoulders slumped, and her head fell forward, but she did not address him.

"I must say, this is rather more shocking than finding you with your cloak and skirts thrown over your head." He was teasing her unmercifully, and he damn well knew it; however, she deserved any jests he made.

His mind swirled with reasons why Lady Edith was in Langworth Inn, outside his bedchamber door—on her hands and knees. None of them boded well for Triston and his need to remain unscathed by the scandal sheets for the foreseeable future.

His teeth ground together, but he was unable to hold back his rising ire. "What in the bloody hell are you doing here?"

At his harsh words, her shoulders stiffened, and her head snapped up, her eyes moving around to meet his as she pushed to her feet unassisted.

"Do not play coy, my lord," she seethed. "You know exactly why I am here."

It was then she took her narrowed glare from his and moved it to his shirtless chest, her eyes widening. Things would have been safe had her gaze stopped there, but it traveled lower, and her face blossomed with the most fetching rose color as her lips pressed together.

It only made matters worse when his manhood decided to disobey him and harden further as her now wide stare locked on his undone trouser flap.

"I have many ideas why I would *want* you here." He raised his brow in suggestion, though her eyes were still stuck far lower than his face…or chest…or waistband.

She snapped from her daze. "You are incorrigible, my lord," she hissed as she pushed past him—into his bedchamber. Into his empty bedchamber.

He had half a mind to shout for Molly to return and act as chaperone until Lady Edith decided she was ready to depart. Because the way she plopped herself down on his bed, her saturated cloak and skirts clinging to her legs, told Triston she was not leaving anytime soon.

Looking from the blessedly empty hallway to his room and back once more, Triston slammed the door shut. He could not risk anyone happening upon her in his private space.

She'd be compromised.

And he'd be to blame.

"Allow me to ask again, what are you doing here?" No, he was not entirely to blame. Edith had made her own way here, though he hadn't the faintest notion how or why, and she had willingly walked into his chambers and threw herself upon his bed.

All while he stood gawking, trying to remain angry even when his body wanted nothing more than to join her on the bed.

"Why are *you* here?" she retorted, crossing her arms.

"Bloody hell. I live here!"

Edith's muscles went rigid, and she leapt to her feet as if someone had actually pinched her backside. Her head turned from side to side as if noting for the first time that they stood in a bedchamber and she had been sitting upon a bed—a man's bed.

"You live here?" She gulped. "Right outside the

gates of Vauxhall?"

"Langworth Inn is not so close to Vauxhall." His father had had the same reaction when Triston had requested funds to secure his room and board at the Langworth Inn. He was aware the area was not known for much else but entertainment; however, Triston had sought distance and space—between him, society, and his father and the duke's new bride. A little lane off Laud Street had given him exactly what he'd longed for. "And yes, I most certainly do live here. However, you do not."

Even flustered with water dripping from her, she was captivating. Her blond hair was secured in a tight knot at the back of her head with several tendrils framing her face that had escaped her coiffure. He barely stopped himself from stepping toward her and pushing the wayward strands behind her ear.

"You are certainly correct, my lord. And I think it best I depart." She took a step toward the door, keeping her stare on the floor at her feet.

Triston stepped into her path, blocking her exit.

As much as he wanted her gone and away from his private chambers, his need to know why she kept appearing wherever he was proved stronger than his good sense to allow her to pass.

A CHILL RAN down Edith's spine, whether from her water-soaked clothes or the intimidating figure blocking her way, she was uncertain. One thing she knew all too plainly was she'd made a dreadful mistake. She'd thought to spy on Lord Torrington, discover his secrets, and hand them over to Ophelia for exposure by way of the *Gazette*'s *Mayfair Confidential.*

She'd gravely underestimated Torrington, and overestimated her own skill. Spying on him was no easy feat. She was now certain he held some scandalous secret, but she would never be permitted to find out what it was. But, now, Edith doubted she would want to betray the formidable man before her.

There would be consequences—dire consequences.

Edith notched her chin higher, not in confidence but to glare at Torrington straight in the eyes. How dare he deny her departure! "Do step aside, my lord," she hissed, placing her hands on her hips. "I find I wish to leave."

"I think our acquaintance has progressed beyond the 'my lord' formalities." He made no move to allow her escape. "You are in my bedchambers, after all. My given name is Triston."

Triston? Edith wasn't sure why the name surprised her. She'd known his title, but it seemed his given name was an intimacy she was unprepared for, nor had any right to possess.

Hell, at this juncture, she'd half expected his given name to actually be Adonis.

"Oddly, the name suits, my lord." Edith hadn't meant to vocalize her musings, and she quickly looked away to the washstand to his left. If her eyes dropped back to the floor, her perusal would travel all the way down his hulking body—his barely clothed body. And Edith did not need to linger on the way his muscles flexed when he tensed or the speckling of dark hair that covered his chest. Far darker than the hair atop his head. And she most certainly did not want to think about what lay beneath the flap of his undone trousers—for she already suspected it fought to gain freedom. The image caused her face to flush with heat, and her legs to quiver unsteadily.

She shouldn't want to look, but despite her best efforts, her eyes returned to his bare midsection.

Luci would likely whistle at the glorious sight.

Ophelia would swoon into a dead faint, and smelling salts would be needed.

But Edith…Edith hadn't any notion what to do or

what to think. In fact, to her horror, she was frozen. She could not move past him, nor would she retreat farther into his personal chambers. Even now, she was helpless to look away from his muscular shoulders, so wide he could easily carry a fallen carthorse across them. Or maybe rescue an entire schoolhouse of children in one fell swoop.

"Do you enjoy what you see?" he said with a chuckle.

Yet she hadn't actually taken in his form at all, but avoided settling her stare on his finely built masculine body.

She wanted to push him aside and flee, but that would put her hands in contact with his bare skin. Instead, Edith crossed her arms and leaned in close, making it obvious she inspected every inch of him, from his trousers, which hung loosely about his hips, up over his stocky midsection, and finally across his chest and to his face.

"I have seen many oxen with broader shoulders,"—she smirked, pulling back and leaning to the side as if to get a glimpse of his backside—"and far more accentuated hindquarters."

She gulped.

No laughter remained as he narrowed his eyes on her. "Did you just compare my physique to that of a farm animal?"

Edith took a step back—damnation, she would not cower to him. "If you prefer, I can select another animal. A donkey, perhaps? They are well-known for their obstinacy. Or better yet, an African lion, I have read they are intimidating creatures."

"You think me intimidating?" It was Torrington who took a step back this time, as if her words had wounded him. "Wait, do not answer that question—I have a far more important one: why do you keep appearing everywhere I am?"

"It is not I who keeps appearing," Edith corrected.

"I was minding my own business outside of Abercorn's townhouse. You are the one who scared me from the tree. And you were the one who caught my eye in the ballroom. And I was enjoying an afternoon in the park when—" She clamped her mouth shut.

"Enjoying an afternoon in the park until…you saw me and decided to follow?" he demanded. "I may very well be as large as an ox, or as stubborn as a donkey, or even as domineering as a lion, but at least I am not a snake—slithering and sneaking about, ready to bite and poison when the mood strikes."

Edith gasped, covering her mouth with her hand.

"Oh, you find it belittling to be compared to a bloody animal?" he sneered. "Well, I find it insulting to be lied to, followed, and scrutinized by a woman I do not know."

Edith sighed. "I have not been following you, I swear to it."

Not a complete lie, or at least she hadn't been at Lord Abercorn's townhouse to spy on Triston—she allowed herself to think of him by his given name—nor had she attended the ball with Ophelia and Luci expecting to see him. And the park, well, that was rather serendipitous. She had decided to keep an eye on him, but she'd never thought to follow him out of London proper.

Edith glanced to the window, but the drapes were pulled securely shut. "The day must be growing late. My parents will surely be wondering where I am when I don't arrive home on schedule."

"I know what you are up to, Lady Edith Pelton." His stance widened as he surveyed her from head to toe.

It was odd because, Edith was baffled at her bravado in following him and sneaking into the inn; however, she still considered Torrington a friend of Abercorn's, no matter he hadn't admitted as much. He hadn't denied his association with the duke either. She could not allow him to discover her ultimate goal for being outside Abercorn's townhouse, nor her interest in him at the ball. Could she?

No, she needs must distract him from the entire mess she'd created.

It was not only Edith's safety in jeopardy, but also that of Ophelia and Lucianna if the duke found out they persisted in proving his guilt in Tilda's death. He would no doubt seek vengeance if he discovered the truth.

"Why do you not live with your father?" Edith hoped to throw him off guard. "He has a lovely townhouse in a fashionable part of town. It is certainly closer to the more favored parts of London. I imagine it is inconvenient to journey all the way to Surrey for your lodging."

He held his stance, blocking her exit; however, Edith was uncertain she was in any rush to leave. It was highly improper and foolish to remain, but the man and his situation intrigued her.

"I am not the first lord to leave his father's home."

Edith pivoted and sat in a chair close to the fire, hoping her relaxed manner would lull him into an easy conversation. "No, but one does not normally find lodging in such an area." Maybe she could use him to gain information about Abercorn, as well.

His posture loosened, and he paced toward the fireplace and back to the door before swinging around to face her. "I will answer your questions if you agree to do the same."

It was an interesting proposition. "I can ask anything, and you will answer so long as I reciprocate?" she asked, her brow raising. She needed to be certain about what he offered.

It would not do to share information that could be used against her and her friends if she gained nothing in return.

CHAPTER 8

"THAT IS EXACTLY what I am saying, Lady Edith."
Triston was playing with fire, and he damn well knew it.
If he didn't watch out, he was likely to suffer burns that
would not heal with time, only fester and spread.
Though there were no secrets the *ton* and the many
sharp-tongued matrons hadn't used as gossip fodder
since his broken betrothal two years prior. Could it be
the lady before him was oblivious to his past? He
moved from his place blocking the door and leaned
down toward her, placing his hands on each of the
chair's arms before issuing his next warning. "However,
allow me to caution you against lying or misleading me
in any way. I do not take well to such actions."

She stared wide-eyed at his forearms, his position
keeping her seated, before averting her stare to her
worrying hands. Lady Edith tilted her head back and
sighed.

The woman was stalling, and Triston did not have
time for any of it. If she were found alone in his
bedchambers, Edith would be compromised...ruined,
her reputation in tatters. And he would once again be
the spectacle of gossip.

Triston could not allow that to happen; however, if
he did not find out what she was up to, she would

continue to plague him and put herself at risk.

Her eyes drifted shut, and he noticed her hand slip into a pouch in her skirt to grasp something.

"I have one question, Edith," he whispered, still only inches from her. When her eyes sprang open, and her chin tilted back down to meet his gaze, he continued, "Why have you been following me?"

"I told you, I was not—"

"If I am to believe that, then why do you keep appearing near me?"

Edith pulled something from her pocket, it was barely larger than the palm of her hand, but she held it out to him.

"What is this?" Triston took the object, surprised to discover it was a leather-bound book. "You enjoy reading? That tells me nothing."

"Open it," she commanded, crossing her arms defiantly and looking to the small fire in the hearth. "You will find what you need to know within."

Standing straight, Triston moved to the candelabra on his washstand for light and flipped the tiny book in his hands several times. The cover was worn, brown leather with tight stitching along the spine as if it had been repaired recently. One corner bent outward—the place where its owner repeatedly opened it.

Triston did the same, opening the book to reveal a hand-scribed, yellowing page.

Lady Edith's name flowed across the page in large, swirling penmanship.

Was it her handwriting? If so, it was nothing like he'd expected from her. On the several occasions he'd made her acquaintance, or watched her from afar, she always seemed rushed and frenzied. This handwriting was painstakingly neat, as if the writer had much time to dedicate to each letter.

Triston glanced back at her, but the diminishing flames licking the underside of the logs in the hearth kept her attention, giving him a moment to study her—

truly *see* Edith.

Certainly, she was the woman who'd fallen out of his father's tree, the female who'd stared unabashedly across the crowded ballroom at him, and the one who had traversed an unsavory part of London to follow him to Langworth Inn.

But there must be more to this… No woman of gentle breeding would put so much at risk for a lark.

He admired her resolve. As yet, she'd never backed down from him, nor treated him as a fool.

Even now, she seemingly sensed him eyeing her, and her chin notched up.

With her petite frame—at least one-third his size—and her blond hair, she appeared little more than a girl just out of the schoolroom, but on the few occasions he'd garnered a closer look into her almond-shaped, whiskey-colored eyes, he saw a depth no innocent maiden should be burdened with.

But she was here. In his chambers. Sitting calmly.

She hadn't fled as she had during their first meeting, and she'd willingly handed him the book he currently held. Truly, it appeared to be a journal.

Perhaps this was her attempt to seek his help.

Triston turned back to the journal and flipped to the next page. In the same neat script, he read:

Mayfair Confidential

His brow furrowed, and he rolled the words around in his mind, searching, attempting to grasp why the words were familiar to him.

Finally, he shook his head and turned to the next page.

One word was written at the top, a name, underlined several times.

Abercorn.

His sister had told him of Lady Edith's and her friends' connection to Abercorn.

What followed was page after page of barely legible notes. Dates, times, places where Abercorn had been seen. There was even a detailed accounting of people coming and going from his townhouse. Another page, only half-filled, noted both the day he'd discovered her on Downshire property—she'd noted Abercorn had been seen through his top-floor window, consorting with a raven-haired woman—and then continued with notes from the ball when the duke had requested a dance from both Pru and Chastity.

She hadn't lied when she'd argued she hadn't been there because of him.

Why did he feel a pang of resentment that Edith was so wholly focused on Abercorn and not him?

The tightness in his chest released, and his stomach twisted the moment he turned the page to see his name across the top, though it was only underlined once.

Below it was simply written: *built as sturdy as a druid warrior, two sisters (?), does not live with family, friends with Abercorn (?), arrogant.*

Was that the summation of his life thus far?

He should be angry to learn she was also watching him, but Triston was only confused.

"Let me see," he mused. "Built as sturdy as a druid warrior? No, my heritage is closer to a Viking warlord. Two sisters, yes, Prudence and Chastity. Does not live with his family." He paused and glanced around the room. "I think we have established the truth of that. Friends with Abercorn. I believe the term 'friends' is stretching our relationship a bit. We are neighbors. When in London, Abercorn is only the man who lives next door. He has no children or family so, naturally, he dines with us on occasion, but there is nothing more than that between our families. And arrogant? Most certainly. Does that answer all your questions, my lady?" He raised his brow when she turned to stare at him, remaining silent. "Oh, I also had a huge cat growing up…he was a bit of a pest and despised my father, but I loved him all the same."

Triston used his finger and fanned through the rest

of the pages—all blank, awaiting either more information about him or Abercorn. Perhaps she sought yet another man to shadow.

"Can you please put on a shirt?" she asked.

"I apologize if my hulking frame is disturbing your delicate sensibilities," he threw back at her. "I was not expecting company in my private chambers and, therefore, was not dressed appropriately. You must excuse my ungentlemanly attire."

"Do not be ridiculous, my lord," she sighed. "But as enlightening as this has been, I will need my journal back, and then I will be out of your private chambers immediately."

She stood as Triston retrieved a clean linen shirt from his armoire and threw it over his head. "You are not going anywhere yet. I have not gotten my question answered."

Triston sensed he'd reached a delicate topic, one Lady Edith was reluctant to speak about. It was so personal, she seemed prepared to flee without gaining any of the answers she'd come for. However, he had no intention of allowing her to depart yet.

"But—but—," she stammered, her eyes lighting with contempt. "I gave you my journal."

"Which told me what you know about me—and Abercorn—but not *why* you seek this information." Triston tied his trouser flap closed, hoping the gesture would put her at ease. "Now, why *are* you so determined to ruin Abercorn?"

Edith took several quick steps until she stood a mere foot from him and turned her glare up to meet his. "Me, ruin him? He is the one who is responsible for my dear friend's death. I presume the better question here is why *you* would allow your innocent sisters to be in the man's presence for even a moment, knowing the accusations against the man."

"As I said, he is my father's neighbor—a harmless old man with no family to speak of."

"He has been wed three times, and he has outlived them all, even though they are usually decades his junior," Edith seethed, her hands securely on her hips, ready to argue her point. "What say you about that? What if he fancies one of your sisters? What then? Do you plan to accept his offer of marriage and hand your sister over to a man who will likely outlive her, as well?"

"What is your proof Abercorn did anything untoward in his previous marriages?" Triston hadn't many dealings with Abercorn, as the man was nearly old enough to be his grandfather; however, the conviction in Edith's tone swayed him greatly.

"Proof?" she asked. "I was there. I saw my dear, beloved friend lying prone at the bottom of a grand staircase—the *duke's* grand staircase—on her wedding night. A night that should have been the happiest of her life. A day that was supposed to be remembered with great fondness as she and Abercorn set off on their bridal tour. But, instead, Tilda suffered a broken neck from her fall. The physician said she was dead before she hit the bottom step. What other proof do you need? I can sketch the scene for you, if that will make you happy."

Triston had never taken much stock in the accusations leveled against Abercorn. Hell, he'd had enough of his own societal ridicule to last him decades—and within those bits of chatter there had been nothing but a grain of truth, yet that did not stop the gossip mills from feasting on him. He'd heard at White's that the rumors swirling about Abercorn were much the same.

"You saw him push her?" Triston asked, shaking his head. If he heard confirmation, he knew he'd be honor bound to see that Abercorn paid for his crimes.

Edith pivoted away from him and paced toward the door. For a brief moment, he expected her to flee—leaving her journal safely in his hands—but she turned again and paced back toward the hearth. "Of course, I did not see him push her; however, Luci heard them argue at the top of the stairs—she saw him standing above before he fled the hall to return a few moments later when his butler summoned him. Or so Luci has claimed since that night."

Triston breathed a sigh of relief. "No one saw Abercorn physically push his new bride?"

"Well, no, but—"

"And you think spying on the man with your gaggle of friends will find justice for Tilda's death, by ruining a man who may very well be innocent of the crime you have levied upon his person?" He chuckled, harshly. "My own father is married for the third time, and I can attest that he caused no harm to his previous wives, my very own mother included. Abercorn may very well be cursed in love, just as my father is."

"And if one of your sisters perishes because of their association with Abercorn, that blood will be on your hands—the weight on your conscience." Her glare narrowed, but she refused to look away. "I do not know about you, but I will have no other deaths permanently staining my soul if I can make known Abercorn—or any other scoundrel disguised as a gentleman—poses a threat to any woman. My friends and I are determined to save others the fate our friend faced and ended her life."

At some point, either Edith or he had taken a step forward, bringing them from a foot apart, to their bodies almost touching. And so they stood, as several long moments past, neither willing to back down.

CHAPTER 9

EDITH WOULD HAVE been wise to agree with Lord Torrington—Triston—and then tuck her tail and run, not stand toe-to-toe with a man over twice her size, especially with another story due to Ophelia by nightfall.

In that moment, she made the mistake of breathing in deeply, allowing his scent to overtake her. Even with the hint of horse, his scent of amber and dark wood was in no way unappealing to her. Quite the opposite. The raw aroma of Triston had her heartbeat spiking, her chest heaving to gain breath, and she feared her knees would buckle before either of them backed down.

"I will do all in my power to see Abercorn gets what he deserves," Edith hissed, breathing through her open mouth. "I will never allow that man to murder again."

Triston's muddy brown eyes flared with anger, but his tone only held annoyance. "And I cannot allow a man to be ruined without solid proof of wrongdoing."

Thump. Thump. Thump.

"Go away!" Triston shouted. "I am otherwise engaged."

Otherwise engaged. Is that what Torrington called a bitter disagreement with a woman alone in his chambers?

Their standoff was ended as quickly as it had begun when another volley of fistfalls hit the door.

"Open this door immediately, or I will have to call for the maid to bring me a key."

Edith risked a glance at the window. What little light peeked through the slit in the draperies told her the sun was setting and the day was growing late. It would not be long before someone suspected she was not where she should be. Did someone see her leave the park following Triston?

Edith clutched at her chest, her heartbeat increasing. "Who is here?" she whispered.

Triston's jaw clenched tightly as his hand massaged the back of his neck. "My father."

Edith gulped. "Your father?"

"Do not think me too old to kick down this door!" the man called, grasping the latch to the door and attempting to barge in. "Open the bloody door."

The color drained from Triston's normally overconfident face, and his demeanor shifted to uncertainty.

Edith knew the feeling well.

She glanced about the room for a place to hide, yet the bedrails made it impossible to squeeze beneath, and the armoire would not hold more than a small child. As a final resort, she hurried to the window.

"We are three stories above the ground," he hissed from right next to her, startling her. "You may survive a fall from a tree, but if you slipped from this height, you would be no better than your dear departed friend."

"Then where shall I hide?" she demanded in a low tone. "I cannot be found here."

He snorted. "Do you think I do not know that?"

"That is it, Triston!" Footsteps could be heard walking down the hall.

"The dressing closet." Triston set his hands on her shoulders and spun her around to face a door she hadn't realized was there. It was little more than two feet wide—certainly, Torrington could not fit through the opening without turning sideways. "Go. I will handle my father quickly, then you must depart."

Edith didn't waste another moment, but hurried toward the closed door, pulling it open and slipping inside. He closed the door behind her, casting her in complete darkness. Yes, she knew the tiny room was likely littered with boots, ballroom shoes, shirts, cravats, and trousers; however, the notion of not knowing for certain was daunting. Pressing her ear to the wood, Edith heard Triston move toward the door and as he unlatched it, and used the sound to cover her own opening of the dressing room door a crack.

From her vantage point, she could not see anything but Triston's hand pulling the portal wide, and a glimpse of a large man—nearly as tall as Triston—stepping into the room.

The door shut behind him, cutting off the light from the hall beyond.

Footsteps sounded, and Edith feared that Triston's father suspected someone hid within the room, and was set on finding her. She took a step back, deeper in the closet and away from the voices. Though, even if she ducked behind the pressed and hung shirts would she not be hidden entirely from view.

"Father, to what do I owe this visit? I was under the impression our meeting this morning was sufficient to count toward your forced weekly conversation." Triston's words dripped with sarcasm. "Am I wrong?"

"You did not show up to escort Prudence and Chastity to their evening entertainment," his father responded with a hint of jest. "I asked three things of you: fall in line, accompany your sisters, and do not outshine their endeavors to find suitable husbands. Why in the bloody hell is that too much to ask?"

Edith stepped forward once more, needing to see Triston's reaction to his father's harsh tone. The need to exit the closet and stand at Triston's side was almost overwhelming. That would not help either of them and would only go to proving his father correct.

"I escorted the girls—and Lady Downshire—to Hyde Park after I left our meeting," Triston countered. "I only just arrived home an hour ago, and I am awaiting a bath. I planned to come for them immediately after."

Edith knew they'd been speaking for more than an hour. It was her fault Triston had failed to appear for his sisters.

"I will dress immediately and come for them; the evening is still early."

Edith saw the elder man wave his hand in dismissal. "Do not bother, Esmee dressed and escorted the pair."

"Father, I—"

"Do you think I allow you to live here and still collect an allowance because of my kind nature?"

Edith shrank back from the opening when footsteps sounded on the wooden floor, coming in her direction.

"Would you prefer I live under your roof and have to see the woman who betrayed me"—the door slammed shut, muffling his response, yet she could still decipher some words—"...did you...my betrothed...seducing her."

"I fear you should not gain too much familiarity with your accommodations, Triston." The other man shouted loud enough to penetrate the thick wooden door separating Edith from the confrontation in the next room. "If you are unable to fulfill my demands, you will be living under my roof once more. Unless you have some source of income I am unaware of."

Triston said something in response, and from the lowering of Lord Downshire's voice, Triston must have conceded to his father's edict.

Edith moved deeper into the dressing closet to think over all she'd heard thus far. What had Triston meant by his utterance regarding the betrayal by his betrothed and someone else seducing her? Maybe he *did* have secrets, and Edith just hadn't known where to look or what questions to ask. The story certainly revolved around why Triston resided in a boarding house and not his family home.

Edith hastily spilled her hand into the sewn-in pocket on her skirt, but it was empty but for the nub she used to write. Blast it all, but Edith wished she hadn't given the journal to Triston, or left it in his possession when he'd rushed her into the dressing room. These were all things she need remember and ask about later.

The door swung open and crashed into the frame, casting muted light on the small space. Edith let out an unladylike screech as she nearly leapt out of her skin, her foot knocking a stack of boxes over, spilling their contents on the closet floor. As quickly as the light flooded into the room, it was blocked once more when Triston stood in her path, his large body framed by the doorway.

With the fire from the hearth lighting his back, he appeared truly fearsome, yet Edith refused to shrink in terror.

He'd had plenty of opportunities to harm her, and he hadn't.

She snatched her journal from his hand and pushed past him. "What was all this about?"

Edith didn't turn to see his reaction but moved to the window and pulled the drape aside to view the front of the inn as Lord Downshire entered his carriage and sped off. Edith made certain to keep behind the heavy window covering to shield herself from sight. Surprisingly, her horse was still tethered to the post where she'd left the mare. Not surprisingly, the sun had set, and the street was dark, except for the light coming from the windows of the inn.

The afternoon had passed, and her parents must be

worried about her. Not to mention Lady Lucianna and Ophelia.

"It is time you leave, Lady Edith." The words were whispered near her ear, and a tingle traveled down her back.

She'd asked Triston a question, but with the feel of his breath upon her neck and his heated body so close to her back, she couldn't remember what it was she wanted to know.

HE SHOULDN'T BE standing so close to her.

He shouldn't have allowed her into his bedchambers.

He shouldn't have attempted to trick his father into an argument.

He shouldn't be surprised that he longed to wrap his arms around the petite, determined, headstrong woman before him. If he were completely out of his mind, he would turn her toward him, take her into his arms, and lay her gently across his bed, showering her entire body with kisses, evidence of the need he hadn't realized he felt for her until now.

A thirst he hadn't felt for any woman since Esmee's betrayal.

Triston needed her gone, immediately. He couldn't worry about her future plans for ruining Abercorn, nor what she'd overheard about Triston's past.

He grasped her hand where it pulled back the drapery, revealing the street beyond and his father's departing carriage. Unfortunately, the movement brought her even closer. Her hair smelled of jasmine and honeysuckle. He knew the fragrances well, they were the same scents his mother favored and were what he'd gifted to his dear sisters the prior Christmastide morning.

His mother was a fine woman. His sisters, even

though they didn't share the same mother, were also noble and kind.

Trustworthy.

Jasmine and honeysuckle reminded Triston of trust.

Esmee's preferred aroma had been dark—berries and bergamot.

The last person he wanted to be thinking of while Edith was so close was Lady Downshire.

Triston leaned closer to Edith's neck and breathed deeply once more, allowing the scent to overtake him. He'd never thought the fragrance a woman chose could speak to their nature.

"I should go." Edith pulled her hand from the drape—and his touch—and turned.

In that moment, they were body-to-body, her bosom pressed securely to his abdomen and her head tilted back so far it could not possibly be comfortable.

"That would be wise, Lady Edith."

"Before anyone sees me here."

"There is most certainly risk of that," he breathed as his arm circled her waist.

"And then we would be in far more danger than we are at present."

Odd, but Triston could not imagine a more dangerous position than this very moment with Edith pulled tightly to his chest. All he need do is lean down and take her lips, but that would cause him to step back, putting distance between their bodies.

Triston wanted nothing between them.

She stared up at him, her eyes begging him to hold her close even as he noticed her body pulling away from him.

"Bloody hell, Edith." He stepped away, intending to let her go, bid her to leave with all due haste, but his body did not listen. His head dipped, and his lips met her soft, plump mouth at the same time his arms wrapped around her once more and lifted her to meet his great height. She weighed no more than a feather in his embrace. "Edith," he moaned against her lips, scared to pull back and have her float away from him.

Her fingers threaded through his hair, tightening and tugging as he deepened their kiss, he dared to drag his tongue along her bottom lip. Her entire body tensed before she quivered in his arms.

Triston released her and pulled back, staring down at her.

Her fingers, no longer entangled in his hair, now pressed to her reddened lips.

"I think it best I depart," she mumbled, her free hand finding her hidden pocket and the journal most likely within once more. "I am sorry for keeping you from your sisters, my lord."

"Allow me to change, and I will accompany you home." His heart nearly beat from his chest. It would be a cold day in hell before he allowed her out of his sight, especially to travel about darkened London streets. He was a gentleman, after all. And *if* it had to do with anything deeper, Triston wasn't willing to think of that now. "It will only take me a moment."

"We both know that is unwise."

She stepped away from him, toward the door, and an entirely new void opened within him.

"I cannot, in good conscience, allow you to leave unchaperoned."

"And I cannot, in good conscience, allow anyone to know I was here."

Was that sorrow in her eyes? Did she want to stay with him as much as he wanted her to remain?

With one final look, she hurried to the door and slipped out.

The sound of her riding boots could be heard running down the hall and taking to the stairs.

Triston sprang into action and was out his door and turning the opposite way Edith had fled. Bloody hell, but she was right. She could not risk being seen alone with him—he understood that much; however, that did not mean he'd allow her to flee into the night without someone to watch over her.

Pushing the door at the end of the hall wide, he shouted, "Ames!"

"Are ye ready for ye bath, m'lord," his manservant asked from the depths of the servants' stairwell. "I can be right up with a basin o' water."

"Ames, have Molly bring the water," he commanded into the darkness below. "I want you to follow the woman who is departing out front. Make certain she arrives home safely."

"I will, m'lord." Ames's feet could be heard shuffling into his boots before a door slammed, and Triston knew his manservant would not disappoint him.

Triston's father had insisted if he wanted to keep his residence at Langworth Inn, he needed to heed Downshire's every wish. And tonight, he'd failed, leaving his sisters to be escorted to the ball by Esmee.

He was torn between following Edith home and washing quickly to attend to his sisters, to get back into his father's good graces. The marquis had told Triston not to bother with the girls this evening, that Esmee was with them. But Triston knew better than to believe his father. The older man still expected his son to hurry and attend to his duty.

Triston had an obligation to Prudence and Chastity—which, most certainly had nothing to do with his father's demands—but after, he would call on Lady Edith and command her to let go of her foolish notion to uncover Abercorn's misdeeds. If the man were truly dangerous, the last thing Triston wanted was Edith—and her friends—anywhere near him.

CHAPTER 10

EDITH STARTLED AWAKE to complete darkness—
and stale air.

Her entire body stiffened with alert even as fear as
hot as a flame coursed through her.

Something caressed her cheek and lips. She wanted
to push into the feeling, remember the way Triston's
mouth had felt against hers and slip back into the dream
she'd been in before waking.

Had she fallen asleep in his dressing closet? No,
she'd departed Langworth Inn. Edith was certain of it.
Right after Lord Downshire had left, in fact. She'd
sprinted to the stairs and out the front door without
anyone noticing.

Her head ached when she tried to concentrate on
what had happened next. Something pushed incessantly
into her hip, causing an agonizing discomfort. Her mind
continued to roll, a stark terror settling around her like a
well-tailored cloak as she tried to identify her location.

Shifting, Edith realized she couldn't move her
hands. They were held securely in front of her, her
palms facing one another with her fingers clasped.
Another excruciating jab sent shooting pain into her
side and up into her back at the same time her head
throbbed. It was the rough wood below her digging into

her side, her hands tied at her waist making it impossible to push off her hip to her back.

A numbness overtook her as her denial settled in.

Edith opened her mouth to scream, but nothing moved past the lump lodged in her throat. Utter disbelief swiftly transformed into panic as her voice ripped from her chest. The high-pitched scream echoed in her confined space, causing terror to take hold.

A bout of dizziness brought spots of bright colors—red, green, and yellow—before her eyes, and her stomach roiled.

She couldn't think clearly, unable to grasp where she was and how she'd gotten here.

Her entire body shook and her teeth chattered—though if it was from the cold or her fright, Edith wasn't sure.

She bent her elbows, bringing her hands to her head. Her fingers clawed at whatever covered her face—a coarse fabric that smelled of hay, causing the stale air that infused her lungs and kept her short of breath. Pushing upward on the hood, she was able to move it high enough to gain a proper breath, yet it did nothing to dispel the staleness of the air surrounding her.

Her heart raced erratically, and her entire body trembled intensely.

Edith opened her mouth to scream once more…or call for help, but the words stuck in her suddenly dry throat.

She attempted to straighten her cramped legs, which protested the sudden movement, causing her head to pound ever more. Thankfully, her ankles were not bound.

The floor beneath her jolted and bumped, raising her body from its place only to send it crashing down again, sending her squarely onto her bruised hip and knocking her shoulder.

It returned quickly to the even sway from before.

Though the gentle motion did nothing to dim the

increasing pain taking over her body from her head to her shoulder and down to her hip. She prayed for the numbness of moments before to return and take it all away.

Yet, she remained awake and alert to every shooting ache coursing through her.

Pushing the hood higher still, she noted the space wasn't as dark as she'd thought. She spied a crack above her head and shifted to her back to gain a better look. Light could be seen above—its brightness coming and going as if swinging like a pendulum.

Back and forth. Back and forth.

Edith focused on the pattern, her screaming mind quieting for a brief time. She released her clasped fingers, tracing the sway of the light in the few inches of movement her ties afforded.

She hastily turned to her side once more when her head exploded in pain and her stomach threatened to revolt.

Reaching out with her bound hands, she felt the darkened space before her—wood, the same as beneath her and at her feet.

It was like she was stowed in a box. A cold, icy chill ran through her.

But there was light from above and a constant jostling as the wooden enclosure moved.

Bringing her legs high, Edith kicked out at the wood above her, but was only rewarded with a shower of dirt falling upon her. Her eyes burned from the filth as she blinked it away, bringing her hands up to scrub at her face. Whatever kept her locked in this tight space was as securely fastened as her hands were bound.

Would anyone realize she'd disappeared? Would someone look for her? If she had no idea what had transpired or where she was headed, how could she expect anyone else to figure it out?

Edith needed to concentrate. Closing her eyes once more, she begged her mind to stop swirling, her panic to subside, and listened to the sounds around her. She needed to think—what was she hearing? What was she feeling?

The churn and fall of carriage wheels along a dirt road. She was in a carriage...the boot of a traveling coach.

The creak of the lamp as it swung on the rear of the carriage...above her head.

Someone had taken her, but why?

Suddenly, Edith remembered detouring away from her home in Mayfair—toward St. James.

Her terror returned with a vengeance, and she shrank into herself, pulling her knees as close to her chest as her skirts allowed.

She vaguely remembered guiding her horse down Abercorn's street, hoping to learn something, anything, for when she returned home, she was certain her parents' fright over her disappearance would quickly morph to anger. Her freedom to travel about London without their attendance would be no more. And so, instead of returning home immediately after leaving Triston, she'd thought to make one last attempt with Abercorn. The possibility of dismounting her horse and knocking on his door had even crossed her mind as a rational course of action.

Unfortunately, Edith didn't recall making it to Abercorn's door.

She squeezed her eyes tighter. She needs must remember what had happened...or anything that would tell her where she was and who'd taken her.

The evening had been darkening, the sun already having fallen behind the tall buildings of London proper. Edith had passed a carriage on her way down St. James, but the curtains were pulled tightly, and she couldn't see within, although the coachman had nodded to her as they passed.

The Abercorn townhouse had come into view—the house ablaze with light as if His Grace were home for the night or had yet to leave. Edith had dismounted her mare and tied it to the tree she now knew resided on Downshire property.

A sound came from behind her, a stick breaking, and then...blackness.

That was all.

Instead of attempting to evoke anything else, Edith focused once more on where she was at present. Her head throbbed again as if trying to block any further memories from resurfacing. The pounding only managed to increase her fear, the hair on her neck standing on end, and her muscles screaming for movement. Panic raced through her, begging Edith to do something—fight to gain freedom, kick, and scream. Whatever it took to break from her prison.

She tried once more, kicking her feet up with as much force as she could muster from her position. But the boards didn't give and the movement only sent waves of throbbing pain up her legs to her shoulder and hip.

Immense pain clouded her vision.

She was in a carriage, that much she was now certain of. With only the sounds of the wheels turning, the horses' hooves, and the swinging of the lamp above the boot, Edith suspected she was not in London proper any longer. There were no voices to be heard, no shouts from passing carriages, or calls of warning from pedestrians walking along the street. The carriage jostled along the uneven road as it hit ruts and bumps along the way. The reins jingled against one another as the conveyance turned sharply.

Edith scooted toward the side and pressed her eye close to another crack in the wood. The glow from the lamp afforded her a view behind the carriage—nothing but the empty road with trees bordering each side and shrubs growing large enough to block the path behind them.

Thankfully, with her nose also pressed to the side

of the boot, her lungs breathed in fresh, clean air, relieving the pressure in her chest. With the fresh breath came something new—a scent she hadn't smelled in many years. Crisp, cold salt.

Whoever had taken her was bound for the sea.

CHAPTER 11

TRISTON STRAIGHTENED HIS cravat as he surveyed the ballroom, attempting to locate his sisters. It would have been wise to remain at Langworth Inn long enough for Ames to return and assist him with his evening attire—and confirm that Lady Edith had arrived home safely. Many would argue Triston was not always a wise man—of that he needed no convincing. Along with his hastily tied neckcloth, Triston's brown jacket did not precisely match his darker trousers—a fact he had not been aware of until he entered the ballroom and the hundreds of candles above illuminated his improper wardrobe selection.

Blast it all but he'd been unable to take his mind from Lady Edith—and their kiss—followed by her quick departure. Not a piece of him had wanted to see her go. Not long before their kiss, he'd been infuriated with her; however, a simple embrace—that was in no way simple—had extinguished his anger and flared another emotion entirely within him.

She'd compared him to an ox—and a druid warrior—an arrogant ox with dubious friends.

Everything had transpired so rapidly, Triston hadn't made the connection between the first page of her journal and the *London Daily Gazette* until he'd called for his carriage to be brought round.

Mayfair Confidential.

It was a weekly column in the *Gazette*, nothing more than unfounded gossip, though the writer claimed to have substantiated all stories. To Triston's satisfaction, the column hadn't come to be until *after* his own brush with scandal.

He'd been shocked and insulted to think Edith had set her sights on him, gone to the great risk of embroiling them both in a new scandal, all for a story. She'd be disappointed to learn, as gentlemen of the *ton* went, he was a rather boring fellow. Triston had seen enough upset and heartache to last him a lifetime. Certainly, he enjoyed himself on occasion, but nothing scandalous or noteworthy; especially with Pru and Chastity joining the marriage market this Season.

Speaking of Prudence and Chastity…he spotted his sisters on the far side of the ballroom, once again hidden behind a large palm.

He shook his head at their foolish notion of remaining unseen until they were ready.

Did they not understand what was at stake if they did not settle on matches this Season? There would not be a next for them. It had taken all of Triston's persuasive tactics to convince his father to allow the girls at least one Season before Esmee became with child and she insisted they all move to the country until after the babe was born. There was no guarantee his father's wife would allow his siblings a future Season after.

Regardless, he was surprised to see Pru and Chastity alone.

He scanned the crowd once more, looking for a familiar raven-haired witch, but a far different—but no less deadly—stare met his. Her eyes not icy blue but a deep emerald.

Before he had enough sense to flee, Lady Lucianna and Lady Ophelia strode in his direction.

If he were a wise man, which he'd even more come to believe he was not, Triston would turn now, return to his lodgings, and not venture into society again.

"My lord," Lady Lucianna hissed, stopping before him, unconcerned a proper introduction had yet to be made between them.

"Lady Lucianna, I have heard a great deal—"

Her narrowed stare had his words catching in his throat.

"Where is Edith?" Lady Ophelia asked, her wavy, deep red hair far more fiery than her words.

"Why in heavens name would you presume I know anything about Lady Edith's whereabouts?" he posed.

He knew his mistake immediately when Lady Lucianna snorted and crossed her arms, and Lady Ophelia gasped, pressing her fan to her chest before quickly snapping it open to cool her face.

"We know she has been keeping an eye on you," Lady Lucianna continued. "We were to meet before the ball, but Lord and Lady Shaftesbury said she left Hyde Park earlier under the guise of spotting us."

"But we were not at the park today," Lady Ophelia replied, looking to Lady Lucianna for reassurance. "And Edith never returned home. Her parents came around looking for her."

Lady Lucianna kept her glare on him. "Which means, she followed *you.*"

"This is preposterous," Triston retorted. He didn't want to mention the likelihood that Edith following Abercorn was just as convincing as the theory Lady Lucianna had settled upon. An inkling of unease settled in the pit of his stomach, despite his proclamation. He slammed his hands into his pockets and rolled back on his heels. "There is no way you can know I was at Hyde Park today."

"Oh," Lady Lucianna cooed, and Triston suspected she was about to snap the trap shut around him. "Lady Prudence and Lady Chastity were more than happy to share the news of their ride in the park today…accompanied by you, my lord."

Triston glanced between the two women, each with their brows raised in question as if they'd expected him to lie and were happy to confront him with the damning proof he'd requested. There was little use denying it. While they suspected Edith had followed him from the park, he knew she had.

But she'd departed Langworth Inn almost two hours prior. That was plenty of time for her to dress and attend to her friends, yet, Ames hadn't returned before Triston had departed. He did not know for certain she'd arrived home without anything going awry.

"Where is she, Torrington?" Lady Lucianna took a menacing step toward him. While the woman was very thin, her height rivaled his. "I can see you know something you are not telling us."

It was none of their concern if Triston were hiding something from them; however, it had been his responsibility to make sure Edith arrived home safely—and he'd forsaken her. He'd failed, as he had with so many things in his life. The notion of pleasing everyone, doing exactly what an honorable gentleman would, was daunting. And everything had gone wrong again. Perhaps he would be wise to not put so much time into helping others. It never seemed to work out.

"I do not think he is going to tell us what we need to know," Lady Lucianna mused. "Ophelia, I think it is time we send for the magistrate. Allow him to handle things before Torrington has the opportunity to change his story and consort with his sisters to gain their cooperation in the matter."

"If you do that, I will tell all of London that Lady Edith is behind the *Mayfair Confidential* column in the *Gazette*." Triston watched the pair closely. He suspected Edith was not the only one behind the column, and he highly doubted her friends would allow her to take the fall if society placed the blame solely on her.

Neither woman moved.

Lucianna scowled at him, her brow wrinkling in displeasure, while Lady Ophelia once again looked as if she'd faint if she did not gain a spot of fresh air.

"Now—" It was Triston's turn to glare. "I think it best we step outside and discuss this matter...in private."

The young women looked to one another before nodding in agreement.

"Since I arrived only a few moments ago, my carriage should still be waiting out front. I will meet you both there after I inform my sisters I will not be able to remain."

"You will come promptly?" Lucianna asked. "This is not yet another charade?"

"I promise to not tarry overlong."

"Ophelia, tell your mother you are ill and I will escort you home," Lady Lucianna instructed. "And I will give my father a similar excuse."

"That is wonderfully ingenious, Luci," Ophela squealed before heading off in the direction of the refreshment table.

"We will wait at your carriage." With a final glare, Lady Lucianna turned in search of her own family.

Triston scanned the crowd once more. His sisters hadn't noticed his arrival yet, and blast it all, he couldn't locate Esmee in the crush.

Edith could be in danger; he had no time to waste in finding her.

His gut screamed Edith had been speaking the truth all along—that Abercorn was indeed a threat. Though, just hours before, he would have assumed it just as likely she'd be set upon by thieves on the London streets as it would be that Abercorn meant anyone any harm. He'd been a fool to dismiss her concerns so swiftly.

Finally, Prudence and Chastity caught his stare and hustled over to him.

"You have arrived," Pru sighed.

"Guess who spoke to us. You will not believe it," Chastity gushed.

"I do not have time to chat, dear sisters," Triston said, continuing to search the room. "Where is Lady Downshire?"

"She deposited us here and demanded we act accordingly until your arrival." Prudence narrowed her gaze on him, likely noting his tense shoulders. "She said you would see us home safely at the end of the night. Why do you ask?"

Blast it all. Triston did not have time for any of this. It was quite possible that Edith had arrived home without incident, but he needed to know for certain. However, he could not leave his sisters here without a chaperone, or a means to arrive home.

"You needs must come with me." Triston pivoted and started for the door, not waiting for any response. "Come along."

His sisters burst into action and followed quickly behind him as he exited the ballroom and departed the front door.

"Our wraps!" Chastity cried, but didn't pause to wait for the servant to find and return them.

"Come," Prudence hissed. "Something is afoot and I, for one, want to find out what. Triston is never in such a tizzy."

A tizzy? At any other time, he would have chuckled at Pru's use of the word, but not this day. He *was* in a tizzy…soon to be a frenzy if they didn't locate Edith with all due haste.

Just as he'd requested, Lady Lucianna and Lady Ophelia waited by his carriage.

Bloody hell, but Triston hadn't realized he'd be sharing the carriage ride with not only Edith's close friends but also his sisters. Four women in one carriage.

They all seemed surprised to see one another.

Pru's and Chastity's surprise showed in overexcited

shouts of glee, while Lucianna and Ophelia gave him quizzical looks but greeted his sisters kindly.

"What is amiss?" Pru asked, taking Lucianna's hands in hers. "Triston is fairly out of his mind with worry."

"As he should be." Lucianna threw an accusatory frown in his direction. "But what are the pair of you doing here? You should be enjoying your evening at the ball."

"I am depositing them at home before we set off for Lady Edith's townhouse." Triston signaled for his coachman to set the steps down for the woman to enter. "Can we be off?"

"Lady Edith Pelton?" Chastity whispered to Ophelia. When the auburn-haired woman nodded in confirmation, his sister clapped her hands in anticipation. "Must we go home, brother?"

"Yes!" Triston replied in unison with both Lady Lucianna and Lady Ophelia. He cleared his throat and lowered his tone. "We will drop you at home, and I promise to gladly escort you wherever you demand in the future."

Pru and Chastity gave him mirrored pouts as he swung his arm wide, motioning for them to enter the carriage.

"Take us to the Downshire townhouse, quickly, if you please," Triston commanded.

Triston took his seat between his sisters with Edith's friends sitting opposite. They tried not to scowl at him and keep their questions unvoiced until they deposited Pru and Chastity, but they were failing miserably at both.

All while Triston attempted to keep his unease at bay.

"Tell me what you know," he demanded. His sister's presences be damned.

"Why do you not tell us what *you* know first?" Lucianna notched her chin high.

"This is outlandish." Did they not understand he cared about Edith as much as they did? He'd known full well the risks she was taking spying on Abercorn, and yet he'd thought the situation harmless, all things considered. As far as Triston was concerned, Abercorn wasn't a scoundrel. He wasn't a man prone to violence. Triston would have known, would have heard something. "Lady Edith did, in fact, follow me from the park this afternoon—all the way to my lodging."

Chastity gasped beside him. "All the way across the river?"

Lucianna and Ophelia shared a skeptical glance. "And what did you do when you found her at your lodging?"

"Yes, brother," Pru begged, clasping her hands. "What did you do?"

Triston was uncertain what luck he still possessed, but mercifully, they arrived at his father's townhouse then. The coachman pulled into the drive, but Triston didn't wait for him to climb down from his perch; instead, he opened the door himself and leapt to the ground.

Holding his hand out, his sisters stepped down one at a time.

"Is Lady Edith in danger?" Pru wrung her hands before her, knotting the handle of her handbag. "Tell me you have naught to do with this. We only just met Lady Lucianna and Lady Ophelia."

"We desperately want to call them friends." Chastity set her hand on his sleeve.

"I cannot say if Edith is in danger or not, but I can assure you, I have nothing to do with her disappearance." He placed a quick kiss to each of his sister's cheeks. "Now, allow me to see you to the door."

His father stood in the doorway when they arrived. "What is the meaning of this?"

"I must return the girls a bit early due to an unforeseen incident." Triston squared his shoulders, prepared for his father's wrath. The man did not disappoint.

"What have you done now, Triston?"

"I cannot speak to the matter at this moment, Father, but I will tell you as soon as I know exactly what has transpired."

"Yes, Father," Pru said, coming to his defense. "It is a grave matter indeed."

"Where is Esmee?" Downshire peered over Triston's shoulder. "Why did you not leave the girls in her care?"

"Stepmother did not remain with us at the ball," Chastity said.

"She instructed us to keep out of trouble until Triston arrived to see us home."

His father eyed Pru and Chastity, a hint of question in his glare. However, though the man always thought the worst of Triston, he loved his children and never questioned his daughters when they spoke.

"Callahan!" Downshire shouted. "Where is Lady Downshire?"

His father's aging butler appeared in the foyer, his lips pressed together in a grimace as his eyes ping-ponged from Triston to Downshire to the girls.

"I must take my leave, Father." Triston gave the man a curt bow. He had no intentions of remaining to hear about Esmee's latest flight of fancy. "Again, I am sorry you had to leave the ball this evening."

"Do not fret," Chasity replied, stepping forward to squeeze his hand. "We only hope you find her."

"Find who?" Downshire demanded as Triston turned to depart.

"We will tell you all, Father."

"My lord?"

Triston halted at the unease in the butler's voice.

"My lady returned after dropping Lady Prudence and Lady Chastity at the ball. I saw her lady's maid rush a large satchel to the marchioness's waiting carriage."

It was nothing more than his father deserved. Esmee was leaving him and running away with another. Much as she'd done to *him* two years prior. He'd begged his father not to trust the viperous woman, but he'd needed to discover the fact on his own.

"Did she tell you where she was headed?"

"I believe her maid said she'd be away for several days."

Triston shook his head. He could not concern himself with his father's hellion of a wife—he had his own wayward woman to find.

Without another wasted moment, he stomped from the house. Movement next to his father's townhouse caught his eye. A horse was tethered to the tree Edith had fallen from over a week prior.

Triston hurried to the animal—a mare.

She pranced in place anxiously.

What was the horse doing here? Edith must be close, possibly eavesdropping on Lord Abercorn once more, but no light shone from his townhouse's windowpanes. There was no way she'd leave without her horse…especially after the sun had set. She must be close.

His heart spiked as he scanned the area. Maybe she'd decided to climb another tree and she'd fallen again—this time injuring herself.

On the ground, not far from the tethered beast, Triston spotted something familiar.

Edith's journal!

She would never depart without her notes.

Triston pushed a leaf from the leather-bound book and picked it up.

"What is it?" Lady Lucianna had departed the carriage and stood a few paces from him. "It looks to be Edith's mare, Poppy."

Triston could not nod, not without taking his stare off the journal he held.

He attempted to flip open the book, but his finger

slipped on something moist marring the cover.

It was too dark to see properly, but he brought his wet finger to his nose.

Salt…and copper. He rubbed his forefinger and thumb together. The liquid making his skin sticky.

Every sense Triston possessed heightened. The night breeze rustled a patch of fallen leaves, the horses neighed to be returned to their warm stables, and his entire body hummed with anticipation.

Panic? Dread? Rage?

Triston allowed each to overtake him in due course. He lived a thousand days in a blink of an eye.

"Is that…" Ophelia gasped, obviously following Lucianna from the carriage.

"Blood?" Lucianna finished.

CHAPTER 12

EDITH'S FINGERS ACHED from trying to pry a nail loose from its hole. The continued bumps and dips in the road did nothing to lessen her pounding headache or the burden on her shoulder and hip. The area was in no way large enough to gain a sitting position.

She groaned, shifting once more to better shield her shoulder.

It was still dark outside, the morning sun not yet risen, but other than this, Edith had no notion if it were midnight or approaching sunrise.

In the hours she'd spent attempting to find a way out of the boot—and the moving carriage—she'd discovered the source of the punishing pain in her head. A knot had formed at her hairline—she'd been hit with something, splitting her skin.

Her ice-cold fear had thawed to frustration.

She'd screamed until her throat was raw. She'd begged to be released with no answers. She'd kicked, pounded, scraped, and banged at the wood surrounding her until every inch of her body ached with unseen bruises.

As the seemingly endless moments passed, Edith determined there was no possibility she'd break herself loose. The best she could do was conserve her strength and hope to gain her freedom once the carriage arrived at its destination.

How had she gotten herself into such a predicament?

The worst part was that Torrington had warned her against spying on Abercorn, had implored her to give up her daring determination to ruin the duke. But Edith hadn't listened. She'd been so focused on making right what had happened to Tilda and helping to prove Luci's accusation correct, she hadn't thought through the risks of her endeavor. Or what might happen if she were caught.

Which, from her current predicament, she had been.

However, did that mean Abercorn *was* guilty of pushing Tilda down the stairs on their wedding night?

If he'd taken her, then it was all the proof society needed to condemn him for his treacherous actions. If she'd live to prove his culpability was an entirely different matter—one Edith was determined not to dwell on.

She only need survive this—but how long would it be before someone noted her disappearance?

If Luci and Ophelia went to her parents after Edith failed to show for their meeting, would anyone have faith in the pair that something untoward had occurred? They'd cried foul once before, and no one had believed them. Would their words of concern be cast aside as quickly as their accusations against Abercorn?

Edith should have stood by Luci's side on the night Tilda died. Shouted as loudly as she could about Abercorn and his involvement—she wouldn't be here now if she had.

She replayed her afternoon with Triston and her departure from the inn in frustration.

No one but Luci and Ophelia would know her disappearance had anything to do with the duke…except maybe Triston. She had to trust he would figure things out and come for her.

This was all her fault. It was maddening. If no one came for her, Edith had no one to blame but herself. There was no one to save her but herself, but how could she figure out her own rescue when she had no idea where she was being taken or how far she'd need to go to escape and find help.

The carriage slowed and turned sharply, causing Edith to slide and her head to slam against the side of the box.

"Ouch!" She instinctively moved her hand to her head, but was unable to reach the spot.

The carriage moved slower down a heavily rutted path. Branches scraped the side of the conveyance as if they passed through what must be a wooded area.

After what seemed like another hour of being tossed about like a helpless ragdoll, they stopped. The carriage shifted as the driver disembarked.

It was time…her abductor—most likely Abercorn or his servant—would remove her now. The time had come to figure out her course for escape. Her heartbeat pounded in her ears as she attempted to listen for approaching footsteps.

Edith pushed back toward the large split in the wood but could not see much beyond what the pool of light from the lamp showed her. A flat grassy area with a sliver of a modest house almost out of view.

Now that the horses' hooves and carriage wheels had gone quiet, another sound could be heard.

She breathed in deeply, confirming that what she heard was correct—sure enough, the salt in the air was heavy with the breeze coming off the ocean. What she heard were waves slamming against a cliff.

She stilled for a moment when another thought struck her.

Abercorn had pushed Tilda down a flight of stairs with several witnesses within earshot *and* eyesight. There was nothing stopping him from pushing Edith off a cliff with no one the wiser. The duke was older than her father. Could she fight back and escape? Where would she go? From what she'd seen as they traveled after she woke, they hadn't passed any villages or journeyed through any towns. She may need to walk for hours before finding help, and there was always the chance Abercorn or his driver would locate her.

The carriage door opened, and the springs on the conveyance barely squeaked when someone alighted.

Suddenly, frigid air reached every inch of her skin as the lid of the boot was lifted.

A masked face came into view as Edith tried to look past the man to identify where they'd taken her, beyond it being a coastal area.

"Sit up, m'lady," an unfamiliar, gravelly voice commanded. "I be help'n ye out, but if'n ye try ta run or harm me, I'll havta club ye again." His eyes narrowed beneath his black mask. "Ye hear, or do I be need'n ta keep a close watch on ye?"

"I—I—I—" Edith worked to string together a coherent response. She did not want to be hit again, and she most certainly didn't want the man setting a hand on her. "I will not be any trouble…if only you will tell me why I'm here."

The man slipped a hand under her elbow and assisted her to the ground.

Edith stilled her body's natural response to pull away as revulsion overtook her.

In the several minutes it took to accomplish this feat with her hands bound, Edith noticed that a quaint cottage stood about a hundred feet from the carriage, yet she could not assess the house in detail because her eyes were drawn behind the building.

A sheer cliff dropped off another three hundred feet behind the cottage, the sea pounding relentlessly against the rocks as the waves splashed over and onto the area surrounding the house.

Her muscles tensed, and a scream ripped from her

throat. Her captor snarled, cutting off her yell as she gasped for breath.

"Scream again, and I be forced ta cut yer tongue from yer mouth." The man pulled the hood back over her head with a sharp tug, throwing her into complete darkness once more. But unlike before, Edith knew what surrounded her and where her fate lie—at the rocky, sea-soaked bottom of a cliff.

Would her death be slower than Tilda's? Edith prayed the hand above took mercy on her and made her demise a swift one.

"Go on." The man grasped her elbow and steered her toward…she was uncertain, but she prayed it was the cottage and not the cliff.

She hadn't been given time to properly process her final moments: what she needed to think over, whom she would miss most, and who would worry about her. None of it truly mattered anyhow. She'd be gone—with little trace. She only prayed her friends, and her family, would not waste time searching for her because she would never be found at the bottom of a cliff. She'd be washed away within minutes.

Her stomach twisted at the thought of never seeing her parents again, leaving Luci and Ophelia wondering what had happened to her, and Triston…oh, blast it all, but she'd been affected by their kiss.

Her face moistened with shed tears. For once she was thankful for the hood that blocked her face from view as it soaked up the sign of her weakness.

Had this been Tilda's final thought? Had she worried that her loved ones' lives would be ruled by her death?

Edith walked as slowly as the man allowed, not ready to know her fate, and needing more time. She'd only, just that evening, had her first, proper kiss. It had been everything she'd imagined, though not with the type of man she'd always dreamed of.

Lord Torrington, Triston—she allowed herself a

moment to repeat his name in her mind. He was arrogant and demanding with a likeness far more alluring than any poet could capture with words. He was Adonis to her, a creature famed to exist, but one which no man had bared witness to except in the pages of books. His chiseled jawline and broad shoulders fell within the dictates of myth, while his extreme height, thick legs, and solid frame were more suited to a warlord of centuries past. His touch had been gentle despite his size. His words soothing despite his deep tone.

Her foot caught on something, and she almost tumbled to the ground, but the man held her arm tightly and yanked her back before she fell completely.

"Wait here an' don't ye move." Two knocks sounded, and Edith heard the door open. "Come on."

She was pulled into the room and pushed down onto a chair. It was far better than the boot; however, the room had a deep chill and musty odor, as if the hearth hadn't seen a fire in many years, and the floors hadn't been cleared of dirt and dust in far longer. The floorboards creaked as the man stood in front of her and untied her wrists. Instantly, Edith flexed and twisted her cramped hands, attempting to banish the numbness that had set in at some point in their journey.

Her freedom was short-lived, however, when he stepped behind her and snapped her arms behind the chair, tying them together there. The motion sent a jolt of pain from her bruised shoulder to her heart, increasing the throbbing to the point where colors once more danced before her closed eyelids.

Yet, relief flooded her. She'd been taken inside the cottage—a reprieve from death, at least for a short while.

"May I have something to drink?" Maybe if she kept the man talking, he would share something that would help her escape. Or, possibly, she could convince him to untie her and allow her to go free.

"M'lady." The man groaned as he walked across the room. "She be secured, an' won't be cause'n any trouble for ye. If ye be certain ye don't be need'n a fire, I will take me leave now."

Edith's head whipped from side to side, attempting to see through the hood over her head, but nothing was clear. She hadn't realized someone else was in the room. Edith hadn't detected any other movement or breathing; however, after the door had shut, she sat very still and listened more intently. The rustle of brocade, the tapping of a slipper on a wooden floor, and the smell of berries assaulted her.

Someone was in the room with her.

And it was a woman—not Abercorn, as Edith had anticipated.

There was no woman who had cause to harm Edith. An unexpected release of tension caused her to sag in the chair. This was a mistake, all of it a misunderstanding.

It was then Edith realized she'd planned to demand answers from the man before he did away with her. She needs must know, even if she were unable to pass on the information to Luci and Ophelia, if the duke was responsible for Tilda's fall.

Edith held her tongue, determined not to be the first to break the silence. She could think of no logical reason for someone to bash her over the head and steal her away from London.

"What is your purpose with Abercorn?" The woman's deep, sultry voice was calm, as if she were asking if Edith wanted cream in her afternoon tea or if she favored sheep's wool or fox hair lining her coats. "How about Triston, Lord Torrington? Why does he keep sniffing about your skirts?"

Her relief was short-lived as a fresh wave of confusion and unease set her on edge. The rope keeping her hands bound cut into her skin when her body tensed.

Edith wracked her memories for a woman who had connection to both Abercorn and Triston, but the only two were Lady Prudence and Lady Chastity, and they were not the sort for mischief. Heavens, the pair rarely left the potted palms bordering ballrooms and shrank from view at other societal gatherings. They were most certainly not ones for kidnapping.

"What, do you not speak?" the woman purred.

A chair creaked, and Edith suspected her captor was coming toward her.

She pulled at her bound arms once more, but her bonds were tight to the point of sending excruciating pain up her arms whenever she moved. Her mind bounced between thoughts of being outnumbered by the servant and this woman—or if a better chance at survival hinged on her remaining silent or giving the woman what she wanted so desperately she'd kidnap a woman for it. Certainly, Edith could find out what the woman wanted and give it to her. A simple, rational conversation would bring this all to an end and have her back in London before too much damage had been done.

"Do not think to escape, Lady Edith." The woman's calm, cultured tone turned to a hiss. "I have no reservations about harming you."

"What do you want?" Edith's voice was muffled by the hood, but the woman's cold laugh said she'd detected Edith's renewed terror. "Lord Abercorn was married to my friend, and Lord Torrington and I are merely acquaintances."

"Abercorn is not wed to your friend now," she stated, her footsteps growing close—slow and deliberate. "But, still, you were meddling about his property a fortnight ago."

Edith wanted to demand how the woman knew any of this.

"And I saw you keeping watch over both Abercorn and Triston at the Gunther's ball." Her captor's footsteps halted, and Edith felt the woman's breath upon her cheek.

She wanted to deny her interest in Triston at the Gunther's ball. It was Abercorn—and Triston's sisters' safety—she'd been concerned with. While she'd been keeping a close eye on Abercorn, this woman had been watching *her*, along with Luci and Ophelia. Were they safe? Had they been taken, as well?

"And then you followed Triston from Hyde Park. Now, this does not appear to me to be the actions of mere acquaintances. Is my thinking faulty, Lady Edith?"

She flinched back at the woman's seething rage.

CHAPTER 13

"OPEN THE BLOODY door, Abercorn, you scoundrel!" Triston released another volley of fist pounds on the duke's townhouse door, the journal still clenched tightly in his other hand. He should have heeded Edith's warning about the man. He should have listened. He should have confronted Abercorn before now. "Open up before I tear this door from its hinges!"

"Mayhap he is not home?" Lady Ophelia whispered.

Triston turned sharply, immediately regretting his scowl when the woman flinched back as if burned.

Abercorn had to be home.

Edith had to be inside. This fiasco had to end now—this night—before anyone became the wiser about her disappearance. He pictured her the day they'd met, the sun reflecting off her golden crown as if she wore the halo of an angel—the image quickly transformed into Edith, hunch in a corner, stark terror etching her face as tears streamed down, falling one by one to the ground at her feet.

His temper flared red hot.

Triston took a step back, preparing to kick the latched door when hurried footsteps sounded from inside. The bolt was thrown, and the door pulled back a crack. No light shone from the dark foyer beyond.

The Abercorn butler's familiar face peeked out at Triston. "Lord Torrington? My master is out and is not expected until the morrow."

"Where is he?" Lucianna demanded from over Triston's shoulder.

"He has been at Lord and Lady Frampton's house party since yesterday." The man pulled the door open farther, his alarm subsiding. "Is there something I can do for you?"

"You are certain the duke is not home?" Ophelia asked timidly.

"I am quite certain, miss." The servant's head bobbed with his words.

"Very well. We will not bother you further." Triston pivoted and marched back toward his waiting carriage, the pair of ladies close behind. "Let us be off."

He waved his arm for the women to regain their seats in the carriage.

"Where will we look next?" Ophelia stared at him, her face blank. "I cannot think of anyone who would seek to harm Edith, except Lord Abercorn...if he knew we were watching him closely."

Something nagged at Triston. He flipped Edith's journal open, but there were no new scribblings since he'd looked through it earlier in the evening. Turning back to the pages filled with notes on Abercorn—notes Triston hadn't deemed important enough to read earlier—he scanned the page and Edith's hurried words until he located the day he'd met her.

The day she'd fallen from the tree.

The day he'd gotten a rather impromptu look at her undergarments.

He thought back to that day. Edith had stated clearly she hadn't been their snooping on him or his father, but Abercorn.

"Do you plan to sit here?" Lady Lucianna huffed, not bothering to truly look at the object he held. "We need to be searching for Edith, not sitting in your father's drive while you…read a book."

"It is Lady Edith's journal," he replied, not bothering to take his eyes off the page he scanned.

There it was. *Abercorn appears to be entertaining a very naked, raven-haired woman in the top, right, east-facing window.*

Triston leaned forward and stared up at the noted window. The drapes were firmly pulled, but he assumed the room to be Lord Abercorn's private quarters. Had this been what had startled her so greatly she'd tumbled from the tree?

He flipped to the final page about him—penned just that afternoon.

Lord Torrington is spotted with his sisters in the park, accompanied by the same dark-haired woman from Abercorn's top window(?).

Abercorn and Esmee?

Triston's heart plummeted to his feet. He was unaware the pair were familiar with one another, more than being passing acquaintances.

"M'lord!" Ames's call came from the shadows of the Downshire townhouse. "M'lord. You are here. I do not know what happened. I was follow'n the miss as ye instructed—"

He pivoted toward his manservant and glared toward the shadows he waited in, his eyes narrowing to see the man. "Ames. What happened?"

"Who is he?" Lady Lucianna leaned out the open window, her eyes also focusing on Ames as he stepped out of the shadows.

"M'lord, I be try'n ta tell ye." Ames cupped his shoulder, his other arm wrapped around his midsection. "I was follow'n the miss when she came ta ye father's home. I thought it be strange, but then I seen ye mother—pardon—stepmother, lurk'n about the drive. Her maid load'n her travel'n coach."

"Slow down. Breathe, my man or you are likely to expire before you can finish."

The man took several deep breaths, eyeing Lady Lucianna, his reservations clear.

"Now speak!" she demanded.

"While I be watch'n the marchioness, the miss be watch'n ye neighbor's home. Then someone bashed me across the back. I fell ta the ground, I did. That big rock over there"—he removed this hand from his shoulder long enough to point to the bounder placed close to Triston's father's townhouse—"I fell and hit that. Knocked me breath right out. When I gained me senses, m'lady, miss, and the coach be gone. Disappeared."

Without another thought, Triston called to his driver, "Southend-by-Sea! Lady Downshire's familial home on the cliffs. With haste!"

"Southend?" Lucianna's brow furrowed. "That is in East Essex, nearly a four-hour journey from here."

"Yes, it is. All the more reason we should hurry." Triston pulled the door closed and sat back. "They have a several-hour lead on us."

"*They* who, my lord?" Ophelia's breathless tone said she might be in danger of fainting. "I should send word to my father—"

"There is no time." Lucianna gave Ophelia a stern look.

"Very true." Triston nodded in agreement as the carriage started out of the drive.

"What will ye have me do'n?" Ames shouted over the moving carriage wheels as he hobbled alongside the conveyance.

"Follow us and stop in Hadleigh. Collect the magistrate and demand he come to the cliffs!" Triston sat back, confident his servant would not let him down. Next, he faced the two women across from him. Lady Lucianna had him pinned with her assessing, narrowed glare while Lady Ophelia sat wide-eyed and visibly shaking. "I will explain everything on the way, but we must be going."

His stepmother and former betrothed, Esmee, was

a callous, spiteful creature. But harming another, especially a woman? That did not seem within her at all. The act would not benefit her in any way, and if Triston knew anything about Esmee, it was she only did what benefited her. However, if Abercorn were with her—and they were embroiled in some sort of illicit *affair*—there was no deducing what the pair was up to.

Triston only hoped he and Edith's friends arrived in time. From the blood on the journal, he suspected that Edith had struggled with her abductor and had been injured in the process.

"We should not have pushed her to continue looking into Abercorn," Ophelia mused aloud, wringing her hands in her lap. "If anything happens to her, it is our fault. The duke is a dangerous man...we knew that, yet still we needed answers."

"Do not say this." Lucianna placed her arm around her friend's shoulders as they shook with a silent sob. "We were all doing our part to prove the man guilty of Tilda's death. Yet, mayhap we should have come together and not allowed her to spy on the duke alone."

"Do you truly think Abercorn is behind this?" Lucianna asked, pinning her glare on Triston as if he should have prevented all this.

Blast it all, he wished he'd been close enough to stop it.

"I am uncertain if Abercorn is solely involved, but we are headed for my stepmother's cottage. It was gifted to her on her sixteenth birthday by her maternal grandmother. It lays mostly unused. I, myself, have only been there once. It is a long journey, and I suggest the pair of you rest. We will arrive by sunrise."

The women stared out the window as they traveled beyond London and into the darkened countryside. The easy, well-oiled sway of the carriage may lull the women to sleep; however, Triston would get no rest until he knew for certain Edith was uninjured and back with her family—and with him.

His jaw clenched at the ludicrous notion. They'd shared *one* kiss—a rather innocent one, at that. There was little possibility he'd so much as crossed her mind after she departed his lodgings. Unfortunately, the same was not true for him. He'd thought of her while he bathed. He'd muddled his cravat more than once preparing for the soiree as he'd searched the room for her sun-kissed pale locks. If he'd hurried and arrived at the ball sooner, he would have discovered Edith's disappearance far earlier than he had.

Pushing the curtain from his window, Triston stared out at the night. A sea of darkness surrounded them with only the occasional glow of the moon through the overgrown trees bordering the rutted road.

He could not think what Esmee was doing consorting with Abercorn—if Edith's notes were correct, and the two dark-haired beauties were truly one and the same.

Hell, Triston had no doubt they were one and the same.

It was Esmee's way of things. She'd claimed an interest in him only long enough to catch his father's eye. She wed Lord Downshire quickly, securing her place as marchioness, but Abercorn could make her a duchess—did she not realize the messiness of divorce?

A part of him felt remorse for his father, duped by a woman he'd loved enough to hurt his own son to claim.

Triston wondered if he'd fought harder to keep Esmee if she'd have seen how much he'd truly cared for her—but, over time, he'd come to realize his attachment to the raven-haired woman was an emotion built solely on lust. It had never been anything close to love between them. He understood this now. The brief relationship he'd forged with Edith was far deeper than anything he'd experienced with Esmee. It only took Edith's disappearance to make him realize the depth of his connection to her.

His blood boiled at the thought of Esmee being responsible for what was happening to Lady Edith. He would journey to the far reaches of England to secure Edith's safety. He'd wage war against a fire-breathing dragon to make certain she was unharmed. And Triston would lay down his own life to make bloody certain Edith lived a life full of happiness and love.

Without a doubt, he was willing to give up his existence to secure hers.

A woman he'd met only a short time ago.

He didn't know her well enough to say if any of his feelings were love, and not more than any chivalrous gentleman would offer; however, he was driven to do far more for Edith than he had ever felt compelled to do for another person.

Triston was certain he could not look back. He could not turn away. He could not live his life as if Lady Edith had not completely taken over his every thought and action.

IT BECAME MORE and more difficult for Edith to draw breath through the thick hood, and her head still pounded while her shoulder and hip throbbed. Every one of her limbs was numb with cold. Intense shaking had overtaken her firm resolve to not show her panic to the woman who kept her bound.

Time was passing, and the servant hadn't returned, but then again, neither had she heard the carriage depart. At least there was someone still about with the power to stop this madness. Edith must speak with him, give him a reason to help her.

Was it morning yet? If her hood was removed would she see the sun had risen while she was tied to the chair?

And the woman currently stalking in front of her was nothing if not mad.

She moved from calm and reserved to angry and shouting to high-pitched laughter with a note of irrationality. The subject of the woman's inquiry seemed to bounce between topics just as rapidly as her temperament changed.

Despite several hours locked in the cold cottage with her, Edith was no closer to determining the woman's identity. She knew with certainty that she'd never heard her voice before. Was she a jilted lover of Abercorn's? Possibly another person the duke had harmed?

Edith was hard-pressed to keep her fear at bay long enough to concentrate on the mystery at hand.

"I am finding it difficult to breathe." Her voice was muffled and Edith was uncertain if the woman could understand her. "Can you please remove my hood?"

Edith had asked the same question several times before, but her captor never seemed to hear the question; instead moving on to another subject as if Edith hadn't spoken. It was as if the woman were wasting time—or waiting for someone to arrive. Everything was beyond Edith's comprehension. She was exhausted, her mind finding it hard to connect thoughts and words after so many hours bound to the stiff-backed chair.

"Mayhap a drink of water?" She attempted once more. "My throat is—"

"After all I have done, all I have suffered through, you and *Triston* think to ruin *me*?" Her voice cracked, and she laughed once more. "I cannot allow this to happen. Never will I allow this to happen. I have come so far, given up so much—I will not allow you, the spitting image of a porcelain doll with hair of pure gold and skin as fair as any English rose, and Triston to take from me what I have always deserved. A proper English rose, imagine that. Never would I have through Triston would favor such a dull chit."

The woman's words were becoming more and

more confusing as the hours passed and morning crept toward them. Edith could see muted light through her hood, something that hadn't been there before. The sun must be rising.

"I suppose it cannot hurt to remove your hood now," she mused, her feet starting again across the room. "He will be here soon. There are many things Triston is, however, lacking intellect is not one of them. Though I am far more clever than the pair of you. He will find your little notebook and come for you. If he needs any further proof, my maid let slip to the butler where I was going. I will have my confirmation that the pair of you will not cause my downfall."

"I can tell you, I have no idea what you speak of. You can set me loose now, and I will never say a word of this to anyone," Edith begged. "This must be some mistake or misunderstanding."

The hood was jerked from her head, the woman's grasp taking with it a thick lock of Edith's hair.

"Ouch!" Edith blinked rapidly to clear her blurred vision as she turned her head back and forth, taking in the room around her. However, the woman was nowhere to be seen.

"Look all you want," the woman hissed in Edith's ear. "Soon enough, you will see nothing but the watery cliffs below."

Her fears confirmed, Edith whipped her head sharply. The woman—the raven-haired beauty from Lord Abercorn's upstairs' window and Lord Torrington's carriage in Hyde Park—stood behind Edith, her long locks tumbling down over her shoulders in disarray, her icy-blue eyes widened in madness.

This must be the woman Triston spoke of, the one who had betrayed him for his own father. "Lady Downshire." Breathlessly, Edith turned away from the lady to hide her utter shock. A window stood directly before her. The carriage that had brought her sat in the drive, the driver now leaned against the side, his mask discarded during the night. "Please, allow me to leave. I will never speak to Lord Torrington again. I will stay far from Abercorn and his properties. You will never see me again."

"Oh, very shortly I will never have cause to see you or Triston again," Lady Downshire cackled. "Mayhap I should be rid of you now? I can't have Triston being the hero and embarking on the folly of saving you."

She needs must keep the woman talking, must stall her. "Do you truly expect Lord Torrington to come for me?" Edith asked, keeping her eyes trained out the window, silently begging the servant to come to her rescue, but he never glanced in her direction. "I am barely acquainted with him. He has no reason to worry about me."

Lady Downshire moved into her line of sight, her hands clasped behind her back. For the first time, Edith gained a clear view of the woman. Young, but her face held deep lines. She could not be more than a few years Edith's senior. The woman's deep hair, unblemished skin, and catlike eyes were alluring in a sensual way. She understood what had drawn Triston to this woman; she was captivating in her exotic appearance.

But why hadn't *he* been enough for her?

"You were betrothed to Lord Torrington?" It was as good a subject as any, and hopefully, one that would keep the woman talking until Edith could discern a means for escape. "I am sorry things did not go as planned."

Lady Downshire's hands fell to her sides, and a sneer settled on her face, marring her lovely features as rage overtook her. "Do not speak as if you know anything. You are a senseless maid with no knowledge of life."

"I assure you, I know much of life…and loss." Edith lowered her eyes to her lap, not wanting Lady Downshire to see how much it hurt her to admit anything about Tilda's death, especially to a woman obviously intimately connected to the man she feared had played a part in her friend's demise. "You can talk to me."

Without warning, the woman lashed out, her flat palm landing against Edith's cheek with a crack. Her neck whipped sharply and heat boomed across Edith's face. She pressed her lips together, determined not to cry out from the pain and shock of the woman's venom.

She turned away from Edith, moving without further word to a chair across the room. It must be the place she'd sat silently when Edith and been brought into the cottage.

Thankfully, Lady Downshire's anger seemed to ebb as she sank into the chair, her shoulders sagging as her scowl relaxed to a mere frown, her thoughts obviously drifting to another time and place.

Edith stared back toward the window, a cloud of dust could be seen in the distance.

Her heart sped up. Someone was coming.

The approaching carriage remained unnoticed by the driver leaning against Lady Downshire's coach as he stared off toward the cliffs beyond the cottage.

The roar and slap of the waves likely drowned out the sound of the coach and four horses.

"Ah, it must be him," the woman sighed pulling back the cloth and staring out the window. "It is indeed. Triston has finally arrived. You know, I thought he would arrive hours ago. Is it possible he does not care for you as much as he cared for me?"

CHAPTER 14

"LOOK!" OPHELIA EXCLAIMED, her nose pressed firmly to the windowpane, keeping out the early morning ocean breeze. "There is a carriage. She must be here."

After long hours of pondering the situation, Triston was certain Edith would be found within the cottage at the end of the drive. His father's carriage waited out front, but no sign of the Abercorn coach could be seen. His elation was only dimmed by his cautious nature—and the need to get his hands on Esmee and demand she give him answers.

The morning fog off the cold North Sea rolled in from the open waters to settle on the cliffs, only burning off once the midday sun crested above the area. If he'd journeyed here under any other circumstances, Triston would halt the carriage and take in the sight from the drive, a bit above the cottage and cliffs below.

Not today. Not ever would he gaze upon a cliff so majestic and not think solely of destruction and chaos.

And loss.

Esmee had taken Edith. There were no more lingering doubts once he spotted his family carriage outside of his stepmother's family home.

He stilled himself from throwing the conveyance

door wide and running the remaining way to the cottage. Triston could outrun the horses, his blood pumping violently through him would push him fast. However, he would not alarm the women across from him before it was necessary. If he raised their nervousness, they could very well find themselves in harm's way. They could not follow him into the cottage. He needed them to wait in the carriage until he'd determined Esmee was no threat and Abercorn wasn't also within the dwelling. He could not rescue Edith while keeping the other two women safe and out of trouble.

If he hadn't been so overcome with the need to find Edith, he would have realized sooner that the pair would have been safer remaining in London and allowing Triston to find and return Edith.

"I must ask a favor, Lady Lucianna." Triston looked to Edith's tall, slender friend—undoubtedly the leader of the group if her command of the situation during Edith's disappearance was any proof—for support. "I need you both to wait in the carriage while I enter the cottage."

"You think we should trust you?" Unease laced the woman's words as she assessed him.

Triston held his hands out, palms up. "I have brought you both this far. I care deeply for Edith's safety, as much as the pair of you." He moved to Lady Ophelia, her pensive expression meaning she was seriously thinking through everything. Maybe he should have addressed her first. "Lady Ophelia, it is imperative I keep all three of you safe—return you home whole and unharmed."

"You were incapable of completing that task when it was only Edith you were charged with. What makes you think we trust you to be able to step up with all three of us hanging in the balance?" Lucianna questioned.

Ophelia set her hand on Lucianna's arm. "Come

now, Luci. Lord Torrington has been honest with us thus far since discovering Edith's journal. We have little idea what we will find in the cottage. Let us allow him to venture in first."

Their carriage pulled up alongside his father's, with Samson leaning against it, his gaze on the cliffs beyond. The servant's family had been in the Downshire employ for three generations.

Triston bounded from the carriage before either woman had confirmed they'd remain out of sight. He needs must make sure they had some semblance of surprise—if Esmee hadn't already seen them. Walking around his father's coach, he immediately had Samson by the collar and twisted, cutting off the man's yelp before it left his throat.

"What have you done?" Triston hissed, bringing the servant's face close to his own.

"Lord Torrington!" Samson croaked, pushing at Triston to release him. "I—this—ye must—" he stammered.

"I *must* do nothing but allow the magistrate to deal with your misdeeds." Triston pushed the servant away, the sudden action sending the man splaying into the dirt. "Is it only Esmee and Lady Edith inside?"

When Samson remained silent, pushing himself back and away, Triston stalked forward. "If one hair on Lady Edith's head is harmed, it will not end well for you or Esmee, I swear to you."

"I—I—I never harmed the girl, m'lord. Swear on me pa, I didna." Samson crawled backwards. "I was only do'n what m'lady said."

"Kidnapping an innocent woman?" Triston seethed, advancing on the man. "Was it you who hit her? There was blood on her journal." Triston bit back the urge to pounce on the man, take out his pent-up aggression that had built during the four-hour journey to the sea.

"I startled the girl, and she bumped her head on a

tree branch. That be all, m'lord."

"What is Esmee's plan with her?"

"She doona be tell'n me much, but I heard her talk'n ta herself—she planned ta lure ye here." Samson tripped over himself, and he rushed to get the words out. "After that, I not be know'n. I swear ta it."

The woman was using Edith as a pawn to lure him to these cliffs.

Triston's lip curled back in a snarl, and his eyes narrowed one final time on the servant before he turned and called for his own driver. When he hurried over, Triston bit out each word as if it were his fist slamming into something—or someone. "Tie him up. Make certain he does not slip away. Ames should be here with the magistrate before long."

"Of course, my lord." The coachman ran back to the carriage and collected a length of rope from beneath his perch.

"You are not to give anyone anymore problems, Samson," Triston seethed. He didn't have time to deal with the disloyal servant. He needed to help Edith. "Do we have an understanding?"

Samson shook his head vehemently, spittle flying from his gaping mouth.

"Good, now give your hands to my driver," Triston demanded.

He barely paused to watch the coachman secure Samson's wrists.

"What is going on?" Lady Lucianna called from his carriage.

"Who is that man?" Lady Ophelia chimed in.

But Triston was already stalking toward the cottage, the cliffs surrounding it on three sides as the morning ocean spray relentlessly hammered the sheer rocks. He was uncertain if it was the din of the waves or the sound of his own blood thrumming through his veins that echoed in his head, blocking out all other noise.

His steps faltered when the silhouette of a woman

passed the large window—a pocket pistol held in her hands.

The tousled midnight hair and hurried, frantic movements did not fit the Esmee Triston knew. Something had broken loose within the woman, sending her into a manic spiral. He wracked his brain, attempting to remember any specific thing—either said or done—that would send Lady Downshire into such a maddened state.

His heart dropped as he looked closer. Edith was bound to a chair, her eyes widened in terror as Esmee advanced on her, the pistol pointed squarely at Edith—the rising sun gleaming off the pearl handle.

Triston moved in slow motion, his body not responding as quickly as he demanded…his breath heaving as he raced to stop Esmee.

The door to the cottage stood ajar, and Esmee's deep, throaty voice drifted toward him, halting his movement.

"…you see, I am to have a baby—the next Marquis of Downshire. My dear husband, Horace, is so deeply excited for our babe."

"Lord Torrington is to be the next marquis," Edith challenged.

"Correction, my dear Lady Edith, for I can see you are a bit daft," Esmee laughed. "Our poor Lord Torrington, my beloved stepson, will fall to his death this day. You see, he will be overcome by grief when he learns I am with child. He is still desperately in love with me. Everyone knows this to be true, even though I chose his father. He cannot handle I am to give birth to another Neville heir."

Triston lifted his foot to kick in the door, ready to remove the pistol from Esmee's hands and untie Edith, but her words halted him.

"And how do you know the child belongs to Lord Downshire and not Abercorn?" Edith's words were laced with conviction.

His pride—and affection—for Edith grew. She'd discovered Esmee's treachery when Triston, and his father, hadn't noticed anything amiss. His stepmother not only sought to dupe his father, but also do away with him to make way for her own child to inherit the Downshire estate. And there was no proof the child even belonged to the marquis' bloodline.

The woman was sadly mistaken if she thought he was so easy to be rid of.

"With you and Triston out of the way, no proof will exist to the contrary." Esmee waved the tiny pistol about.

Triston leaned close and peered through the crack in the door.

Esmee lowered the weapon and paced back toward the hearth. The tiny shot certainly wouldn't kill Edith from any distance, but up close, the pistol could cause serious injury. Especially if Esmee's aim were true.

"What of Abercorn," Edith asked. "Will he not suspect the babe is his?"

The woman threw her head back and cackled, it was the only way he could describe the sound, as if Edith had said the most insane thing.

His hair stood on end, and a shiver ran down his spine at the sound—so cold and emotionless.

"Enough." Esmee sobered, lifting the pistol once more and pivoting back toward Edith. Crossing the five paces to stand before her, she shoved the weapon in Edith's face. "You will keep your mouth shut!"

Triston noted that her hand shook, and the pistol wavered slightly.

He needed to end this charade.

Glancing over his shoulder, Triston saw Lucianna and Ophelia staring at him from the safety of the carriage.

Bloody hell, what had possessed him to travel without a weapon of his own? He clenched his jaw. Regardless, Esmee should not be hard to overpower.

Taking a final deep breath, Triston pushed through the door.

CHAPTER 15

EDITH SHRIEKED AT the same time Esmee turned sharply toward the door as it slammed against its frame. The shiny pistol slid from her grip and clattered along the floor until it hit the far wall.

Triston. Relief flooded Edith when he finally entered the cottage.

Both he and Lady Downshire followed the weapon's progress across the room, and Edith sighed, comforted to know the woman no longer held the gun.

Both Triston and Lady Downshire took off after the pistol; the woman scurrying across the room on her hands and knees, attempting to arrive at the far wall first, but Triston was quicker. He took hold of the weapon and held it high, out of the woman's reach, and she clawed at him and pulled on his shoulders to bring it back down. A deep sense of compassion welled inside Edith to notice that Triston did not aim the pistol at Lady Downshire, but only sought to keep it from her.

"Enough!" Triston commanded, his tone filled with power and leaving no room for argument; however, Lady Downshire seemed undeterred—and out of control—continuing to beat at Triston's chest.

Edith could not take her eyes off Triston—his hulking presence overtaking the room, commanding all present to heed his fury. His intense stare took her in next, from the obvious knot on her forehead, which ached with a fierce intensity that matched his stare, to her bound wrists, her uncontrollable shaking, and finally, coming to rest on her petrified gaze.

She knew exactly how she appeared—Edith had had a few opportunities to taken in her reflection in the window before her. She knew her hair was knotted, a twig tangled in her golden tresses. Her face was smudged with dirt from the carriage boot. And worst of all, her journal was gone, her hidden pocket ripped at the seams. Lady Downshire said she'd left it in London—odd to be concerned with a silly journal in such a terrifying moment.

Finally, Esmee stepped away, her heel catching on her gown, sending the woman tumbling, her arms pinwheeling and grasping for anything to stop her fall.

Edith watched as the woman's mouth opened in a silent scream as her head hit the table and she crumpled to the floor.

"Are you well, Edith? Tell me if you are injured." Triston set the pistol down and rushed to her side, reaching behind her to untie her wrists. "If she so much as—" He breathed.

"I am as well as can be expected after spending several hours in a carriage boot and many more tied to this chair, but nothing that will not heal with time and rest." Edith flexed her wrists, bringing them before her as Triston gently massaged the indentations from the rope. Feeling and warmth quickly returned to her fingers. "I shouldn't have been so foolish as to journey back to Abercorn's before going home…"

Triston placed a quick kiss to her lips, his heat banishing her chill.

"As heartwarming as this is, I will need to ask you to step away from Lady Edith, Triston," Esmee purred, rubbing the side of her head.

Glancing over his shoulder, she saw the woman

had collected her pocket pistol and held it aloft once more; however, this time, her hand was steady, and her gaze alight with a fury so deep, her icy blue eyes glowed in the dim cottage.

"Triston!" Edith couldn't say anything more before he flipped around.

As Edith stood, he pushed her behind him. "Go, Edith," he whispered. "Out the door, now!"

She didn't want to leave him, couldn't imagine fleeing and letting him get hurt—or worse yet, killed—because she wasn't here to help.

Her gaze assessed the room, looking for anything she could use as a weapon.

Triston slowly advanced on Lady Downshire. "Esmee, put the pistol down. You do not need to do this. It is over. Do not give me reason to restrain you."

"I am with child, you brute," the woman wailed, swinging the gun wildly at Triston. "You stay back from me. Your father will never forgive you if he learns you assaulted me in my delicate condition."

Triston sidestepped, attempting to keep one step ahead of her as she swung her pistol and he moved in a circle, leading the woman away from Edith. She knew the wise thing would be to hurry to the carriage as she'd been told, but her desire to remain and help Triston would not allow her to depart. It was her fault he was in danger in the first place. If she hadn't gone to Abercorn's townhouse again, if she hadn't followed Triston from the park—heaven help her, if she hadn't climbed into the tree all those weeks ago—he would have never been dragged into any of this.

And she never would have discovered how much she could care for a man. Her heart ached at the very thought of a life without him.

Lady Downshire would have continued her trysts with the duke, unbeknownst to her husband or Lord Torrington.

They would not currently be in the wilds of Essex

in a cottage overlooking sheer rock cliffs—a severe drop Esmee thought to cast both her and Triston over. All to save herself the embarrassment of being exposed as a lying, cheating adulteress, pregnant with another man's child.

The entire debacle was preposterous. Edith, and her friends had been in the business of collecting gossip and exposing the next scandal for almost a year now, but this was nothing Edith had ever wanted to be embroiled in.

Triston's Hessians scraped along the wooden floor, and he led Esmee away from Edith toward a door that opened in the kitchen.

Her pulse raced as she scrutinized the room one last time. The cottage was empty except for a lounge, table, chairs, and a few tarp-covered objects. Not so much as a fire poker to grasp if the need arose. It'd been too dark outside when she'd been let out of the carriage boot and her hood replaced before entering the cottage. There had to be something to use as a weapon outside. Maybe an ax to chop firewood or a long piece of wood…anything.

Triston was backing up through the door into the kitchen area with Esmee following, her pistol trained on Triston's heart.

If Edith hurried, she could find her own weapon and return within moments.

Edith followed Triston's lead and began backing up toward the front door which remained open, but kept a watch on Lady Downshire. The woman was mad enough to change course before either Triston or Edith suspected her switch in target.

Suddenly, an arm wrapped around her neck, and a voice hissed, "Where do ye think ye be makin' off ta?"

The servant's stale breath assaulted her neck, hot and sour.

Why hadn't she thought about what had become of the man who'd brought her in from the carriage?

Edith begged herself to remain still, to not say a word to distract Triston from his target. The servant began to pull her from the cottage and out toward the cliffs beyond, her feet coming out from beneath her as she tried to gain purchase. His free hand snaked around her waist, firmly pulling her to his body to cut off her struggles.

Glancing around the yard, she saw another man lying unmoving on the ground. Edith would never forgive herself if she were the cause of anyone else being injured.

Within a moment's time, they were around the house, and the prone man was blocked from her view by the cottage. The violent thrashing of the waves against the cliffs made it impossible for any screams to be heard. At least if she kept the carriage driver occupied, it was only Lady Downshire whom Triston need overtake before coming for her.

All hope was not lost.

Edith trusted Triston—he came for her even after learning she'd been spying on him.

Blast it all, she more than trusted him.

He would come for her again; she only need slow the driver down.

"Do not do this," Edith said, the man's arm tightening around her throat. "You will lose everything. And for what? That senseless woman inside the cottage?"

"Shut ye mouth!" He pulled up with the arm around her midsection, lifting her feet off the ground and moving faster toward the cliffs, no longer pulling but carrying her. "M'lady has never been senseless, ye best bet. She be a wondrous lady—who not a single soul appreciates. Not her husband, nor that nob Abercorn."

"You are in love with her," Edith croaked, her windpipe slowly crushing under the servant's tight hold. It wasn't a question…there was no other way to explain why a man would throw away his life to help a woman who'd kidnapped an innocent woman and lured a gentleman—a master within his household—to his death. "She does not love you."

Edith needs must make the man see reason. Lady Downshire loved nothing but herself and the status that came from marrying a wealthy, titled man.

"As soon as you do as she says, she is going to leave you—blame everything on you. You will be the one locked away at Newgate or hung for your crimes. Not her. She will return to London and live as if nothing happened." At her words, he tightened his grip even more, cutting off Edith's air and sending her head swimming.

"You, there!"

Edith's mind cleared instantly when Luci's voice thundered from behind them, causing the man to speed up.

"Duck!" Ophelia shouted.

Edith didn't need any more encouragement. She whipped from the man's hold and fell to the ground, rolling to the side and away from the cliffs.

There was no time to ponder how Luci and Ophelia had gotten all the way to Essex or even knew she'd been taken.

Thwack.

Edith turned and attempted to push herself to stand. Her friends were immediately at her sides with Ophelia grasping her elbow to help her stand. From the corner of her eye, Edith watched Luci throw a long piece of wood to the ground before nudging the servant with her slippered toe.

Luci turned back to Edith with a shrug when the man didn't move. "I guess he wasn't expecting that."

Edith's chest burned, and she sucked down a large gulp of air before doubling over in a coughing fit. The pounding in her head intensified once more, and her throat ached.

"How—I mean when—I cannot—"

"Shhhh." Ophelia rubbed her goose pimple-covered arms. "You are freezing. Let me get you back to Lord Torrington's carriage. There is a wrap waiting for you."

"Lord Torrington! Have you seen him?" Edith pulled from Ophelia's hold and started back toward the cottage. "Lady Downshire had a pistol trained on him. We must stop her!"

Luci bent to retrieve the wooden branch she'd hit the servant over the head with, but Edith shook her head.

"She is with child. We cannot harm her, or the babe might be injured, as well."

"But she kidnapped you." Luci's words were laced with disbelief. "How can you feel any sympathy for this woman?"

Edith hadn't contemplated her feelings for Lady Downshire; honestly, she only knew her for this one action. Though it was deplorable, she longed to know the many actions that came before it to bring the woman to such a place where she sought to harm a woman she'd never met—or Lord Torrington.

"It is not sympathy, Luci, but a sense any of us could have ended up in a similar position." Edith turned back toward the cottage as a set of double doors on the back side of the house were flung open, though the never-ending slap of the waves covered any sound. "We can discuss this later. We need to help Triston."

The women shared a knowing look, but Edith didn't pause long enough to question it.

Triston was slowly backing toward the cliffs with Lady Downshire in pursuit—her hands steadily holding the pistol. He didn't allow his eyes to stray toward Edith or her friends, though by the way his shoulders tensed, he'd seen them.

If they didn't act quickly, Triston would be forced over the cliff—taking Edith's hope for the future with him.

Waving to Luci and Ophelia, the trio sidled close to the cottage wall and followed it until they were directly behind Esmee, who pressed forward toward the cliffs at a slow pace.

Edith couldn't imagine the horrible, senseless, and hurtful words the woman spouted.

Lady Downshire's voice was swallowed by the increasing wind, only heard by her and Triston.

EDITH, WITH LUCIANNA and Ophelia close behind, edged their way along the cottage wall until they were directly behind Esmee. He was torn between pride at their bravado and a desire to shout at them to save themselves. Triston could not comprehend how Esmee hadn't noticed the trio or Samson lying prone on the ground only fifty feet away.

She'd always had a one-track mind, focused on the thing she wanted at that precise moment. It had been winning him once upon a time, but it had quickly changed to snaring a marquis—Triston's father—and eventually, having her own family. Odd he hadn't realized how much she'd changed over the years. She'd been willing to bed another man to make certain she carried a child as soon as possible, but Triston doubted she'd slaked her lust only with Abercorn.

Had Samson fallen prey to Esmee's viperous ways?

If Triston hadn't been able to resist the woman's treacherous charms, there was little possibility a mere coachman would turn away if his mistress took an interest in him. The depth of her manipulation sickened him. He felt an immense sense of pity for Samson, though that did not overshadow his part in Edith's disappearance.

"Esmee." He held his hands out, not wanting to incite her further. "Let us return to the cottage and discuss this. I am certain things are not as dire as you suspect."

He'd kept up the pretense that what had been said before he'd entered the cottage was still unknown to him. She thought him still pining away for her, continuing to miss what they'd briefly shared two years prior. No lit candle was held for the woman before him—it had been snuffed out the moment he'd caught his father in a compromising situation with Esmee in his study.

Shaking his head, Triston had to concentrate on the present, not the wounds from his past. They had healed, but if Esmee pulled the trigger on her pistol or caused him to fall from the cliffs, it would be the end of him…and Edith.

"Did you think I wouldn't find out what you and your little strumpet were up to?" Esmee waved her weapon before her, her grip so tight her knuckles were white. "There is no more time for talking, and I will not allow you to alter my course. The decision has been made."

The term *strumpet* incited Triston once more. Esmee, the woman who's easily betrayed him and his father thought to use such a word when speaking of Lady Edith?

She'd been seamlessly altering from composed to livid to a babbling mess making little sense. It had always been Triston's belief Esmee was a determined, persistent lady. She knew what she wanted, and she went for it. The woman stalking him toward the cliff's edge was not that woman.

"You do not need to do this, Esmee," he shouted to be heard above the growing noise of the waves at his back. "Lady Edith and I—"

"Are trying to destroy me!" Her eyes grew wide with madness. "I will not allow it. I am Lady Downshire, a marchioness. I will give my husband an heir."

"But he *has* an heir."

"*You?*" Spittle flew, and Esmee threw her head back in laughter. "My son will be the next Marquis of Downshire, not you, Triston."

"You plan to kill me?"

"Oh, no. You will jump from the cliff willingly." Esmee halted, her lips curling into the innocent smile Triston remembered from years prior. "You will be so distraught over the news of my pregnancy. You brought me here to declare your love, you see, but I rebuffed your advances. In the end, you could not handle the rejection, and unrequited love made you take your own life." She shrugged as if she'd painstakingly planned the entire situation and now only needed him to be the honorable gentleman and do as she said.

Did she think him the sort of man to beg, either for his life or for her love?

His chest tightened. He hadn't fought or begged for Esmee before or now, but he would for Edith. He needed her, and she needed him. For that to happen, he must be alive.

"Now, can we not get this over with?" she asked. "When I am done with you, I still have need to deal with your ladybird; though I am certain Samson has her occupied at the moment."

Triston focused on Esmee, not wanting his eyes to stray toward Edith and her friends, who were currently whispering amongst themselves. He only prayed the trio did nothing foolish to put them at risk. A wish he had a dreadful feeling would not go without frustration as the ladies had already proven themselves reckless.

Out of the corner of his eye, Triston saw Samson starting to regain his wits, though he hadn't managed a sitting position as yet.

If the servant were able to rejoin Esmee in her endeavors, the odds would be less in Triston's favor. He couldn't allow this to happen.

Bloody hell, Triston should have insisted his father make the journey with him, but there hadn't been time to convince the marquis. Belatedly, Triston hadn't even thought of the idea until London was far in their wake. The marquis would be hard-pressed to think his beloved wife capable of any of this.

Triston took another small step back, the overspray from the cliffs hitting the back of his neck and saturating his jacket. The lip of the sheer drop could only be a few paces away...and he was no closer to getting Esmee to see reason.

Edith and her friends fanned out behind his stepmother, moving slowly into a semi-circle of sorts as they blocked her in. They surrounded her on three sides with Triston taking the fourth position.

He shook his head slightly, hoping they'd see his silent plea and find their own safety.

Instead, the women only moved closer, trapping Esmee but also putting each of them at a greater risk of being the woman's new target.

Edith had taken the position directly behind Esmee—in Triston's line of view.

He took in the sight of her. Edith commanded all of his attention, holding him hostage. If these were his last moments, he would perish happily, knowing the images of Edith would be forever burned into his memory.

The woman was beautiful, her appearance nothing but sunshine and brightness with her delicate skin, sun-kissed, pale locks, and honey eyes.

He was helpless to do anything but watch as the trio shared a nod and all shouted in unison, their voices carrying high above the din of the ocean behind him, and echoing around them.

Esmee halted her advance, her head twisting this way and that to find out where the noise had come from. Her hand clutching the pistol dipped to her side, and Triston took the opportunity to pounce into action.

Triston leapt forward and took hold of Esmee's hand, wrenching the weapon from her.

Lucianna and Ophelia quickly stepped forward and grasped each of Esmee's arms.

Esmee's eyes widened in utter shock as she looked from one woman holding her to the other and desperately tried to tug herself free. A long, black strand of hair fell over her eyes, and Triston reached forward to brush it aside.

"It is over, Esmee," he sighed, uncertain if she heard him over the crashing waves. "There is no use struggling."

Esmee crumpled to the ground, the two women struggling to keep her from completely falling.

A deep, wrenching sob escaped her as her head fell forward and her damp, raven hair veiled her face from sight. Her shoulders shook, and her body trembled.

Edith stepped forward and knelt next to the woman who'd had such nefarious plans for her, and laid her arm around Esmee's heaving shoulders, leaning in close to whisper something in his stepmother's ear.

When Esmee nodded, Edith slipped her arm around the woman's back and helped her to stand.

Triston would have gladly taken Edith in his arms and walked away, but here she was, helping the woman who'd only an hour ago intended to push her off a cliff.

His heart swelled, and the despair of the previous night dissipated.

Edith led Esmee back toward the cottage with Lady Lucianna and Ophelia close behind. Her compassion for his stepmother baffled him. How could Edith want to be anywhere near Esmee?

When the group disappeared into the cottage, Triston turned toward Samson, but the servant was being led away by Triston's coachman.

His carriage still waited in the drive, but another plume of dust traveled toward him, another carriage approaching. It must be Ames with the Hadleigh Magistrate.

Bringing his arm to shield the sun from his eyes,

Triston watched the coach's harried approach with its four large, spotted horses pulling at the reins.

"My lord?" He turned away from the approaching carriage to see that Edith had returned to his side. "You must be cold. Luci is starting a fire inside. I think you should warm yourself."

"You always think first of others." He turned to her, tucking a lock of hair behind her ear before leaning down to kiss her forehead.

Edith pulled back and stared up at him, her brow furrowed. "It is what I have always been taught. If I put others first, my happiness will naturally follow."

Triston remained silent, running his thumb along her hairline where a large lump was forming. She was so innocent and pure—and because of him, that was shattered. He stared into her eyes, waiting for the moment her innocence would disappear and be replaced by darkness. With that, Edith would turn away from him. She had no other option—she exposed scandal, she did not live it herself. Unfortunately, things were to become far more complicated, and the risk of society finding out grew more pressing as the carriage carrying Ames and the magistrate arrived.

He doubted her coming happiness would include him.

CHAPTER 16

EDITH HEARD, RATHER than saw, yet another carriage arrive at the tiny cottage on the cliffs. It was as if the sea had realized the danger had passed because the roar of the waves subsided, bringing an almost peaceful hum to the tiny yard in front of the cottage.

There was nothing Edith wanted more than this moment.

She'd thought only an hour before her time with Triston was forever at an end. The chance to tell him exactly how much she cared for him would be taken from her; however, here they stood.

Both whole and safe.

Which meant Edith would have plenty of time to express to Triston everything her heart held for him. Speaking of her heart, it raced as he continued to stare down at her, his look softening and holding a meaning she couldn't quiet decipher.

A mixture of sorrow...and what?

Esmee and her loyal servant were being held inside the cottage with no danger of escape or chance of harming anyone else.

There was no reason for sadness—or regret—which was what she saw in Triston's eyes.

They should celebrate.

Without giving herself time to change her mind, Edith stood on her tiptoes, but his face was still out of reach. She encircled his neck with her arms, feeling that the hair at his nape was still damp, but this did not stop Edith from drawing Triston down to her.

She peered into his eyes. "Thank you for coming for me."

"I—"

Her lips met his, silencing his reply. Edith would not be able to go on if he told her he'd come out of any other reason but love—for her. His warm lips banished the cold that had settled on her long before the morning sun had risen. As she'd sat tied to the chair, the hood over her head, Edith truly believed she'd be cold and overrun by shivers forevermore; however, when Triston's arms wrapped around her waist and pulled her close, she knew, without a doubt, she'd never feel the icy tendrils of cold run through her again.

"Triston!"

He pulled back with the call of his name and set Edith back on the ground. However, their brief kiss was enough to give her hope there would be more to come. If not today, then tomorrow, or the day after. She was not allowing Triston to go.

"Triston!" They both turned to see Triston's father running toward them, his arms outstretched as if he did not touch his son, hold him quickly, he may disappear. "You are safe. Where is Esmee?"

The man, so much like his son with his great height and strong jaw, stopped and placed his hands on Triston's shoulders.

Behind them, a haphazardly dressed man, likely the Hadleigh magistrate awoken from his slumber, and another man sauntered toward the open cottage door where Ophelia shouted for their attention.

"She is inside, Father," Triston confirmed, and his father relaxed, the strain of the long carriage ride draining from his shoulders. "She is unharmed, physically."

The marquis shook his head. "I do not understand…"

Edith wanted to take Triston's arm, give him someone to lean on when he told his father the damning truth, but to her surprise, it was he who stepped free of his father's hold and pulled Edith close once more.

"Esmee is not well. Her mind…it is addled." The sorrow returned to him, and Edith thought maybe this was what had weighed on him since his stepmother was thwarted. "She, with Samson's assistance, kidnapped Lady Edith and brought her here, thinking to lure me to my death. She says she is with child."

"It cannot be," Lord Downshire mumbled, looking over Triston's shoulder to the cottage. "I must go to her. Have a physician summoned. I cannot…I am sorry…it is too much…"

"Go to her, my lord," Edith whispered. "Having you near will calm her, I am certain."

The marquis looked down at her, as if noticing her for the first time, and his eyes widened.

"Lady Edith… I cannot tell you how sorry I am for all this—"

She held up her hand to stop him. "Do not worry over me, go to your Lady Downshire."

Edith suspected her dirty clothes, knotted hair, and the atrocious lump on her forehead made her appear far worse than she actually felt.

With a nod, and another pat to Triston's shoulder to confirm he was truly solid and well, the marquis dashed inside the cottage.

Edith remained quiet and still at Triston's side as he watched his father go.

"I cannot believe he came," Triston mumbled.

"He loves you. You are his son, after all." Edith was only privy to the one exchange Triston had shared with his father at his boarding house before she was taken. The man did not seem one to show his affection for his offspring, but the love was there. Edith was sure of it. "Shall we go inside and help?"

"Heavens no," Triston said, his hand caressing her cheek. "I think we have done our part for the day."

She held her breath, waiting for him to say more. When he didn't, Edith sighed. "I am sorry for causing you and your family so much trouble. If we hadn't been so fixated on Abercorn, none of this would have happened."

Triston leaned down and placed his lips to her forehead, being sure to keep away from the knot. "No, I should have heeded your warnings about the man."

"You do not think us foolish for our continued persistence with Abercorn?" She closed her eyes, concentrating on the feel of his mouth as it trailed from her forehead, to her cheek, to her jaw with an aching slowness until he reached her lips.

He kissed her right there, not caring who saw their intimate moment—and her question dissipated. It no longer mattered as he lifted her from the ground, and Edith ran her hand through his hair, pulling him ever closer to her.

CHAPTER 17

EDITH ALLOWED HER eyes to drift closed, the sway of the moving carriage tempting her to sleep, safely tucked against Triston's side. She was exhausted, yet it had taken nearly an hour for her nerves to settle enough for the tension to drain from her. Her head still ached, throbbing in time with her hip.

However, she was unharmed.

Both she and Triston were unscathed, while they'd left Lady Downshire in the care of her husband, the Hadleigh magistrate, and a local physician. Samson had confessed all—including his own tryst with his mistress. Edith despised watching the hurt in the marquis' eyes as he learned of his wife's treachery firsthand.

Esmee was a gently bred lady of the *ton*, married to a wealthy, influential lord.

Which meant, if Triston's father did not deem her actions worthy of punishment, then Lady Downshire could very well return to her place among society with impunity for her deeds.

She was obviously demented and in need of a physician's care, especially if she were with child. Seeing as how Triston's father—at Prudence's and Chastity's insistence—had accompanied Ames to Lady Downshire's home in Essex, she doubted the woman would continue as she had before—or planned to after doing away with Edith and Triston. At the very least, she'd be removed from London to the Downshire country estate, Carlton Curlieu Hall in Leicestershire, until after the babe was born. Triston had reassured her of this after handing her, Luci, and Ophelia into their carriage.

As they'd started back toward London, they'd each fallen into their own silent musings as the miles passed. Luci and Ophelia were tucked tightly under a woolen blanket on the opposite seat, while Edith had selected to sit beside Triston as opposed to between her friends.

Yet, neither woman seemed to judge her harshly for the choice.

Triston was ever so warm, giving her the heat she'd lacked after the cold night she suffered. He pulled her a bit closer at that moment, and Edith couldn't stop her smile.

Unexpectedly, his lips pressed to her forehead.

Edith couldn't prevent her sigh of contentment from escaping.

"We will be back in London before we know it," Triston mumbled to no one in particular.

"And how are we to explain our disappearance to our parents?" It was unnecessary for Edith to open her eyes to know Luci sat across from her, her arms crossed and a scowl on her face. "And arriving home in your carriage…we will all be ruined."

"Better ruined and alive than dead and forgotten at the bottom of a cliff," Ophelia chimed in.

Edith giggled at Ophelia's impertinent comment, knowing it would only further inflame Luci.

Her friend only huffed. Cracking her eyes, Edith watched as Luci turned to stare out the window, her arms—as suspected—crossed.

"Do not fear, ladies," Triston replied.

"We have everything to fear, Lord Torrington." Luci's cool demeanor broke wide. "We cannot trust you to fix all of this for us."

"Did I not tell you to have faith I would rescue Edith?"

"Yes," Luci reluctantly agreed. "But—"

"And did I not follow through on that promise?"

"Oh, my lord, you certainly did…with our assistance!" Ophelia exclaimed, tugging the blanket away from Luci to cover her own legs. "You were quite dashing and a regular white knight. You must admit, Lucianna, Lord Torrington did know where to find Edith, and he kept that madwoman distracted long enough for us to bash the poor coachman over the head."

Luci snorted. "I will admit nothing of the sort."

"Then I suppose I should direct my driver to head for Gretna Green." Triston shrugged.

Edith's shoulders straightened. There was only one reason for a person to travel to Gretna Green, and Edith could not entertain the very notion for fear it would lead to her disappointment.

"Gretna Green!" Ophelia sat up straight, her eyes as wide as tea saucers, mirroring Edith's own startled look. "Why would we journey to Scotland?"

"To avoid scandal—I will wed Lady Edith, and you two will be our witnesses." He spoke as if the idea weren't completely outlandish. "When we return to London, it will be as husband and wife, and you two will be properly chaperoned."

Husband and wife? Edith allowed the preposterous notion to settle within her. To have Triston by her side for all eternity? It seemed too much for her to hope for.

"You think a hasty marriage across the border will stall the gossips?" Luci narrowed her glare on him.

"If that does not stop any whisper of scandal, then I am certain the trio of you can say…" He tapped his chin in thought. "Have a letter posted in the *London Daily Gazette* to clarify the circumstances surrounding Edith's hasty marriage to a man more handsome than any lord in decades. You can also reassure your readers that though I am a sturdy man, I am not, in fact, as strong as an ox nor as arrogant as a London dandy."

"I believe I compared you to a Greek god—Adonis—not oxen." Edith leaned away from Triston and stared up into his molten cocoa eyes, his humor evident in his smirk.

"My dear Lady Edith, you still possess the skills of a snake with your lightning-quick ability to persuade." He pulled her close once more, this time, bringing his lips to hers.

Not caring that both of her friends gasped in surprise, Edith pushed herself ever closer to Triston, not daring to allow him room to pull away from her. She'd allowed him to send her away once, and they'd almost lost each other. It would not happen again.

"I suppose we do owe you our sincerest gratitude for assisting us in finding Edith; however, let us keep in mind she would not have been taken had it not been for you, Lord Torrington."

Edith released Triston's lips long enough to laugh. "That is the best you will get from Luci, my lord. I would take it as a 'thank you' and move on."

"I think I will take your advice." He brought his hands to cup her face, his thumb lightly grazing the spot where she'd been hit. "Oh, and I intend to have that blasted tree removed from my father's London drive."

"Just because you have proven yourself worthy, does not mean we will stop our pursuit of Lord Abercorn—and other men who think to cause women harm." Luci leaned back in her seat, tugging a portion of their wrap back from Ophelia.

"I cannot stop any of you from this course; however, I will caution you against writing any piece that is not solidly grounded in facts."

"You will not demand we stop?" Ophelia asked.

"Of course, not," Triston replied. "My dear sisters happen to enjoy the *Mayfair Confidential* column greatly. I will not be the cause of their displeasure. Now, I pose the question once more: where do we go from here? I can instruct my driver to London, or on to Scotland."

Edith's heart spiked as she waited for her friends' responses.

"You truly mean to wed Edith?" Luci asked, eyeing him closely.

Even Edith felt a measure of uncertainty under her friend's intense stare.

"If she will have me, yes. However, I prefer a more traditional approach than a Gretna Green wedding." He turned to Edith once more. "If you will have me, and your parents agree to our match, I would insist on a proper betrothal and a large wedding—as quickly as possible. Unless you prefer Gretna Green, that is."

Her heart fluttered once more, and Ophelia sighed dramatically.

"And what if my parents object?" She would not share with him that her parents would never object to a match Edith wanted. "What then?"

"It will be my turn to kidnap you!"

"Oh, Lord Torrington, I think you may have convinced me noble men exist, after all," Edith sighed. "And love is certainly possible."

"Love?" Luci hissed as if saying the very word burnt her tongue.

Edith pulled back and stared across the carriage at her dearest friends. "Yes, love. We must remember, no matter how much we long to discover what truly happened the night Tilda fell down those stairs, we cannot forget to find our own happiness. She would have wanted that for all of us, far more than spending our lives reliving her passing and never moving forward to secure our own futures."

"You expect me to easily forget that Abercorn caused the demise of our friend?" Luci asked. "To act as if it didn't happen and go on enjoying the endless soirees and nights at the opera, all while my heart is heavy and burdened?"

"We will never forget Tilda." Ophelia nodded.

Edith knew Ophelia risked Luci's wrath if she openly agreed with Edith.

"I am not asking you to forget—or stop keeping a close eye on Abercorn—however, we can also seek our own futures in the process." Edith needed her friends to understand that while they were all burdened with grief and guilt over Tilda's death, that did not mean their hearts should be closed off to finding their own paths in life. "Please, just consider the possibility that we can continue helping others remain free from the clutches of evil scoundrels, but also find our own peace with life."

"I will do everything in my power to help," Triston offered. "I will contact Bow Street and have Abercorn followed until we learn if he is responsible, or the trio of you are satisfied he poses no threat to others."

"That is very kind of you, but far too kind. We cannot put you at risk." Tears threatened to fall, but Edith held them back. "*We* have issue with Abercorn, not you. I cannot ask you spend your resources to help us."

Triston already lived in a boarding house under the weight of his father's generous allowance. She could not ask him to spend coin he did not possess; however, he would have rightful use of her dowry if they wed.

"Edith," he sighed. "I care very deeply for you—your well-being and that of Lady Lucianna and Lady Ophelia—therefore, I would not be an honorable man if I allowed you to continue without offering assistance. And because my sisters have set their sights on the trio of you. I promised no harm would come to any of you."

"It seems your life is full of domineering, undaunted women, determined to continue along their chosen paths, Lord Torrington," Ophelia offered with a laugh.

"I would have it no other way." He placed another

kiss on Edith's forehead. "But I will request something in return."

Luci's brow rose in question. "I assumed as much."

"I expect both of you to speak fondly of me to Lord and Lady Shaftesbury." He winked. "I have my own path in mind, and I am determined to bring Lady Edith along, as my wife."

EPILOGUE

London, England
February 1815

THE EVENING WAS exactly as Edith had always dreamed it would be: the musicians played each piece to perfection, the ballroom was decorated in lovely shades of pink and gold, the chandeliers above the crowded room glowed with light, and everyone was enjoying their evening of merriment, celebration, and revelry to honor Lady Edith Pelton's betrothal to Lord Torrington.

Especially the besotted groom and his wife-to-be, as they twirled about the dance floor.

Triston's hold was a bit too tight to be proper, but not so close their betrothal would commence with talk of scandal.

Besides, no one dared speak of any indecent activities if the *Mayfair Confidential* column had yet to comment on it. And the *London Daily Gazette*'s gossip column had advertently allowed slip that Lady Edith Pelton, with her dearest friends in tow, had suffered a devastating carriage accident on a darkened route outside London after they'd snuck from their homes for a midnight excursion. If the dashing Lord Torrington hadn't happened upon the stranded women, they likely would have been set upon by thieves or, worse yet, wild beasts. Furthermore, it was stated any other man would not have had the brute strength to lift the back of the carriage high enough for their driver to replace the broken wheel.

Ophelia had giggled openly as she'd written that portion of the column.

Thankfully, Edith had been present to see Triston roll his eyes heavenward and chuckle at the obvious mention of his immense proportions.

Even now, swirling around her family's townhouse ballroom, Edith felt tiny in his arms as he towered over her.

Imagine her parents' shock when Triston had asked for Edith's hand in marriage only a fortnight after their return from Essex—or as Lord and Lady Shaftesbury still believed—her night stranded alongside the dark road outside London.

"Your smile shines brighter than a million candles, my love," Triston whispered, pulling her to his side as the musicians played the final note. "Our lives will never know a moment of darkness as long as you are near."

"You are a shameless flirt, my lord." Edith smiled up at him, placing her hand upon his arm as they departed the dance floor and made their way toward Luci and Ophelia. "Whatever am I to do with such a man?"

"Keep him close at all times," he teased.

Edith and Triston both nodded a greeting to the Marquis of Downshire as they passed, Pru and Chastity keeping close to their father's side.

"Has his melancholy lessened?" Edith whispered, smiling at Triston's father as they moved on.

"I fear he may never recover from Esmee's betrayal. He loved her deeply, even though we all knew her to be flawed." Triston slowed his pace. "However, he was relieved to learn that she was not with child in the end. He has settled a property and allowance on her, and Esmee has agreed to never return to London if Father does not turn her over for her crimes. In return, my father will handle all her medical needs in the future."

"That was kind of him," Edith said. "Does your father not wish to seek a divorce?"

He shook his head. "Sadly, or maybe thankfully, he has declared he does not intend to wed again."

"I think you gained your kind heart from him."

"A short month ago, I would have adamantly disagreed with you; however, upon recent introspection, I believe that to be true. I also believe I love you as deeply as he does Esmee."

"Which I can never think to be an objectionable trait." She risked a glance up at him. "Especially since that is what led you to me."

"To be candid, it was your undergarments that caught my eye long before I knew the beauty of your long, golden locks, amber eyes, and quick wit."

Edith swatted him with her free hand. "My lord!"

"But in all fairness, I have come to realize I love and adore you...almost as much as the sight of your knickers!" Triston's deep chuckle echoed through the room, drawing envious stares from lords and ladies alike.

"You are certainly lucky I love you in return...and can overlook your outrageous comments."

Ophelia and Luci motioned for them to follow as soon as they were almost upon them, before turning quickly and hurrying out onto the terrace.

Edith was helpless to do anything but trail the pair out the doors and into the refreshing night air. The moment she and Triston stepped over the threshold, Luci and Ophelia rounded on them.

"You will never guess who arrived only moments ago!" Ophelia nearly sang in delight.

"Who?" Edith inquired. She'd compiled the guest list and handwritten the invitations herself.

She made to look back into the ballroom to search the crowd for anyone who didn't belong.

"Do not look," Luci hissed. "He is coming this way, and he is certainly angry!"

"I can only imagine what trouble you ladies are embroiled in now." Triston scrutinized the woman. "However, this night belongs to Edith and me, and I will not have anything distracting me from her beauty and our future happiness."

With a grand flourish, he twirled Edith back toward the ballroom, his hand firmly at the small of her back, and guided her straight to the dance floor, giving her no opportunity to glance about to see who was headed for her friends on the terrace.

And it suited Edith marvelously as there was nothing she wanted more than to keep her attention on Triston.

Her friends could care for themselves for this one night.

"Triston," Edith sighed, relishing the warmth of his hold on her as they joined the other dancers' motion.

"Yes, my dearest ray of sunshine." He pulled her a few inches closer, and Edith allowed it. They were to be wed, after all, and who cared what gossip started now.

"Why do you call me that?" Edith bite her bottom lip when he smiled—that mischievous grin she'd come to adore.

"Do you remember the first time we met?"

"How could I forget, my lord? You saw my knickers before you knew my name." To Edith's great surprise her face did not flame with shame at the thought of her skirts tossed over her head due to her fall from the tree.

"Well, before I was afforded the handsome sight of your underpinnings, it was the reflection of the noonday sun off your golden hair that caught my notice."

"So, you are saying if I had my hood drawn, we might have never met?" she asked.

"My love." He shook his head as the final chord of music rang through the room. "Let us not ponder that possibility for then who would have been close to notice the disappearance of Lady Edith?"

"Perhaps there would have been no disappearance if..." Edith allowed her voice to trail off as Triston tucked her into his side once more and moved off the dance floor.

"Thankfully, there are only a few who know of your disappearance at all." He guided her toward a grouping of potted ferns, changing course when Lady Prudence and Lady Chastity came in to view. "My, my, Lady Edith, my dear sisters are determined to keep a close eye on you—however, I find myself in need of a kiss."

"Then you are lucky we did meet because I know the perfect place." Edith didn't hesitate before continuing through the potted ferns and along the wall, exiting out the servant's door that lead to the back staircase. "Come..."

THE
Misfortune OF
Lady
Lucianna

THE UNDAUNTED DEBUTANTES
Book 2

CHRISTINA
McKNIGHT

DEDICATION

To Theresa and Debbie

You're always there when it counts.
Thank you for believing in me and this series!

PROLOGUE

Devonshire, England
December 1813

Lady Lucianna Constantine sat beside her dearest friend, Lady Tilda Abercorn, formally Miss Tilda Guthton—at least before her morning wedding to Lord Abercorn, a duke. Luci wanted to be happy for Tilda; she longed to feel an ounce of the joy and merriment evident in her other friends—Lady Edith and Lady Ophelia—but she simply could not find the emotion within her. So, for the moment, she settled a less than genuine smile on her face and prepared to send Tilda off for her first glimpse of what a marriage bed held.

If Tilda's shoulders appeared a bit too stiff or her posture a bit too straight, none of her friends mentioned it.

"I truly must return to my chambers before His Grace suspects I have slipped out…before our marriage was so much as consummated." Tilda leapt to her feet from the lounge.

When Lady Ophelia giggled, Lucianna joined in. The sound far lighter than her normally husky chuckle. It should be Luci preparing for her wedding night, not Tilda, the mere daughter of a baronet. As the daughter of the Marquis of Camden, Luci had always thought she would make a match long before Tilda. Or even Edith and Ophelia. It irked her to see her friend find a match before her father had even so much as mentioned any possible suitors for her.

Not that Luci would ever consider taking Abercorn, a man old enough to be her father, as husband; however, she'd always imagined she would be the first one to share all the delectable secrets found behind a closed bedchamber door.

The tall clock nestled between the bay windows had chimed midnight at least five minutes earlier.

"You will tell us everything on the morrow? At breakfast and not a moment later. I truly must know if everything is as I've been told." Luci suggestively raised one brow, wrapping Tilda in a tight embrace before withdrawing and taking in her appearance from head to stocking-covered toes. "You look breathtakingly innocent."

And utterly terrified.

Quite possibly ready to expire from her nervousness.

The other women liked to think Tilda possessed a backbone of fortified whalebone, but Luci knew differently. They'd been bosom friends since they could barely toddle about in their families' townhouses in Mayfair.

It was Edith's turn to console Tilda. "You are beautiful. You are smart. And today was a perfect way to start your married life. I only hope Ophelia, Luci, and I are blessed with such generous husbands."

Generous husbands? Tilda's spouse would be lucky to see another five years upon this earth. Luci hoped the man didn't pass to the hereafter, leaving his widow to care for an unruly horde of children—or worse yet, no offspring, and needing to find a new home when Abercorn's closest relative and heir came to claim his due.

"Thank you, Edith. You have always been a great

friend." Tilda found compassion in Edith's arms, melting into the blond-haired English rose's hug. It was an emotion Luci struggled to offer—empathy for others.

She'd been taught from a young age that one fought for what they wanted. If they did not get what they desired, then it was because they hadn't wanted it badly enough. Or so her father, Lord Camden, had drilled into his four children's heads since they were knee-high.

Tilda pulled back, her smile wobbling. "I must hurry. It will not do for my *husband* to arrive in my room to find that I have fled."

Luci slipped her arms through Tilda's, while Ophelia retrieved her book and followed a few paces behind them. Luci knew Ophelia was there because the girl, no matter how many times she'd been scolded, did not see the need to lift her feet high enough to avoid shuffling.

"I will extinguish the candles," Edith called.

"Always the responsible one," Luci said over her shoulder with a smirk. The only thing that irritated her more than Ophelia's sluggish footsteps was Edith's sensible demeanor.

Luci pulled Tilda close as they walked toward the main staircase. "Now, Tilly, when I said I want to hear every word, I meant every detail!" she cooed. "Since you insisted on wedding first and rushing the ceremony before your first Season was even half over, you owe us."

Tilda's feet slowed, and the stare she turned on Luci was laced with concern...and doubt. "You know as well as I this match was my father's doing, not my own. I would have gladly waited until the end of the Season to announce my betrothal."

She placed a quick kiss on Tilda's cheek. "I know, I know. My father would have done the same had Abercorn shown an interest in me." Luci gently turned

Tilda toward the stairs and swatted her bum. "Now, get up there and greet your new husband properly."

"Luci!" Tilda hissed. "I must admit, I have no notion what you mean by that."

It did not irk her at all that Abercorn favored demure, reserved, soft brunette beauties over Luci's tall, slender frame and midnight-black hair falling all the way down her backside. No, Luci had no doubt she'd claim a dashingly handsome, witty lord as her husband. She could already picture the envious stares from other eligible men—and unattached ladies. Maybe a prince…

Tilda started up the stairs, hesitant at first, but Luci gave her a wink when Tilly glanced down at her, which gave the woman the confidence to dash up toward the final landing.

A shadow stepped into view at the top of the staircase, a hand grasping Tilda's arm.

Luci moved to better see who had stopped her friend. All the other guests had been in their chambers abed for several hours. Not even a servant had been seen since a footman had stoked the hearth over two hours before.

"No, I swear to it. I did not…" Tilda's whine sounded from atop of the stairs, a firm shake from her companion muting the remainder of Luci's friend's words.

A shock of greying hair over a red dressing robe came into view, the man's face coming within an inch of Tilda's as she pulled back.

"Tilly?" Luci called as her friend's foot slipped from the top stair, sending Tilda's arms swirling as her body fell backwards.

Tilda's mouth opened, a bone-deep scream escaping before her head hit the ground, returning the manor house to the silent stillness of a moment before. Then, Tilda's body thumped three times, finally settling on the polished floor at Luci's feet.

Luci stood silently for a moment, her mind racing

to catch up with what she'd just witnessed.

Glancing up once more, she expected the man to hurry down the stairs to help Tilda, but all she saw was a flash of red and then…nothing. He was gone, vanished.

Her stomach turned as her mind raced to connect what she'd seen at the top of the stairs.

"Edith!" Lucianna's pulse raced, her scream high-pitched as she knelt by Tilda. "Ophelia!"

Another thump sounded on the floor.

Luci looked up to see Ophelia frozen in her place, her book splayed open at her feet, causing the final thump. Edith rushed in a step behind her.

"Luci." Edith stepped around Ophelia. "What is it—"

She stood, shaking her head gently.

"No, no, no," Edith sobbed as she hurried to Tilda. "This cannot be—"

"He did this." Luci couldn't hold back the accusation in her tone. Edith looked away from Tilda to where Luci stood. She pointed toward the top of the stairs, leaving no doubt who had been responsible for this.

Following Luci's indicated direction, Edith narrowed her eyes on the darkened landing above them, but Luci knew her friend would see no one lingering in the shadows.

Abercorn had fled.

"Whom?" Ophelia squeaked, walking forward to stand behind Edith.

"That is not important at this moment," Edith whispered, kneeling beside Tilda, much as Luci had done a moment before. "We must wake her up, make sure she is all right and call for the duke—and a physician."

"There is no point." Luci knelt next to Edith, sweeping Tilda's hair from her face. "She is gone."

Luci held in the sob that threatened to escape. It was imperative that she contain her emotions, at least until the magistrate was called and an accounting of the fall recorded.

Her dear friend, so nervous—yet alive—only moments before, now stared up at the ceiling, her sightless, vacant, chestnut-brown eyes forever frozen in terror.

Anger ignited within Luci, and she begged her simmering blood to cool—at least long enough for her to speak.

"They argued." Luci grasped Edith's arm as she reached forward to touch Tilda. "He was up there, and he pushed her. I swear it."

Luci was helpless to do anything as Edith took in the mangled sight of Tilda, her white nightshift tangled between her legs, and her head tilted at an odd angle.

"Wha-wha-what should we do?" Ophelia wailed.

"We will rouse the house and tell them all what the duke did!" Lucianna shot to her feet once more. "Someone must have heard the commotion."

The foyer was deserted except for Luci, Ophelia, Edith, and, of course, Tilda.

"You are correct. I heard her scream and then the thump"—Edith visibly cringed at her choice of word, and Luci wanted to comfort her—"as she fell down."

"She did *not* fall." Lucianna knew her voice reached a dangerously high pitch as she narrowed her glare on Edith; however, she was helpless to calm the rage within her. "She was *pushed*. By Abercorn!"

Luci stared between her two remaining friends, her eyes softening, begging them to believe her.

"How could this happen?" Ophelia asked, collecting her book from the ground.

"That is a question for him. You saw him, right, Ophelia?" Luci looked toward Ophelia, her loose hair cascading over her shoulder.

The color drained from the girl's face, making her pale complexion turn almost green.

"Tell her what you saw," Luci demanded. "You

were standing right here."

"I—I—I was reading." Ophelia turned to Edith, her book held tightly as if it could protect her. "I swear it, Edith, I did not see anything. I was reading about Xavier and—"

"What is going on here?" Townsend, the Abercorn butler, bustled into the foyer, his hair askew as if the noise had pulled him from slumber. "Your Grace!" His eyes widened on Tilda as he rushed across the room to where she lay. His hands moved to find her wrist and settled. "No pulse. She has no pulse!"

The servant shuffled to his feet, teetering for a moment before gaining his balance after the shock of seeing his new mistress dead at the bottom of the grand staircase—on her wedding night.

"Petunia, Petunia!" Townsend shouted, his tiny feet rushing toward the kitchens. "Petunia! We must summon His Grace. Petunia, where in all that is holy are you, woman?"

Doors opened, and voices sounded above from the guests' wing as Townsend continued calling for Petunia.

In any other situation, the scene before Luci would have incited a least a slight chuckle as the butler mimicked a bird in flight. There was no humor to be found—for anyone.

"Oh, Your Grace!" Townsend said, staring toward the top of the stairs. "Please, do not look. This is not for your eyes."

The duke stepped into view at the top of the stairs. He'd likely only retreated to the shadows down the upper hall and waited for the alarm to be sounded. However, he was still garbed in his wedding day finery with a tumbler in his hand. It could not be… He'd worn a red robe only moments before. He started down the stairs, a grey lock of hair falling before his narrowed glare as he scrutinized the scene below.

As if he hadn't watched Tilda fall backwards after pushing her.

Luci's hands balled into fists at her sides, and her face heated in rage.

The man had pushed his new bride down the stairs and had the audacity to lumber upon the scene as if he were unaware of the death his shove had caused.

Tilda deserved better. Certainly more than the devil-may-care attitude of the scoundrel she'd wed.

Luci would see the man punished, if it were the last thing she ever accomplished.

CHAPTER 1

It is hereby announced that this writer has born witness to the Marquis of Camden scandalously parading his mistress about in polite society.

As this writer can also attest, Lady Camden and Lady Lucianna were also in attendance at the soirée the marquis saw fit to escort his mistress to.

Shame on a man who does not value family over his own pleasure.
-Mayfair Confidential, London Daily Gazette

Hanover Square, London
March 1815

"PREPOSTEROUS, SENSELESS RUBBISH." Roderick Crofton, the seventh Duke of Montrose, pushed the *London Daily Gazette* away from him on the breakfast table and scowled at his now cold morning repast. "Nothing but a scandal sheet, I tell you. Get this out of my sight."

"Certainly, Your Grace." A footman hurried forward to remove the paper. "May I bring you anything else? Tea, perhaps?"

Tea? No. Roderick did not desire tea. He craved a newspaper that took an interest in reporting true and accurate facts regarding current events, not another gossip rag that took great pleasure in ruining upstanding gentlemen.

Not that Roderick personally knew the Marquis of Camden; however, the *Mayfair Confidential* had set its sharpened teeth upon *him* only two months prior.

"Your Grace?" the footman asked once more.

"No, no, Joshua." Roderick waved his hand in dismissal. "Unfortunately, you cannot provide what I need." When the servant's shoulders slumped, he continued. "However, that is no fault of yours, I assure you."

When Joshua took his place against the wall, Roderick took hold of his utensil and pushed the cold eggs about his plate. If he did not consume at least half the food, Cook would likely chase him down and demand he eat—or else. He'd never discovered what she meant by "or else," and he damn well didn't plan to. He speared a sliver of pheasant and placed it into his mouth and then chewed slowly. Perhaps it would appear he'd eaten more if he remained at the table longer. Blast it all, but he was no longer a boy in knee breeches.

He did not need a woman, no matter that she'd known him since birth, following him like a clucking chicken. If Roderick found he was not hungry, then he would not eat.

Period.

End of story.

Until Cook gained word and saw his untouched plate.

With a sigh, he scooped a mouthful of tepid porridge from his bowl and crammed it into his mouth before he could change his mind.

He supposed someone looking after his well-being was appreciated.

For all the headaches the woman caused him, he was grateful to have her.

Joshua yelped in surprise when the sound of the

front door slamming, followed by pounding footsteps, approached the Montrose townhouse dining room.

He raised his brow in question as the dining room door slammed against its hinges, revealing his stable hand, Lucian, his clothes disheveled and his cap clutched to his heaving chest. For all his bluster, he stood silently, staring at the floor, waiting for Roderick to address him. This was the same lad Roderick had gotten into trouble with in their youths for leaving tops on the upper-floor landing—causing not one, not two, but *three* maids injury. And now, he cowered before Roderick as if he would rip the stable hand limb from limb if Lucian spoke out of turn.

"Speak, Lucian," he finally commanded.

"I have news, Your Grace," he mumbled, keeping his eyes trained on the floor.

"And are you worried this news will displease me?" Roderick pushed his onyx hair from his eyes, tucking it behind his ear. He needs must make a note to have his valet trim it or procure a stronger pomatum to keep the blasted strands from falling into his face. "Out with it."

"Your Grace, I…" Lucian started again after taking a deep breath.

"Enough with formalities," Roderick said, pushing his chair back to stand.

"I think I have finally determined the source of the *Mayfair Confidential* column." He dared a glance at Roderick and seeing his pleased expression Lucian continued. "There is a woman. She's come and gone from the *Gazette* on five occasions over the last fortnight. She was there in the late-night hours, and while I have not confirmed, I suspect a new column was printed in the *London Daily Gazette* today."

"You are correct." Roderick nodded to Joshua to remove his plate of hardly touched food. "Have you ascertained the woman's identity?"

A moment of excitement hung in the air.

"No, Your Grace." Lucian shook his head. "I

wanted to make certain you approved of me looking further into the matter. I do know she does not find full-time employment at the paper, nor does she have relatives within the *Gazette*. I asked about the business, but no one was familiar with her—or they refused to comment."

"Of course, I want you to investigate further." Roderick's command thundered, and once again, standing against the wall, Joshua flinched. "This woman, whoever she may be, is responsible for destroying my life. I will see she pays for her actions." He needs must calm his anger, especially if he wanted to keep his footman from expiring from fright. "What can you tell me of this woman? Is it possible I am acquainted with her?"

Lucian pulled at his coat as if noting for the first time his ramshackle appearance. "She arrives in a fancy carriage each time, leaving it down the street. She enters the business without so much as a glance over her shoulder. This was why it took me so long to figure her out. If I were the one exposing men of the *ton*, I would be paranoid and watching my back at every turn. But this woman, her chin is always high, raven hair always perfectly groomed, and her gowns are impeccable, likely made by the finest modiste in London."

"You suspect she is of noble birth?" Why hadn't the notion crossed his mind before? Roderick had suspected the culprit to be a jealous lord, not a woman—especially not a lady of class.

"I have little doubt of it, Your Grace."

"Then you have my permission to look into the woman further; however..." This was not an entirely new venture, sleuthing. He'd been investigating random men and businesses for several years now; though it was imperative that he not draw attention to his activities. "Do not let the woman know we are on to her, or she is likely to vanish."

"Certainly, Your Grace. I will bring you

information as soon as I know anything more." Lucian bowed and turned to leave.

"And, Lucian."

"Yes, Your Grace?"

"Do bathe and get some rest before going back out."

The servant smiled, wearily. "Thank you, Your Grace."

Roderick glanced back toward the footman pressed against the far wall; he seemed unimpressed and no less anxious by the kindness Roderick had shown Lucian.

No matter, he had many important things to accomplish, far more dire than convincing a new servant he was not the beast he appeared to be despite his jet-black hair, severe jawline, and penetrating ice-blue eyes. He only knew these terms for a gentleman's appearance because Lady Daphne was always going on and on about his dashingly handsome face.

His gut twisted at the thought of the young woman, so innocent and shy. It would have been a pleasure to take her as wife and make her the Duchess of Montrose. Yet, that had been another thing stripped from him by the *Mayfair Confidential*. What his father's dastardly friends hadn't stolen from him, the person who'd published the damning column in the *London Daily Gazette* had.

He could remember every scandalous word:

It is hereby stated that this writer has born firsthand witness to the 7th Duke of Montrose, scandalously alone with a golden-haired nymph in his private opera box, all whilst betrothed to Lady Daphne.

As this writer can also attest, Lady Daphne's hair is pure night, compared to the observed doxy's crown of light. Let this article stand as proof that Lady Daphne would do well to find herself another eligible lord to take as husband.

-Mayfair Confidential, London Daily Gazette

Lady Daphne's father had decided to do just that: secure another eligible lord for her to take as husband.

Roderick had been so hell-bent on finding out the truth of his family's missing fortune, he hadn't even thought about the repercussions of being seen in public with another woman. At first, he'd pondered the idea that the *Mayfair Confidential* writer had actually done him a glorious favor. He hadn't loved Daphne. She was sweet, innocent, and beautifully angelic even with her dark locks. And with time, he had no doubt an affection would have grown between them, despite the girl's lack of passion for anything of substance.

Bloody hell. His fury over the situation returned whenever he thought of it; his pulse beating erratically, and his blood hammering through him.

There was no more Lady Daphne in his future. And with her gone, so was the dowry he'd counted on to restore at least a portion of his family's coffers. Admittedly, it was much less than he needed to secure the Montrose line and keep it from ruin, but it would have bought him enough time to find the men responsible for swindling his father out of every coin not nailed down.

He should be donning riding garb and Hessians for an afternoon at Hyde or Regent's Park to socialize and search for a new bride. If he had half the sense he claimed to have, Roderick would be doing just that. Unfortunately, he'd inherited more than just his midnight looks from his father. Apparently, he'd also gained his lack of wisdom.

The time would come to begin his search anew for a wife, but that wasn't now. Perhaps he'd look through the few invitations that had arrived over the last few days and select a few social gatherings to attend. Maybe a ball or a recital.

At the moment, Roderick needed something to ease his fury and cool his heated blood. That was something a ride in Hyde Park could not do.

However, he knew the exact place it was acceptable to thrash another—and it was called sport.

CHAPTER 2

LUCIANNA WANTED NOTHING more than to strike down the man before her; however, he was not the cause of her rage. Nevertheless, he would do for now. She gracefully stepped back as her opponent lunged at her. Behind her mask, she grinned as the man's foil thrust into empty air.

Recovering quickly, he returned to the *en garde* position and awaited her next move.

She took a deep breath, though it did nothing to calm the raging current within her.

The nerve of her father, bringing his mistress to a ball when he knew bloody well his wife and daughter would be in attendance. It was the height of embarrassment. What galled her further was the way her mother, Lady Camden—a pillar of London society—had shrugged and moved on to the refreshment table as if there were nothing she could do about it. As if she weren't utterly mortified by her husband's scandalous actions. At one time, her mother, Eloise Constantine, had been the envy of every woman at the ball. The rare, dark beauty every woman wanted to be and every man wanted to bed. But nearly twenty-two years with Luci's father had broken something in the woman.

Not broken…utterly obliterated.

With time, her dark locks had lost their luster and finally given over to grey, her shoulders were not as straight as they'd once been, and her friends had, one by one, distanced themselves from the marchioness.

Did they think Luci's father's rakehell ways would rub off on their own dear husbands?

Luci didn't doubt for a second her father would corrupt any man that gave him a speck of devotion. She'd spent years outraged over her mother's situation, but what could a mere child do to change anything, especially when Lady Camden appeared unconcerned with her position.

Luci held her foil out in a point-in-line manner. She tired of this match.

She could have bested her opponent in her sleep.

This would force him to defend himself by enforcing a beat, a tap to her blade to either initiate an attack or provoke a reaction from her.

There was nothing more she wanted than for her opponent to force her to react.

The match had been one of parry and counter thus far. No grand moves, no unexpected *flèche*, and certainly no feint.

Luci had come to Bentley's to work off her aggression and anger from the night before; instead, she felt as if she were matched with an amateur. After returning home, she'd hastily hurried to Ophelia's townhouse and instructed her friend to write the *Mayfair Confidential* column about her father. Lady Ophelia had done her best to persuade Luci not to write such damning things about her own family—that it could ultimately harm her own reputation. Luci didn't care. She was beyond giving a whit about her future prospects. Not to mention, she'd failed to make the acquaintance of a man worthy of her love, let alone her respect.

Lord Torrington, Lady Edith's betrothed, was the exception, though she was loath to admit the fact aloud.

The man had an overinflated, arrogant notion of his own self-worth as it was, and there was absolutely no way Luci would give the man more fodder with which to build himself on.

Regardless, it was her father whom Luci truly wanted at the tip of her foil.

Comical since fencing was the one thing her father had taught his eldest daughter. The only thing of worth the marquis had passed on to her as yet. The memories flooded her; not many fond ones surfaced, overshadowed by hours spent at the tip of her father's foil as she learned harsh lesson after harsh lesson.

Never had her father taken compassion on her, even during her first years of learning.

Her opponent hadn't made the decision to attack or force her to attack.

Taking one step forward, she thrust the tip of her foil in his direction—a challenge, of sorts.

Their masks made it impossible for her to tell what the man felt—either reluctance or renewed confidence. And, she knew, neither did he suspect his opponent was a woman. Which was for the best. Luci didn't desire for anyone to go easy on her because she was female—they were all sportsmen at Bentley's. Her tall stature and wide shoulders were only embellished by her outfitting.

Her opponent lowered his foil tip to the ground at his side, admitting defeat.

Bollocks.

It appeared she was not to gain the vigorous match she'd desired.

A part of her longed to place her tip at the man's heart, forcing him to defend himself; however, unsportsmanlike conduct would have her membership revoked. It was something she'd never jeopardize.

Luci rolled her neck from side to side, dispelling the stiffness that came with hours on the strip. No doubt also partly due to her forgoing sleep the previous night to make certain the column reached the *London*

Daily Gazette in time to be printed in this morning's post.

No matter that Edith was distracted by Lord Torrington and their coming betrothal ball, and Ophelia would rather have her nose in a book, Lucianna was still determined to fulfill their promise from the night of Tilda's death. She would expose any scoundrels for their misdeeds, and her own father was not beyond her vengeance. The man she longed to rip apart before all of society—Lord Abercorn—remained just out of reach. But she was certain he could not escape for long.

Her opponent bowed stiffly and departed the strip.

Luci was capable of biding her time. Abercorn would misstep eventually—she was certain of it—and Lucianna would be there to take him down. Permanently.

Turning, she surveyed the room for her next match partner; however, the pickings were slim this early in the day. Many men—the lords who could afford the dues at Bentley's—were barely breaking their fast at this hour.

"Are you prepared to take on a skilled opponent, my lord?" A man stepped from the shadows created by the rack holding spare foils and other gear. He was tall, even by her standards, with massively broad shoulders. Thankfully, a man's sheer size normally spoke of their less than agile abilities. His mask in place and his foil at the ready, he didn't wait for her response but joined her on the strip. "*En garde.*"

His impertinent manners were overlooked when she noted his expert stance and strong hold.

This was the opponent she'd been waiting for—and his disregard for proper etiquette only fueled her ire.

Exhilaration hummed through her, but she focused her entire being on the match to come—the correct footwork, the perfect hold on her foil, and, lastly, the appropriate set of moves to gain the win.

Luci lowered her chin and immediately advanced,

her need to take control of the match overpowering her common sense to bide her time and assess the fencer's skill set.

He expertly parried her action.

She'd learned years before to always knot her waist-length hair tightly and securely under her mask—or face the consequences. Namely, male opponents treating her like a weak female as opposed to the accomplished sportswoman she was. Thirteen years of daily fencing lessons would turn any girl into a fierce competitor—either that, or break their spirit. Luci allowed no one and nothing to bring her down, especially not her father's relentless need to best his children at the one sport he could muster any talent for.

Very advantageous for her father that business was not considered a sport.

Regrettably for Lord Camden, Luci, his eldest child, had mastered the art of fencing by the young age of fourteen.

After a year of lost matches, Luci's father refused to spar with her and had instead purchased her membership at Bentley's.

The buzz of her opponent's foil sounded close to her ear as he advanced, forcing her to back step or risk injury. His skill was something she hadn't witnessed at Bentley's before, nor did she recognize the man's voice.

She needs must keep her head on the match—not on her father's scandalous activities or their rough past as father and daughter.

And most positively not on attempting to identify her opponent.

Concentrating on the set of her feet, she knew a match could be won—or just as easily lost—because of footwork.

Luci cross-stepped, bringing her farther from his dominant hand, but he was too quick and had anticipated the novice move, bringing his foil around. She was forced into a *passata sotto*, twisting and lowering herself under his weapon and holding herself balanced with her free hand upon the ground. She moved to attempt an upward thrust with her own foil, hoping to catch her opponent off guard; however, he'd deftly accomplished a riposte and outmaneuvered her point.

He was a worthy opponent, indeed.

Recovering quickly, she prepared her next move.

It had been many months since she'd located a fencer with half the skill she possessed.

But his retreat gave her ample time to reset and contemplate her next move.

She must think two steps ahead. She quickly advanced with a straight extension, knowing any decent opponent would parry, and she'd be forced to disengage, twisting her foil. But she expertly changed tactic to an expulsion, successfully opening the man's defenses. Before he knew her course, the tip of her foil was aimed directly at his heart. Victory surged through her. The thrashing of her heart as she allowed herself several deep inhales and exhales, echoed through her head.

She expected him to enact some practiced maneuver, removing the tip from his breast, but instead, he chuckled and flipped up his mask.

Luci was not fool enough to think her opponent had no other moves planned, and she kept her tip trained on him until he lowered his foil in surrender.

She had the oddest sense it was not a move of defeat but one of promise for another time.

She narrowed her glare on him, her irritation only growing. The man had not shown her his true capabilities on the strip, but had only seen the match as spirited fun. Luci did not have the same opinion, and she wished to slash her foil before his face to remove his smug grin.

"To whom do I owe the honor of my first loss in too many years to count?" he asked, his blue eyes sparkling. A nagging sensation of recognition filled her.

He completely removed his mask, revealing hair of the darkest black—so deep, Luci thought she saw hints of blue. It was a shade darker than hers, which Luci hadn't thought possible. His locks were midnight obsidian, while his eyes were as clear as the blue sea. "Come now, lad. You are certainly skilled and deserve to be commended."

She studied the set of his jaw, his extreme height, and commanding presence. Where had she seen the man before?

Her rule was to never, ever remove her mask while on the strip. Never reveal that she was a lady. And, under no circumstances, allow any man the opportunity to go soft on her during a match based on her femininity. She entered Bentley's prepared to fence and only removed her mask when she'd once again gained the safety of her carriage. Bentley's proprietor had never betrayed her confidence, which she suspected had more to do with her father's money as opposed to any loyalty to Luci.

However, a piece of her needed to show the arrogant man that a mere woman had bested him. Longed to show the haughty lord that no matter his superior demeanor, he was no competition for her...

Slowly, she pushed her mask up and completely off her head. A tumble of dark waves cascaded down her back and over her shoulders. Luci flipped her head as she tucked her gear under her arm, sending her long tresses out of her face.

His mouth gaped, and his brow rose in question.

Luci knew well the sight he beheld: ebony waves of hair, piercing, intense green eyes, and sun-kissed skin. She was tall in stature, and every inch the lady many women envied—just as every woman had envied Luci's mother in her day. This man now took in her regal stare and supple curves in her masculine garb—though it was tailored to hug every inch of her body.

From the lust in his open stare, he had noted every

womanly curve he'd only moments ago attributed to the form of a young lad.

It was Luci's turn to smirk.

And smile she did. "You may show proper honor to my skill by collecting your senses and closing your gaping mouth, or I will think you find it offensive to be bested by a woman." Luci outright grinned, pride swelling inside her to finally have the nerve to expose her face to one of her defeated opponents. "You may issue your accolades whenever you are ready…and it is my lady, not my lord."

He stalled for a moment before speaking. "I must say, the only thing to overshadow your skill with a foil is your beauty, *my lady*." He bowed slowly, his eyes traveling the length of her as he did.

Luci could feel the heat of his stare as it took in her form for the second time.

She'd never had occasion to overthink her preferred fencing attire, that of her male counterparts, to be scandalous or revealing in any overt manner. But his intense scrutiny scorched her from her face, down to her toes, and back up again. It was not hard to imagine her face blossoming with heat, as well. She would give him due credit for his eyes only lingered at her bosom— barely noticeable under her tightly bound cloth wrap—a brief moment before returning to her face.

However, his inspection gave her time to look closer at him. He was as tall as she'd suspected, and just as broad, his fencing attire not adding to his size as hers did. His hair hung nearly to his shoulders in a way far less gentlemanly than was preferred in London's premier ballrooms. But it was his eyes that attracted her notice most. Their blue depths held something she couldn't quite place her finger on. Hurt? Anger? Betrayal?

What could this lordly arrogant man know of these things?

His examination of her person sent a shiver down

Luci's spine, and all her defenses, bred through years of dealing with her father and competing in fencing, jumped into action. She should pivot, turn and flee Bentley's immediately; instead, she asked, "Your name, kind lord? I wish to add it to my extensive list of conquests."

She would never allow him to know of his appeal. When a man was given the upper hand in any situation, it was Luci's experience that they used it to exploit others and gain exactly what they searched for. Though there couldn't be anything the dark-haired lord sought from Luci. Only a moment before, he'd had no notion whom he sparred against, let alone that she was the eldest daughter of the Marquis of Camden.

His grin only widened when he snorted with laughter.

Was the man overly familiar with such blasé commentary from the women he associated with?

Luci was in the presence of a rogue—a taker of the innocent, a philanderer with no moral compass, a charlatan in lord's attire. The set of his crooked, self-assured grin, and his open appraisal of her was something Luci had witnessed on at least a dozen occasions.

She knew the type well, had lived under the roof of such a man her entire life—and called him *father*.

"What is so amusing?" she asked when he continued to grin at her after this laughter had ceased—likely due to her penetrating stare and uplifted chin. "Do you think it luck that handed me the win today?"

"Oh, certainly not, my lady." He moved and set his mask and foil on the bench against the far wall and then proceeded to remove his gloves, his back to her. "For a lad, your skill was at an expert level, but for a woman?" He shook his head and turned back to face her. "It was complete mastery—a practiced prowess many men never achieve in all their years at the sport."

Her face flushed—from the compliment or the

overt use of the word *prowess*, she was uncertain. "I am overjoyed to see that we are in agreement of my skill, and furthermore, your need to study the sport more thoroughly before our next match." She rocked back on her heels, not attempting to hide her smugness over her victory and her mastery of their back and forth banter.

As he paced back toward her, he tapped his bottom lip with his forefinger. "And what, my lady, makes you think I would agree to another match only to be bested soundly once more?"

It was Luci's turn to laugh. Her deep chuckle filled the room, empty except for her and the jet-black-haired man before her. His shoulders stiffened when she expressed her own merriment with the situation. "Are you saying you would turn down another round of sparring?"

"I said nothing of the sort; however"—he halted several feet from her—"I am not in the routine of agreeing to things if there is no chance of them working in my favor.

"Well, I never offer if I do not know I will win." Luci tilted her chin up a notch.

"Your name, my lady?" he requested again, his stare returning to its former intensity and never leaving hers. He was not appreciating her womanly curves nor waxing poetic prose about her silky hair and vibrant green eyes. It appeared he truly wished to learn her given name. "My lady?" His brow arched in question.

She should not give her name, but there was something about the man that pulled the words from her. It could be his sincerity, his forthright nature, or possibly his confidence in being bested by a woman at a predominately male sport. "Lady Lucianna Constantine, my lord."

"Your Grace."

"Pardon?"

"It is *Your Grace*." His smirk returned as he seemed to go from intense to playful with each breath he took.

"The Duke of Montrose, but you may call me Roderick—you have bested me with a foil, after all."

All thoughts of her own coy nature disappeared quickly with the one damning name.

As she'd suspected, he was a rogue, a rakehell, and a debauched man.

And the very first lord she'd taken down with the *Mayfair Confidential*.

The exhilaration from her victory on the strip dissipated.

CHAPTER 3

RODERICK WHISTLED AS he stepped through his townhouse door just as the sun was setting on the day. The shock on his butler's face was evident; however, he was still wholly focused on the nimble beauty that was Lady Lucianna. He'd attended Bentley's for several years now and had never crossed paths with the woman. Or had he? Would he have known a woman resided under her fencing attire?

Their time together had ended quickly when he'd given his name, as she'd no doubt recognized him from the scandal two months prior, when he'd been falsely accused of being unfaithful to Lady Daphne—his betrothed. But the gossip sheets had gotten it all wrong.

Unfortunately, Lady Lucianna hadn't given him the time to explain anything. Bloody hell, he wasn't even certain that was the reason her entire demeanor had changed and she had hurried off.

Blast it all, but he couldn't resist thinking of her tightly clad legs that had seemingly gone on forever. No skirting with petticoats and underpinnings to hide the muscular curves of her calves or the toned expanses of her thighs.

He shook the image of said thighs wrapped tightly around his waist from his mind as he handed his overcoat to the waiting servant.

He'd thought of her well-trimmed, slender frame—while she'd been plotting her escape.

"Your Grace, Lucian awaits you in your study." The butler dipped his head and hurried off.

Lucian had returned already?

Roderick had expected the servant to rest and return to the *Gazette* on the morrow, or by earliest that night.

"Inform him I will see him now." His words echoed in the empty foyer; his butler having departed for parts unknown. "I suppose I can inform him myself," he mumbled, starting down the hall toward his study.

The man's news could only serve to further brighten his day after so many months—nay, years—of desolation caused by his father's reckless investments, and then that bloody column.

The tides were turning.

They had to at some point, and the closer he came to the study the more hope surged.

Roderick could practically feel the weight being lifted from his shoulders. Not that knowing the identity of the *Mayfair Confidential* authoress would solve all his financial—and social—problems; however, it would be a start; a way to gain some semblance of control over his life, which had been spinning endlessly out of his control for some time.

He strode into the study, pushing the door closed behind him, and smiled at Lucian. "I hadn't expected to see you for a few days."

Lucian stood from his chair before Roderick's desk, wringing his hat in his hands once again. Roderick needs must remember to explain to the servant that the nervous gesture did not invoke a sense of confidence. If Lucian ever expected to gain employment with Bow Street as a runner, he need hold his head high and meet every man's eye, regardless of their station and status.

"I have news, Your Grace." Lucian's head dipped.

"You have secured her identity?" Roderick still found it hard to believe a woman—a gently bred lady at that—was behind the atrocious column that had stolen his future. Though, after his morning at Bentley's, Roderick now understood women sometimes exceeded what men thought of them. Their roles not so specifically fitting into the neat square society and generations of teaching had created for them.

"I have, Your Grace." For the first time since agreeing to take on the assignment, Lucian smiled. He'd successfully completed a task Roderick had assigned to him. "The authoress is none other than Lady Lucianna Constantine, eldest daughter of the Marquis of Camden."

Roderick felt like he'd been punched in the gut...and pushed off a cliff. The name dispelled any light that had begun to peek through the gloomy haze that had settled over his life.

"Are you certain?" He half expected the servant to laugh, slap him on the back, and jest about the look of horror that'd crossed Roderick's face before informing him that he'd seen him leave Bentley's earlier in the day.

However, that was not to happen.

"Yes." Lucian nodded severely, completely sober. "I sketched the crest on the carriage door a few nights ago and I finally found another servant—in Lord Esquire's employ—who knew the family name. It did not take long to locate the Camden townhouse in Mayfair, and I saw Lady Lucianna return home at midday."

The irony of her townhouse location and the name of her column was not lost on Roderick.

"Does the marquis have other children, perchance?"

"Yes, Your Grace, but I have been told they are all still in the schoolroom."

She'd known all along whom he was at Bentley's.

Her coy, playful manner was all a jest at his expense. The entire time, he'd been mooning over her skill and beauty, she'd known full well he was the man she'd ruined with her fallacious ramblings in the *London Daily Gazette*.

Breathing deeply, Roderick attempted to suppress his anger.

He'd enjoyed almost an entire day without the need to slam his fist into a wall or throw a door closed until it fell from its hinges.

He'd been a fool to think any weight had been lifted or that his days living under a cloud of scandal were to be dispelled so easily. All so simply vanquished by learning the identity of one alluring, captivating, and utterly enchanting beauty.

The back of his throat soured at the thought.

The woman would pay for the havoc she'd caused in his life.

"Where is she now?" he asked.

"I left her at the Earl of Shaftesbury's townhouse," Lucian said. "She arrived in a fine blue gown with her mother. I suspect they will be there until the end of the evening. I asked a coachman, and he said they were gathering for Lady Edith Pelton and Lord Torrington's betrothal ball."

"Wonderful," Roderick seethed. She'd ruined his life, made a fool of him at Bentley's, and now she planned to spend her evening twirling about a dance floor and drinking spiced sherry? Oh, no. "You are dismissed."

"Thank you, Your Grace." The servant turned on his heels and stalked from the room, a rare moment of confidence infusing his long stride.

Unfortunately, every ounce of the confidence born and bred into Roderick as the heir to a Dukedom had fled the moment Lucian had uttered Lady Lucianna's name. He'd scrutinized her with longing not long before—had thought of future matches between them.

All impossible now as he'd misjudged her interested in him.

Roderick would not cower. He would not hide his head in shame. He had done nothing wrong by escorting the widow Cavendish to the opera. They were friends—the former Duke of Montrose being close to the widow's late husband.

Blast it all, but he was a duke…and no mere slip of a debutante would be the cause of his thorough ruination.

Not without severe consequences.

He'd been debating whether to accept an invitation to a soirée or garden party that very morning. It was long past time Roderick donned his ballroom finery—and attended a betrothal celebration…with or without a proper invitation.

CHAPTER 4

THE NIGHT WAS purely magical. Everything that Edith and Triston—Lord Torrington—deserved in their betrothal ball. The *ton* had turned out in droves, not an invite turned down as they all clamored to the Earl of Shaftesbury's Mayfair townhouse to gain a look at the new couple. Their love story, or at least what society had been told, started when Lord Torrington had dashingly rescued Edith, Luci, and Ophelia from a carriage accident outside of London.

Thankfully, no one had inquired as to why the ladies had ventured into the English countryside unchaperoned, or how their parents had not discovered they'd been missing an entire day, which was advantageous for the trio because there had been no carriage accident. However, Lord Torrington had rescued Edith from the clutches of his evil stepmother, who'd kidnapped her from the London streets and whisked her off to the seaside cliffs of Southend.

All had been set to rights since her rescue the month before, and now, Luci adored Torrington as much as Edith and Ophelia did. He was a man above all men, and one not tarnished by scandalous misdeeds—all too common in Englishmen.

He was perfect for Lady Edith.

"It is allowed for one to be envious of a friend so long as it does not cross the line to jealousy," Luci recited quietly as she watched Edith, held securely to Triston's side as they greeted guests and walked the perimeter of the ballroom.

Everything was perfect.

As Luci knew the couple's future would be.

"I am surprised you are not dancing this set," Ophelia said, handing Luci a flute of champagne as she turned to examine their dear friend and her betrothed greeting yet another couple who'd joined the ball.

Luci stifled another yawn. "I am exhausted. After staying up all night to deliver and make certain the column was posted, and then my morning at Bentley's, followed by helping Edith prepare for this grand soirée, I am falling asleep on my feet."

Ophelia fanned her face and took a sip from her champagne. "Mayhap, if you'd listened to me and not been in such an uproar over your father's actions and your need to harm him, you would have gotten at least a bit of sleep last night."

"And we both know how I excel at taking orders from others." Luci glanced at Ophelia out of the corner of her eye. The woman with her auburn hair, fair skin, and pale blue eyes was as exotic as Luci was, but in a wholly different and more innocent manner. Luci was all dark with her long, black hair, startlingly green, catlike eyes, and height as tall as most men. Ophelia was pure light—if she would ever come out of her shell and allow herself to shine.

"Oh, look!" the woman exclaimed, pulling Luci's attention back to the crowded room in time to see her father depart the card room with none other than Lord Abercorn. "What is your father doing with that vile man?"

"A better question is: why was Abercorn issued an invitation at all?" Luci seethed.

"Come now, Luci," Ophelia chastised. "Abercorn

is Lord Torrington's neighbor. And no one would want to offend the man, lest he spread rumors about what truly happened when Edith was taken. And, as far as Edith is concerned, she thinks it best to keep her friends close and our enemies closer."

"Very true." Luci narrowed her gaze on the men, wishing her look would set the pair ablaze. While her father hadn't killed anyone—that she knew of—the Marquis of Camden and the Duke of Abercorn were identical in many ways. "When he drops his guard, we need be close and ready to expose him. The man will not get away with Tilda's death, I assure you of that. He should have been hauled off by the magistrate the very night it occurred."

"You know I agree with you, but there just was not enough proof that he pushed her, Luci." Ophelia snapped her fan shut and turned her stare back to Edith and Lord Torrington, who were now moving in their direction.

Ophelia could refuse to discuss the topic all she desired, but Luci knew full well what she'd seen. Abercorn and Tilda had argued, he'd shaken her, and then Tilly was plummeting to the ground floor at Luci's feet. How Abercorn had changed from his red dressing robe back to his formal attire, Luci wasn't certain, but she knew he had been the one to kill Tilda.

If only her two friends had spoken up that night, aligned with Luci and pointed the finger at Abercorn, none of this would be happening now. Then again, the *Mayfair Confidential* column would not exist, Edith would not have met Torrington, and Luci would not have had to run from her fencing club after learning the name of her opponent that morning.

So many things would be different. Maybe the trio of them would have completed their first Season and found loving, honorable husbands, instead of observing the appropriate mourning period for Tilda.

Unfortunately, none of them would know how

things could have turned out.

"You are scowling, Luci," Ophelia hissed, nudging her elbow into Luci's hip. "And people are starting to notice."

"Let them stare. The girl who cried wolf," Luci mimicked the name she'd heard society call her behind her back; however, she attempted at least a look of passivity as opposed to an outright frown. "I will not be happy until Abercorn has been punished."

"Be that as it may, tonight is not that night." Ophelia drained her glass before continuing. "Tonight is about celebrating Edith and Lord Torrington and their upcoming nuptials. Do you think you can find an agreeable demeanor for at least another couple of hours?"

"For Edith, I can." But that did not mean she could stop the fury she felt over her father and Abercorn from heating her insides.

"Very good. Now, look, a new guest is arriving." Ophelia stood on tiptoes as the butler announced the new guest. "I do hope it is Lady Prudence and Lady Chastity. They are great fun."

Lord Torrington's younger sisters were acceptable as debutantes went. They weren't vain or featherbrained, which were things Luci could not tolerate in a friend. However, Luci hadn't taken the time to truly get to know the women. It would behoove her to try. After Edith's wedding, the pair was likely to be underfoot a lot.

"...the Duke of Montrose."

Luci's eyes snapped to the ballroom entrance as Montrose took the first step into the room.

Her heart stopped for what seemed like several long moments as he searched the crowd. He was looking for someone—and it was highly likely it was she.

Had he discovered her to be the woman who'd exposed him? Certainly not. No one knew who was behind the *Mayfair Confidential* column in the *London Daily Gazette*. They'd been extremely careful with the entire activity. They'd only delivered under cover of night—Luci having taken over the duty of bringing Ophelia's final column to the *Gazette* building while Edith was occupied with preparing for her wedding.

Blessedly, Edith and Torrington arrived at that moment, and Luci slipped her arm through Ophelia's and motioned for the couple to follow them.

The terrace doors lay open and only a short distance away. Luci practically dragged Ophelia toward them, skirting lords and ladies as they went until the fresh night air surrounded them.

Luci turned, keeping Ophelia at her side and hoping Lord Torrington would block her from view.

"Did you hear who arrived only moments ago?" Ophelia said a bit enthusiastically for Luci's liking.

"Who?" Edith made to look back into the ballroom to search the crowd.

"Do not look," Luci hissed. "He is coming this way, and he is certainly angry!"

"I can only imagine what trouble you ladies are embroiled in now." Triston scrutinized Luci and Ophelia, seeming to forget that his own bride-to-be was just as entangled as they were. "However, this night belongs to Edith and me, and I will not have anything distracting me from her beauty and our future happiness."

With a grand flourish, he twirled Edith back toward the ballroom, his hand firmly at the small of her back.

The action gave Luci a clear line of sight into the space.

Which meant Montrose was also able to see her. And he was stalking her way, unaware of the people who leapt out of his way or the people who stared in his wake.

"Ophelia," Luci whispered, unable to remove her eyes from the man. "I need you to cause a distraction."

"Me?" she squeaked. "I do not—"

"Yes, you. Only long enough for me to hide in the garden."

"But, why ever would you—"

"There is no time." Luci pushed the auburn-haired woman toward the terrace door. "I will keep out of sight by the cherub fountain. Come and get me when he leaves."

Luci didn't wait to see if Ophelia did as she demanded. She grasped the skirts of her midnight-blue gown and hurried down the stairs into the Shaftesbury's gardens. The paths were unlit, keeping other guests from exploring the natural wonders, but Luci knew the area well. She and her friends had enjoyed spring and summer picnics between the many rose bushes and gardenia plants during their youths. They'd learned to play lawn bowls and the game of graces on the expanse of green bordering the gardens.

Even by moonlight, Luci had no trouble finding her way.

The moment she stepped onto the lawn-covered path leading around the statue she sought, her delicate, black slippers soaked up the evening dew. Her footwear was ruined, and her stockings would likely be stained beyond repair. It mattered naught.

Luci ducked behind the fountain, a towering monstrosity of curiously entwined, nude cherubs. They'd inspected the piece at great length in their childhoods, Edith being the first to notice that two of the three angels were not fashioned properly. They had an extra *attachment* below their extended bellies.

They dared to question Lady Shaftesbury about the oddity only once—the woman's face flaring scarlet before declaring the question was not fit for young girls to ask.

Kneeling behind the statue, Luci no longer cared about ruining her gown. She needs must remain out of sight and undiscovered. Montrose must certainly be upset about her besting him with a foil. There was no other reason he could be here. Could there? Edith would never invite a man they'd exposed; which left only the possibility that he'd stormed into Lady Edith betrothal ball without invitation—specifically to find Luci.

CHAPTER 5

RODERICK HAD GAINED entrance to Lord Torrington and Lady Edith's betrothal ball without incident. No household in the *beau monde* would dare turn away a duke, invited or not. He hadn't bothered to stop long enough to remove his jacket and hand it to the footman. His purpose and course were clear: he would find Lady Lucianna and make her admit her part in his ruination.

Then what?

The woman was not capable of setting things to rights; she could not fix his broken relationship with Lady Daphne, nor could she restore his family's missing fortune. Lady Lucianna was not in possession of the information Roderick sought.

Nevertheless, he was certain he would find peace with this current situation once he confronted the woman responsible.

And she had to be in this very room.

Sure enough, Roderick spotted Lady Lucianna on the terrace of the Shaftesbury's townhouse. The terror in her widened stare told him she knew exactly why he had come. He continued across the ballroom. If he cut directly through the dancing couples, he paid no mind. His sights were set on one thing…and one thing only.

Vengeance.

In the form of Lady Lucianna.

A couple reentered the ballroom and hurried past him, but he kept his narrowed glare on the object of his ire.

A wisp of pale green, followed by the face of an auburn-haired woman moved to block his path—and his sight—as she stood on her tiptoes just inside the double doors, wavering from side to side.

"Excuse me, miss." Roderick made to step around the woman, but she stepped in the same direction, blocking him once more.

The slip of a woman giggled—giggled!—but finally stepped around Roderick with a simple word of apology. "Do beg my pardon."

He nodded curtly to her, but she'd already flitted farther into the room.

Leaving Roderick free to pursue Lady Lucianna on the terrace.

He stalked through the open doors, his narrowed glare sweeping across the outdoor patio and back again.

His hands clenched at this sides as he inspected the two couples on the terrace. Neither included Lucianna.

"Where in the bloody hell has she made off to?" he muttered, gaining a puzzled glance from one of the couples.

There was no way to escape but back into the ballroom—or down the steps into the unlit gardens below. The collection of shrubs, hedges, rose bushes, various flower blossoms, arches, benches, and statues seem to go on forever from his vantage point, at least until the night cast everything into utter darkness.

She was down there, Roderick could sense it.

It was possible she watched him even now; getting a laugh that she'd outmaneuvered him once more. His irritation swelled to the point of boiling over at her avoidance of a situation she'd caused.

She may have had the last say earlier in the day, but

they were on even ground now. She'd known who he was at Bentley's. And now, he knew who she was.

Tonight, *he* was determined to have the final word.

Roderick shoved his hands into the pockets of his evening coat, thankful he hadn't stopped to hand it over to the footman, and started down the steps into the cold, dark gardens below.

The second his Hessians hit the soft, damp grass of the nearest path, he was also glad he'd forgone his ballroom shoes. It was enough that his valet would give him hell for the disrepair his boots would surely be in by the end of his excursion to find Lady Lucianna.

Nevertheless, he pushed onward. The dew from a blue blossom clung to his sleeve, and he brushed it away.

Each path he ventured down was empty.

Each hidden seating area was vacant.

Finally, the narrow path he'd selected opened into a large, circular area with a statue depicting rounded, naked cherubs, spouting water into the fountain below. The moon above lit the open space and reflected off the pool of water.

Serene. Quiet. Peaceful.

Roderick could not enjoy any of what the picturesque garden landscape had to offer.

Not when his entire body tensed in anticipation of locating Lady Lucianna.

The only sound was his footfalls as he stalked farther into the night and away from the ball at his back. A rose thorn caught his trousers at his knee, digging into his skin and sending pain shooting down his leg as he pulled free.

The music from the betrothal ball had receded, as had any light given off by the terrace torches. The full moon afforded him little help as he passed under a topiary arch into yet another courtyard with benches and several statues—this time featuring animals.

Scanning the open area, Roderick looked for any

movement, listened intently for any sound that would betray Lucianna's whereabouts.

Nothing.

No movement.

No sound.

How had she disappeared so quickly without a trace?

Roderick refused to allow a sense of disheartening hopelessness to fill him once more. He'd lived too long with that weight upon him.

He'd seen no marked path leading to the townhouse drive and around to the street in front of the row of Mayfair homes, but there must be. Perhaps Lucianna had found it and fled the ball entirely.

It was time he returned, gave his good tidings to the betrothed pair, and departed.

There was time to find her on the morrow. He'd send his man to keep watch on her, and Roderick would approach her then.

He turned back toward the well-lit house set high above the gardens below, wishing it were possible to slip out of the party without notice; however, the growing crowd on the terrace told him his entrance had gained much attention.

Sighing, he started back, taking the same paths he'd taken when entering the gardens.

A wisp of midnight blue caught his eye as he passed by the cherub fountain.

Roderick didn't think, didn't pause. He took off after the figure as it fled back in the direction of the house. Catching her was not an option. He pushed faster, but she was more familiar with the paths as she turned and crisscrossed across the garden, her skirts gathered high to avoid tripping.

Triumph flooded him at the same time his irritation flared at having to chase the woman.

Roderick was knocked in the side of the head when he failed to duck under a low-hanging branch. He only allowed it to slow him for a mere second before pushing on.

Lady Lucianna was a few paces ahead of him now, her strides as long as his.

Not much farther, and the glow from the townhouse would light his way once more and he could increase his pace without threat of injury.

Exiting the garden path, Lady Lucianna veered sharply to the left and onto a walkway he hadn't noticed when he stepped from the terrace.

He lunged forward and grabbed her arm, halting her.

A quick tug brought her round to face him, and Roderick took her in his arms to keep her from breaking away.

Damn it, but she fit perfectly in his embrace. Lucianna's height nearly matched his, though she kept her eyes trained on his chest. Her silky, black hair was piled high atop her head, but Roderick longed to see it flow down her back.

He loosened his hold enough to bring his hand to her chin, nudging it upward, coaxing her to meet his glare.

She tried to pull her face from his hand.

"Look at me," Roderick sighed. The fight drained from him when a shiver went down her spine. Was she afraid—of him? "Lucianna?"

Reluctantly, she lifted her narrowed, moss-green eyes to him. They fairly glowed in the darkness.

"Why did you run?" he asked.

"I am not one to linger in the path of an angry man." She scowled up at him before turning to gaze at the terrace with disinterest.

She'd seen him, knew he was angry and looking for her, and so she'd run as opposed to facing the consequences of her actions. If she'd been a man, Roderick would have suggested they meet at dawn on the expansive lawns of Hyde Park to settle the matter between them. He would not have had to resort to chasing a female down during the middle of a social gathering.

His temper rose once more at her deception from that morning.

And her part in his ruinous fall from grace.

Not that his position as a duke was in jeopardy; however, there was a certain stigma that clung to a man who had been accused of unbecoming behavior with a woman not his wife or betrothed. It was easy, less complicated, to look the other way when a gentleman visited his mistress in private, but it was another thing entirely for the couple to be seen in public together.

Roderick had made the mistake of meeting his informant in a very public place.

He had caused the gossip; however, no one had thought to ask whom the woman was he consorted with, or what his relationship with her entailed. They would have learned that she was the wife of his father's dear friend—not a common harlot, nor his mistress.

The ill-advised meeting, and the gossip it had caused, would have lessened with time; talk of it replaced as another scandal occurred. But Lady Lucianna had decided to post it in the *London Daily Gazette* under the ludicrous guise of the *Mayfair Confidential*.

In one fell swoop, she'd stolen his chance to find out who was responsible for stealing his family fortune…and caused the end of his betrothal.

Roderick would not allow Lucianna to continue unscathed.

Glancing over his shoulder, he noted their proximity to the terrace. Happy to see that a few more people had joined the crowd watching them. From this distance, he and Lady Lucianna likely appeared in a loving embrace—a couple in the midst of a tender moment. However, they did not feel Lucianna's tense posture in his arms. They could not see the frown she turned on him. There was no way they saw the sparks of anger shooting from her glare.

"May I go, *Your Grace*?" she seethed, attempting to take a step back.

The woman was beautiful—an exotic, midnight rose.

But her hoyden ways and senseless destruction of his life were not acceptable.

Roderick pulled her close, causing her glare to snap back to his, her mouth opening in an *O* of surprise.

Yes, a lesson could prove very beneficial for Lady Lucianna in tamping her wayward tendencies.

And Roderick may be the best gentleman to do it.

He leaned down and took her mouth, his lips settling against hers.

Gauging her reaction, she did not pull away nor did her compressed lips soften under his. Roderick waited. If she jerked away, he would not stop her—he was not a brute. To his delight, she melted into him after only a brief moment, and he parted his lips, their mouths joining in a rhythmic dance of push and pull, give and take, exploration and conquest.

Everything around him faded away.

His entire body heated with the sensual movement of their caress.

When he ran his tongue across her bottom lip, her mouth blessedly parted, allowing him to explore further. He would show her how it felt to be trifled with, to have one's weakness discovered and exposed.

Tentatively at first, Roderick slid his tongue between her lips to taste her.

Honeysuckle and fruit berry. She was pure sweetness.

Everything about the night surrounding them faded to a distant memory.

He pulled her closer as his tongue set a rhythm with hers, much as their lips had, their bodies pressed tightly from knees to chest.

Lucianna fit perfectly against him—not too short, not too willowy.

His arm loosened, falling to cup her bottom as his other left her chin to rest on her neck, her skin soft as the finest cotton to his touch. In the moment, Roderick didn't long to have her—as had been the case at Bentley's—he needed her close to survive. Better yet, he craved to have every soft inch of her pressed against every hard line of his body.

His body was not only warm, it was on fire.

Lucianna pushed closer to him, demanding more, and Roderick gave it.

His entire body throbbed with need. Need for her.

The intensity grew to the height of severe pain.

Suddenly, his eyes sprang open as his tongue throbbed.

The blasted woman had bitten him—drew his tongue deep into her mouth and clamped her jaw shut.

His arms were suddenly empty, and the night breeze cast cool air upon his heated face. He stood alone, watching Lucianna flee down a path that ran parallel to the back of the house.

She paused several yards away. The woman would return. She would beg his forgiveness, and the entire wretched situation would resolve itself. Though he sensed his pride had taken the biggest hit.

Instead of making her way back to him, she settled her hands on her hips, her anger evident even from this far away despite the dim night and the barest illumination the moon cast on her.

"Your rakehell ways and heavy-handed manners will not prove my downfall, you scoundrel!" Her shout echoed across the space between them and rose up into the night as if the stars above sought to memorize her accusation and rain it down upon any woman who gained a familiarity with the Duke of Montrose.

She flipped back around, her black hair having come loose from its pins and cascading down her back as she lifted her skirts and ran.

Finally, she disappeared.

A loud cheer of celebration sounded from the terrace as the guests laughed at the scene he and Lucianna had unwittingly created.

He felt his mouth as she disappeared around the corner—thankful the hellion hadn't drawn blood.

Bloody hell. He hadn't meant to cause a scandal, only teach Lucianna the damage that could be caused by meddling in others' lives.

Taking in the sight of the terrace once more, Roderick set off at a leisurely pace down the same path she'd fled. He had no intention of catching her, only departing the party without attracting more attention. The entire walk, he pondered her accusation. A high-handed scoundrel and rakehell?

Roderick was nothing of the sort.

However, every person present with decent eyesight knew it had been the Duke of Montrose who'd stalked from the garden. He only hoped it was not too much to wish for that Lady Lucianna's identity remained a mystery, for if the *ton* recognized the woman he'd held in his embrace and kissed, there would be no chance of preventing the scandal to follow.

CHAPTER 6

LUCI CRINGED WHEN the door to the breakfast salon slammed open, then set her fork aside and took a sip of tea to clear her throat. The morning was early; however, that did not stop her father from moving through the house similar to an angry elephant. His rage had yet to diminish after the post in the *Gazette*, but neither had he taken his mistress out in public again.

It was a boon in Luci's mind.

She allowed herself a secretive smirk, keeping her attention focused on her plate. There was no need to incite her father's wrath while her siblings, Derek, Matthew, and Candace, were present.

The chair next to her at the head of the table was pulled back, and her father sat. Another footman set a heaping plate of pickled eggs, bread, ham, and cheese before him.

She glanced away quickly, at least confident it would not be she who brought the Marquis of Camden to anger first thing in the morning.

"Pickled eggs?" He pushed the plate away, causing his bread to slide onto the table and an egg to roll off his plate and across the pristine white linen between Derek and Matthew before finally hitting the floor.

Her mother, the marchioness, would be beside

herself when she saw the blemish on her rug when the thing broke open and spilled its yellow center.

The boys laughed, and Candace, Luci's youngest sibling, giggled.

Luci shot a warning glance in their direction. If they were not careful, the marquis' fury could just as easily land upon them. That was something Luci avoided whenever possible. They were too young to understand their father's shifts in mood and his black temper—or the destruction and injury that followed when someone continued to poke him.

A new plate was delivered to the marquis, and after a quick inspection, he proceeded to eat.

Her brothers and sister released a collective sigh. Even Luci gathered her fork and resumed her meal.

"May we be excused, Father?" Derek inquired. "I have studying to do. My tutor will arrive shortly."

Neither Luci nor her siblings knew the temperament of their father when he entered a room. If they did not request to be excused from their meal, the marquis would rant and rave about respect and proper etiquette. If they did ask to leave, their father was just as likely to punish them all for interrupting *his* meal.

From the set of her father's shoulders and his grim demeanor, today, the marquis was waiting and wanting an argument...no matter where he found it.

"Do you all think to scurry away the instant I enter a room?" the marquis seethed. "Oh, I am certain the useless lot of you will run off to your mother's side, pet her like an injured bird, and whisper sweet words of compassion to her."

"Derek, Matthew, Candace," Luci said in an even tone, making certain to keep her breathing regular, despite the anger seeping from her father's every pore. "Do hurry along and prepare for your tutors."

Luci kept her stare on her father, his head lowered over his plate, but there was no disguising the stiff set of his shoulders or his flared nostrils.

The door closed quickly behind the trio, leaving her to handle the marquis.

"Do you think to overstep me? Take command of this household?" His glare snapped to hers, their green eyes a matching set as the marquis attempted to stare her into submission and tempt her to break eye contact. "I am the lord of this house—and of your life. It would be wise for you—and your siblings—to remember that."

"I will certainly keep that in mind, Father." Luci notched her chin higher, refusing to look away or cower before him.

The marquis scrutinized her, his brow pulling tightly as he frowned. Luci was normally very cautious about saying the right thing to appease the man. And today was no different. She'd said the correct words, but her demeanor was not to his liking. There was a chance he would fall into a deeper rage. Or he could turn back to his meal, the fight over. One never knew.

However, Luci would not look away until he did one or the other.

She would never cower before him—never allow him to rule her as he did his wife.

Whether it was her own pride or her lack of self-preservation that kept her narrowed stare trained on her sire, she was uncertain.

Lucianna refused to be the broken woman her mother was.

She would not allow her father, of all people, to extinguish her flame.

It startled her how similar the man was to Abercorn. Though her father had never physically harmed his wife or children, he'd come close. Who was more dangerous? A man who did not hide his temper, or a man who remained calm and reserved at all times.

"Lady Lucianna?" The Camden butler, McMahon, cleared his throat. Neither she nor her father had noticed the servant enter the room. "You have guests in the blue salon."

Finally, the marquis returned to his meal, and Luci made to stand, smoothing her gown as the footman pulled out her chair.

"Make yourself available this afternoon," the marquis muttered, slathering his toast with marmalade. "You will attend me at an important meeting."

"Yes, Father." Luci nodded. The marquis had never included her in a meeting, whether concerning his many business endeavors or those family-related. It was not unknown to the Camden clan that the marquis—and his decisions—ruled everything. "Do send for me when you are ready to depart."

She hurried from the room before her father could halt her for not requesting permission to be excused.

Edith and Ophelia were waiting in the blue salon.

Luci had expected them since she'd departed Edith's ball the previous night without notifying her friends. They had every right to be angry with her, but Edith appeared downright furious, and Ophelia...her face was red and puffy, her eyes filled with unshed tears.

"A-choo!" Ophelia brought a kerchief to her nose as she sneezed.

Edith set her arm around Ophelia's shoulder before turning to Luci. "Where did you disappear to last night?"

Luci recoiled at the blonde's angry tone.

It was usually Luci who raised her voice amongst the trio, and Edith who was collected, never daring to allow her decorum to waver.

"Yes." Ophelia sniffled. "I went to the cherub fountain, but you were not there. I waited in the cold for over an hour, calling for you, until I gave up and returned to the ball. And now—a-choo—I have a cold."

"Ophel—"

"Do not Ophelia me!" She wiped at her dripping nose before turning her glare back to Luci. "I am now sick—sick!—and for what? Where did you run off to?"

"You left my betrothal ball, Lucianna," Edith jumped in, her fury dimming to something closer to hurt. "It was an evening, only one night, to celebrate Triston and me—and you deserted us. For what?"

Luci proceeded into the room and sank into the nearest chair, the upcoming meeting with her father forgotten. It was Ophelia's turn to comfort Edith as she wiped a tear from her cheek. This was not at all what Luci had thought would occur when next she saw her dear friends.

"Please accept my sincerest apologies. I had no intention of leaving you out in the cold...or departing your ball." Luci clasped her hands in her lap, hoping she properly conveyed how sorry she truly was. Her head hung in remorse, but she peeked up at her friends, desperate to hear them voice that they'd forgive her. "I was in trouble. I had to leave or risk scandal for all of us. Please..."

Both women melted at the sorrow in Luci's tone.

"What happened?" Edith asked. "Ophelia told me it was Montrose who stormed across the ballroom. I didn't so much as set eyes on him."

"Oh, I tried to distract him." Ophelia coughed, swiped at her watering eyes, and continued. "But he marched right around me. Were you able to escape him?"

Luci was uncertain how much to share with her friends. Obviously, not how muscular and secure his arms felt as they held her. Nor would she speak of her desire to run her fingers through his silky black hair as he pressed his body firmly to hers, his hand cupping her posterior. And especially not that a pool of warmth had gathered between her thighs when Montrose had set his lips to hers.

However, she did owe them some form of explanation.

A smidgen of truth, without all the glorious details.

"Montrose kissed me!" Luci covered her mouth in

utter shock.

"He, what?" Ophelia yelped.

"The nerve of that scoundrel!" Edith's outrage would have been comical were it not for the sparkle Luci saw in her eye. Could her dear friend know precisely how much Luci had enjoyed their embrace?

"What did you do?" Ophelia's eyes widened, her hands pressed to her bosom, still clutching her kerchief. "This is much like a real-life novel!"

Luci sniffed. "Then it would be a gruesome one."

"Why?" Edith eyed her intently.

"Because I bit the fool."

"Bit him?" Ophelia sat forward, her cold forgotten. "Where? On his hand?"

"No." Lucianna shook her head, her hair loosening from its pins at the action. "His tongue."

"How in the heavens could you bite his tongue?"

Luci frowned—and Edith giggled uncontrollably— as the auburn-haired woman pondered how one could bite another's tongue. It was easy to identify exactly when Ophelia realized the only possible way for Luci to do such a thing.

"He...put *his* tongue...in *your* mouth?" she stammered, sending Edith into another fit of laughter. "But that would mean..."

"Yes, Ophelia." Edith patted the woman on her back when she sputtered, breaking into a sneeze. "The Duke of Montrose slipped his tongue into Luci's mouth. And, I suspect, she enjoyed the experience greatly— though she is obviously loath to admit it."

"I most certainly did not—"

Edith waved her hand, silencing Luci's protest. "Now, how did this kiss end in your deserting me and leaving Ophelia out in the cold?"

"Does he know we wrote the article about him?" Ophelia asked. "Oh, Lord Torrington promised not to tell, but Montrose owes us nothing, especially after we caused Lady Daphne to break off their betrothal."

"No, he did not allude to knowing about our activities as the authoresses of the *Mayfair Confidential.*"

"Then why was he so angry?" Ophelia sat back once more, wiping at her eyes. "He was so furious, he almost ran me over in the ballroom."

"There was no time to ask before he kissed me, nor after I bit him." Luci hated her body for betraying her. Her face flared red, and that blasted tingling sensation between her thighs returned. She clenched her knees tightly together to keep the feeling from spreading. "That is when I ran down the path along the back of your townhouse, then down the drive to the alley, and home."

"*You* walked home?" Edith's brow scrunched.

"Of course. Do you think me incapable of finding my way home?" Luci retorted, offended by her friend's disbelieving tone. "We only live five townhouses from one another. Both of our stables back up to the alley. It was simple enough to reach my home and slip inside without notice."

It was Ophelia's turn to snort—as well as a woman could with her nose blocked by congestion. "You demanded your carriage follow you about the shopping district to avoid walking to the end of Bond Street to hand off your packages."

It was exactly what Luci had demanded on several occasions. "Last night was not a shopping excursion, I will have you know, though it will be necessary to obtain a new set of black ballroom slippers. Mine were utterly ruined by the mud and filth littering the alleyway, not to mention the dew from the lawns."

"What of your mother?" Edith demanded. "You must have worried her so."

"I sent word as soon as I arrived home that I'd left ill." Her mother was likely relieved to escape the ball early after her embarrassment several nights prior.

"And you did not think to have someone tell me— a-choo—I could come out of the cold?"

"Again, I am immensely sorry, O," Luci stood and then knelt before her friend on the lounge opposite her chair, taking her hands in hers. "I never meant for you to become ill, nor did I think I would need to go to such extreme measures to get away from the brutish man. What happened when he returned to the ballroom?"

Edith and Ophelia shared a questioning look.

"What?"

"I think we should tell her…" Ophelia glanced at Edith. "She should know."

Edith sighed. "If we must." Edith turned back to Luci. "A large gathering of guests witnessed Montrose kissing a woman in the gardens. They said she fled before anyone could discover her identity, and he left shortly after."

Ophelia smiled for the first time. "But now we know it was you."

"Is that supposed to make me feel better?" Luci demanded, releasing Ophelia's hands and returning to her seat. Her mind whirled with the possibility that someone at the ball had recognized her as she'd fled.

"At least no one suspects it was you." Edith's cheerful tone irked Luci.

"But Montrose!" Luci's mind was reeling. "He will pay for embarrassing me."

"Again, no one knows it was you."

"*I* know it was me. The rakehell has some nerve." Luci's hands balled into fists. "Yes, he will be seeking my forgiveness when I get done with him."

"I think it best you stay far away from the man," Edith pleaded. "What if he speaks the truth? You could be ruined—and put the *Mayfair Confidential* in jeopardy."

"All before we are able to prove Abercorn killed Tilda!"

"I can promise you, the man knows naught about our agreement with the *Gazette*." If Luci's friends noticed her words didn't hold any conviction, they didn't comment on it. "Now, I must ready myself. My father has requested my attendance at a meeting this afternoon. I must change my gown before he calls for me."

Luci stood, her friends following suit.

"Just promise us you will not say or do anything hasty until we know for certain exactly what Montrose knows," Edith said pointedly.

Shrugging, Luci embraced Edith and then Ophelia. "I promise to not act in a rash manner."

The women said their good-byes, agreeing to meet at Oliver's Book Shoppe the following day.

Neither Edith nor Ophelia noted Luci's phrasing: she would not act in a rash manner. But who determined if a manner was rash or well thought through?

CHAPTER 7

RODERICK SAT, NOT moving, behind his neatly organized, mahogany desk; at times, forgetting to breathe. He'd remained awake all night, pondering his situation and a way out of it—or, as best he could, a way *through* it. His drumming fingers broke the silence that had descended upon the room sometime that morning after he'd penned the letter to the Marquis of Camden.

Not a person had disrupted him in hours.

Though that did not stop him from jumping to attention at any little noise that penetrated his study door.

He'd informed his butler no one was to cross the threshold of his study until his guest arrived.

The solution to his many problems had been easily achieved, especially after he'd reassessed what actually needed fixing.

First, his financial status. He was low on funds; therefore, could not afford to keep an investigator on retainer. This made it no simple task to track down the men who'd played his father for a fool and left the Montrose estate with barely more than enough coin to keep the servants' salaries paid and wax for lighting. Yes, the key to rectifying this was far easier to attain than Roderick would have thought before the previous night.

His second problem would unwittingly solve his first. The hellion, Lady Lucianna. She was a woman in need of taming—and Roderick would be the man to offer for her hand. Their match—and her dowry—would not completely solve his financial woes, but it would give him ample funds for an investigator.

His chest tightened at the thought of possessing Lady Lucianna and all her fiery spirit.

No longer would it matter about the article she'd posted in the *Gazette* bringing scandal upon him. She had stolen his family's good name and honor with her foolish article, but now, she would correct the problems she'd created in his life.

If Lady Lucianna's father were as peeved by his wayward daughter as Roderick was, the man would willingly agree to the match. The betrothal agreement would be drafted with all due haste. The banns read as quickly as was allowed. Before long, both Lucianna and her dowry—a sizeable amount no doubt, if the Marquis of Camden's legendary eye for business deals and cutthroat ventures were to be believed—would belong to him.

The marquis would be gaining a duke for a son-in-law and have Lucianna taken off his hands.

And Roderick would insist that she reform her hellion ways or retire to the country.

Simple.

Now, he need only wait for Camden to arrive.

He glanced at the clock—nearly two in the afternoon. It wouldn't be long now.

Either the man showed, or he didn't, and Roderick was back to square one with solving his financial woes. However, if Camden came, all Roderick's dilemmas could be eradicated by mealtime.

He tilted his chin up and brought his arms up, interlocking his fingers behind his neck to support the weight of his head. All the while, his muscles relaxed, and he breathed easier, certain Camden would come.

He smiled. He hadn't been filled with an ounce of hope since he left the widow Cavendish the night before the scandal had hit. She'd agreed to meet with him several nights later and hand over the ledger of names, accounts, and bank locations for each gentleman involved in the damning ring of hells. Those lords had convinced his feeble-minded, gambling-and-drink-addicted father to hand over all of his family's fortune to invest in a new gaming hell in the Rookeries.

Roderick's grin faded at the memory. His father, the late sixth Duke of Montrose, had thought to settle his own gaming debts and invest in a business venture that would benefit his son—and his son's sons—for years to come.

He'd been utterly and unceremoniously swindled.

By men he'd likely considered his friends.

Men Roderick had never met nor knew anything of.

It was the main reason Roderick kept to himself. That, and he had no idea who was involved in the charade that now had him offering to wed a woman who he had little in common with, had only seen on two occasions, and who angered him to no end.

Lady Lucianna had thought herself cunning, no doubt. Luring him into the darkened gardens only to assault him and flee.

Little did the woman know Roderick was becoming quite adept at finding people and locating the information he sought. He was not his father, and would not be trifled with, especially by a mere slip of a lady.

Plus, he most likely would have already caught the men responsible for stealing his family's money if it hadn't been for Lucianna sticking her nose in his affairs. Or if finding the men were impossible, then he would have wed and used Lady Daphne's dowry to continue his quest for justice.

He massaged the ache in his neck. Maybe he should have sought his bed—or at least a warm bath and a change of clothes—after sending the missive to the Marquis of Camden. Roderick glanced to his liquor-stocked sideboard, longing for a tumbler to fortify his resolve; however, he needed to keep his wits about him if he were to best the marquis during the betrothal negotiations. His confidence was overly high his *guest* would not turn down the proposal.

A knock echoed from the foyer, and his grin returned.

Footsteps hurriedly moved to open the front door, and his butler welcomed Roderick's guest before the pair started in the direction of Roderick's study.

His butler's usual shuffle could be heard, followed by the solid, confident steps of Camden—and another, much lighter step. Had Camden brought his wife?

It hadn't occurred to Roderick that Camden would include anyone else. The match made sense on paper: the daughter of a marquis to wed a duke. Roderick's grin faded once more, and his jovial mood soured at the notion of convincing Lady Camden of his affection for Lady Lucianna.

LUCIANNA GLANCED AROUND at the gaudy, almost abhorrent foyer as the butler ushered them in. A large monstrosity of a chandelier hung overhead, dripping with dozens of candles. The floor shone as if it were waxed only an hour before. The table at her side was free of dust, and its vase filled with fresh, blue blossoms.

"His Grace is expecting you, my lord." The butler closed the door behind them, and a footman hurried forward to accept their coats. "Right this way."

Following her father, Luci moved deeper into the house. She had no idea whose townhouse it was nor why they were there. Hanover Square was an area even more prestigious than Mayfair, the houses far grander with sprawling lawns and extravagant gardens and stable houses. This property seemed a bit less cared for than others on the street, but nonetheless, its station was much loftier than her family home.

"Father?" She set her hand on his sleeve. "Who lives here?"

"You will find out soon enough, child," he snipped back, halting to take in her emerald gown, neatly pinned hair, and white gloves. "You should be thankful I have brought you along on such a momentous occasion." His brow furrowed. "As your father, I have every right to handle your future in any way I see fit."

Her future? She was only attending her first Season after the tragedy of her friend's death had cut her previous London Season short. As yet, no gentleman had shown any overt interest in her. Not that she planned to wed anytime soon. An honorable man was nearly impossible to find in a sea of scoundrels, rakehells, and rascals. Men drank too much, gambled exceedingly, favored women of the night, or lived day by day, hoping to keep out of debtor's prison.

Luci had no intention of being forever tied to an unsavory man.

With no suitors to speak of, she could only assume her father meant to sell her to the highest bidder—wealth, and stature—as a business deal.

Not uncommon and certainly not something she'd think was above her father's ilk. The Marquis of Camden was known for his vicious business dealings and cutthroat practices during venture negotiations. Luci owed him a bit of gratitude as he'd settled large dowries on both her and Candace. Though all that did was bring forth fortune hunters and men who would not give a whit about her once he held her money.

Every speck of common sense within screamed for her to beg her father to reconsider whatever matter had brought them to this house, plead with him to depart and never return.

Luci was helpless, a feeling she'd felt on one other occasion, a time she wished she'd tried harder to convince her friends and the magistrate that there was a villain in their midsts, not a grieving bridegroom. Very similar to the day Tilda had been pushed to her death, Luci was walking into a situation out of her control.

"Do not tarry, Lucianna." Her father glanced over his shoulder at her. "When a meeting time is set, it is highly improper to be late, especially with the significance of today."

The man's foul demeanor from that morning had vanished, replaced by a man who knew his worth and position. Confidence and arrogance dripped from his every word. The set of his shoulders was one of haughtiness. His easy manner told Lucianna that whatever awaited them in this home, her father was certain he held the upper hand.

And that terrified Luci.

No matter how much she despised her father, as the head of the Camden household, he was her master; just as he commanded and demanded respect from his servants, so were Luci and her siblings to follow his every edict.

She only need look to her mother to see the consequences if she ever actively sought to refuse her father's orders.

A shiver went through her at the penalties she'd face if the marquis ever learned it was by his own daughter's hand he had been exposed in the *London Daily Gazette*.

Luci squared her shoulders and notched her chin high—every ounce the daughter of the Marquis of Camden—as she marched down the hall after her father.

The servant opened a door at the end of the hall and announced their arrival. "Your Grace. The Marquis of Camden and Lady Lucianna to see you."

"Show them in, Danvers."

That voice…

Luci froze mid-step, every nerve in her body revolting against moving another inch. If she took another step, she'd enter the room, and her greatest fear would be realized.

"Come, Lucianna," her father hissed, stepping into the room and leaving her alone in the hall.

She suspected all color had drained from her face as icy tendrils reached toward every limb of her body.

The Duke of Montrose. They were meeting with the one man who more than likely knew all her secrets.

Luci suspected after witnessing Montrose's anger the night before that he'd stumbled upon her truth. The identity of the person behind the *Mayfair Confidential*. She hadn't been able to admit it to Edith or Ophelia that morning, but the fury Montrose had focused on her as he stormed through the garden could only mean he'd discovered she posted the article exposing his disloyalty to Lady Daphne.

The only thing left to do was stall him from telling her father.

Luci stepped into the room, greeted by Montrose's cocky grin of victory.

CHAPTER 8

RODERICK STOOD TO greet the marquis, his welcoming smile returning to cover his shock at Lady Lucianna's presence. Camden strode into the study, taking in the room around him before acknowledging his host. Lucianna was blocked from view behind her father.

Danvers gave Roderick a curt bow, and he nodded for the butler to depart and close the door.

This discussion demanded privacy, even from his household.

He knew full well what he'd asked Camden here to discuss, but Lucianna was a wild card. Roderick was uncertain if her father had shared the purpose of this meeting. If he hadn't seen fit to enlighten his daughter, it was possible she would be very upset when she learned of the reason behind the appointment.

Roderick did not want his entire household eavesdropping and spreading the news within the servant's gossip mill before an agreement was signed.

Hell, it might become necessary for Roderick to inform Camden of Lucianna's unsavory activities as the *Mayfair Confidential* authoress, which he was loath to do, as it could cause a scene within his house that would not be easy to mask.

Lucianna stepped from behind her father; her emerald gown matching her eyes, and her black hair framing her face angelically. Though Roderick knew from the glint in her eye that the woman was anything but angelic. Beguiling and witty, yes. Sharp-tongued and elegant, for certain. Demure, reserved, and modest, however, were not words he'd ever use to describe Lucianna.

She seemed as shocked to see him as he was to see her, and judging from the look of contempt that settled on her face, she was prepared to do battle with him once more. It was a shame they were not at Bentley's. He couldn't help but wonder who would have the upper hand this day.

"My lord," Roderick greeted Camden, refusing to allow his eyes to stray toward the marquis' daughter again. "Thank you for accepting my invitation to discuss this"—how to describe the matter at hand?—"delicate matter."

He risked a glance at Lucianna to see her frown deepen. It was the only sign the woman gave at her discomfort of the situation. He admired her ability to keep her emotions under such tight control, though the corner of her lips turned up in a confidence smirk.

Roderick was unable to harness his own shock, his brow lifting in a silent question as to what she found so comical.

"I see there is no need to introduce the pair of you," the marquis muttered. He looked back and forth between Roderick and his daughter. "Please, wait outside, Lucianna. I will speak with Montrose and call for you when we have settled on the details."

Her mouth gaped open as her face reddened. The woman was not used to being so easily dismissed, and Roderick would be fooling himself if he didn't admit he enjoyed her stunned expression.

For once in their brief acquaintance, she had no sharp retort, no sugar-dipped reply, and no way of refusing her father's command without causing a scene.

Lucianna, no matter her hellion ways, was still a woman born and bred into the highest society in England. She knew her role as the daughter of a marquis and played it well.

Would continue to play it well until she was no longer in a position for playacting. It was that time that should concern Roderick.

If she were anything like him, her memory was long, and her need for vengeance patient.

Finally, she nodded. "Yes, Father."

With arms crossed and one last lingering, scathing glare for Roderick, she turned on her heels and marched toward the closed door. She paused for the span of a single breath, as if expecting someone to jump forward and open it for her. When it did not happen, she reached forward and pulled the door wide, stepped out of the room, and slammed the door in her wake.

She was not happy. From Camden's slight cringe, he knew it as well as Roderick.

The marquis masked his irritation with his daughter by taking the seat before Roderick's desk. "Now, Montrose—"

"Do call me Roderick," he said. "If you are here, I assume my proposal is agreeable to you. We might one day be family."

Camden chuckled. Outright laughed in Roderick's face.

Roderick's brow rose. "Should I assume you are not here to speak about a betrothal between me and Lady Lucianna?" The hair lifted on the back of his neck, and his confidence lessened for the first time since sending the letter to Camden that morning.

The marquis sobered, eyeing Roderick. "Do you think you are the only duke sniffing around my daughter?"

Roderick sat heavily in his chair, taken aback. He hadn't even considered another offer for Lucianna's hand. "Well—I—I am certain it does not surprise me, my lord. Your daughter is charming and very beautiful, with quite possibly dozens of suitors clamoring for her attention."

"But she has the attitude of a dour matron, I assure you." Camden crossed his legs and reclined in his seat. "However, she is well-connected, schooled in the fine art of managing a household, and comes with a sizeable dowry. So, I should have expected the men to come calling, despite her less than agreeable nature."

Did the man not note the regal, graceful, perfection that was Lady Lucianna? Roderick supposed wealth did not lend itself to a keen eye for value and quality.

And make no mistake, no matter how angry he was at Lady Lucianna, how betrayed he felt by a woman who did not know him from the King of France, she was a woman of worth. It only took one look—and a few seconds in her presence—to know she was something special. Something worth having…and keeping.

"I must warn you, this auction may very well see a betting war the likes of Tattersall's best." The man chuckled again. "But before we speak of such important matters. Let us toast our new association with a drink."

Roderick leapt to his feet and moved to the sideboard, not because the marquis had commanded it, but for the sole purpose of hiding his flabbergasted expression—and growing anger—from the man.

The Marquis of Camden had just sat in his study and compared his daughter's betrothal negotiation to that of a horse at auction.

Devil take it, she was worth more than any horse!

Turning two tumblers right side up, Roderick filled each with a healthy portion of amber spirits. If the marquis' entrance was any indication, Roderick's afternoon would not be proceeding as expected.

Camden took his tumbler gratefully and sniffed at the liquor, as if the quality and age of the stuff would lend a good air on the man who'd served it. The brandy they held was aged longer than Camden himself.

How could Roderick have thought making a game of taking Lucianna as wife would be a simple, uncomplicated matter between two men?

Lady Lucianna was complicated at her core; a woman who fenced as well as any accomplished man, a lady who did not shy away from exposing her own father's misdeeds, and a hoyden who dared invite a gentleman to deepen a kiss only to bite down on his tongue.

"Now, I must admit, your offer to take the girl off my hands is much appreciated," Camden began, swirling the brandy in his glass. "I fear she has become a handful since her coming out—gallivanting about London, speaking out of turn, and Lord knows what else she does when I—or my staff—are not keeping watch over her."

Roderick only nodded in agreement. The woman was certainly entangled in far more than her father knew.

"And most recently, Lucianna has seen fit to turn my entire household against me. My younger children, always so obedient and well-mannered, have begun to challenge my authority and even look to Lucianna before adhering to my command. Honestly, I cannot have such mutiny in my home."

"My lord, I—"

Camden brought his narrowed stare to Roderick's, cutting off anything he'd thought to say in Lady Lucianna's defense.

"So, Montrose, in other words, I am very interested in your marriage offer. Unfortunately, I have gained another offer for Lucianna's hand, though I am not entirely hard-pressed to pick the better lord. She is like any wild filly. She will need a firm hand; possibly need to see the end of a whip every once in a while to keep her in line."

Roderick's skin crawled as if a thousand ants

marched along every inch of his body.

He was repulsed.

What father instructed his daughter's suitor to use cruel methods for harnessing her wayward tendencies?

The mere thought was baffling.

And Camden was obviously entertaining offers from other gentlemen. At least Roderick knew he would never raise a hand—or a weapon—against any woman, no matter how irritating their actions or words.

Roderick sat a bit straighter in his chair. Had another perspective husband agreed with Camden: a firm hand and a whip here or there when necessary?

Bloody hell, the marquis sickened Roderick; however, if he withdrew his interest in Lady Lucianna, she might very well be left with a man far less honorable than he.

Roderick would not forsake any woman to that fate—even Lucianna who'd stolen his only opportunity to find his family fortune.

However, marrying Lady Lucianna also meant tying himself to Camden.

He shuddered to think whom Lucianna would find herself betrothed to if it weren't Roderick. There were many cruel men living within London. Men who by no stretch of the imagination could ever be considered gentlemen. Men who spent their nights in scandalous brothels disguised as legitimate gaming hells. If a gaming hell could ever be *legitimate* in nature.

Lucianna was helpless to disobey her father's decision on whom she would marry.

"Ah, well." Camden emptied his tumbler in one swift gulp and slammed the glass on the desk between them. "I can see you are not the man for her. Which is a pity. I suspect Abercorn will have to do, even though he is as old as Corinthians."

The Duke of Abercorn?

What would the old duke want with such a young bride?

Neither alternative was acceptable. Turn away from a betrothal to Lady Lucianna and leave her in her father's clutches—and likely betrothed to Abercorn within a fortnight—or agree to Camden's conditions and be tied to Lady Lucianna and beholden to her father.

Roderick would never give the impression he'd abuse a woman, no matter what she may do to incite his anger; however, leaving her in Abercorn's clutches was the same, even if he were the one holding the whip.

"My pursuit of Lady Lucianna is very serious, my lord." Roderick commanded his shoulders to relax, to look at ease and not alert the marquis to the danger he was in even speaking of injuring a woman. "I am prepared to have the documents prepared and signed whenever you wish it."

"I will need to discuss it with my daughter. She is unaware of the nature of our business here."

Roderick wanted to laugh. He suspected Lady Lucianna was never fully unaware of anything.

"I have one request, my lord."

"Of course, Montrose." Camden stood, signaling their meeting was nearing an end. Roderick followed suit.

"I wish to call on Lady Lucianna." It had been many years since he'd attempted to court a woman. Even with Lady Daphne, it had all been arranged and handled behind closed doors. "I think it best she and I become acquainted more before we formally announce our betrothal."

"*If* you are to be betrothed," Camden corrected. "However, a stroll in the park or trip to Bond Street for ices would not be unacceptable."

"Very well. I will call on her presently." Hell, he would call on her this very evening, if it would not be seen as too eager. The last thing Roderick needed was for Camden to change his mind and give Lucianna to the Duke of Abercorn. "Shall we bring Lady Lucianna in and tell her about our agreement?"

Roderick wouldn't mind a bit of time in Lucianna's presence. Hell, maybe he would be so bold as to request a moment alone with her. They were to be wed, after all. Her father would be a fool not to accept Roderick's offer and nor could Camden be against allowing the soon-to-be betrothed couple a moment together.

"That will not be necessary, Your Grace." Camden shook his head and bowed. "I will inform her of my decision, and she will be prepared when you call on her. I will have my man draw up the paperwork for your signature."

"Of course, my lord."

There was nothing more Roderick could say or do as the marquis departed the room, soundly closing the door behind him. Truly, there was little Roderick suspected needed to be done at this time. Camden would handle informing Lady Lucianna, and when next they met, she would have no cause to deny him her company.

The sound of two sets of footsteps retracing their way back to the foyer was all Roderick heard as Camden led Lady Lucianna from the house.

For not the first time, Roderick wondered why the marquis had brought his daughter if only to instruct her to wait in the hall until they departed.

He refilled his drink and collapsed back into his chair.

He should feel a measure of relief to know that a formal betrothal between him and Lucianna was almost guaranteed, which meant his coffers would be full once more—or at least, back to a more agreeable amount—and he could resume his endeavors to locate the men responsible for stealing from the Montrose estate.

Relief flooded him. A bone deep sense of rightness filled him.

He would have his money—and Lady Lucianna.

His troubles were coming to an end. The

confidence that had filled him earlier returned.

CHAPTER 9

"WHAT WAS THIS all for, Father?" Luci asked as she settled her skirts. The carriage dipped as the marquis entered and took the front-facing seat. "Dragging me from the house only to wait in some lord's hallway seems peculiar."

Her father, ever the arrogant marquis, only stared at her before shouting to their driver to return them home. No matter her question or her rising temper, the man would not be prodded into answering any of her questions until he was ready to speak.

It was a trait Luci long suspected she'd inherited from the marquis.

She crossed her arms and stared out the window, prepared to wait for her father to speak. Arguing and insisting answers would get her nowhere. Maybe disinterest would lull him into a false sense of security, and he'd speak of what he planned to gain from meeting with Montrose?

Luci kept one eye on him. He didn't appear upset or furious, so Montrose hadn't spoken of the *Mayfair Confidential* and her part in the articles. She was thankful for that much.

Finally, her father sighed, and she turned from the carriage window to see him scrutinizing her. They were much alike, all darkness. Yet, Luci suspected her father's darkness was far deeper than surface level.

"You have been out of the schoolroom for nearly two years now."

Truly only fifteen months, but Luci kept that bit of information to herself.

"And you are spending my coin to furnish your second Season."

As if the Camden coffers were in jeopardy of running dry. Besides, Luci hadn't the time to spend any money beyond her basic wardrobe last Season before she and her friends went into mourning for Tilda. More accurately, Luci was enjoying just her third month as a debutante.

"Have you found a suitor to your liking?" he asked.

There it was. He wanted Luci to take a man to husband—and depart his household. The marquis would relish that. In one fell swoop, he'd have his hellion of an eldest daughter gone, and no one would stand in his way of treating his wife, Luci's mother, any way he saw fit.

It would be all the more satisfying when she delivered her next—and finale—blow to the marquis.

"I do not plan to wed, at least not this Season." After Tilda's death, and everything Luci had learned about the other unscrupulous men of the *ton*, she had little hope a decent man existed—with the exception of Lord Torrington. Plus, if she were to wed and move away, who would care for her siblings? There would be no one willing to step between them and their father's fury.

"Then we are both lucky I have found not one but two suitors for you." He picked a piece of lint from his sleeve as if his declaration were nothing more than him expressing his love of carnations, while Luci sat still—frozen—unable to process what he'd said. "Obviously, the Duke of Montrose is an influential, shrewd lord, who would make a great addition to the Camden lineage."

"You think to wed me to…Montrose?" Luci stumbled over the words.

"What did you think our meeting was concerning?" His tone said her father thought her dim-witted.

Luci hadn't given the meeting much thought beyond her father requesting her accompaniment, which was anything but normal. She and Montrose would make a most disastrous pair—she'd bitten the man, for heaven's sake.

"He requested an audience to discuss the joining of our two families." Camden spoke of her betrothal as if he were agreeing to discuss the purchase of a new carriage. "I cannot say I am against the match; however, I have other offers to consider."

That had Luci pushing back into the cushioned seat. "Other offers?" she squeaked, repulsed by the weak tone in her voice.

"Yes. Abercorn." He continued to gaze out the window. "Though I am uncertain if Abercorn is the man for you. Three wives and no children. What is to say you won't marry the man and grow old, never producing an heir—his Dukedom would pass on to another relative and forever be out of Camden control."

A business arrangement.

Her future had been reduced to nothing more than deciding what would gain her father more in the long run. A virile, robust lord like Montrose, who simply exuded potency and prowess. Or an aging, very wealthy duke like Abercorn, who would bring many business connections but no guarantee for a future including children who would be linked to the Camden name via their mother.

Luci shouldn't have thought any other option was open to her—unless she'd been able to stall long enough for her twenty-first birthday to arrive; however, she was two years from the date.

Montrose or Abercorn. Was that truly any choice at

all?

"Abercorn killed Tilda…and Montrose is a known rakehell," she hissed, gaining her father's full scrutiny. "You would make me choose between a murderer and a philanderer? You would enjoy that greatly, wouldn't you? Men of your own ilk, the pair of them."

"Lucianna!" he warned in a harsh tone. One that in her youth would have had her mouth clamping shut and her eyes averting to his feet. Not today. Not in this coach. And certainly not in matters dealing with her future. "You—and those silly, foolish women you call friends—caused quite the scene last Season. You are lucky either gentleman will have you. You are tarnished goods, to say the least."

She'd taken aim at her father and levied her most unforgiving insult; however, she'd said what needed to be said. If her father correlated her words with what had been printed in the *London Daily Gazette*, it would be a wonder.

Leaning back, Luci crossed her arms and turned her attention to the passing London street.

"Do not sulk, it will cause wrinkles," he mumbled. "You will marry either Montrose or Abercorn. Whomever I see fit to select for you."

Luci would rather a coin be tossed into the air to seal her fate.

"And if I will have neither?" she dared ask.

The marquis chuckled, a light, wheezy snort. "I did not raise a chit fool enough to think she has any say in whom I chose for her marriage. Do not be dim, Lucianna, it is very unbecoming."

"Abercorn killed Tilda," Luci said. Images of her lovely, bright friend lying lifeless at the bottom of Abercorn's staircase filled her mind. "You honestly cannot expect me to overlook that damning fact, no matter how *tarnished* you think I am."

"That was a sad, unfortunate occurrence. Do not think I completely lack sympathy for the girl. However, that is in the past. I am speaking for the future of the Camden name." His stealthy glare landed on her, almost begging her to argue further.

"Father, I…" She sucked in a deep breath to stop from sobbing.

"You will marry. And it will be either Abercorn or Montrose."

"And if I refuse?"

"Then I will drag you before the clergyman and see that the deed is done," he said with utter calm and composure. He was a man used to getting exactly what he wanted, when he wanted it. That he was prepared to hand his daughter over to a murderer, only meant gaining access to business deals that were before out of his reach. "Now, put a smile upon your face. We are almost home, and you will speak of your two suitors with vigor to your siblings. You will be overjoyed to learn whom I will ultimately offer your hand to."

"And then you will finally be rid of me."

Her father sat a bit straighter, an odd grin and faraway look entering his eyes. "Yes, yes, that is another boon I have yet to fully think through, though I will find great happiness in having you out from under my roof."

Luci could not blink, would not allow her father to think she would go quietly into a marriage she did not agree with—or any marriage at all.

But his stare matched hers in force. Her hurt mirrored in his determination.

Suddenly, the footman pulled the carriage door open.

They'd arrived at home.

"Smile, my dear daughter," he hissed. "I am certain you would not want to anger me into a hasty ceremony by special license."

Luci hated herself for giving in, but she smiled. This game was one of finely executed moves, parried by advanced defensive tactics.

Much like fencing.

And that was one sport she would always best her father at.

CHAPTER 10

ONE DAY.

One full day.

Roderick raised his hand to shield his eyes from the blazing sun. Well, it had been at least twenty-three hours.

That was an acceptable amount of time to wait before calling on one's intended, soon-to-be-betrothed.

Roderick slammed his hand into his jacket pocket to stop the shaking. His other held a large bouquet of yellow blossoms—he hadn't any notion the variety, but he felt like a coxcomb pacing before the Camden townhouse, scared to knock and face Lucianna.

The idea of her yelling and screaming at him was not what he feared.

No, he feared one question from her: why?

…and that would be the first time he'd be forced to lie to the woman he'd take as his wife.

Roderick would not tell her it was because he needed her dowry. There was no way he would be honest enough to tell her it was because he feared leaving her in Camden's household. And neither would he start off by asking her to write a retraction to the article in the *Gazette*.

Not that an apology from the *Mayfair Confidential*

would change anything.

Regardless, he was coming up to snuff. No matter what the marquis asked, Roderick was prepared to comply.

It struck him as odd he'd willingly agree to any conditions Camden set forth, but Roderick was appalled at his father's mismanagement of the Montrose estate—and he needed funds as soon as possible if he did not want his creditors to come knocking. What if his father had been working under the guise of doing what was right and honorable, but found himself waylaid in the process or even misguided by those he trusted?

The sleeve of his jacket moistened, and belatedly, Roderick realized the bottom of the bouquet had opened, and water was saturating his cuff.

Blast it all, but he shouldn't have gone through the trouble of procuring flowers…hell, what if she did not favor these exact blossoms? He would look like the fool he already felt he was.

He switched his hold to the other hand and shook his arm, water splattering the closed door in front of him, only leading to the continued leakage of moisture on his other sleeve.

Roderick leapt off the stoop to avoid more water marring the entrance. "For the love of—"

"May I help you, my lord?"

The tips of his ears heated, and Roderick shuffled his feet to hide the marks on the stoop. It was as if Cook had found him with his hand in the cookie jar.

He cleared his throat and smiled. "Good day. I am here to call on Lady Lucianna."

"My lady is not accepting visitors at this time."

As simple as that. Roderick had gone out of his way to do something special for the confounded woman, and she *was not accepting visitors*.

He fought to keep his temper under control. Circumstances had changed—he now needed her. Proving a point or teaching her a lesson was no longer important.

"I am certain if you give my name, Lady Lucianna will agree to see me." To help with his point, he held out the flowers before him and gave them a solid shake. "I would hate to see these beautiful blossoms waste away before Lady Lucianna has time to appreciate them."

The butler looked from Roderick to the flowers and back again, his brow pinched in a peeved manner before he sighed and held the door wide for the duke to enter.

"Whom may I tell her is calling?" he asked.

"Montrose!" Lady Lucianna's unmistakable hiss sounded from behind the servant. "How dare you—"

"I can call a footman to throw him out, my lady," the butler said, starting to close the door in Roderick's face, but he was already over the threshold, and the door only knocked his hand, the flowers falling to the stoop.

The servant's manners presented themselves once more. "Oh, my lord, allow to me collect—"

Roderick swatted the man away. "I can collect them without assistance." He knelt to the floor. "But thank you, all the same."

"What are you doing here, Montrose?"

Roderick cocked his head to the side to stare up. Lady Lucianna stood several feet behind the butler, her toe tapping as she pulled on her gloves.

"Your father gave me permission to call on you," Roderick replied, pushing awkwardly to his feet, the flowers once again clutched in his hand, although several blooms were either bent or missing altogether. "So, here I am."

"And here I go." Lucianna tied the strap of her hat under her chin and took her handbag from a side table. "I fear I have a previous engagement." She glanced over her shoulder and nodded. "Charlotte, come along before we are late."

"Lucianna!" The marquis' thundering voice preceded his solid footsteps as he descended the stairs. "Where are you—" Camden took in Roderick at the threshold. "McMahon! Step back and allow His Grace entrance. What is wrong with you? Take the damned flowers to the housekeeper."

Roderick nodded to the butler, regretful for his part in angering Lord Camden. "My lord. I was in the area and thought to call on Lady Lucianna, but it seems I should have sent word ahead, asking for an audience."

The man looked between Lucianna, buttoning her walking cloak, and back to Roderick, his arms damp from the flowers. "Where are you going, girl? I do not remember you asking for permission to leave."

Lucianna's chin lowered as if to convince everyone present of her meek nature. "I am to meet Lady Edith and Lady Ophelia at Oliver's Book Shoppe in less than an hour."

"You are taking your maid with you?" Camden's brow furrowed.

"Of course, Father."

"Then I see little reason why Montrose cannot go along, as well."

It was the first thing the marquis had ever said that Roderick agreed with.

Roderick smiled, clasping his hands behind his back and rocking on his heels.

"It is settled. Now, I have work to do," Camden nodded to Roderick and headed down the hallway with not so much as a "by your leave" for Lady Lucianna.

"Do not look so pleased, Your Grace." Lucianna pushed past him toward the door. "Come, Charlotte."

He glanced around the empty foyer—Camden had slammed a door down the hall, the butler had disappeared with the flowers, and Charlotte had followed her mistress outside.

Pulling the door closed, he followed the women to the drive. "We can take my carriage," he called, hurrying to catch up and assist the women, his driver caught off guard.

Lucianna halted, assessing his coach. "I think Charlotte and I would be far more comfortable in the Camden coach."

"Do not be stubborn, my lady," Roderick sighed, as the triumph of being included in her outing evaporated at her sour expression. "My coach and driver are ready and at your service."

She glanced at the conveyance, and Roderick expected her to turn down the offer; however, she surprised him by nodding and holding out her hand for assistance. Charlotte followed suit, and he entered the carriage last, galled to find the pair on the forward-facing seat. Roderick clamped his mouth shut, his teeth grinding, but he would not comment on the rudeness.

"Where to, Your Grace?" his driver called.

"Oliver's Book Shoppe off Bond Street."

At Lucianna's raised brow, he continued, "Do you think me so uncivilized that I am unfamiliar with local bookshops?"

"Humpf." Lucianna jerked her handbag onto her lap and busied herself flapping her fan.

Her maid had the good sense to stare out the window and act as if she were not present.

THEY DEPARTED THE carriage in much the same manner as they'd entered, with Lucianna hesitantly allowing him to assist her.

He then tucked her hand into the crook of his arm and pulled her close before whispering, "Do not bite again or you will fast learn I bite back."

Lucianna made to pull away, but he laughed and held her firmly in place. The woman needs must learn that while he was an understanding man, he would not put up with her hoyden tendencies.

Charlotte trailed them into the shop, a bell chiming overhead as they entered.

"Do wait for us here," Lucianna called over her shoulder as they walked farther into the bookstore.

The smell of worn leather and old ink surrounded Roderick, and he remembered his childhood spent in his grandfather's library. Shelves lined the room from floor to ceiling, each cluttered with books of every size. The hiss of conversation drifted on the air, and he noticed the shopkeeper and an older gentleman deep in discussion by the register. It had been a long time since he'd allowed himself the opportunity to wander rows of books, searching for adventure in written form.

"Are you looking for anything in particular, my lady," he asked as they meandered down a deserted aisle, putting distance between them and her maid. He noted the hair on the back of her neck prickle, exactly as he'd intended when he leaned in close with his last words. "I am here to assist you in any way."

"Do stop doing that," she hissed. "We are not in your private coach nor a secluded garden."

"But, nonetheless, alone." Roderick peered down the aisle and then back the way they'd come. "There is no one to see—or hear us."

Lucianna pulled from his grasp and turned her pointed stare on him. "That is very advantageous because I find I have much to say to you." Her glare traveled down his form and back to his face. "You are a scoundrel, a man in the habit of taking advantage of women when they are out of options. And I, Your Grace, will not abide by any of it."

"So, that is it?" he asked. "You will not *abide* by my offer, and instead, agree to wed old man Abercorn?"

"I have agreed to nothing, Your Grace."

"Roderick."

She stumbled a step at the change in conversion, her back pressed against a shelf of books labeled: *Adventure*.

"Call me Roderick. And I assure you, Camden is quite adamant you wed, and soon." He could not look away as her brow pulled sharply down, and then her face relaxed as if her thoughts were far away…all to return her eyes to him. "Come now, you cannot think a marriage to Abercorn would suit you."

"I am uncertain a marriage to any man will suit." She pressed her gloved finger to her lips as if she didn't trust herself to go on.

Blast it all, but he wanted her hands exploring his neck, tangling in his dark locks, and traveling down his back.

"However," she continued, drawing his attention back to the present—their reality, as it were. "I do see the merit in agreeing to your proposal." His spirits soared at her words, but why? "At least until I can find a way out of this nonsense."

Her meaning was clear: marriage to him was not to her liking.

"And marriage to Abercorn would be what, precisely?"

"Unthinkable." Her shoulders sagged. The weight of it all finally too much for her.

Roderick could imagine the taxing weight upon her given no option but to wed, and to select between two men not of her choosing. His betrothal to Lady Daphne had been done under similar circumstances; a duty to uphold his family's honor by securing the necessary funds to steer clear of debtor's prison. They'd made the best of their bad situation, he and Daphne. She was sweet, demure, and proper. Everything a man should long for in a wife; however, not once did he have the overwhelming sensation, the all-encompassing need, to take her in his arms and kiss her.

However, at this very moment, an irresistible craving drew him to Lucianna. He wanted to pull her against him, set his lips to hers, and give her the proper kiss he'd attempted in the gardens. However, this exotic

English flower came with thorns—barbs capable of mortal injuries to any man who attempted to pluck her.

The question was: Did Roderick think it worth the wounds to try and claim her?

"If I am unable to waylay my father or speak some sense to him, I will wed you, Montrose."

For the second time in as many minutes, Lucianna seemed to change before his very eyes. Her shoulders were now stiff with resolve.

"I am certainly happy you would choose me over the aging duke."

"I cannot say I did not consider many things in this decision."

"I would very much like to hear what sets me apart from Abercorn."

She eyed him closely before responding, as if gauging his off-guard manner before speaking. "Are you a murderer, Your Grace?"

"Not that I am aware of, my lady." He kept his voice neutral, refusing to show the shock that coursed through him at her absurd question. "Are you?"

She waved her hand and stepped away from the shelf. "Heavens no, do not be obtuse."

Him, obtuse? The woman had an odd way of deciphering who was being dim-witted.

She took his arm and continued down the long aisle, her free hand dragging along the spines of books as they passed. "Do you have a tendency to lie to your peers and the magistrate?"

"I cannot say the opportunity has ever presented itself, so I am unsure how to answer that question honestly."

"Are you for or against pushing someone down a flight of stairs?" Her steps slowed further with this question.

Roderick pulled her to a stop. Her eyes widened as if she sensed she'd gone too far—said too much. "What in the bloody hell are you speaking of?"

Lucianna averted her stare, remaining silent.

"For the love of all that is holy, Lucianna, what is this all about?" Roderick demanded. He reached out and placed his fingers gently on the side of her face, bring her stare back to his. "Lying…murder…what are you trying to say?"

She lowered her eyes, staring at his neckcloth. "These are all things Abercorn is guilty of."

"Then why would you write scandalous articles about others—false stories, mind you—thus ruining the lives of other men, if you know for a fact Abercorn killed someone?" Why this was the first question that came to mind, Roderick didn't know.

"You know of the *Mayfair Confidential*?" she breathed, her face going pale. "What do you know of anything?"

Her voice grew shrill—not an ounce of denial to be found.

An unspoken truth between them. Lucianna was behind the article that ruined his life…and now there was no denying he knew the depths of her misdeeds. She would not be offering any apology, just as he had no forgiveness for her.

"That is not important at the moment." Roderick pulled her close, the tip of her nose nearly touching his chin. "Did Abercorn murder someone?"

Her arm tensed under his hold, and she pulled her chin away, breaking eye contract.

It was all the confirmation Roderick needed. He did not need her to say the words. Lucianna was scared; of the situation her father had placed her in, and the likelihood she would be forced to wed the Duke of Abercorn.

Roderick would not allow it. Never had he harmed a woman. Never would he. Neither did it please him to see Lady Lucianna in such a terrified state.

CHAPTER 11

LUCI SHOOK HER head from side to side. She shouldn't have spoken of the events surrounding Tilda's death, or her hatred of the duke. She, with the help of Edith and Ophelia, was determined to see that Abercorn paid for his misdeeds.

Montrose would not interfere with that plan.

For now, allowing him to think she was in agreement with their betrothal would keep Montrose occupied, and her father satisfied—and Luci out of Abercorn's reach.

"Tell me what Abercorn did."

The duke's steel blue eyes drew her, wrapped her in a blanket of security. No matter how false that comfort was or how much she longed to tell him everything, Luci knew it was not true. She did not know him beyond his skill at fencing and his scandalous activities at the opera all those months ago.

Trust was something earned.

The Duke of Montrose had secured nothing with her.

"If you are in danger, I will handle this." He moved closer still, as if she were in peril in the middle of the bookshop.

His scent of sandalwood and oak washed over her,

and Luci breathed him in—deeply. She wanted to believe he would help her. Needed to trust she wasn't alone in her task to bring Abercorn down and make him pay for the loss of Tilda.

But, first, Luci would need to confide in Montrose...Roderick.

Luci was certain even her dearest friends were hesitant to believe her account of Tilda's fall down the stairs and Abercorn's hand in the matter.

Her father was well aware of her hatred for Abercorn but still thought to barter her hand in marriage to gain some measure of control. The marquis thought so little of his firstborn.

"If you wed me, you will be forever indebted to my father." She leaned back, needing distance. Surprisingly, she cared that her father would have some kind of hold over Roderick. "I cannot ever ask that of anyone. He is my sire, but he is every inch the horrid man Abercorn is."

"You cannot expect me to walk away after learning all this, not now." Roderick set his hands on her shoulders and gently caressed away the tension. "If he hurt another person, I am now bound by duty, and my honor as a gentleman, to see he is punished for his crimes."

A lock of hair fell loose from its pins, and Roderick brushed it back behind her ear, never taking his eyes from her as a shiver ran down her back.

Why did this man seek to help her?

Roderick owed her nothing. He was a pawn in her father's game to bring more wealth and prestige to the Camden name, just as she was.

"There is much you do not know about me—and my friends."

"I have witnessed enough to know you are not one to shrink away from the truth."

He was right, though she wished some days that she could forget Tilda, forget her wedding, and forget the gruesome sight of her falling down the stairs. Most of all, Luci wished she could forget the vacant stare from her friend's sightless eyes after her soul had left her body. Every moment, Luci dwelled on what she could have done had she noted Abercorn's ruthless, abusive ways before that night. Yet, as Edith and Ophelia repeatedly told her, none of them had noticed anything off with Abercorn—and Tilda had certainly not shared any disreputable things about her betrothed.

"None of this is your responsibility, Your Grace." Lucianna moved away from him. If she stayed near him another second, she would come to truly believe he could fix everything, repair her, and make certain Abercorn was brought down. There was no one who could see that happen but her—with Edith and Ophelia's help.

"If you will not tell me, I will search out my own answers," he called as she reached the end of the aisle. "I assure you, I will not stop until I find out exactly what happened."

Luci halted, clutching her handbag before her. Staring at the floor, she knew she had two options: step from the row and into view of anyone else in the shop or turn back toward Roderick. If she returned to him, she could not trust herself to keep her own secrets.

There was so much more to her than what Abercorn had done.

Roderick knew, or at least suspected, her involvement with the *Mayfair Confidential*. How could he tie himself to a woman who'd written such a scathing article about his scandalous behavior? Did he think to exploit her once they were unequivocally tied together?

And, more importantly, how could Luci even think to confide in a man guilty of such unsavory activities as being seen at the opera with a woman he was not betrothed to?

Her chin lowered.

She was no better than he.

They both had secrets; however, sharing hers would put her—and her friends—in jeopardy.

And Luci knew Roderick's secret. In fact, she'd made certain all of London knew it.

Why did a tendril of remorse flicker inside her? Never had she experienced even a hint of doubt or guilt over exposing gentlemen of the *ton* for what they truly were: scoundrels.

"Lucianna?" he pleaded. The raw nature of his tone pulled at her. Begged her to return to his side.

But for what purpose?

To enter into a sham of a betrothal to appease her father and keep Abercorn at bay.

Turning, Luci notched her chin high. "Lord Abercorn killed my friend. He pushed her down the stairs on their wedding night. I am the only person who saw the entire tragic scene clearly. And no one—with the exception of my friends—believes my tale of the events."

There. She'd said it.

Now she only need wait for him to laugh, chuckle at her absurd accusation. Roderick would insult her in similar fashion as her father; call her a feather-brained, dim-witted, reckless chit. There would be no need to start the charade of a betrothal because even a man marred by scandal would not allow his name to be linked to a delusional female.

Not that it mattered a whit to her. Luci didn't trust Montrose. It was far more likely she spoke of Tilda's death to push him away, not draw him close in confidence.

However, he didn't turn away from her. Nor did he so much as avert his stare or take a moment to think through what she'd shared.

Instead, he closed the distance between them, taking her into his arms and pressing them tightly together.

"Roderick," she breathed. "What in heaven's name

are you doing?"

"The only thing I know how to do…keep you safe."

His head dipped, and their lips met.

Not like before. Lucianna was not calculating her next move, preparing for a counter-attack, nor planning her escape.

She did not want to flee.

In fact, she wanted nothing more than to be lost in Roderick's embrace, sheltered from the cruel world around her. Away from the reach of Abercorn, and no longer her father's pawn.

Here, with the duke's arms wrapped tightly about her, and his lips upon hers, she could put the need for vengeance behind her. She'd never forget Abercorn's misdeeds, but they did not consume her.

Roderick consumed her now.

His embrace. His scent. His delicious, crushing hold on her.

It didn't matter that she'd ruined him before all of society.

It didn't matter she'd been tarnished by her need to publicly ostracize Abercorn.

Nothing mattered but his arms around her.

Luci was helpless to pull away, to push him away, to fight the connection she sensed forming with this man.

They needed to discuss everything: her involvement with the *Mayfair Confidential*, her spying on Lord Abercorn with her friends, and her father's need to control everything he touched. But not now, not here.

Luci's handbag fell forgotten to the floor, and she clutched at Roderick's back, pressing her entire length closer to him.

"A-hem?" The male voice cut through the haze surrounding Lucianna, and she reluctantly pulled back from Roderick, fearing the shopkeeper had found them in a most delicate position.

Glancing over her shoulder, it was not Oliver, the shop owner, but Lord Torrington grinning back at her, Edith at his side, while Ophelia hid behind the couple to mask her embarrassed and reddened face.

RODERICK FAIRLY GROWLED at the interruption when their lips parted.

As quickly and surprisingly as it had started, Lucianna leapt away from him as she stared over his shoulder.

His rebuff died on his lips when he turned to see a gentleman so large he filled the aisle with his sheer size, a petite blonde woman tucked into his side, and an auburn-haired nymph doing her best to hide from view behind the couple.

Roderick eyed the lady doing her best not to be seen. He had, in fact, seen her before.

"You." He pointed to her. "You were the one from the ball. You blocked my path and almost allowed Lucianna to escape."

"Which would make us," the massive man interrupted, "the couple whose betrothal ball you attended without invite."

"Lord Torrington, Lady Edith, and Lady Ophelia," Lucianna stepped in front of Roderick. "May I introduce the Duke of Montrose?"

"You may, but that will not be enough to pacify our curiosity at his presence." Lady Edith placed her hands upon her hips and scrutinized him as if he were a costly, rare bolt of fabric. One she hesitated to stare at for too long and didn't dare touch.

"Yes, Luci, what is going on?" Lady Ophelia asked, her head bobbing around Torrington's shoulder.

"I—well—he—" She glanced between her friends, a rosy hue blooming on her cheeks.

"I arrived at the Camden townhouse to call on Lady Lucianna. Unfortunately, my manners escaped me, and I did not send word ahead, asking for an audience." Roderick felt, rather than saw, Lucianna's eyes on him. "And so, I offered to transport her and her maid here."

Though if he'd known he was going to face a battle squad, Roderick may have departed the Camden townhouse alone, his flowers still in hand.

"Why were you calling on Luci?" Lady Edith pried, her eyes narrowing on him once more.

"It is a long story." He waved away her question. "But since you have arrived, I will bid you all ado and leave Lady Lucianna in your company."

Lucianna's arm shot out and snagged his sleeve, mercifully dried from the earlier flower incident. She held him in place at her side. "Montrose will remain. This is not as much his issue as ours. It seems my father is entertaining an offer from Abercorn."

"For what?" Lady Ophelia finally pushed in front of Torrington.

"For my hand in marriage."

Both women gasped, and Torrington's shoulders stiffened. "That cannot be true."

"I assure you it is, my lord," Roderick replied.

"The Duke of Montrose has graciously also made an offer for my hand." She glanced up at him for confirmation. When he nodded, Lucianna continued. "And, so, I will accept his offer…for now. But we must find the evidence we need to see Abercorn taken in by the magistrate. Then this whole charade can be put behind us and Roder—the duke—can return to his own endeavors."

"What in the bloody hell is that supposed to mean?" Roderick didn't have any other endeavors, at least not the emotional kind—or any other he was willing to share with Lucianna and her companions.

And why did he care if Lady Lucianna and her friends thought he was involved with another woman?

Three sets of rounded stares turned toward him.

The shopkeeper appeared behind Lord Torrington and the women, holding his finger to his pursed mouth, silently demanding silence.

"Oh, I find I like this man very much," Torrington barked with laughter.

"He does seem quite useful, doesn't he?" Lady Edith nodded in agreement.

"But he is rather imposing with his dark features and cold, blue stare," Lady Ophelia said, inspecting him from head to toe. "However, Luci looked like a storybook heroine in his arms. I could hardly tell where her black locks ended and his onyx hair began."

Were they seriously discussing *him* in front of *him*?

"Imposing?" Roderick could not keep up with the group's banter. "At least I am not the size of a bison."

All eyes turned to Torrington, not a single person mistaking *whom* he spoke of.

"Ah, well, I have been called much worse by a far lovelier person, Montrose. You need to do better if you think to wound my delicate sensibilities." He tapped his finger against his cheek in thought. "I believe an ox was the comparison, though that is very much in line with a bison. Oh, and arrogant and demanding, of course. Am I forgetting anything, my love?"

The blonde, Lady Edith, giggled, lifting on her tiptoes to place a kiss on Torrington's cheek. "I have apologized many times for calling you arrogant. I still stand behind my oxen reference, though."

"My lords, my ladies," the shopkeeper called, bustling down the row toward them, his own silence forgotten as his heeled boots clacked against the hardwood floor. "Please take your rambunctious assembly elsewhere, you are disturbing my patrons who are here for serious pursuits of knowledge."

"My apologies, Oliver, we will keep our voices down and not disturb anyone." Lucianna smiled at the shopkeeper, flashing her most angelic, innocent grin, and the man practically wilted where he stood. "If we promise, may we stay?"

Oliver eyed the group, his stare lingering on Lord Torrington a moment longer than the others before he conceded with a nod. "But keep it down, and don't clutter the row if someone comes looking for a book. I have bills to pay, after all."

"Of course, sir."

"We wouldn't dream of costing you business."

And finally, from Torrington, "Thank you."

"This way," Ophelia waved toward the back of the shop and pushed through the group, making certain not to make eye contact with Roderick. "There is an alcove toward the back where we can speak privately."

Roderick raised his brow at Lucianna, who only shrugged but followed her friends.

He hung back to allow the women to proceed him into the rear of the shop. That it allowed him a moment to take in the sway of Lucianna's hips as she linked arms with Lady Ophelia and Lady Edith was only good timing. With their heads tilted together, the trio of women whispered as they hurried to the alcove.

What wasn't as advantageous, was Torrington matching his slow strides, his hands clasped behind his back.

"They are a formidable group, are they not?" Torrington said in a low tone.

Roderick eyed the women, uncertain what he'd gotten himself involved in and what type of trouble awaited them. "Are they always this…aggressive?"

"Only when they have their minds set on something," Torrington replied, nudging Roderick onward. "Not long ago, it was me. Thankfully, now, it is…well, you."

"Me?" Roderick halted as they exited the row of books, and Torrington was able to step next to him as opposed to walking a step behind.

"Oh, make no mistake, Lady Lucianna has her

sights set on you."

The woman was confusing. One moment, she was running from him, the next she'd bitten him, and then she agreed to wed him. "Only a moment ago, she made it very clear she would only agree to a feigned betrothal."

Torrington patted him on the shoulder and turned toward the women, who'd each taken a seat on the alcove bench as they spoke quietly. "Yes, Lady Lucianna is a bit hard to read; however, she trusts you. It took her weeks to even speak to me."

Trust was an unfamiliar concept to him, so much more so since his father's passing.

"I thought this was all about Abercorn and finding proof of what he did...not that I can even say with any certainty what Lady Lucianna is accusing him of." He watched as the women's conversation became more intense as their voices rose. Lucianna scowled, and Lady Edith slashed her hand through the air, silencing everyone.

Torrington shook his head. "I fear it took me some time to figure it all out, as well, and it wasn't until the woman I love"—he tilted his head in Lady Edith's direction—"disappeared, that I wised up and took this whole Abercorn thing seriously. I'm uncertain if he is guilty of what they are accusing him of; however, the man is guilty of something dastardly."

"Do you think—"

"Triston." Lady Edith waved them over, her brow furrowed.

"We best join them before they decide to burn Abercorn's townhouse to the ground. Or something far worse."

"What could be worse than setting a house ablaze?" Roderick asked, his shoulders stiffening at the thought.

"Judging from the scowl on Lady Lucianna's face and the abject terror on Lady Ophelia's, I think we are about to find out." Torrington leapt into action far quicker than a man his size should be capable of and called over his shoulder, "We should hurry, before their minds are set."

Roderick caught up to Torrington as they both entered the alcove, the space having appeared far larger until they joined the women.

"We have decided how to proceed." The set of Lucianna's chin and her straight posture was all confidence.

"*They* have decided," Lady Ophelia interjected before her cheeks blossomed with heat, almost matching the hue of her long locks.

"There is no other option." Lady Edith set her hand on Ophelia's and squeezed. "Our time has run out, and we cannot risk the marquis favoring Abercorn's pursuit of Luci over yours, Your Grace. The Duke of Abercorn is known for moving quickly to secure what he seeks. His courtship of Tilda only lasted a fortnight before they were properly betrothed, the banns read, and a wedding date set."

"I still believe there is—"

"There is no other way, Ophelia," Lucianna cut off the woman's protest.

"Then what has been decided?" Torrington asked, lowering himself to the bench between Lady Edith and Lucianna.

Roderick ignored the spike of possessiveness that coursed through him at Torrington's proximity to Lucianna.

"We will knock on his door and simply ask him if he pushed Tilda." All three women nodded at Lucianna's proclamation.

"You think it is as simple as all that?" Roderick knew little about the old duke, but outright asking him if he killed a woman did not appear to be the most sensible course of action if they sought to discover what truly happened. "Why would he tell the truth now?"

"Because we plan to expose him in our next *Mayfair Confidential* column if he refuses to give us answers about the night Tilda died."

All four nodded in agreement as if writing a risqué column used to ruin men of the *ton* was not outlandish in any way, but completely commonplace among the group.

CHAPTER 12

LUCI STARED OUT the window as Montrose's coach turned into her drive and halted before her door.

The journey home had been tense, filled to brimming with awkward silences and averted eyes. Roderick, along with Lord Torrington, had venomously discouraged the women from confronting Lord Abercorn, especially in his own home.

A footman hurried to assist Charlotte down, but Luci waved him off when he offered her his hand.

She needed to speak with Roderick—privately.

Without her maid present, without the fear of an eavesdropping shop owner or her friends close to ask questions she didn't want to answer. In fact, it was Roderick who *owed* her answers.

And she would have them, even if she were forced to remain in his coach all night.

The thought sent a tingle through her as she touched her lips, no longer swollen from their kiss, yet she could still imagine the heat of his mouth against hers. Maybe all night with the intense man sitting across from her was not such a discouraging notion.

Luci shook the thought from her mind. Ever since he'd appeared at her door, flowers in hand, she sensed she'd judged him far too harshly and made assumptions inaccurately. It was a trait she despised in others, and she did not take kindly to it in herself.

"Your servant is waiting, my lady." Roderick shifted on the seat across from her. "There is little doubt the marquis awaits you across the threshold, as well, just out of sight."

"My father awaits no one, Your Grace." Luci reclined on the bench, setting her hands lightly in her lap. She was not going anywhere. "If he were home and had any need of me, he would simply drag me from this carriage."

She glanced toward the open door, and Roderick followed suit.

"See, the marquis is likely not in residence, or is ensconced in his study."

"I suppose you are correct," he conceded. "Your father is a formidable man. I think you take after him in that regard."

"That is highly insulting." Luci retorted. Never did she want to be her father—nor her mother, for that matter, but especially not her father. "The marquis is ruthless in business and merciless with his kin. He knows not the meaning of empathy or compassion. I would hope that is not the way you see me."

Despite all her agitated bluster, he only gave her a toothy grin and chuckled. The odd smile should have added a comical air to his appearance, but it only confirmed that there was a part of him Luci was unaware of.

But if she found out, what would that mean for her determination to see all unsavory men exposed and scandalized?

"While I know my status as an honorable lord has been called into question recently, I have not fallen so far as to think it acceptable or appropriate to insinuate that a woman is lacking in any way. I assure you of that, my lady." He sobered quickly at her narrowed glare and held up his hands, warding her off. "By formidable, I only meant undaunted by circumstance."

Her chest tightened at his words. That could only be taken as a compliment.

"May I ask you a question?" He sat forward, her answer seeming to hold immense weight. When she nodded, he continued. "Would it be improper to ask you to accompany me on a stroll down the lane? I find myself thinking you have many questions you wish to ask, and I cannot think to remain in this heated carriage overlong. I believe a spot of fresh air would do us both a lot of good."

Some time outside, still a private walk, but without the overwhelming urge to place her lips against his once more did sound wise.

She'd never been one to wilt into the arms of a man—especially one with a sordid past.

Admittedly, a disreputable past she had exposed…and was by the minute seeming unlikely for the man she'd come to know during their excursion to the bookshop. But how could she have misjudged him? He was at the opera with a woman who was not his betrothed. What explanation could there be for his action other than a scandalous one? Still, she had the feeling she'd been wrong about him.

"I think I would enjoy a stroll, Your Grace." *Roderick*, she thought to herself. Forever in her mind he would be Roderick. Not Your Grace, and certainly not the Duke of Montrose. "You are correct in assuming I have many things I'd like to discuss with you."

And many apologies to offer, though a mere spoken act of contrition could never repair the damage she'd done by posting the article in the *Gazette*. She'd still been grieving the loss of Tilda, wrecked with guilt over her passing. Bloody hell, she would forever be plagued by remorse at her dear friend's death; however, she could still attempt to make amends with Roderick.

Though he had every right to rebuff her.

He leapt from the carriage and held his hand out to

assist her down. "Shall we?"

"We shall." Luci couldn't stop from smiling at his gallant behavior.

She nodded to the footman when Roderick tucked her hand into the crook of his arm and led her back down the drive to the street beyond. There were no horses or carriages stirring up dust. No gardeners lingered in the yards of neighboring townhouses. It was as if they hadn't left the privacy of the Montrose carriage at all—until Luci noticed her maid, Charlotte, trailing at a discreet distance.

All thoughts of dragging Roderick behind the nearest shrub and imploring him to kiss her fled as they settled into a slow, steady walk. Besides her friends, Luci had never experienced such easy companionship. She watched over her younger siblings, but they were just that, brothers and sisters, not confidantes. She was their guiding light, and she struggled every day to search deep within to keep that light shining.

She had to be strong in every sense, or she feared turning into her mother; a woman so battered and beaten by years of neglect and harsh words she'd given up the fight. It was a pity Lady Camden, Eloise Constantine, once the daring, mysterious debutante had lost every ounce of fight within her.

That was not to be Luci's fate.

Her shoulders stiffened with resolve.

Never would she allow a man, any man, to bring her to such a low point. No matter if it were her father, a suitor, or the gentleman she pledged to serve for all her days.

But here, with Roderick, she could just be. Walk at her own pace. Remain silent if she so desired. There was no need for her to take control, lead the way, or carve a path.

She almost let slip from her mind the many nagging questions she had for him, in favor of simply enjoying this rare moment of ease. The late afternoon breeze pulled at her pinned hair, desperate to free it. The sun heated her skin, raining comforting kisses of warmth along her neck. A matching set of collared doves chirped and cooed from a tall tree as they strolled past. Roderick's hold on her arm tightened, tugging her closer to his side as if the breeze would blow her out of his reach, or the sun would scorch her delicate skin, or the birds would draw her attention too far from him.

In that brief moment, Luci was wanted. Cherished. Adored. She was worth more than her role as her father's bartering chip. Her sibling's protector. Her mother's champion. And Tilda's voice from beyond.

She was Roderick's prize. He was her protector. He would champion for her future. And he would supply voice when hers could not long speak loud enough to be heard.

Yet, he was still, in almost every way, a stranger.

It was nearly impossible to grasp that a man could stumble into her life and usurp her every thought. Make her long for things she hadn't wanted since her innocence had been shattered.

Since departing the coach, Luci had yet to dwell on their coming visit to Abercorn's townhouse. The overwhelming pressure to prove the man's guilt before all of society did not seem as all-consuming as a few hours before. No longer did she worry about Abercorn being the victor for her hand. Roderick, her defender, would never allow it.

He'd said as much, and she believed him with every ounce of her being.

She sighed.

"Do you wish to return home, my lady?" he asked, tentatively.

"Surprisingly, there is no other place I'd rather be than right here, right now." She stared ahead, scared to see his reaction to her forthright comment. Perhaps, it was he who wished to return her and be on his way. "Unless you have other matters to attend to?"

She risked a glance up at him from under lowered lashes. In the past, it would have been seen as coquettish, a feigned timid manner filled with doubt and reservations; but in this moment, Luci was terrified he did want to return her to her father's townhouse and escape the trouble she'd dragged him into.

"I have not another place to be today. Or any day, for that matter, Lucianna." He stared straight ahead, a pleasant smile overtaking his intense nature. "I think we have much to discuss, and the time is now before things progress further."

Luci was helpless to concentrate on anything after he'd said her name—Lucianna. The name had always signified the striking, rare, courageous woman she felt like on the inside. An outward sign to others that she was not a typical, pliable, demure maiden but something far more.

A woman destined to be remembered.

For her fierce love. For her loyal nature. For her invincible pride.

Not as a woman bought and sold at the discretion of any man.

Because of those exact qualities, she needs must make amends for the wrongs she suspected she'd done to Roderick. "What were you doing at the opera that night?"

His shoulders tensed, and Luci feared she had been right all along about him, that the disparaging accusations she'd levied against him in the *Gazette* were not misrepresented or false, but true.

"I was there seeking information." He kept his focus straight ahead as a coach turned onto the street and ambled by. "I was not there to be with another woman, nor did I ever seek to hurt Lady Daphne or tarnish her reputation."

"What type of information can be found at the opera?" She'd witnessed men, like her father, seeking out the willing, nimble bodies of ladybirds. She'd once stumbled upon a couple in an intimately scandalous embrace off a well-lit path at Covent Gardens. She was not fool enough to think that the sirens littering the playhouses and outdoor parks did not tempt gentlemen.

He sighed, and she sensed that he'd made an important decision, one he'd been debating since they started their walk.

Suddenly, the breeze blew no more, the birds were eerily silent, and a cloud passed over the sun, casting a large shadow over them.

"I was there to meet the widow of my father's best friend." He halted and turned toward her. "I was not there to betray Lady Daphne. Quite the opposite, actually."

"One might think it suspicious that a man would believe being seen in a very public setting with another woman on his arm would not harm the woman he is purported to love."

Roderick rubbed his jaw and pushed his hand through his hair. "I was thinking of none of that, only securing the information I needed to…" His words trailed off, and he dropped Luci's arm, pacing a few steps down the walk and pivoting to return and face her. "Lucianna, it was not my intention to bring Lady Daphne into the muddled mess of my life. Neither did I plan to levy that weight upon you. My family, everything my ancestors worked so hard for, was taken…and I have charged myself with getting it back."

Luci understood him a bit more in that moment. Roderick was searching for something, much like she was searching. "While that is very kind of you, it is my decision, as your betrothed, to decide what burdens I share with you and which ones I leave on your shoulders. I have little doubt we can assist one another."

He looked away, focusing on a house farther down the lane, and Luci feared it would be the end of their discussion. He would share no more and would refuse her help.

"I need to be honest with you. When I decided to offer for your hand, it was done out of a sense of vengeance, a need to hurt you—to take away your opportunity at a match of your choosing—much like your post in the *Mayfair Confidential* did to me."

He kept his eyes averted, but Luci was helpless to look away from the pain etched across his face.

She should feel an immense betrayal at his confession, laced with anger and outright indignation at his deceptive plans; however, none of these filled her.

"I know," she admitted. She'd known from the time she walked into his study with her father, though she'd tried to deny it, even to herself. "But what do you seek to gain from our marriage now?" Luci had little doubt Roderick would one day be her husband, the man who would protect her for the rest of her days.

And she longed to do the same for him.

His breath left him in a loud whoosh. "I wish I knew, Lucianna. Unfortunately, I've lived my life one day at a time since my father passed away, never planning past tomorrow because, well, the future is too bloody unpredictable. I thought I had things figured out that night at the opera, or at least, the means to sort through everything. But just as quickly, it was all stripped away."

"By my hand." Luci glanced down at the ground, ashamed of her part in ending his previous betrothal. "I am sorry you lost Lady Daphne."

He placed his hand beneath her chin and lifted her face, their eyes meeting. "While I cared for Lady Daphne—she is a sweet girl, everything that most lords require in a wife—we had nothing but a friendly fondness for one another. Love was not a part of our association, or at least, it hadn't matured to that point before our match was called off."

Roderick caressed her cheek, and Luci's eyes drifted closed, the warmth of the sun returning, his touch seemingly pushing the clouds away. It should seem scandalous to be so connected to this man, all while he spoke of his past fondness for another woman.

"In all our time together, I never felt for Lady Daphne what I've come to feel for you in the past several days," he confided. He placed a delicate kiss on her forehead before his hands fell away. "A coach is coming."

The words escaped him on a sigh.

Roderick had wanted to say more—and Luci was desperate to hear it.

Luci opened her eyes slowly, knowing once she did, whatever had been blossoming between them would need be stowed away for another time, another moment of privacy.

If and when it happened again, Luci would be ready.

Glancing down the street, she noted the Camden crest on the approaching carriage. From the quick manner in which Roderick put a respectable distance between them, he'd also recognized the coach and prepared for who would be within.

Luci turned toward the carriage and waved. There was no reason to hide—she and Roderick were doing nothing wrong. Charlotte followed them at a discreet distance, and it had been her father who'd suggested the duke accompany her for the afternoon. If anything, her father should be proud of her for coming to accept his dictates without further argument.

The conveyance slowed as it came abreast of them as they turned to return to the Camden townhouse.

"Good day, Father," Luci called with a smile when the marquis glared out the open window. "Beautiful day, is it not?"

Her father's scowl was all Luci needed to see to enforce that her jovial mood only irritated the man.

"Montrose," her father greeted Roderick curtly. "I thought you would have departed hours ago."

Why did he care if Roderick and she became better

acquainted? After all, if things continued down the path her father had set, they would be formally announcing their betrothal before long.

Luci had to applaud Roderick on his skill at playacting, as he grinned at her father, ignoring his dour stare. "We returned not long ago but, as Lady Lucianna commented, the day is too marvelous to spend trapped indoors. We decided on a stroll down the lane. You are welcome to join us for the return walk, my lord."

Luci nearly burst with laughter as her father recoiled in shock at the offer.

"Certainly not," the marquis said, leaning back into his coach. "Home, Rogers."

Without another glance, her father's driver put the horses back into motion, and soon disappeared into the Camden drive, several houses down the lane.

"Your father,"—Roderick pulled her close once more and set a slow pace—"he is a peculiar man."

"Is that another trait you will proclaim I inherited from him?" Luci let out the deep laugh she'd been holding inside. It didn't matter that her father thought he was using her as a pawn. She would not concern herself with worries over inciting her father's anger with her joyous mood.

No, for the next several minutes, Luci was determined to bask in the sun with the cool breeze on her face and Roderick by her side.

Tomorrow, she would fret once again about Abercorn and proving his guilt. When she sat down to her family supper table that evening, she would think over the truths Roderick had shared with her, and dwell on the secrets he still kept. As she prepared for bed that night, she would allow her own culpability in Tilda's death to wash over her and extinguish her spark of happiness. After Roderick's carriage had pulled away, Luci would reenter her family home to guide her siblings, protect her mother, and distract her father from his unavoidable fury.

But this moment, and the next fifty or so paces, belonged to her.

She lifted her chin to look at Roderick at her side and smiled—the most sincere grin she could remember since she'd watched her future shatter into a million tiny pieces as Tilda tumbled down those stairs.

"Your Grace," she sighed. "Thank you."

His brow furrowed in question, but he returned her smile. "What for?"

"For reminding me that it is acceptable to carve a moment out of life to stop—or stroll—and appreciate the warm sun, the call of the birds, and the afternoon breeze in my hair."

Silently, she added, *And the kiss of a most dashing man.*

CHAPTER 13

"STOP FIDGETING, OPHELIA," Luci scolded as they arrived at the Abercorn townhouse stoop. "We have yet to even knock on his door. He will see through our ruse if you keep that up."

The girl was a nervous Nellie if she'd ever seen one, afraid of her own shadow, and prone to picking at the stitching of her gowns. Despite all that, Ophelia was Luci's dearest friend since Tilda's passing, and she loathed putting her in this predicament; however, they all needed to confront Abercorn.

Edith patted Ophelia's shoulder. "Everything will be all right, do not worry."

"There is no need to coddle her," Luci hissed. "If the pair of you would have agreed to expose Abercorn in the *Gazette* months ago, none of us would be here right now."

"You cannot possibly know that," Edith snipped.

"Oh, I most certainly do know that."

A whistle sounded behind them, letting Luci know that Roderick and Lord Torrington were in place, keeping a close eye on the trio from the shadows of Torrington's father's townhouse, directly neighboring the duke's property.

It reassured her to know Roderick was close and

would allow nothing to happen to her. He didn't have to say it. After their time together the day before, Luci was confident Roderick had more in common with Lord Torrington than her father. He was not guilty of what she'd accused him of—escorting his mistress to the opera while betrothed to another. She would do what she could to polish his tarnished reputation. But right now, she had to keep her focus on Abercorn.

"Is this the best place to speak with him?" Ophelia tugged at her gown. "We saw what happened the last time we were in his home."

"There is no other place the man will be as complacent—feel as secure—as in his own surroundings." Edith and Luci had heavily debated this part of the plan, deciding that approaching the duke in a crowded ballroom or at the opera would not lead him to speak freely. "Besides, we have all agreed to remain downstairs."

Luci was confident in their decision to confront Abercorn, even though Ophelia appeared so nervous she'd likely fall over at the littlest breath of trouble.

"Are we ready?" Edith asked, plastering a smile on her face, ever the fearless one since she'd fallen in love with Torrington.

"As ready as we will ever be." Ophelia fanned her reddening cheeks.

"Remember"—Luci eyed both of her friends—"we are here to speak with Abercorn about his generous offer of marriage. This is a purely social visit with you both serving as my chaperones. Everything is above reproach."

"Until we get our feet in the door," Edith whispered.

"Exactly." Lucianna grinned.

Their plan was as solid as it could be. After they had entered Abercorn's townhouse and were led to a receiving salon, the women would make certain the drapes were pulled back, allowing Roderick and

Torrington a clear view to keep watch over the trio.

If anything went awry, they would kick in Abercorn's front door, if necessary, to reach the women.

Luci knocked on the door, and footsteps were instantly heard from within.

An elderly butler pulled the door wide, his eyes scrutinizing the trio.

"Lady Lucianna Constantine, accompanied by Lady Edith Pelton and Lady Ophelia Fletcher, here to see Lord Abercorn." Luci handed the butler her calling card, determined that they not be turned away. "Is the duke receiving visitors?"

At the butler's continued silence, Luci worried Abercorn was not in residence at all and their carefully crafted plan would be thwarted by their own mistake.

The servant finally stepped back, holding the door for them to enter.

Edith and Ophelia both sighed with relief.

Luci glanced over her shoulder as the two women entered the Abercorn townhouse. Roderick gave her a reassuring nod.

Their idea may very well be harebrained and without chance of success, but at least Roderick had enough faith in her to allow her the opportunity to lure the truth from Abercorn. There was no doubt Roderick had his own secrets. She'd be a fool not to notice the way his shoulders appeared to hold the weight of a thousand pounds or the hard lines around his eyes, a product of sorrow and loss. Or the way he analyzed everyone as if outlining every way they could injure him if he allowed them close.

Luci shuddered to think she'd caused some of that burden with her piece in the *Gazette*.

"My lady?" the butler asked when she remained on the stoop. "This way, please."

Putting Roderick from her mind, Luci entered the foyer, surprised by the many candles lighting the area. It was certainly a waste of coins to burn this amount of wax on a daily basis.

The servant shuffled, his feet never actually leaving the floor as he walked across the foyer and opened the room to a similarly lit salon. Upon entering, Luci was pleased to see the drapes were open, and a clear view of Lord Torrington's father's townhouse was in sight.

"I will let Lord Abercorn know of your presence. His Grace will be with you momentarily." He bowed stiffly as the women glanced about the room. "I will ring for tea. Do have a seat."

He pulled the door closed on well-oiled hinges, leaving Luci to inspect the room as Edith hurried to the window and waved in Torrington's and Roderick's direction.

The salon was decorated in bold shades of yellow and blue, complete with striped drapes, polka dot pillows, and matching plaid lounge and stuffed chairs. The obnoxious sight had Luci's head swirling at the odd pattern contrast and color combination. Upon closer inspection, the pieces in the room, including the tables, lamps, and wing-backed chairs close to the hearth appeared fairly dated. Even the pillow on the lounge was frayed at the edges.

This room had been appointed long ago, likely before Abercorn was out of the schoolroom.

Edith and Ophelia selected a low-slung sofa in sight of the large, arched window, remaining visible to the men outside, while Luci continued to stand. She was unsure why, but something told her standing was the best way to face the opposition.

And Abercorn was most certainly their opponent.

Luci would not allow herself to be fooled into a false sense of security based on her friends being near and Roderick being just outside the window. That was exactly what had happened to Tilda. The duke had presented himself as an honorable, kind, and worthy lord when he held none of those traits.

If she were utterly honest, the man might have duped any of them into marriage.

A shiver went down her spine to think it could have been her lying at the bottom of those stairs—or Ophelia, who would have been even less likely to defend herself than Tilda.

No, Abercorn would not remain free to harm another woman, especially Luci.

She would take Lord Torrington's suggestion and run off to Gretna Green before she'd allow her name to be forever linked to Abercorn. Though wasn't it already? She'd caused the scene at the duke's country manor, demanding the magistrate investigate Tilda's fall and pointing the finger at her friend's new husband.

Luci crossed her arms in defiance. She would sound the alarm again without a second thought—only this time, she would protest louder...and longer. Until Abercorn was removed from polite society and never given another opportunity to harm someone.

Tears stung her eyes.

Poor Tilda.

Again, they should have noted something not quite right about her bridegroom.

But Luci hadn't...and her friend had suffered the consequences.

"Lady Lucianna, my dear. What a charming surprise."

She pivoted in time to see Abercorn enter the room and close the door behind himself.

"And Ladies Edith and Ophelia?" He paused, his stare widening on the women sitting close to the window. "I must say, this is *very* unexpected—but in a good way, nonetheless."

"Your Grace," Luci said, dipping into a curtsey. "My father spoke of your betrothal offer, and I thought it time I pay you a social visit."

Both Edith and Ophelia sprang to their feet and dipped low in greeting. Luci couldn't help but notice the duke's eyes stray to Edith's bosom as she curtseyed.

"No matter the reason." He waved his hand, dismissing her words. "It is a pleasure to have you all in my home. I know there is much in our past; however, I am certain it can all be discussed with time—and a measure of patience. Please, do have a seat."

Edith and Ophelia looked to Luci with hesitation, but she nodded, and the pair regained their seats by the window. She noted Edith glance toward Torrington with a weak smile. Blessedly, Abercorn seemed preoccupied and didn't appear to notice Edith's fascination with the landscape beyond the windowpane.

Luci followed suit and sat upon the lounge, facing her friends and hoping the duke would take the seat across from her. That would put his back to the window and allow her friends' attention to go unnoticed.

She crossed her feet at the ankles and arranged her skirts, biding some time before it became necessary to speak. The cushion crackled with disuse beneath her when she shifted to tuck her feet under the lounge.

"Your home…" Luci paused, debating how to continue. She was loath to insult Abercorn before he'd even begun speaking. "It is very antiquated."

Outdated and in need of renovation was what she'd been thinking; however, antiquated was the best she could do.

"Yes, well," Abercorn sighed. "My mother renovated this townhouse, selecting every piece from the wall sconces to the rugs, even hand-stitching the pillows in this room, and I am hesitant to undo all her hard work." He glanced around the room, obviously attached to the yellow and royal blue trimmings with many years of fond memories. Finally, he returned to the present. "Of course, once I take a wife, she will have control over the entire household, and an unlimited purse to make any changes she deems necessary to make this her home."

Abercorn sat a bit straighter in his chair as if

expecting her to applaud his generosity and kind nature. His lips pulled back in a wide grin, showing off his stained teeth, yellowed almost to match the furniture his mother had selected decades before. Could she have guessed what the man would be reduced to in his old age?

"It would please me greatly if you'd accept my courtship, Lady Lucianna—or may I call you Lucianna? Mayhap Luci, as Tilda was fond of calling you?" The man appeared a hound waiting for a well-deserved treat.

A pain stabbed deep at her middle, as if the man had used his words to stake her. The duke did not deserve to utter Tilda's name—not today and not ever.

Abercorn would receive no reward from her. "Lady Lucianna will do fine."

"Very well, but you have leave to call me Francis." Reclining in his seat, the duke glanced at the door. "My apologies for my staff's inadequacies. I thought tea would have been delivered long before now. You all must be parched." He stood, pulling the servants' bell cord several times. "Another item my wife will be charged with rectifying."

"Tea is not necessary, Your Grace," Ophelia chimed in from her seat by the window.

"Of course, tea is necessary, far more than that, it is expected." He tugged at the cord several more times before returning to his seat, avoiding her wrinkled nose and pinched lips. "It will not be long now."

The charade was wearing thin on Luci, and the tension was growing thick—it seemed only Abercorn hadn't noticed the unease in the room.

"Lord Abercorn, may I speak freely?"

He broke eye contact as he smoothed his necktie with a chuckle. "Lady Lucianna, England has known several female monarchs. No matter what the colonists spout, our country is a progressive state. Women have the right to speak of what they wish, just as men, especially with a man who—with luck—will one day be your husband."

Edith burst into laughter, drawing Abercorn's attention as if he'd been so absorbed with Luci he'd failed to remember they were not alone.

At Luci's scowl, Edith clamped her mouth shut and stared at her lap, but her blonde curls bobbed with silent mirth.

"Thank you, Your Grace," Luci said with a grin, luring the duke's attention back to her. "It is only I wonder why you seek to wed *me*."

His expression grew pensive as if even he hadn't thought about why he desired to court his dead wife's best friend. Rubbing the back of his neck, he glanced at the door once more, but there would be no reprieve from her question.

The door remained solidly shut.

And her question hung openly between them.

"You see, while Tilda and I were very close, we are also exceedingly different people." Luci couldn't help but acknowledge the many dissimilarities between them. Tilda was sweet, caring, and compassionate—a true English rose of pure innocence. In contrast, Lucianna was, admittedly, jaded, cynical, and not the least bit demure. Not to mention, Luci's insistence that *he* had pushed his new wife to her death. But all Luci could verbalize was, "She was petite with hair of the softest brown and eyes that matched, while I…well, we can all see I am nothing like Tilda with my midnight locks and moss-green eyes."

It was almost insulting to both women to reduce their differences to the purely physical—meaningless, skin-deep, external attributes.

The duke cleared his throat, the direction of the conversation causing a gleam of perspiration to break out across his forehead. "It is, well, that is a rather difficult question to answer; however, I will endeavor to do my best." His hand twitched, and he reached out to smooth the fringe on the side of his seat.

"It is not a difficult question at all, Your Grace." She bit the inside of her cheek to hold back further comment.

"You are quite stunning in a dark, exotic way. Also, well-connected with the grace and poise I seek in my future wife and duchess," Abercorn declared with a satisfied grin, as if comparing her to a bird trapped in a gilded cage was a future any women would seek out. "You are witty, intelligent, and possess a strong will I admire greatly. We would make a fine match—the marriage-minded mothers will be envious of your ability to catch a duke, as it were."

Luci swallowed back a smart retort. The man certainly was daft if he thought she would pay any mind to his flowery words.

A fine match, indeed.

She forced an innocent smile, relishing the spark of unease that lit his face.

CHAPTER 14

RODERICK LEANED AGAINST the three-story townhouse at his back and crossed his arms, keeping his stare on Lucianna through the window. Lady Edith and Lady Ophelia sat close to the arched panes, hardly taking their focus off Roderick and Torrington.

The sun was high overhead, the eaves from Torrington's family home shielding them from the harsh heat of noonday. He took his eyes off Lucianna perched on the lounge in Abercorn's home for a brief moment to take in the bright blue sky above. Since their morning sparring match at Bentley's, not a single rain cloud had dared cross the London landscape—this fact had not escaped his notice.

"We never should have agreed to allow them anywhere near Abercorn without us present." Torrington sighed heavily, pacing in the shadows of his father's townhouse. "Anything could happen before we are able to get to them."

While nervous, Roderick was confident in Lucianna's ability to care for herself. The blasted woman had bested him with a foil and survived all these years under the control of Camden. She was no demure, fragile creature.

However, Torrington's lovesick, puppy dog

demeanor, fretting over Lady Edith's decision to accompany Lucianna and Lady Ophelia into the duke's townhouse was fast growing cumbersome and annoying.

"If it would make you feel better, you are welcome to press your nose to the windowpane, mayhap you will even hear a bit of the conversation," Roderick jested. "Oh, and you can look upon Lady Edith with your smitten stares of affection."

He half expected the man to round on him and throw a fist at his face, but instead, he chuckled, breaking the tension that had stiffened his shoulders. "Is it so apparent?"

"Is what so apparent?"

"That I can hardly take my eyes off her for a moment."

"Only to anyone blessed with sight." Roderick wanted to reach out and halt the man's pacing, but instead, he turned back toward the window.

"This is not a normal occurrence for me, I assure you," Torrington gushed, turning once more. His feet trampled the vegetation as he continued his stalking. "It took nearly losing the bloody woman for me to realize I'd fallen unequivocally in love with her."

"So you mentioned." Roderick casually pushed away from the wall, attempting to hide his interest in the direction of their conversation. "What happened?"

The question halted Torrington mid-stride. "Lady Lucianna did not tell you?"

He shook his head.

"You did not read of it in the *Gazette*?" Torrington's brow rose in question.

"If I had, I now know not to believe a word of it," Roderick said with a shrug. "Likely, Lady Lucianna did not see it as her place to share."

Roderick was loath to admit that, in fact, they'd had scarce moments alone to discuss anything more serious than the matters transpiring between them.

"My father's wife kidnapped Edith and absconded with her to her family's Southend home, determined to toss us both over the cliffs to our deaths."

He waited for Torrington to laugh at his joke, but his expression remained serious.

"Your mother did—"

"Not my mother," he corrected. "My father's third wife."

"Why in heaven's name would anyone wish to harm Lady Edith?" Roderick inquired, suddenly feeling the need to pace himself.

"She thought Edith and I had spied her with her lover," Torrington turned his attention back to the window—and Lady Edith's copper stare—and Roderick feared the man would fall silent, but he continued. "But, with Lady Lucianna's and Lady Ophelia's assistance, I rescued her…and then Lady Lucianna rescued all of us from scandal with her story about a carriage accident and my gallant appearance to save them from a night stranded along a deserted country road."

"What happened to your stepmother?"

"Oh, she has since retired to the country and will never cause Edith harm again."

"I would suspect her lover has noticed her disappearance," Roderick prodded.

When Torrington didn't immediately answer, Roderick turned toward him, fearful he'd insulted or angered the man, but Torrington only nodded to the window. "It doesn't appear as if Lord Abercorn is pining away for his lost lover."

"Abercorn?" Roderick didn't even attempt to suppress his shock. "Your stepmother's lover was Abercorn?"

"Afraid so," Torrington nodded in confirmation. "And to make matters even more scandalous, my stepmother, Esmee, was once *my* betrothed…until she took a liking to my father's title and decided not to wed me and wait to become a marchioness instead."

"And I thought society eyed me with concern," Roderick mused. "If I keep you by my side, I never have to fear they are staring at me."

Their chuckles were cut short by a loud crash and two female screams.

"Bloody hell!" Torrington shot into action, not pausing a single second to see if they could deduce what had caused the commotion. He was already running toward Abercorn's front door—with Roderick close behind.

Within a few yards, Roderick passed Torrington, his feet pounding down Abercorn's cobbled drive. It didn't matter who saw him thundering toward Abercorn's door.

They'd taken their focus off the women for only the blink of an eye.

And something had gone seriously wrong.

Roderick didn't bother to knock or await the butler's answer. He gasped the door latch and pushed. Thankfully, the door was unlocked, or Abercorn would have returned to the foyer to see a splintered, used piece of wood that could no longer be confused as a door.

The entrance was dripping with candles, and the sconces were lit along the three halls Roderick glanced down. It was a bit odd for only an afternoon social call. Even the chandelier above held the maximum candles, glowing brightly and gleaming off the polished floor.

"What are you waiting for?" Torrington shouted, knocking Roderick on the shoulder when he continued into the foyer and turned left toward the salon the women had been shown to. "They are this way."

Bloody hell, but Roderick knew which direction Lucianna was in. Even if he hadn't been watching from outside, he was drawn to her. Her very essence called to him. She was a siren—his very own siren.

Torrington flung one door open, but the room was empty.

Roderick hurried past the man and opened the next

door with a bit less force.

"Lucianna?" Roderick stepped into the room, taking in the sight surrounding him.

Lucianna still sat on the lounge, but Lady Edith stood near the window, her hands clutching at her throat. Lady Ophelia trembled, eyes wide as she fanned her face, the color having drained from it. But he didn't spy Lord Abercorn as his narrowed stare surveyed the room—though it was possible the offensive color scheme played tricks on his eyesight.

"What is going on?" Abercorn called gruffly, his head popping up from behind the lounge Lucianna sat upon. "Why, I never—"

"I can ask you the same thing, Lord Abercorn," Roderick thundered, the tone so deep and menacing it shook the portraits on the walls. "What is the meaning of this?"

Lady Edith stepped hesitantly around Abercorn as he struggled to push himself to his feet, and she hurried to Torrington's side. They began to whisper between one another, but Roderick couldn't take his attention off Abercorn. The man was dangerous, Roderick was certain of it.

He was at Lady Lucianna's side within the blink of an eye, and he took her hand, pulling her to her feet and dragging her into his arms. "Is everything as it should be? I was so worried."

"I am well, Roderick, I promise."

He could barely hear her words over the thrashing of his pulse, but he pulled her tighter to him, his embrace only softening when she pulled away to stare over his shoulder.

Lady Ophelia gasped and collapsed onto the bench near the window, and the color drained from Lucianna's face, leaving her looking green.

Thundering footsteps sounded from the hall, entering the room behind him.

"Lucianna, girl," the Marquis of Camden's voice

boomed into the room. "What is the meaning of all this?"

"Father, I—"

"Your daughter," Abercorn said, back on his feet and moving closer to where Roderick continued to hold Lucianna, though not as closely as he'd like. "Arrived a few moments ago, her two friends in tow"—Abercorn paused for a moment, nodding to both Lady Edith and Lady Ophelia—"to accept my proposal. She said she is honored to become the Duchess of Abercorn. I fear I was so overjoyed, I tripped over a settee in celebration."

"What?" Lady Ophelia exclaimed, jumping from her seat on the bench.

"That is preposterous," Lady Edith shouted, setting her hands on her hips.

"That is not at all what transpired," Luci said, pulling away from Roderick to stare at her father, her head shaking back and forth. "I would not accept Lord Abercorn's offer of marriage."

"Then what is happening here?" Another woman, far more matronly than Lucianna and her friends, cut in. The adornment on her hat bobbed precociously as she pushed her way into the room and rushed over to Lord Abercorn. "Are you hurt, Frannie?"

Roderick looked to Lucianna and then Torrington, but no one seemed to know what in the blazes was going on.

"Oh, do not fret over me, Sissy," Abercorn pushed the woman's hands away. "I am only filled with excitement and was not careful enough. Can you believe Lady Lucianna has agreed to be my wife?"

Abercorn and the elderly woman shared a quick embrace before *Sissy* placed a quick kiss on the duke's cheek and receded back toward the door—where Camden still stood, silently watching the room.

"There is a mistake. This is a mistake. Abercorn is addlebrained," Lucianna said, moving toward her father. "I was not here to accept Abercorn's proposal."

"She is only embarrassed to be caught in my home by so many." Abercorn chuckled. "She is such a delicate lady; however, there is no need to keep hidden what we have any longer, Luci."

Roderick wanted to pull Lucianna back to his side and punch Abercorn in the jaw at the same time. Unfortunately, only one was possible.

"I assure you, Lord Camden,"—Roderick grasped Lucianna's arm, but he didn't need to tug to have her return to his side—"Lady Lucianna and her friends were not here to accept any form of courtship or betrothal from Abercorn."

Camden's shoulders stiffened, and his narrowed stare landed solidly on Roderick as if he were the unsuitable, unwelcome occupant of the room.

"Lucianna," the marquis seethed, never taking his glare off Roderick. "What is the meaning of this? I did not instruct you to call on Lord Abercorn, nor did I allow you to spend more time with Montrose. Did you seek to thwart my plans, much like you do in our home?"

He advanced on his daughter, but Roderick took a step also, pushing Lucianna behind him as he held up his hand. "Lord Camden, allow us to sit down and discuss this—mayhap without so many prying eyes?"

"I do not see what we would need to discuss," Abercorn blustered, looking between Camden and Lucianna, the first hint of doubt crossing his face. "Lady Lucianna and I are ready to make our betrothal official. Camden and I were just in the library going over the agreement."

Roderick's stomach sank when Camden made no move to deny Abercorn's words.

"Father," Lucianna said, her voice laced with hurt. "Tell me you have not decided my fate."

CHAPTER 15

LUCI DID HER best to glare at her father, but inside, she was falling apart, crumbling, caving in. She blinked rapidly to hold back the tears that threatened to cascade down her face. Crying before Roderick was bad enough; however, she adamantly refused to allow her father or Abercorn to see her weaken. Or show any sign of giving up.

The situation had spiraled so quickly, Luci could barely understand what was transpiring. Her father had made it seem as if he were pushing Luci toward Montrose as a suitor when all along, he was set on Abercorn. But why? There could be very little besides an added two decades mingling with the upper crust of society that Abercorn had to offer her father.

And there was no doubt, the Marquis of Camden's goal when marrying off Lucianna was to increase his connections; both within society and in the business. It begged the question: what had Abercorn offered Roderick could not?

"Things are decided," her father said with a confident nod. "I think it best if you and your *friends* leave, and you return home. I will arrive shortly to speak with you."

She didn't like the way he sniffed at the word

"friends" as if Edith and Ophelia were little more than rodents riding her coattails.

"I will not leave, Father," Lucianna seethed. When she felt Roderick's hand caress her arm, she cooled down a bit. "I have no intention of wedding Abercorn."

"That is not up to you," Abercorn said with a smug smile before looking to Camden for confirmation, but his grin fled when he saw the scowl on the marquis' face. "What I mean to say is—"

"It does not matter what you mean, Abercorn," Camden hissed, for the first time allowing his cool demeanor to fall. "Who I choose for Lucianna is my decision. Neither of you has any say in who that is—nor when things will be officially settled."

It was the only bright spot in the conversation. Abercorn had sparked her father's displeasure, and Luci only hoped it was more than the transgression her father laid upon her shoulders. Maybe he would see reason, understand that in no world should she be required to wed a man who might very well have killed her dearest friend.

"I think it best if Montrose, Abercorn, and I speak privately." Her father pivoted sharply and stalked from the room, expecting Roderick and Abercorn to follow.

Abercorn and her father had given her matching smiles, and Luci swore they would have continued with an explanation of letting men handles the business at hand while the ladies returned to their tea and needlework.

Abercorn and Sissy were the first to snap into action and hurry after the marquis. "My lord, we can use my study, if that pleases you."

"Do keep your nose above trouser level, Francis," her father huffed.

Luci held tightly to Roderick's sleeve, knowing she should allow him to go—to speak with her father quickly and not cause the marquis' anger to settle on him if he were tardy to the study; however, she needed to speak with him.

There were many things they hadn't discussed, namely, their association after this feigned betrothal ended. Was he even willing to continue with the charade?

More importantly, could Luci ask him to make that sacrifice?

Once their betrothal was called off, Roderick would face another round of scandalous gossip—once again caused by Luci and her petty actions. There would be no chance that Roderick would forgive her twice for ruining his chances of securing a wife.

"Roderick, please…" She looked up into his eyes, eyes she'd always seen as icy and closed off, but now, they appeared crystal blue with a hint of desperation. "I cannot wed Abercorn, but neither will I expect you to throw away your future to save me."

A reassuring squeeze on her shoulder brought Luci's attention to Edith and Ophelia, both at her sides with looks of determination. Even Lord Torrington's dour scowl spoke volumes.

"I—we—will never allow Abercorn to get his hands on you," Roderick assured her, taking her icy hands into his warm palms. "We will think of something."

"If all else fails, the pair of you are welcome to my original plan to wed Lady Edith," Torrington offered with a grin, but it quickly faded when he realized the stark expressions on everyone else's faces. "Honestly, it is a solid plan and would not be hard to see done."

"I agree with Triston," Edith said with a nod. "Gretna Green may be the only answer."

"Gretna Green?" Roderick stared between Torrington, Edith, and Luci. "But that would mean—"

"We would actually have to wed," Luci finished, shaking her head. "I cannot ask that much of you, Roderick. A fake betrothal is one thing, but a legally binding marriage? I could never ask you to sacrifice so much."

Nor was Luci certain she could live with such a grand sacrifice on her part. A future with Montrose as her spouse, neither having agreed to the match willingly, could very well prove a disaster.

"But we will not know anything until Montrose meets with the marquis and Lord Abercorn." Ophelia's low, hesitant words cut through the many emotions flooding Luci. "Let him meet with your father. Then we shall convene again and decide our next move."

"Since when did you become the voice of reason, Ophelia?" Edith asked, clinging to Torrington's side.

Ophelia's brow rose. "Likely since you became so smitten with Lord Torrington your sensible nature has been all but forgotten. Besides, I have always been infused with much sense, though I rarely need express it. That is what I have you and Luci for."

Nervous laughter filled the room as the group started toward the door.

"I think you all should wait at Lord Torrington's father's townhouse," Roderick instructed as they entered the foyer. "I will meet with the marquis and join you immediately after."

"I will stay here with you." Luci pushed her shoulders back and paced toward the study door that stood ajar, not bothering to glance behind her to see her friends depart or Roderick trail her.

This was her life—her future—and she would not see her fate decided by her vengeful father or Abercorn and his delusional, self-absorbed tendencies. Neither man was the least bit concerned with her well-being or happiness.

"Slow down, Lucianna, or you will stumble and injure yourself." Roderick grabbed her arms to halt her, but did not hold her so tightly she could not pull away. She adored that about him—he wanted her to listen to him, yet he would not force his ideas, concerns, or opinions on her.

Roderick *did* care about her happiness.

Of that, she was certain.

He might even willingly sacrifice his future to make certain Abercorn never touched her.

What kind of woman would Luci be if she allowed him to throw away his life to make certain she wasn't forced into a marriage not of her choosing?

He stared down at her, imploring her to stop and listen, but Luci couldn't do that. If he spoke, gave her all the many reasons he should go through with their betrothal, Luci might be convinced to allow him to sacrifice himself. Hell, after their walk yesterday, she'd even led herself to believe he actually cared for her beyond the retribution he sought for Luci's hand in ruining him.

For those many minutes, Luci envisioned a future wrapped in his arms, always safe and protected. She dreamt of a home all their own—and children with their midnight hair. A girl with her father's intense blue eyes, and a baby boy with Luci's moss-green irises.

Both were tanned beyond what was proper because Roderick insisted they spend a great deal of time outdoors, picnicking in the park or hiking the trails along the Thames.

It was foolish and self-serving to even think about the possibilities and future to be had as the Duchess of Montrose.

"I will come with you to meet with my father and Abercorn." Every muscle in her body tightened, but Luci refused to allow her calm demeanor to slip. "I think my father will listen if I am present."

RODERICK STARED INTO Lucianna's deep green eyes—taking in the desperation and hurt that lingered just below the surface of her calm exterior. He had no right to demand she depart with her friends, nor ask her to wait outside the study.

The marquis and Abercorn were, even now, discussing Lucianna's future. Something her father may legally have control over, but not if he sought to hand her off to an unsavory, despicable lord. No woman should be lowered to play the pawn between gentlemen.

Roderick's honor as a nobleman would not allow such a thing.

Luci was everything any English gentleman should long for in someone they called wife, though not because of increased social status, or wealth, or even because of her exquisitely dark beauty. She had a wit superior to most men, the smarts to know her own worth, and the cunning to make her own way if her father's chosen path did not suit her.

"We will confront your father and Abercorn together," Roderick compromised. It was Lucianna's decision in the end. "But if you feel the need to depart at any time, we will leave together, as well."

When she nodded, a lock of hair came loose from her pins and hung down along her cheek to caress the top of her shoulder. For not the first time, Roderick longed to run his hands through her unbound hair and bring the long tresses to his nose. They must certainly smell of lavender or vanilla.

There would be time for that. Bloody hell, but Roderick would make certain there was plenty of time together in their future. Their brief walk hadn't been enough. His chaste kiss to her forehead was not nearly sufficient to extinguish his desire for her. Not even a fortnight wrapped in her embrace, staring into her deep, complex, green eyes, with unlimited hours talking about their pasts, the present, or the future they envisioned for themselves would satisfy him.

She grasped his arm, notched her chin high, and squared her shoulders, signaling that she was prepared to face her father.

Roderick wished he felt even a small measure of

the confidence she displayed as they walked the several paces across the foyer and entered Abercorn's study.

Even together, they were on uneven ground—the advantage going to Abercorn.

Roderick pledged silently to take that benefit from the other duke.

Entering the room, Lucianna pulled close to his side, Roderick realized he'd held the upper hand the entire time. Abercorn may have his title, his wealth, and his many business ventures, but Roderick had Lucianna.

On his arm, at that moment. And if he had his way, every day hereafter.

Roderick had successfully broken through the tough exterior Lucianna had built up to keep her heart safe from both her father and others who meant her harm.

The way she held his arm tightly, her fingers squeezing through his sleeve, told him she'd allowed Roderick in, expecting him to reinforce any weak spot in her defenses. And bloody hell, he was loath to disappoint her.

"Camden." Roderick nodded before turning to Abercorn, who scurried behind his desk, a place of perceived safety, no doubt. "Abercorn."

"Lucianna," Camden said, his narrowed glare settling on her. "You will depart immediately and await me at home."

Lucianna stiffened. "I will—"

"Lord Camden," Roderick cut in, giving Lucianna a reassuring smile. "Lady Lucianna has a right to be here. This is her future we are discussing. Do you not believe she should be heard?"

Camden lifted his palm loosely as if to say it mattered naught to him before he turned away and took one of the seats before Abercorn's desk, leaving only one chair open. "Sit, Montrose."

Roderick led Lucianna farther into the room and pulled the chair out for her to sit as he stood behind her.

It was as much to show Lucianna the respect due her—that these two men ignored—as it was to keep Camden off guard during the coming negotiation.

"I see no reason for Lady Lucianna and Montrose to be present." Abercorn tapped a stack of papers on the desk surface before him. "The agreement has been drawn up, reviewed, and only needs your signature, my lord."

"While I partly agree with you, Francis," Camden spoke slowly, "I do not agree the present agreement is acceptable."

"But that is not what you said before Lady Lucianna and her friends arrived."

"That was before I was aware of the seriousness of Montrose's pursuit of my daughter." Camden sat back in his seat, folding his hands in his lap as if greatly satisfied by the change in circumstances. "Two men, dukes no less, seeking Lucianna's hand in marriage? I think it best I retire and allow you both to meet with your men of business to submit new agreements if your goal is to call my daughter wife."

Roderick snorted.

The man actually expected a bidding war to ensue for Lady Lucianna's hand. Roderick did not disagree that she was worth the effort on both his and Abercorn's parts if they wanted to pursue her. However, she was being treated like cattle whose highly valued lineage and sires demanded men offer all they had to own her. These men, Abercorn and her father, seemed not to realize the priceless value of his midnight English rose—but he knew all too well.

No one would ever own Lucianna.

Not even Roderick.

CHAPTER 16

WHAT OF MY heart? Lucianna wanted to scream as Charlotte led her to her bedchambers. The maid kept up with a litany of mumbled nonsense, "There there," "Get some rest," "Allow the men to handle things," and the most infuriating, "Your father will choose wisely."

Luci didn't remember bidding Roderick farewell nor entering her father's coach.

A servant steered her clear of Lord Torrington's family townhouse and made certain she was settled before the conveyance took off toward Mayfair.

Now, she sat at her dressing table as Charlotte brushed out her hair as if Luci were preparing for bed. It was only late afternoon. A time when fashionable men and women were strolling in the park or shopping on Bond Street, not being carted away by the powers that be—namely, her father—without so much as a fight.

She was a beautiful, fragile bird in a cage made for two—her mother and her.

Luci snorted. She'd truly thought to escape it all, carve her own way in life, never being reduced to that of a captive. The many times she'd underestimated her father had finally caught up with her. The overwhelming pain in her chest told Luci her determination had waned to desperation. And, finally, hopelessness.

She looked around her childish room with its frilly, lilac bedding and matching pillows. The window drapes were several shades darker, more of a violet. The hues should clash, throwing the room into disarray, as a pure lilac color was no match for an overpowering dark violet. However, her mother had insisted that every piece of furniture in the room be white—pure, untouched, and innocent.

Had Lady Camden tried to reclaim her own innocence as she'd designed this room when Lucianna was in short skirts and pinafores?

If it had been Lucianna's choice—and nothing thus far in her life had been—she would have decorated the room in dark burgundy with blue accents, and the occasional gold trimming. The room would evoke a need to bow to the power held by its occupant.

However, the castle did not make the king.

It went much deeper than that. It was a sense of rightness everyone around the sovereign felt with such a man in power. The security of knowing that the correct person could be trusted to make a well-thought-out and conscious decision that would benefit all.

No matter how hard she attempted to take control of the situation with Abercorn, her friends questioned her. No matter how many times she'd declared she would not wed that murdering lord, Luci felt her voice blowing on the breeze, heard by no one.

Not *no one*, precisely. Roderick was aware of her wants and needs.

He was conscious of the fact that Luci would rather run to the wilds of Scotland than be joined in matrimony with Abercorn.

Did he suspect she had no such aversion to him as her husband?

Secrets and all, Lucianna still cared deeply for him. Even now after such a short time. It was his wounds, the ones he'd shared with her on their walk, and the many he still kept inside that drew her to him. However, long after the mystery of him vanished, she would want Roderick still.

A tap at the door had Charlotte setting down her brush and hurrying over to open the portal.

The housekeeper swept into the room with a full tea service, but the wooden slab did not close.

Luci tilted, narrowing her eyes on the darkened hallway beyond, as Charlotte prepared her normal cup of tea: Earl Grey, cream, and one lump of sugar with extra-hot water.

When not a sound came from the hallway except for the receding footsteps of their housekeeper, Luci focused on her beverage, which Charlotte held out to her before resuming her chore.

Lucianna closed her eyes as the brush moved through her long locks with nary a knot or tangle. It was much as she longed for her life to be: predictable, even in course, with only the occasional concern. She didn't want a life plagued with arguments, doubts, hardships, and, worst of all, regrets.

It was the main reason she pushed so hard to prove Abercorn's guilt. Until that day came, she would be weighed down by regrets, held down by daily reminders that she'd failed her friend not only in life but also in death.

"Lucianna?" a quiet voice called from behind her. A tone that never failed to soothe her when she doubted herself or was sad or even overjoyed. Today, it infused the finality of things. "May I come in?"

"Of course, Mother." Luci opened her eyes to see the marchioness take the brush from her maid and nod for Charlotte to depart. With a sigh, the older woman took over the lady's maid's chore, brushing Luci's thick, onyx hair from scalp to tip as she had when Luci was younger before it was deemed improper for a woman to spend so much time with her children as companions.

For the span of a heartbeat, she thought to

unburden the weight on her shoulders; throw herself at her mother's feet and beg she do something to right the situation.

However, her weak smile of greeting died on her lips.

Lady Camden never made eye contact with her eldest child but preferred to keep her stare on the brush in her hand. The action was all too unfamiliar for Luci. Even at meals, with all her children gathered, the marchioness did not speak to anyone beyond a comment on the weather or a question about the schoolroom. She'd given up her role as matriarch of the family many years ago, around the time her magnificent black hair had turned grey, seemingly overnight, and her deep green eyes had dulled, any spirit they'd once held vanishing with her last strands of self-respect.

She was a woman born into a world that afforded her no decisions beyond those allowed by her father— and later, her husband. Certainly, she was charged with planning the meals for the household, securing the proper clothing for the children, making sure they attended their studies and prepared for University. Beyond that, Luci knew the marchioness lived a solitary life; cut off from her family years prior with no friends to speak of now beyond her four children. And even they had become silent observers to their mother's pain.

All while the man she'd pledge to love and service was serving other women.

That was a fate worse than death for Luci.

No matter the fury inside her, Luci was incapable of changing the course of Lord and Lady Camden's marriage; however, she could never resent her mother for the life she'd chosen. Lady Camden's four children were well taken care of, educated, and would make fine matches—even if Luci's match was to a man over double her years.

"Mama," Luci sighed, her eyes drifting closed once more, desperately needing to be a child again, to go back to before her mother was broken—or maybe it was just before her children noticed how injured and beaten down she was.

"Yes, my fox." Her mother set the brush aside and stared into the dressing table mirror as Luci's eyes fluttered open.

Smiling, Luci said, "You haven't called me that in years."

"I haven't felt the need to remind you of your wit, your cunning, and your intelligence for some time." Her mother sighed, and she appeared far older, if not wiser, than her thirty-seven years. "You are able to see through deception and take swift action to change any situation. You are very brave, my fox."

"This may be beyond my control, Mama." Luci reached up and grasped her mother's hands that hovered directly over her shoulders. "I fear Father is not one to be trifled with, especially when he believes this match will benefit his many business ventures."

The marchioness clicked her teeth and shook her head. "I have long thought you would be the one to rescue us all from your father's domineering, cruel ways. Especially with your secretive activities since Tilda's death—"

"You know, Mama?" Suddenly, Luci had to see her mother's eyes, know if her mother detested Lucianna's means for handling the unsavory man in their lives.

"I was uncertain, at first, but then, after the night your father brought his mistress to that ball, well..." Her mother focused once more on her task of brushing Luci's hair. "When the *Gazette* soundly thumped your father, I knew you had had a hand in the deed. And while I said nothing, inwardly, I cheered your spirit and your bravery for calling out the man." She went silent for a moment, and Luci's heart skipped a beat. It was the first time, in many years, Luci felt she had an ally in her home instead of more people to protect. "You will save us all, I have no doubt."

It was much to ask of a mere slip of a girl, barely venturing into womanhood; however, Luci never wanted to let her mother down. She feared that if she did, the woman would lose all hope for her future and that of her younger offspring if left solely to the devices and whims of Lord Camden.

There was so much pressure in her mother's few words.

Lady Lucianna was to be her mother's only hope for survival.

Her chin lowered as she pondered the greatness her family expected of her. Anger raced up her spine to think everyone seemed to believe it was her responsibility to prove Abercorn had killed Tilda, to stop her father's overreaching abuse of his family, and to find a way to stop her betrothal to Abercorn.

She was only nineteen. She'd never been outside of England, and even more rarely away from London proper. How could anyone think her strong enough, witty enough, cunning enough, to do anything to help them—let alone drastically alter her own life's path.

"Mama," Luci asked, pressing her mother's hand to her cheek. "When did you decide to give up, allow Father the reins, and step back into the shadows?"

She knew from the tears brimming in her mother's eyes that she'd hurt her, but still, the question hung in the air. "I have never given up, Lucianna."

"But Father does whatever he wants. He parades around one mistress after another, rarely accompanies us to societal gatherings, and we hear him shouting at you when you think we are all fast asleep."

Luci watched as a small smile spread across her mother's face, making her appear not much older than Luci herself. "I think you have the wrong impression, my little fox."

"How?"

"He parades around his mistresses because I give him leave to. He decided early in our marriage he was not cut out to be the husband I desired, and so, he's lived all these years without me by his side."

"That is your choice?" Luci was shocked, stunned almost into silence. "Does it not hurt to see him showing off his mistresses?"

"At first, certainly." The marchioness sighed. "I thought, 'what have I done? I pushed my husband away because I could not bring myself to accept him for the man he is.' Over time, this did not concern me because I have always had the task of raising you and your siblings in proper fashion."

Luci doubted she knew her mother at all.

If one did not know their own flesh and blood, what would keep her from doubting every person she met and the society she'd been born into?

"Your brothers will grow to be kind, compassionate, humorous, loving, and loyal men. It is sad it took your father's disloyalty to his family to show Matthew and Derek all the things they did not want to be."

"What of Candace and me?" Luci asked. "Are we growing and learning in your image?"

"Heavens no, my child." The marchioness came around and sat next to Luci on the bench. "I have raised the pair of you to be independent. Taught you to make your own decisions. Never fear risk—or the rewards that might come from it. Oh, and most importantly, I've taught you both to never allow a man like your father to dictate your life. Lucianna, use your cunning and your wit to take hold of your fate." She squeezed her daughter's hands.

"And what happens when I am gone?" Luci sighed. "You, Candace, and the boys will be alone against that monster."

Her mother's chuckle was infused with a deep hurt, driving Luci to apologize, but her mother held up her hand to silence her. "You cannot worry about us. Your brothers will leave for University before long, and

Candace still has many lessons to learn, but I will endeavor to keep her away from your father."

"And you?" Luci looked into her mother's deep green eyes, so much like hers though they held an exhaustion Luci hadn't noticed.

"I will continue as I always have, loving the man I married and praying every day he returns to the kind, honorable lord I was proud to wed all those years ago."

Had her mother had a plan all this time?

An ache settled deep in Luci's chest at the thought that her mother had known her goal all along but had not thought enough of her daughter to share. Luci could not believe that to be true.

"He is a horrible man, but you still love him." Luci leaned her cheek on her mother's shoulder. "That is—"

"The place that hope begins, draws strength."

"How can you be so certain he will return to the man you married?" Luci begged.

"I am certain of nothing except where my own heart lies. And that is with your father."

"Even if he does horrid things? Even when his temper gets the best of him? Even when he demands your daughter wed an unsavory, dishonorable man?"

"Just because the Marquis of Camden demands something does not mean it is to be."

A rattle at her terrace sounded, pulling Luci's attention from her mother to the windowpaned French doors leading onto her private veranda overlooking the street below.

"Did you hear that?" Luci asked.

Her mother tilted her head and listened, just as another round of rattling assaulted her panes.

She shook her head. "No, I am sorry. I do not hear a thing. However, I will request that Charlotte and the housekeeper allow you to rest. Someone will be by later this evening to stoke the fire."

The women stood and embraced. How long had it been since she'd set her arms around her mother and pulled her close? She'd half expected to find the older woman's shoulders gaunt and bony, as if she wasted away due to neglect, but her mother's shoulders were as solid as Luci remembered them.

Another handful of pebbles clattered along the veranda and hit the window.

"Are you certain you hear nothing?"

Her mother smirked before pecking Luci on the cheek and turning to leave. "Have a *restful* night, my little fox. Do not forget, a fox always knows their way, even in the dead of night."

Luci swore she heard her mother chuckle as she closed the door to her daughter's room.

Pushing her waist-length black hair over her shoulder, Luci hurried to the door and turned the lock before facing the unmistakable sound coming from her veranda.

Her heart thumped nearly out of her chest as another spray assaulted the window.

For only a brief moment, Luci considered fleeing her room and calling for a footman to explore where the noise had come from.

Even with that plan still solidly in mind, Luci moved toward the French doors and reached for the latch.

CHAPTER 17

RODERICK HUFFED, TOSSING yet another handful of pebbles toward the lit window above. His head pounded relentlessly following his meeting with Camden and Abercorn. His arm ached from throwing so many bloody rocks at Lady Lucianna's veranda. And blast it all, he was sick and tired of the pitying looks from Torrington, Lady Ophelia, and Lady Edith. To make matters worse—much, much worse—at some point, Torrington's younger sisters had joined the party.

Lady Chastity and Lady Prudence were agreeable enough young women; however, they talked a lot. They spoke of never having met Roderick before. They spoke of Lady Edith's grand ball. They chattered on about Lady Ophelia's new hairstyle.

The veranda they all stood on was large, yet the group's combined excitement seemed to reduce the area to that of a confined, closed carriage.

Giving Roderick little time to ponder his next move—and there had to be a next move, and fast. His blood boiled at the thought of the alternative…

Lord Camden had settled on the Duke of Abercorn as the best marriage prospect for Lucianna.

He hadn't even entertained any additional offer from Roderick.

Lucianna's fate had been secured and signed before Roderick could ask for a drink. His interest had all been for show, to push Abercorn to offer more and make more business agreements to have Lucianna as wife.

Bloody hell, but that was not the end of things.

Lucianna deserved far more than to be bartered like an old boat in jeopardy of capsizing due to her hellion tendencies and disagreeable nature.

She was not disagreeable, only adamant against the misdeeds of others.

She deserved to be cherished and loved. She deserved a home and a family of her own. She deserved to never fear the man she was wed to.

Roderick was unsure if he could give her everything she ought to have, but right now, at this moment, he was the best option for her.

"Mayhap if you aimed a bit higher, Your Grace," Ophelia said, mimicking her improved throwing style. "The pebbles are certain to hit the window then."

"What if she isn't in her room?" he asked, worried the auburn-haired nymph had used up her daily supply of words.

"Then Pru and I will go to the door and knock," Lady Chastity offered.

It struck Roderick as odd a woman he'd met less than an hour before would risk anything to help him gain a word with Lucianna.

"Shhhh," Edith swiped at the air. "I think I heard the latch unlock."

"Oh, the door is opening," Pru and Chastity said in unison, clapping their hands.

"Do quiet that noise." Torrington turned a scowl on his sisters, but it vanished quickly. "It might not be Lady Lucianna who steps out—and we will all need move quickly to hide."

"Who—who—who—" Lucianna's normally deep, confident tone echoed down from above. "Who is it?"

Roderick stepped from the shadows at the tree line

and into the pool of moonlight below her veranda. They'd arrived when it was still light outside, but the day had passed to twilight as they'd bided their time.

He despised hearing the fright in her tone.

"It is I, Lady Lucianna."

"The grim reaper!" At Luci's sharp inhale, Ophelia elbowed Edith, and the two fell into a fit of giggles.

"Montrose, Edith, Ophelia?" She moved farther onto the veranda to look over the edge and see them all standing below. "What in heaven's name are you all doing here?"

"We are here, too!" Lady Chastity chimed in, not one to be left out. "Pru and I."

"Again, what are you all doing here? My father deposited me at home and returned to the duke's residence. He should return shortly," she sighed. "He will find you."

"With luck, he will find none of us." Montrose moved around to the stone steps leading up to Lucianna's private veranda. He took the stairs two at a time and was standing before her in an instant.

She was gowned in a fine nightshift of pure white—all innocence, only broken by the waves of onyx hair that hung clear past her waist. Her toes peeked from beneath her night rail, blessedly bare. She was everything Roderick knew her to be—except her chin no longer tilted upward slightly, and her shoulders sagged.

"My lady," Montrose croaked. She was far more beautiful than he remembered, but he loathed her air of sorrow. "I am here."

"Shall I assume my father officially gave Abercorn leave to announce our betrothal?" Lucianna sobbed, a deep, heart-wrenching cry.

Every emotion from the long day drained from him at her cry; anger, fury, desperation, longing, and hurt—he could not grasp and hold onto a single one. His resolve shook, barely holding together.

"What your father says means naught to us," he soothed, running his hand down her back before pulling her close. "I have a plan—with the help of your friends."

"What? We will just run off to Gretna Green and be wed in disgrace?" She cringed at the word, knowing she'd brought the term down on his head. "My father will likely expect that move and send a group of servants to catch us before we reach the border."

"There are other ways." His mind swirled, trying to land on another option for them, but he could only think of Lucianna in his arms—and keeping her there. "We will find another way."

"Or mayhap it would be best to return to my chambers and await my father's decree that will solidify my future." She pulled away slightly as if to do just that.

But Roderick had her in his embrace, and it would take far more than the Marquis of Camden to take the woman he loved from him.

He stiffened.

The woman he loved?

Blast it all, but he *did* love her.

It had been many years since he'd experienced anything resembling love, and never a love like this. Yes, he'd loved and adored his mother. He'd respected and loved his father.

But never had he dreamt of loving a woman, especially a female as deserving of love as Lady Lucianna.

There would be no compromise. She belonged to him, as his heart belonged to her.

Never again would he allow her to entertain the notion that she might be forced to wed Abercorn.

"Lucianna, I love you," he said as he kissed her forehead.

"Love makes wise people do foolish things." She pulled back to look up at him.

Her eyes were clouded with confusion, yet

Roderick didn't feel confused at all. He set his hands against her cold cheeks. "And it makes a foolish person do wise things. Like finding the woman they love and holding on, no matter what consequences lay ahead."

"Can it be so simple?" she asked.

A shiver ran through her, and her teeth chattered.

Roderick hadn't thought about how chilled the evening had grown, especially with Lucianna gowned in nothing but a thin nightshift. "Let us return inside, and I will show you."

In her chambers, he would have all night to convince her that finding love and holding onto it was just that simple, as long as she felt the same.

But first, he needs must share with her the rest of his sordid past. She needed to know everything before she decided to thwart her father.

Even Roderick had enough integrity to discourage allowing a woman to fall in love with him until she knew the whole truth.

Taking her hand, Roderick turned toward her open veranda door and the warmth that certainly lay within. Surprisingly, she followed without resistance. If she hadn't, he'd been prepared to sweep her off her feet and carry her back to the heated bedchambers.

CHAPTER 18

LUCIANNA ALLOWED RODERICK to guide her back into her bedchambers as she walked on shaky legs. She still held out hope that her father cared about what she wanted for her own future, but when Roderick—with all her friends in tow—had shown up below her veranda, she more than suspected that her father had chosen Abercorn to be her husband.

She'd been mastered, conquered, and bested by the one man who should care most for her. To know the man she'd grown up trying to impress, the man Luci currently did her best to emulate, didn't care a whit for her…hurt. Her father didn't bother himself with grandiose thoughts of love, devotion, commitment, and friendship.

Her head spun when she lowered her chin to hide her feelings.

The Marquis of Camden did not have those things in his marriage, and so, he did not think it of value to his daughter.

Well, the marquis was gravely wrong.

Those were the qualities Luci searched for in not only her future husband but also her friends.

She and Roderick stood before her hearth, facing the flames, their fingers entwined; everything and everyone receding as she could only see him.

This was exactly how Luci saw herself with her husband: at peace, trusting one another, and forever entwined.

She wanted not only their fingers intertwined but also their minds, bodies, and souls.

So fused together people around them wondered how had they achieved such elevated love.

It would never be about one dominating the other—not with she and Roderick. Never would they make the other feel insignificant, unheard, or unwanted.

"Roderick," she gulped. When he looked down at her, his normally intense blue eyes were a meadow of blue blossoms, welcoming and inviting. "I am ready to see what simple looks like. Show me?"

He needed no other encouragement. Roderick swept her into his arms and crossed the room to her lilac fabric-covered bed and pushed aside the white, eyelet drapes.

The feeling of her of bed coverlet against her back had never been so soft or welcoming. In fact, she'd always seen the room as childish, but with Roderick's dark presence in the small space, the room took on an entirely new feel. The lilac and deep violet were exotic hues—begging for the couple's weight.

Roderick paused above her, fanning her dark hair out around her on the bed before pressing a kiss to the tip of her nose. "I have long wondered how beautiful you would be with your hair spread across my bed. I'll compromise for your bed, just this once."

"Your Grace!" Luci's cheeks heated at the meaning behind his words, only to flame further with his final words. He planned to take her to his bed soon. "What if someone enters my chambers?"

"Let them," he mumbled, placing tiny kisses along her cheek, down to her jaw, and over to her ear.

He was unafraid of the scene they'd cause if caught tonight in her chambers, and neither was she concerned.

Luci and her friends had spent years whispering about what happened behind closed bedchamber doors…and Roderick was the perfect—the only—man to show her, teach her.

Her body melted into the contours of the bed at the confidence in his words.

Roderick placed several kisses on her neck before pushing back and balancing on his hands above her.

"There is something I need to tell you before we continue," he sighed.

He was going to tell her he loved her again.

And by all that was holy, Luci would have to admit she loved him too or risk seeing him leave her and pull away for good.

And it would be what she deserved. To love someone meant to trust them implicitly. Luci wondered how long love could last when trust was unspoken…

"I am bankrupt, without funds beyond those necessary to keep my lands and tenants' homes out of disrepair." He lowered his head, their foreheads touching. "When my father died, I found out that he'd willingly given over all of my family's money to a corrupt gambling hell ring. No paperwork, no names, no way of finding what rightly belongs to me and mine."

She gasped, and he instantly pulled back further, sliding his body off hers to lie beside her.

Love was not about money or belongings.

It was about belonging to someone who loved you more than money.

The void above her made her long to cry out, demand he return and lay his body atop hers once more.

"And the woman at the opera?" It was Luci's one reservation about Roderick. He'd been more than clear and honest about Lady Daphne—he had no feelings for her, but what of the woman she'd spied him with that night months ago? "Do you love her?"

"Love her?" Roderick gave a deep, twisted chuckle, and Luci's chest seized.

Would she be able to accept his current words of love and put out of mind his past love?

"I told you, Lady Cavendish is my father's best friend's widow." He stared into her eyes intently. "She also lost everything when her husband died, and she found out he'd promised it all to this underground gambling hell, as well—including her widow's settlement. She had found a lead, and I was meeting with her to discover what she knew. The woman had no funds to hire a Bow Street runner to track down her inheritance, but, because I was fated to marry Lady Daphne and have use of her dowry, I figured I could investigate what she found further."

"And I ruined that for you…"

"No," he said, shaking his head and placing a kiss on her forehead to ease her frown. "You may have slowed me down and made it impossible to discover the lead Lady Cavendish discovered, but with Lucian's help, I have continued searching."

"You did not learn what she knew at the opera?"

"She was fearful of bringing the documentation she'd discovered to such a public place in case we were discovered. I was to meet with her the following day in a secluded area of Regent's Park."

"But the *Mayfair Confidential* article wrecked that plan?"

"Yes, Lady Cavendish did not show up for our appointment," he admitted. "Her townhouse is vacant. There is no one at her country estate. She has disappeared from society, just as she'd planned to do after she gave me the information I needed." Roderick sighed, averting his eyes and taking in the room for the first time. "I suppose Abercorn is not looking all too unsuitable now, huh?"

"Even if we were made to live on the streets of London, and I was forced to push an orange cart outside Vauxhall, I would still favor you over Lord Abercorn." Lucianna pushed from her back and slung her leg over Roderick, forcing him to lay flat. "There are many things in this world I question, but that, I do not."

It was her turn to lean down, halting an inch before their lips touched. "I am eternally sorry." She placed a kiss against his lips when he tried to silence her. "There is not a day I would choose another."

"Even if your father demands it?" he asked hesitantly.

Was he scared of what her answer would be?

Suddenly, Luci was terrified to say the words because once said, she could not take them back. Her course would be set. Although, her path had been unalterable since she'd bested Roderick at Bentley's only several days earlier.

So little time had passed, yet everything had changed for her. She'd never thought to wed after what Tilda had gone through. Yes, a spark of hope had started when Edith met Torrington and fell madly and deeply in love, but that spark had turned to a flame when Luci had stumbled upon Roderick. Even now, it pooled in her belly—and lower—growing with intensity by the minute as she stared down into the eyes of the man she'd never dreamt of loving.

With her hair falling on both sides of his face, she bent down and placed her lips to his. There was no better way to give her answer than to show him.

Luci had no need to fight for control where Roderick was concerned. He allowed her to explore at her leisure, her lips trailing across his cheek and to his neck; however, she kept going until her mouth met his ear. She flicked her tongue out and drew the lobe between her lips, gently sucking.

Tendrils of need coursed through her, and she released his flesh.

His whimper told her he wanted her to continue, but she had many other places to explore. Sights she'd never seen.

Roderick's hands caressed her backside, traveling

lower to rest on her rounded bottom. The feel of his strong hands through her nightshift was unmistakable. The heat coursing through the thin fabric warmed her.

Gently, she rotated her hips and rubbed against the flap of his trousers, surprised at his manhood's hardening. The desire rolling through her had Luci pulling back and sitting straight, enabling her to push her most delicate place closer to his hard length.

She was the hellion she'd always been accused of being, but this—everything about her and Roderick— was right. Her pulse fluttered with her weakness for him, at the same moment her heart soared with empowerment.

His hands left her backside, caressing up her sides to cup her breasts, his thumbs circling her nipples through her shift. He set a slow pace as he stared up at her, and his movements sent her heart thundering as she continued to move against him.

Her yearning intensified until Luci feared she would burst into flames and perish from desire, taking Roderick with her.

"You are beautiful, Lucianna," he mumbled as if drunk off the sight of her above him.

And he never took his stare from hers as his hands halted and he drew down the front of her shift, exposing her breasts.

For the measure of a heartbeat, she moved to cover herself, but he stopped her when he took hold of her hands, placing them on his chest. She couldn't keep them still as she massaged the muscles along his chest and shoulders, sculpted from years holding a foil.

His breath hitched as she untied his cravat and moved to unbutton his shirt and expose him as much as she was visible to him.

Finally, she spread his shirt wide and smoothed her hands over his chest, sprinkled with fine, black hair. Luci shouldn't be shocked by the striking look of her white hands moving across his tanned skin. The contrast was erotic, and Luci was helpless to look away. His skin was as smooth and unblemished as her hands. His tan led down his chest…disappearing into his waistband.

How did the sun's rays touch every inch of his body?

She almost asked, but Roderick shifted below her, pushing up onto his elbows.

She flung her head back when he took her hardened nipple into his mouth, his tongue playing in circles, mimicking the motion she'd inflicted on his earlobe.

Ecstasy.

Pure, scorching hot desire flowed from her head to her toes.

Her core pulsed, demanding no clothes separate them, their bodies needing to be skin to skin.

"What is the bloody meaning of this?" her father's voice thundered, bouncing off her walls and rattling the windowpanes at the same time the latch burst on her door. "Lucianna, what have you done?"

Roderick pulled back, releasing her nipple and returning her shift to cover her exposed breasts.

"Father…I…" She fumbled to refasten the buttons on Roderick's shirt, but her fingers shook, and he pushed her hands away. Thankfully, her long, black hair shielded them from sight. "Do give us a moment."

"Give you a moment?" The marquis fumed. Luci heard rather than saw him stalk into the room. Roderick lifted her from him and set her on the side of the bed before finishing with his shirt. "So you can continue to sully what is mine? In this ruined state, you are worthless to me. I fear I will have to pay—and pay handsomely—just to be rid of you."

Luci realized her father thought her utterly compromised and beyond saving.

She opened her mouth to correct him but clamped it shut again, not bothering to hide her grin.

CHAPTER 19

RODERICK STARED INTO Lucianna's face, expecting all color to drain as panic set in...instead, a coy grin had settled on her, and her shoulders straightened as she scooted to the edge of the bed and stood.

The pristine white nightshift billowed around her legs, covering her naked calves and teasing her bare feet.

The tilt of her chin and narrowed stare had Roderick thinking she was almost happy to face her father's rage. Brushing her long hair over her shoulder, she slowly walked across the room toward her father.

When Roderick sensed his desire had subsided enough, he moved from her bed and trailed in her wake until he stood directly behind her. He set his hands on both of her shoulders.

"Lord Camd—"

She held up her hand, cutting off his words.

He watched Camden's face redden, and his nostrils flare in anger, his hands clenched into fists at his sides. The man had every right to be furious, but not with Lucianna. If retribution were owed, it would be claimed from Roderick.

Roderick had been in the wrong. He'd known his course when he entered Lucianna's bedchambers, though he never would have acknowledged it before.

"Father." Her tone was laced with steel and conviction, as still and confident as the set of her shoulders. "You are too late. I am ruined. Solidly, unequivocally tarnished."

Her chin only lifted farther when Camden narrowed his stare on her. "You have been trouble since the day your mother gave birth to you. I always imagined you doing something foolish to scandalize this family."

Camden shook his head, feigning sympathy for Lucianna.

Roderick wanted to curse the man, tell him his daughter had lost nothing being caught in his embrace. If anything, she'd gained the world.

His world and everything he possessed.

Which wasn't much, but his love was worth more than riches.

"You will leave this house immediately. You have brought disgrace upon your mother, your siblings, and me." Camden pivoted and started toward the door, halting before he crossed the threshold. "And, Montrose, you can see your way out the same way you got in."

Without another word, the marquis stepped into the hall and shouted for the family butler.

A shiver ran down Lucianna's spine, and Roderick stilled himself from wrapping her in his arms, dispelling the chill that had settled along her arms.

Lucianna turned toward him, her shoulders stooping and tears threatening to fall.

Remorse weakened him for his part in her ruination.

"McMahon!" the marquis shouted as hurried footsteps sounded down the hall outside Lucianna's bedchambers. "See that my daughter leaves this house at once. She is to take nothing but a jacket to hide her damaged person."

"Yes, my lord." Reluctance was clear in the servant's voice.

"I will fix this, Lucianna. I swear to it." He stared down at her as she brushed away her unshed tears.

"There is nothing to fix." She shook her head, leaning into him. "This is what I wanted, exactly what I'd hoped for."

"But, your father…" Roderick sputtered, attempting to understand what she meant about it being exactly what she'd hoped for. "You've been cast out by your father…with nothing."

"I will stay with either Edith's or Ophelia's family. Do not fret," she said flatly.

"And what of your things?"

"They are just that, things." She turned a lopsided smile up to him, her cheek never leaving his chest. "But the one thing I will never have to deal with is Abercorn. He would never take a ruined woman to wife. No matter how large her dowry."

The woman, *his* woman, was a smart one.

Roderick had dwelled on all Lucianna was losing…and not on what she'd gain from a tarnished reputation.

"But how will he know of your ruination?" he asked.

"You do not know my father very well, do you?" Her brow rose. "He does not take kindly to parting with his money. If he shuns me publicly, he will remain in possession of my dowry."

"And not have to put up with your hellion ways."

"Correct, Your Grace." She pulled away from him and placed a kiss on his cheek. "You are certainly catching on."

"Yes, it is a positive thing that I am no dullard…and I happen to adore your hellion ways."

"Do you?" she asked with a deep, throaty laugh.

"Oh, yes." He pulled her against his chest. "I do believe your misfortune is to be my grand blessing."

"Did he call her a blessing?" A hiss sounded behind him.

"No, I think he called her depressing," Lord Torrington's unmistakable tone could be heard from the open veranda door.

"Why would he call her depressing?" Lady Edith chimed in. "I do believe he is instructing her in her undressing."

A round of female giggles echoed as the group all but fell into Lucianna's chambers.

"Tell us, Montrose," Torrington called, pulling Edith to his side. "Is Lady Lucianna a blessing, depressing, or in need of undressing?"

"You all have magnificent timing." Roderick leaned down and placed a kiss to Lucianna's forehead, which gained a sigh from Lady Prudence and Lady Chastity, while Lady Ophelia looked ready to faint on the spot. "I was actually professing my adoration and love for Lady Lucianna and hoping our night would end with her acquiescing and accepting my marriage proposal."

"Marriage?" Lucianna squeaked. "But we just thwarted my father's plans to hand me over to Abercorn…there is no need for you to continue your charade and our sham of a betrothal. I will not be responsible for you taking on a dismal future and a bride you never wanted."

"That is wonderful news; however, I have never been one for charades, nor one for 'taking on a dismal future and a bride.' I've longed to have you since that early morning at Bentley's. That did not change after our meeting in the gardens at Lady Edith's betrothal ball."

The women sighed again, but Lucianna flinched back with a frown.

"Lady Lucianna, I love you. I am in love with you." Roderick released her and brought his hands to cradle her face. "I do not care if you come to me with little more than your nightshift. I will live every day showering you with all the possessions your heart desires."

Her bottom lip trembled, and Roderick's breath hitched, thinking she'd turn away from him. He was no more than a poverty-stricken duke, while she'd been raised by one of the wealthiest men in all of England.

"My heart desires only you, Roderick."

He pulled her close, fearing she'd never be near enough to satisfy him, and doubting he'd ever be able to let her out of his sight.

"Say you will marry me, Lucianna," he pleaded. He needed to hear her say it in front of all these witnesses. It would make everything real.

"Roderick, seventh Duke of Montrose, I, Lady Lucianna Constantine, love you," she declared loudly. "I will wed you and be a fierce duchess, the likes of which London has never seen before."

A cheer went up behind him as he crushed Lucianna to him, no longer caring who witnessed their display of affection for one another.

All of London best prepare; the Duke and Duchess of Montrose were sure to leave a trail of fainting matrons and fawning men in their wakes.

EPILOGUE

LUCIANNA WALKED ARM in arm with Ophelia from the bedchambers they'd shared since the marquis had cast her from her home. Never in her life had she felt the depth of contentment she did since being thrown out of her family home without a shilling to her name and agreeing to wed Roderick.

The Duke and Duchess of Atholl, Ophelia's parents, had gladly taken Luci in and given her a place to stay until she and Roderick were properly wed, affording the couple a much-needed air of propriety.

The girls took the stairs two at a time, each holding tightly to the railing.

Roderick should arrive at any moment to collect them for their late-morning shopping excursion to Bond Street. It had been over a fortnight, and Luci had grown tired of letting the hems out on Ophelia's gowns—and having to see her friend's scathing looks each time she noticed another of her gowns gone.

When an envelope arrived for her the night before, Luci had worried her father was demanding she return home and insisting she fulfill his wishes to wed Abercorn; however, the paper held her mother's elegant script, and inside, was a note for one thousand pounds. Not nearly enough to secure a favorable future for her and Roderick, but a more than adequate amount to afford her a shopping trip and to pay a Bow Street runner to track down Lady Cavendish and the men who'd stolen from Roderick's father.

That was, if Roderick allowed her to spend her funds helping him.

There was also Abercorn to think of. Would it be possible to hire the same runner to keep watch on the duke? They'd all determined it was not wise—or safe—to spy on the man themselves any longer. However, Luci had come close to being wed to the man. Another woman would fall into his trap sooner rather than later...and they had a duty to prevent that from occurring.

Luci's mother's letter went on to express her well wishes for the betrothed couple and contained a promise to see Luci's father released her remaining dowry upon her wedding day. Luci had little hope that the marquis would ever acquiesce where money was concerned. She only dreaded her father taking his anger out on her mother and siblings.

A loud knock sounded at the door as Ophelia and Luci took their overcoats from the footman.

"Lord Montrose is certainly a punctual gent," Ophelia mumbled, glancing at the tall clock in the hall.

Ten-thirty sharp.

Not a moment early, and not a second late.

The butler scurried from his pantry to greet their guest, but when he opened the door, it was not Roderick's dark-haired form waiting on the stoop, but a man with hair of pure spun gold.

"Who is that?" Luci leaned in and whispered to Ophelia. "If I were not deeply smitten with Roderick, I think I would find this man very handsome."

Ophelia put her finger to her lips to shush her friend and stepped back into the stairwell and out of sight. Lucianna followed Ophelia's lead as the butler ushered the man toward Ophelia's father's study.

"I haven't the vaguest idea who he is." Ophelia leaned forward, catching a glimpse of the man's back as he entered the study. The door closed behind him, just as another knock sounded at the door.

"That must be Roderick." She leapt from the stairwell and hurried into the foyer as the butler returned to answer the door, but when she glanced over her shoulder, Ophelia hadn't followed.

She stood still, staring at her father's study.

"Good morn, ladies." Roderick stepped over the threshold. "You both look fine today. Are we ready for an exhaustive day of shopping?"

"Hello, Your Grace," Luci called, stepping into her betrothed's open arms. "I can say I have thought of nothing else since my mother's note arrived."

He placed a quick peck on her cheek. "And I am certain Lady Ophelia has grown tired of you ruining her gowns."

Lucianna laughed, turning to Ophelia, but she'd moved in the direction of her father's study.

"Are you coming?" Luci called to her friend's retreating back.

Ophelia waved over her shoulder. "I think I will remain home," she said over her shoulder. "Edith and Lord Torrington will be meeting you, correct?"

"Yes, but—"

"No one likes a fifth wheel, as they say."

Roderick shrugged, and Luci turned back to see her friend press her ear to her father's door.

"Shall we be off?" Roderick took Luci's gloved hand and set it on his arm. "I believe she is duly occupied, and we have a bridal *trousseau* to gather before we depart for Scotland."

Luci nodded, her mind already swirling around the notion of her and Roderick being properly wed and free to live as husband and wife. They'd leave for Gretna Green in two days' time, with Edith and Lord Torrington, as well as Lady Prudence and Lady Chastity, coming as their witnesses.

Ophelia would stay behind, being an unmarried maiden; her mother forbidding her travel to Scotland.

"Are you having second thoughts?" Roderick whispered, his mouth a scant hair's breadth from her ear. "Because, if you are, I can always cancel—"

Luci swatted at him as they started out the door. "Of course, I am not having any second thoughts. However, I was thinking a great deal of you laid across my bed, your shirt undone, and me atop you."

"You minx," he said with a chuckle. "Though I would be less than honest if I didn't admit I have thought of the same thing nonstop for the last fortnight. Do you think after we are wed your father will allow us entry to your old bedchambers?"

Lucianna winked as he handed her into his coach. "No need to ask permission. I learned long ago that the lock on the veranda door is rather easy to dislodge."

"Heaven help us if our children are blessed with your cunning and smarts." He entered the coach after her, and Luci used that moment to spring onto his lap, straddling his legs with her thighs on each side.

She gave him her most practiced coquettish smile and batted her eyelashes for good measure. "Bond Street is at least a ten-minute drive with morning traffic."

"You hellion, we will be lucky to make it to Scotland!" Roderick said with a chuckle before leaning forward to capture her lips.

"And I'm sure that won't be a hardship, Your Grace," she said with a wink as she pulled back.

"I love you, Luci. It may have taken my misfortune to bring us together, but having you in my life makes me the richest man alive."

THE Misadventures OF Lady Ophelia

THE UNDAUNTED DEBUTANTES
Book 3

CHRISTINA McKNIGHT

DEDICATION

For my readers~

The Undaunted Debutantes heroines are very near and dear to my heart. I do so hope you have loved them as much as I have. They are strong, confident, and deserving of love and happiness...just as every woman is!

PROLOGUE

Devonshire, England
December 1813

AS THE RESOUNDING gong subsided, Lady Ophelia Fletcher glanced up from her book to note the fire in the hearth had died to mere glowing embers and a cold draft blew through the room, raising the hairs on her arms.

The other women in the salon, her dearest friends, all laughed, and Ophelia joined in, having lost the train of conversation long ago.

"…you will tell us everything on the morrow? At breakfast, and not a moment later. I truly must know if everything is as I've been told." Lady Lucianna Constantine raised one brow with a wicked grin. Her green eyes sparkled with mischief as she wrapped Lady Abercorn, formally Miss Tilda Guthton in a tight embrace. "You look breathtakingly innocent."

Ophelia glanced at Tilda, their newly married friend, and was surprised to notice that the young woman did, in fact, look far too innocent for her new status as a duchess. Her mousey brown hair was tied back with a simple white ribbon, the pure shade matching Tilda's nightshift perfectly, making it all the more clear that at age seventeen, barely introduced to society, their friend was far too young to wed a man over twice her age.

Again, it was none of Ophelia's business—the heart loved who the heart loved.

She only found it peculiar that Tilda, the daughter of a mere baronet, had been the one to capture a duke's notice. She was lovely enough—adequate at household matters, graceful as expected, and cultured in her speech—however, Abercorn was a worldly, wealthy, and influential lord.

The duke had seemingly plucked Tilda from obscurity, their courtship developing far quicker than normal.

But, that was none of Ophelia's business either.

She was happy for her dear friend, even if her love match did not resemble that of the star-crossed lovers in her current novel.

Ophelia stood, along with Lady Edith, Lady Luclanna, and Tilda, preparing to leave the room—at least, that was what Ophelia assumed they were doing at such a late hour. Tilda's bridegroom would certainly start to wonder where his young duchess had disappeared to if he approached their marriage bed only to find it empty.

Edith stepped forward and wrapped her arms around Tilda and whispered something in the new bride's ear. Ophelia wasn't privy to the private exchange, but an easy smile lit Tilda's face, removing any trace of unease that may have been there, however subtle.

"Thank you, Edith. You have always been a great friend." Tilda hugged Edith a bit tighter before pulling back. "I must hurry. It will not do for my *husband* to arrive and find that I have fled. He said he would arrive by half past midnight, after attending to a few business matters."

Luci slipped her arm through Tilda's, while Ophelia

grabbed her book from the settee and held it to her chest as she followed her friends toward the door, suppressing the tingle of envy that began to blossom at Luci and Tilda's close relationship.

Now was not the time to allow the hurt of being left out to surface and thus drag her into despair.

"Now remember that thing we spoke about, with your ton…" Luci's whispers trailed off as the women departed the room, their heads leaned together much like conspirators, as if Ophelia could not possibly understand the things they tittered about. The pair had likely never even opened a book and lost themselves to an adventure, or a sensual tale of exploration and discovery.

Such a pity, but Ophelia would not be the one to share her private collection of leather-bound tales of love, lust, and escapades.

"I will extinguish the candles," Edith called as Ophelia reached the threshold.

She paused, turning to the petite blonde who'd long been the only one in the group to understand Ophelia's thirst for knowledge and her reserved tendencies. "I will help you."

"No, hurry along," Edith said, waving her off. "I know you are eager to return to your book. It will take but a few moments. I will meet you in our room as soon as I am done."

"If you insist." Ophelia smiled before glancing over her shoulder to see Luci and Tilda had reached the stairs. "I am eager to see how the fair Lady Daniella escapes the rogue pirate, Xavier."

Edith laughed softly. "Well, do get back to their story."

She needed no further encouragement as Ophelia stepped from the room and opened the blue, leather-bound volume to the place she'd marked with a slip of stationery, always hesitant to mar the pressed pages of her books.

Oh, how Lady Daniella flipped her long tresses over her shoulder before giving Xavier a narrowed look and demanding he listen to her, heed her words well, or the pirate would never again taste Daniella's womanly charms.

Ophelia longed to be so bold, commanding, and beautiful as to gain the notice of…well, anyone.

Instead, Ophelia's hair was an ungodly shade of bright red, her nose sprinkled with freckles, and her hips far too curvy to fit with popular fashion. Never could her wild tresses be tamed, unlikely was her complexion ever to be clear and pale, and it was doubtful she would ever embrace London elite's current affection for bold fabric choices.

She sighed, focusing on her place on the page.

A scream pulled her eyes from the author's description of Xavier's bare, hair-covered chest.

Thump, thump, thump.

"Edith!" Luci's blood-curdling scream stopped her in her tracks. "Ophelia!"

A sob escaped her as her book slipped from her grasp, hitting the polished floor with a resounding thud, unlike the hollow noise from a moment before. Her slip of personalized stationery drifted across the floor, coming to rest only when it partially slid under a closed door.

Tilda lay sprawled at the bottom of the staircase, her head turned at an odd angle, her eyes open wide.

Ophelia blinked several times.

She waited for Tilda to move. Or Luci to help her up. Or the floor to open and swallow them whole.

But nothing happened.

She blinked again when her sight blurred with tears.

Suddenly, time started again. The distant *tick-tock* of the mahogany clock in the room they'd just departed could be heard. Edith appeared at her side, and Luci crouched over Tilda, her black hair cascading over her shoulder to—mercifully—block the sight of their friend.

"Luci." Edith stepped around her toward Lucianna. "What is it—"

Edith's words cut off.

"No, no, no," Edith sobbed as she hurried forward. "This cannot be—"

"He did this." Desperation laced Luci's tone when she pointed toward the top of the stairs.

Ophelia looked to the darkened landing above them but saw nothing of consequence.

"Who?" Ophelia asked, swallowing the sob that threatened to escape if she opened her mouth again.

"That is not important at this moment," Edith scolded her, hurrying to Tilda's side. "We must wake her up, make sure she is all right and call for the duke—and a physician."

How is it not important, Ophelia longed to ask. However, she pressed her lips together and remained silent—as was expected of her.

If she were Lady Daniella, Ophelia would lift her chin until she stared down her slightly crooked nose at her friends and demand to be heard and answered. However, she was not Lady Daniella, a woman abducted from her village on the Scottish coast by a pirate most fierce. She was merely Lady Ophelia, a passably comely, reticent, self-professed bookworm. The women before her were beautiful, clever, and captivating. Everything the heroines in her novels were. Not red-haired, freckle-faced, and rounded.

"…he pushed her. I swear it."

Ophelia shook her head, feeling guilty at the continued wandering of her thoughts when she should be listening to Luci and attempting to make sense of the scene before her. She'd studied many novels where the hero, a shipwrecked man, had been forced to do battle. She'd read of blood-thirsty Amazon natives and murderous clansmen laying claim to neighboring villages, but witnessing the prone body of a friend was much different.

Actually, it was in no way the same.

Never could any tales have prepared her for the sight before her.

The way Tilda's eyes stood open but lacked any life. The angle at which her arm was bent. The thin trail of dark red blood leaving the corner of her slack mouth.

Uncertainty, confusion, and denial all waged war within Ophelia as her stomach tensed and her breath caught in her chest, locking her lungs and preventing the air from escaping. Perspiration broke out across her forehead and her neck heated at her collar.

Ophelia swallowed past the lump in her throat. "Wha-wha-what should we do?" She hated hearing the weakness in her voice, confirming what her friends already proclaimed about her. She was scared of her own shadow. Likely to faint at the slightest shock.

"We will rouse the house and tell them all what the duke has done!" Lucianna quickly stood, drawing Ophelia's eyes from Tilda. "Someone must have heard the commotion."

Edith glanced around the foyer. "You are correct. I heard her scream, and then the thump as she fell."

"She did *not* fall." Lucianna's tone reached hysterics, sounding much like Ophelia felt on the inside—panicked and terrified. "She was *pushed*, by Abercorn!"

They stared at one another. Hot tears began to stream down Ophelia's heated face, while Luci appeared to regain her composure. Her widened green eyes held no hint of the waterworks Ophelia had been reduced to. Edith reached out toward Luci, but the woman ignored her hand.

"How could this happen?" Ophelia asked, stooping to collect her book as she dashed the unbidden tears away.

"That is a question for him. You saw him, right, Ophelia?" Luci turned imploring eyes on her.

The heat drained from Ophelia as cold overtook

her, and her stomach roiled with unease.

"Tell her what you saw." Luci took an intimidating step toward Ophelia. "You were standing right here."

"I—I—I was reading." Ophelia turned to Edith, her book held tightly against her bosom as if she loosened her hold, Luci would snatch the volume from her. "I swear it, Edith, I did not see anything. I was reading about Xavier and—"

"What is going on here?" Townsend, the Abercorn butler, hurried into the foyer, his hair flopping from side to side like the caricatures depicted in the comical pages of *The Post*. He'd certainly been pulled from slumber. "Your Grace!" His eyes widened at the sight of Tilda as he rushed across the room to where she lay. His hand moved to her wrist and settled. "No pulse. She has no pulse!"

The servant shuffled to his feet, glancing around the room as if expecting someone to step forward and solve this major dilemma—his new mistress, lying dead at the bottom of the stairs on her wedding night.

"Petunia, Petunia!" Townsend shouted as he flapped his arms to and fro, rushing deeper into the Abercorn house. "Petunia! We must summon His Grace. Petunia, where in all that is holy are you, woman?"

Doors opened, and voices called from above as guests exited their rooms, hearing the commotion as Townsend continued calling for Petunia.

"Oh, Your Grace!" Townsend said, staring toward the top of the stairs. "Please, do not look. This is not for your eyes."

Ophelia pressed herself to the wall, praying she could escape notice for a few minutes.

As she took a deep breath, Ophelia watched Luci's hands ball into fists at her sides, and her face redden. Ophelia cringed. An angry Lady Lucianna could raise Satan from the depths of Hell with her fury.

Leaning away from the wall, the duke could be seen

making slow progress down the stairs.

The man seemed oddly unaffected by the sight of his dead wife only five steps below him. Truthfully, his gaze barely took notice of her before he stepped clear of the blood beginning to pool under Tilda's head.

Ophelia spun away from the foyer and hurried toward the sitting room they'd departed a few moments before.

Could it have been only precious minutes ago that they'd all sat close, gossiping about the night to come?

She'd been so distracted by her book she hadn't embraced Tilda one last time. She hadn't whispered good tidings before the new bride had left the room on Luci's arm.

Shame caused Ophelia's face to flush once more as she entered the darkened room and rushed to the windows overlooking the garden. She threw the windowpane open and allowed the cold night air in. Ophelia should return to the foyer, be there for her friends. Did they even notice she'd fled? She'd failed Luci and Edith, and especially Tilda.

If she hadn't been preoccupied with her reading, would she have seen Lord Abercorn atop the grand staircase? Surely, Luci was not mistaken, but Ophelia had been unable to voice her support of her friend's accusations.

Ophelia had frozen, her mind tangled and confused.

CHAPTER 1

It is with great pleasure that this writer speaks for the young women of the ton. Ladies who will not be taken for granted nor misguided by men of unsavory character. And with this article, this writer will no longer glorify the misdeeds of men, but celebrate the accomplishments of young, bright, charming females.

It is this author's opinion that lords far and wide heed th knowledge imbued by this column, as there is little doubt there will be postings regarding.

-The Mayfair Confidential

London
April 1815

LADY OPHELIA FLETCHER sat primly in a chair set against the wall, her ankles crossed and tucked under her with her hands folded lightly in her lap. She was the epitome of the proper miss as she watched Lady Lucianna discard yet another stationery sample. This time it was the color, the last was not an acceptable texture, and the one before that smudged when her friend placed quill to paper.

To all who viewed Ophelia, she most certainly looked at ease with a confident, serene smile.

Inside, she wanted to scream. She breathed deeply and released the air slowly to remain calm and in control. Her smile didn't falter, and her hands didn't so much as twitch, though she longed to clench something, even the delicate muslin of her morning gown.

If she'd brought her reticle, she would have thrown it against the wall.

Luci held up a thick, cream-colored stationery with gold leafing to elicit Ophelia's opinion, silent raising one brow.

"It is lov—"

"No, it is far too *cream* and not thick enough." Luci sighed, turning back to the proprietor and cutting Ophelia off. "Do you have anything with ebony trim?"

"Lovely," Ophelia finished in a whisper. The paper *was* lovely, as were the five other options presented during their hour in the stationery shop.

Her knees ached from sitting for far too long, so Ophelia stood and turned toward the storefront windows. The sun was nearly directly overhead, and Bond Street was now busy with the *beau monde* hurrying in and out of shops, their servants trailing behind, their arms heavy with purchases. It was the way of London. The only thing the *ton* enjoyed more than being seen was spending money on purchases one did not necessarily need and being observed doing it.

Certainly, stationery and calling cards were important, and since Luci was to wed the Duke of Montrose in under two weeks, it was imperative she select something with all due haste before she, Montrose, Lady Edith, and Lord Torrington left for Gretna Green.

Lady Lucianna's father, the Marquis of Camden, had refused to allow a proper betrothal between Montrose and Luci. The man had gone so far as to throw Luci from her home and ban her from seeing her mother and siblings.

And so, instead of waiting until her father agreed

and consented to the marriage, thus having the wedding blessed by her family, Luci had chosen to travel to Scotland to see the appropriate ceremony done. Odd for a woman who, only a few short weeks prior, was determined never to wed, let alone trust a man with her future.

Ophelia shook her head and focused on the passersby.

She breathed in and out. Deep inhale, slow exhale.

It would not do to allow unease to overtake her in such a public place—her cheeks flushing, her eyes widening, and her pulse racing to match the pace of a galloping thoroughbred. It would inevitably end with her vigorously fanning herself, or worse yet, falling into a dead faint. And would only serve to impress upon Luci—and Edith, once she heard of the incident—that Ophelia was less than capable of, well…anything.

Glaring out the window, she noticed an urchin slip past a finely dressed man, the boy's grimy hand snaking into the gent's pocket and back out again before the imp veered away and turned sharply, entering a shop across the street. By the time Ophelia tried to spot the thief's mark, the gentleman had disappeared, as well.

"…what about another choice with gold leaf on the edges?" Luci asked the proprietor.

Ophelia had been mistaken when she believed inviting Luci to live with her until the wedding was a grand idea.

If anything, it was tedious.

She sighed, meaning to turn and regain her seat, but a familiar gentleman strolled past the stationery shop with an elegantly garbed woman on his arm, causing Ophelia to press her face against the glass to watch the man as they moved farther down the street with their heads tilted together in a conspiratorial manner.

Glancing over her shoulder, Luci was busily flipping through another stack of samples on her quest to select the perfect paper product to announce her coming status as the Duchess of Montrose. There was little doubt she'd remain occupied for at least another hour.

Ophelia slipped out the open shop door just in time to see Lord Abercorn, the man responsible for their dear friend's death the Season before—and the man Luci's father had demanded she wed—step into Oliver's Book Shoppe with the spinster, Lady Sissy Cassel, at his side. It was not hard to peg Lady Sissy as Abercorn sister, although her greying hair and stooped shoulders made her appear more the age of the duke's mother. Ophelia had met the older woman only once, the previous month at the Abercorn townhouse, and Sissy had left little lasting impression on Ophelia.

The walk to the shop three buildings down took only a moment, but Ophelia didn't risk entering the business. She pressed herself to the wall bordering the shop and leaned around to peek through the windowpane, freshly cleaned to a shine. She pulled back when she noticed Abercorn turn down an aisle. Her nose left a print on the clean window, but Ophelia stilled herself from rubbing it off with her sleeve.

It would be possible, if she hurried, to slip into the shop and down another aisle without Abercorn noticing her. She needed to see what the man was up to.

As far as Ophelia and her friends were concerned, Abercorn should not be allowed out in polite society. She didn't trust him.

A bell sounded overhead as she entered the shop, and the owner, Oliver, issued a greeting from somewhere deeper inside.

The smell of old leather and candle wax assaulted her. She always enjoyed the mixture of scents, the comfort row after row of books provided, and, most of all, the silence of the bookstore; however, Abercorn's mere presence did away with any security and serenity she gained from being surrounded by her most favorite thing: books. This shop was not her safe haven or her sanctuary when Abercorn was near.

Safely in the aisle, she paused before hurrying toward the back of the shop. She'd been to Oliver's more times than she could count and knew the place well. Abercorn and Lady Sissy were three rows down in the History of the English Coast section. She'd scoured the section many times but found the books mainly about their country's many sea ports, including import and export routes favored over the last three hundred years. In short, the titles nestled on the shelves in that row lacked adventure beyond the mundane. No tales of swashbuckling pirates sailing across the seven seas in search of hidden treasure and their ladyloves. No tales of Arabian nights with hooded thieves and enchanting maidens. Not so much as a tale of a long-ago Robin Hood, stealing from the wealthy upper class and giving to the downtrodden paupers of Nottingham.

Abercorn was a shrewd businessman and tales of fancy were certainly not to his liking, but why would he be interested in trade in and out of England?

If she were utterly honest, Ophelia had little knowledge what men of vast wealth and power busied themselves with all day in their offices. Even her father, a duke much like Abercorn, did not concern himself with family matters, nor did he share news of his business ventures with his children.

"Can I help you with something, miss?"

Ophelia yelped with fright as she swung around to see the shopkeeper only a few feet away from her at the end of the aisle.

"No, sir, thank you," she hissed, putting her hand to her chest as her bosom heaved. "I am merely having a look around."

"If you need anything, I will be behind the counter." The shopkeeper nodded in the direction of the tall desk along the far wall toward the front of the shop before returning to his post.

Ophelia sighed in relief.

Taking in the shop—or the areas she could see through the opening in the shelf before her—it was only Ophelia, the shopkeeper, and Abercorn and his sister in the shop. She watched the duke closely as he moved down the row, scanning the shelves, his back to her. When he reached the end, he turned and started down the next aisle. Another row on England, these mostly featuring large, handwritten volumes depicting various countryside landscapes and their native plants and animals. The duke pulled a book from its place, and Ophelia shifted to see the cover; however, Abercorn moved down the aisle toward Oliver's desk before she could make it out.

"Good day, my lord," the shopkeeper greeted Abercorn. "And my lady. Will this be all?"

Abercorn responded, but his voice was too low for Ophelia to hear.

Oh, bother.

"Ask him, Franny," Lady Sissy whined, but again, Abercorn spoke too softly for Ophelia to hear what was said.

The shopkeeper and Lord Abercorn spoke for several minutes before Abercorn handed over his coin for the book he purchased.

Perhaps Edith and Luci were correct, and Ophelia was unequipped to undertake anything more than writing the articles for the *Mayfair Confidential* column in the *London Daily Gazette*.

The front bell chimed as Abercorn and Lady Sissy exited. Ophelia watched as they promptly entered his parked carriage. There would be little hope of keeping further watch on the man today.

Ophelia allowed her fingers to caress the spine of a book as she stepped around the tall shelf and into Oliver's line of sight. His eyes bulged, and his breath hitched. She'd startled him—and that might be enough to throw the proprietor off and allow her to ask the information she sought. She was here for a reason, after all. It was not enough to simply *follow* Abercorn. They were in dire need of information. Anything that could lead to the apprehension of the man for Tilda's death.

"Good day, Lady Ophelia. I did not know you were still here." Oliver busied himself with a stack of papers on his desk, giving her the privacy she normally needed, but she would not be turned away so easily. When she continued to stare at him, he set the papers aside and faced her from behind his desk. "Can I assist you with locating something?"

"I think you can." She smiled at the man.

"Anything, my lady."

Anything? She supposed she'd put his words to the test. "What was that man"—Ophelia glanced over her shoulder and pointed toward the door Abercorn and his sister had left through—"asking about? And what book did he purchase?"

The duke's trip to Oliver's Book Shoppe may very well have naught to do with Ophelia, her friends, or Tilda's death, but she needed to know. At least, for her own sake.

A measure of confidence infused and emboldened Ophelia. "It would be very helpful to know what Lord Abercorn was doing in your shop, Mr. Oliver."

The man's eyes narrowed on her, and Ophelia suspected she'd gone too far. But hadn't Edith risked it all when she'd climbed into Lord Torrington's father's tree? And hadn't Luci endangered her reputation by kissing Lord Montrose in that well-lit garden? It was Ophelia's turn to chance her name.

She could do this.

She had to do this.

She not only owed it to Tilda's memory but also to Edith and Lucianna.

"Come now, Mr. Oliver," Ophelia coaxed as she took a step toward the proprietor in the dim shop. "We have known one another for many, many years. My father used to bring me here when I was still in short dresses and childish frocks. I dare say, my hair mayhap still plaited. Please, I just want to know the reason for Lord Abercorn's visit to your shop."

His lips pressed into a fine line, and he tapped one finger on the desk. "I pride myself on keeping my clients' acquisitions private, my lady. I am certain you can understand that."

"I can; however, I am more than a client, am I not?" Ophelia's brow rose, and she stepped closer to Mr. Oliver. "It is a simple, unimportant, morsel of information I seek. Nothing more."

His eyes followed her as she advanced on him.

"My lady, you must—"

"My father will be greatly angered if I return to him without what he seeks." Ophelia detested bringing her father, the Duke of Atholl, into the matter, but she was running out of options, and Oliver seemed no closer to speaking. "He is a valued patron of your bookshop, is he not?" There was little need to wait for a reply, but Oliver nodded all the same. "What can it hurt to tell me what Abercorn was here in search of…that is, unless it has to do with my father's collection?"

Oliver's brow shot high, and Ophelia had the sense that she'd stumbled upon something completely unintended, but she pushed the notion from her mind. Her father had nothing to do with Abercorn.

The shopkeeper rubbed the back of his neck and sighed, pondering the limited options she'd given him. Certainly, the man would speak, and Ophelia would have the information she needed, as useless as it might be.

"Lady Ophelia, while your father is a valued client, he will understand I am unable to give you the information you seek." He glanced over Ophelia's shoulder toward the door. "Besides, would you want me sharing news of your purchases with anyone?"

Bloody bollocks. Ophelia certainly would not want

Oliver sharing with all and sundry her adoration for adventure tales or her love for romantic stories. She would not want her recent purchase of Coleridge's *The Rime of the Ancyent Marinere* to be known by anyone in polite society. She was not embarrassed by her reading pleasures, but she did enjoy anonymity regarding her purchases.

Glancing back toward the door, she noted that Lord Abercorn's carriage remained at the curb outside the shop. Lucianna would be completing her transactions very soon, no doubt. Ophelia headed toward the back door of the bookstore, knowing she could depart and re-enter the stationery shop where she'd left Luci without being seen by the passing carriages. She was nearly there when the front door sounded yet again.

Ophelia ducked into a small reading alcove she'd never noticed before at the back of the store and hastily pulled the drape closed to block her from view.

Heavy footfalls sounded across the wood plank floor and echoed through the empty shop.

Peculiar, Abercorn had made no sound as he traversed the rows in search of his book. Nor had his boots made any noise as he'd departed Oliver's. And Lady Sissy's slippers only shuffled along the floor.

A measure of relief flooded Ophelia, allowing her to take a deep breath before grasping the curtain. Her hand stalled when a deep, raspy voice sounded after Oliver's customary greeting.

She peeked through the slit in the hanging drape.

A man stood before Oliver, his hands hanging stiffly at his sides. His side profile showed a strong jaw, tanned skin, and fair hair that hung a bit too long over his collar. While Edith's hair was the color of pure spun gold or morning rays of sunshine, this man had hair so fair it was nearly white, though it could be the deep tan of his complexion that cast the illusion. His stance was wide, and he moved his hands to his hips as his voice rose.

"I would appreciate if you could check your records, sir," the man huffed, running his hand through his hair to return it to its place. "I have, on good authority, word you were at one time in possession of the book I seek."

Oliver's eyes narrowed, and he retrieved a ledger from the shelf next to his desk. "When did you say I might have had the book?"

"Ten years ago, perhaps longer," the man replied, his cultured tone and finely tailored jacket spoke of wealth. "It is called *Smuggling: A Journey from Kent to Denmark*, by Fair Wind Parnell."

"Ten years, you say?"

"There about, yes."

Ophelia dared pull the curtain open a bit further to hear Oliver's quiet reply.

"My apologies, but my ledger does not span more than five years of acquisitions, my lord."

The man rubbed his jaw and turned toward Ophelia's hiding spot, causing her to shrink back to avoid being seen eavesdropping.

"But you have other ledgers?" he asked. "This is of the utmost importance, and time is of the essence."

The man was clearly agitated, but why would a book, especially one over ten years old, be of any import?

Ophelia nearly giggled at the thought. Most of her collection was made up of books twice her age, and all were still relevant and captivating. She scooted closer to the curtain again as the man stared at something to the left of the alcove she hid in.

His eyes.

They were the most entrancing hue of green. They fairly glowed in the dimly lit shop and were only accentuated by his dark complexion—and the irritation rolling off him.

She envisioned that he must be the spitting image

of every pirate ever written.

It did not take much imagination to picture the man bare-chested, the salty sea breeze blowing his hair back as the noonday sun heated his skin. His grip on the helm of his impressively large vessel firm as he barked orders to his crew who worked frantically about the deck. His men would fear him, yet respect his leadership. He would be valiant, courageous, and chivalrous.

Was not every riveting man written of in books—tales of love and adventure—marked by those three traits?

He would be a captain in command of his men and his ship—or at least that would be how the tale went. But would he be a pirate? A naval captain? Or a mere merchant?

Certainly not a smuggler as intimated by his inquiry to the shopkeeper.

No, a smuggler would not sail into battle to win the heart of a woman.

Oliver offered the man a slip of paper and a quill, which the man gladly accepted before scribbling something.

Ophelia exhaled her pent-up breath as Oliver promised to inspect the ledgers kept at his home for the sought book and assured the customer he would send word to the address provided.

With a curt nod of thanks, the man returned the quill and paper to Oliver and strode from the store, the chime signaling his departure.

She exited her hiding spot and hurried to the middle row and a clear view of the front of the shop and the happenings outside the window.

The man, whoever he was, waited as his footman opened his carriage door and then entered the conveyance. Barely enough time had passed for the servant to leap back onto the perch before the carriage pulled onto Bond Street and out of sight.

Leaving Ophelia staring after him, puzzled and highly interested in his plight to secure a book.

CHAPTER 2

COLIN PARNELL, LORD Hawke, departed Oliver's Book Shoppe in no better mood than he'd arrived. He jammed his fingers through his hair, reminding himself for the tenth time he was in serious need of a trim as he threw himself against the velvety soft cushion of his father's town coach.

Blast it all, but the situation irritated him to no end.

"Well?" a raspy voice asked from across the enclosed carriage as it jerked into motion. "Did that fool Oliver have me book?"

"*Our* book," Colin corrected, bringing his glare to the woman. His tone and narrowed stare softened immediately when he took in his grandmama's hopeful look. "My apologies, Molly, it is only I am frustrated and tired of hitting dead ends with our search."

The old woman smiled, her teeth perfectly straight but stained by her love of Turkish coffee.

"Bollocks, but I detest disappointing you," Colin huffed. "Pardon my speech, Molly."

"Do not ye be worry'n 'bout disappoint'n me, lad," Molly chastised, crossing her thin arms over her nearly flat chest. Since the sickness had taken hold, she'd slowly diminished in size, though her demeanor was in no way less frightening, especially when she turned her anger on a subject. "None of this would be necessary if'n your scoundrel of a father was not so determined to prove your grandpapa, me dear Fair Wind, a debauched smuggler."

Colin massaged his temples, praying his headache did not return. Molly had arrived in London only a week prior from his family's country estate in Tintinhull, Somerset, under the guise of requiring a physician, but it hadn't taken long for her true purpose to present itself.

"You know how it angers Father when you call Grandpapa 'Fair Wind'."

"What do ye expect me ta call him, child? Porter? Lord Coventry? M'lord?" The woman huffed as her knuckles whitened on the head of her walking cane. "He be Fair Wind ta me, always has been, and always will be since the moment he entered that tavern in Sheerness. He was no gent then, nor when he went ta the good Lord."

The woman tapped her chest and left shoulder before winking twice and nodding her chin.

It had been the same superstitious ritual she'd performed Colin's entire life. As a child, he'd thought it peculiar and laugh-worthy, but as a grown man with twenty-three summers come and gone, he cringed each time Molly executed the foolish deed when his grandpapa, Porter Parnell, the first Earl of Coventry was mentioned aloud.

Colin desperately longed to make Molly happy. She'd been like a mother to him since his birth as his own parents had been far more interested in partaking of London Seasons and holidays in Bath than rearing their only child.

"I just cannot believe Oliver would sell the book," Molly sighed, shaking her head. "He and me Fair Wind were dear friends."

"If it is any consolation, he promised to review his old ledgers and determine who purchased the tome." It was the best Colin had been able to accomplish—and far more information than he'd expected to obtain. Who would have thought the old bookshop would still be operating after all these years, or that the proprietor would remember the book in question. "He has assured me he will send word, regardless of what he finds in his records."

"He best, or next time, I be forced ta speak with him," Molly threatened.

Yes, the woman was a force of nature, even at her advanced age, but her health was indeed failing.

She thumped her cane against the carriage floor, and her hat fell forward over one eye. She reached up, her fingers shaking slightly, and pushed the cap back. "I will bash him in the knees until he be remember'n exactly what he did with our book."

"You cannot go about hitting people, Molly." It had been a point of contention between Molly and Colin's parents for years. She lived by the old rules, the governances followed by the hardworking Englishmen and women of Kent during a time when she and Colin's grandpapa did all they could to survive. "And, I beg of you, do not cause another scene, or Father has made it clear you will be returned to Somerset where an adequate physician will be retained for you."

She snorted, a decidedly unladylike sound for a dowager countess. "Ramsey, my wayward son, would enjoy noth'n more than leave'n me ta rot in the wilds of Somerset while he lives like the grand nob he is."

The carriage hit a particularly large pothole, and Molly bounced from her seat, landing askew.

Colin immediately moved across the carriage to assist her back to a seated position, but she swatted his hand away.

"I'm not at death's door yet, lad," she scolded. "The carrion hunter won't be summoned for me today. I have important business ta attend before that day comes, and your rascal of a father won't be stop'n me."

And around and around it went.

"Of course, you are not in jeopardy of going to the hereafter as yet."

"And I won't be meet'n my love only ta tell him his son still thinks him a no-good smuggler." Molly turned sharply, likely to hide her teary eyes from her only grandson. "I won't be allow'n that ta happen, Colin."

"Neither will I," he said in agreement.

Colin allowed the silence to cloak him, to settle around him like a well-worn garment as he watched Molly, her head leaning back against the cushion as she continued to stare out the window.

Sometimes, he found himself beginning to believe his father's rantings surrounding Molly's mental state. The Earl of Coventry used words such as demented, addlebrained, and senseless when he spoke of his mother, Molly Parnell. However, Colin only saw a woman who'd cared for him during his infancy and childhood and who continued to dote on him even after his time at University. No one who came into contact with Molly could deny the old woman was set in her ways, or that she had a mouth worse than most seamen, the demeanor of a shrewd merchant, and the crass nature of a bar wench. And she'd been exactly that when she met and fell in love with Porter Parnell all those years ago.

Though before giving birth to her only son, Ramsey, Molly—and Porter—had been bestowed an Earldom by King George II with lands and a fortune to match, she'd never forgotten her humble beginnings in the coast town of Sheerness, Kent.

"Molly." He had the urge to say something, to reassure her that he was doing all in his power to find his grandpapa's book—the volume Molly was certain would prove that Fair Wind was not just a mere smuggler, but an honorable, king-fearing man who served his country well during the Seven Years' War. When his grandmama turned to him, Colin noted how much she'd aged since he last visited her. Her eyes were…tired. It was the only way to explain her heavily sagging lids. Her hair was now solid gray, though she'd always prided herself on her silky brown tresses. And her fingers firmly grasping her cane were gnarled. "I have not given up hope. Never will I give up hope."

"So much like me Fair Wind, ye are, lad." Her smile returned, but it was not meant for Colin. No, she was thinking of Porter "Fair Wind" Parnell, her lost love.

Colin was almost hesitant to call her mind back to the present, but they were nearly to Knightsbridge Townhouse—the Coventry home while in London— and he needed to remind her of the sensitive nature of their search. "You will keep this between us, correct? Father will return you to Somerset without a second thought if he learns we are trying to locate that bloody book again."

"Discretion is me middle name, boy," Molly replied with a grin.

"I thought you said it was Arabella-Louise," Colin teased.

"And ye are a far better listener than your father." She glanced out the window once more, and Colin was filled with a sense of pride—of accomplishment. His grandmama Molly was a determined woman, and with his help they would set history straight and prove that Fair Wind Parnell, later the first Earl of Coventry, was much more than a no-good, scallywag of a smuggler. They would establish that he was, in fact, the trusted friend of one of the greatest monarch's England has ever seen.

…if only they could hide their activities from his father for a while longer.

CHAPTER 3

OPHELIA SLIPPED INTO her room and leaned against the door, her eyes closed. She was beyond ready for a couple of quiet moments alone—and a few scarce minutes to lose herself in her current book, *The Buccaneer's Bounty*, without Luci droning on and on about the silly nature of adventure novels or, worse yet, her upcoming nuptials to the Duke of Montrose. Ophelia in no way felt ill will for the new pair, but she was rather jealous she'd been forbidden to accompany the couple on their trip to Scotland.

Another escapade she'd be left out of.

Oh, she'd known brief moments of adventure—their spying on Abercorn, their hand in the *Mayfair Confidential* column, and their trip to rescue Edith after she'd been kidnapped a few months prior—but none of those had been *hers*. Ophelia had had no control over any of those events, and a sense of helplessness came with that thought.

She sighed and pushed away from the door as she opened her eyes.

Only to recoil in horror.

The small bookshelf near her bed had been emptied of Ophelia's most treasured volumes.

She rushed around the mattress as dread heated her

skin.

Her books…they were haphazardly strewn on the floor with no regard for their value.

Glancing at her shelf once more, Ophelia was stunned to see several lengths of ribbon and a pearl-handled comb and brush set nestled where Ophelia had lovingly placed her collection of poetry.

The door opened and closed behind her with a resounding thud.

"Ah, there you are!" Luci's voiced rose the hairs on the back of Ophelia's neck. "I left the receiving room to call for tea, and when I returned, you had vanished."

Ophelia took a deep breath and exhaled slowly, reciting to herself that she only need share her private chambers for a few more days before Luci would be off to Scotland with Montrose, Edith, and Lord Torrington. Her bedchambers would once again be hers, and her friendship with Luci would return to normal.

"Oh, you are admiring my latest gifts from Roderick." Luci knelt before the shelf and caressed the handle of the delicate brush. "He is such a generous man, and he truly loves me," Luci sighed.

Yes, and before long *he'd* be giving up his personal space to accommodate Lucianna.

Ophelia *was* overjoyed that both of her dearest friends were betrothed to such fine, noble lords.

"Did you hear the brilliant news?" Luci moved to the wardrobe and collected a pressed set of cream gloves to match her sage-green gown—*Ophelia's* walking dress, the hem let out several inches to accommodate Luci's tall stature. "My stationery arrived this morning," she continued without waiting for Ophelia to answer.

"Splendid," Ophelia mumbled.

"When I return from Scotland, I am taking you to Mademoiselle Katerina for an entirely new wardrobe." Luci dragged her fingertips across the neatly hung gowns in Ophelia's dressing closet. "These colors…they are atrocious and in no way complement your complexion."

"But they are the same gowns I've been wearing all Season," Ophelia retorted, but even to her ears, the words held no bite.

"Yes, but now you are the bosom friend of a duchess and a soon-to-be marchioness." Luci pulled a muddy-brown riding habit out of the wardrobe and held it out for Ophelia to see. "You cannot possibly believe this dreadful excuse for a proper fabric is acceptable, O."

"I, well…"

"Do not fret." Luci rehung the habit and turned back to Ophelia with a reassuring smile. "I will outfit you properly."

A peculiar promise from a woman who was in all regards without a home at present.

Ophelia glanced at her still open closet behind Luci and then noted the pair of blue satin slippers protruding from beneath her dressing table, the pile of books continuing to collect dust on her floor, and the stack of shawls strewn across her normally neatly made bed. Luci moved through every room much like a windstorm, wreaking havoc as she did, and leaving destruction in her wake. Ophelia needs must remember to give her maid extra thanks for tidying up after her friend.

"Are you ready?" Luci took in Ophelia from head to toe.

For a brief moment, she had the urge to take in her appearance, as well; however, Ophelia had been dressed since shortly after dawn. She'd broken her fast with her siblings and mother. She'd written another article for the *Mayfair Confidential,* and she'd selected her next book to read—all before Luci had seen fit to crawl from her bed.

"Roderick will be here shortly to collect us for our outing."

"And we certainly don't wish to keep him waiting." Ophelia slipped her coin purse into the pocket of her cloak. "I am ready."

The way Luci's eyes lingered on her, told Ophelia her friend thought her anything but ready.

But, with no other protest, Luci slipped her arm through Ophelia's and pulled her toward the door as if Ophelia were a puppy to be manhandled and led about on a leash.

Not that Ophelia had anyone to blame but herself for the way Luci and Edith treated her—she'd always been happy to follow their lead, listen to their instructions, and do exactly as she was told. It was the same with her family. Ophelia's mother bid her keep watch on her younger siblings, and she readily agreed. Her father demanded she remain in London and not accompany her friends to Scotland, and Ophelia had not issued so much as an argument in favor of what she longed to do. When Luci had quickly taken over her chambers, making them her own, Ophelia hadn't objected.

They departed their shared chambers arm-in-arm and made their way to the main staircase. When an envelope had arrived containing a healthy amount of pounds, both Luci and Ophelia had gasped in surprise. The gift was from Lucianna's mother and was to be spent on proper clothing until such time that Lady Camden could convince her stubborn husband to hand over the rest of Luci's dowry after she wed Montrose.

Another day of shopping did not sound nearly as appealing as an afternoon spent reading. However, with Montrose, Edith, and Lord Torrington in tow, at least Ophelia wouldn't be alone in her plight.

AN EXASPERATED SIGH escaped as Colin pondered for the thousandth time why he'd agreed to allow Molly to accompany him to Atholl's townhouse. He leaned back against the velvet squabs of his father's finely adorned landau and gave his grandmama his most charming smile. Allowing the woman to know he was irritated would be unwise.

"You cannot accompany me into Lord Atholl's home," he repeated for the third time since they'd pulled into the drive. His footman waited outside the carriage to open the door, but Colin refused to depart the conveyance until Molly had agreed to remain inside and unseen.

"Why can I not go in?" Molly huffed, pounding the end of her cane against the floor to punctuate each word. "It is me book the man stole, and I will have it back."

"Atholl stole nothing," Colin said slowly, his imploring stare begging Molly to understand. "He purchased the book at Oliver's, bought and paid for."

"He is a bloody pisser, and ye won't be convince'n me no different."

"Molly." Colin pinched the bridge of his nose. Growing up on the docks of Sheerness, his grandmama's less than proper upbringing presented itself with increased intensity when she was angry or met by opposition. "This is exactly why I cannot allow you to accompany me. If you start in on one of your tirades, Lord Atholl will have no reason to give us any information about the book—that is if he even so much as remembers purchasing the blasted thing."

With a *humph*, Molly trained her eyes on the head of her cane. "We are too bloody close, Colin, me lad."

"I understand your impatience, I do. However, barging into Lord Atholl's home and demanding the book will not gain us what we seek." He was helpless to remain irked by her demeanor. "Besides, Oliver gave me the information in the strictest of confidence. It would harm his business if any hint of gossip escaped, concerning him giving out the personal information of his clients. Tell me you understand and will remain in the carriage until I return."

She took her narrowed stare from her cane and met

his eyes, her countenance immediately softening as she eased into her seat. "Ye are your grandpapa's offspring, that be for certain."

Colin smiled, knowing Molly could never refuse him anything when he presented her with his toothy grin—the mirror image of Fair Wind's smile, the mischievous smirk she'd fallen in love with all those years ago in a tavern taproom full of unsavory seamen.

At that moment, Colin did not feel a single ounce of guilt using the tactic against her to gain her cooperation.

"I know, Molly, and just as you did with Grandpapa, trust me to take care of you. Believe I will find Fair Wind's book and return it to you," he said on a rushed exhale. "Can you do that for me?"

She turned her head sharply to stare at the curtain-covered window.

"I will have your word, or we will leave now and I will return you home." He shrugged, content with either option depending on the choice she made. If she insisted on accompanying him inside, they would return home, and Colin would journey back to Mayfair without her in tow.

"I will wait here," she sighed.

"Thank you, Molly. That is a wise decision."

She snorted, refusing to look at him. However, she'd given him her word, and there was little his grandmama valued more than a promise.

He rapped on the side of the carriage, and his footmen opened the door and placed the step for him to depart.

"I love you, and I will return quickly with any information I discover." He leaned forward and pressed a quick kiss to the cheek she offered.

Colin leapt from the carriage, pausing to have a word with his footman and driver.

"Keep a watch on her. Whatever you do, do not allow her inside Lord Atholl's townhouse."

Both servants nodded in understanding and resumed their posts by the waiting carriage.

His clenched fist pounded on the door, quickly bringing a butler to greet him.

"Lord Hawke to see Lord Atholl," Colin announced, reaching into his jacket pocket for his calling card.

The servant accepted the offering but didn't take his eyes off Colin. "Is His Grace expecting you, my lord?"

"No. However, you can inform him that I've come in regards to information about Sheerness." The butler's brow rose, certainly familiar with the town on the Kent coast, known for its long history of smugglers. "It is a business matter."

"Of course, my lord, this way please."

Colin expected to be shown into the foyer or an empty receiving room, but the servant led him through the entrance, past two salons, and down a wide hall farther into the house.

"His Grace is in his study, sir." The butler stopped and opened a door to Colin's left before stepping into the room, leaving Colin in the dim corridor. "Your Grace, a Lord Hawke"—he glanced down at the card for the first time—"Baron Hawke, is here to speak with you in regards to Sheerness."

Bloody hell. He'd used the information as a ploy to gain entrance. Colin hadn't imagined the butler would announce his interests so boldly. When he'd gotten word from Oliver with regards to who had last owned the book, Colin had had his man of business look into the lord.

"Sheerness, you say?" The voice did not boom and echo down the hall, nor sound forceful in any manner— the robust volume Colin thought a duke would possess. "Do show him in."

"He is right here, Your Grace." The servant glanced over his shoulder to where Colin awaited. "His

Grace, the Duke of Atholl, will see you, my lord."

The comical nature of the exchange was not lost on Colin as he stepped into the room. The door shut behind him with a quietness not found in many homes—the hinges did not protest, nor did the latch clink.

"Your Grace." Colin bowed abruptly as the duke stood, his rounded spectacles and soft brown hair framing his heart-shaped face. "It is a pleasure to make your acquaintance. I apologize for not sending word before calling on you."

The man waved his hand toward the chair before him. "Do sit. I always relish the opportunity to meet and discuss locales of great British import. What do you know of Sheerness?"

Colin took a moment to take in the room around him, the walls were covered in maps spanning from England to Denmark and even Sweden and Russia. A wall lined with tomes of all sizes held titles of world travel and history. On any other day, he'd ask to walk the room and explore Atholl's fine collection.

But not this day. He was here on important business, though whether he should clue the duke in on that fact had still not been decided.

Sitting, Colin noted Atholl scrutinizing him from behind the large desk, its impressive size making the duke appear no larger than a child in comparison.

"My family is from Sheerness, or at least my grandpapa and grandmama on my father's side hailed from the area." Colin was satisfied when the man nodded at the information, making it unnecessary to share any further details surrounding his family's past in Kent. "I have heard you are purchasing property there."

A simple, innocent enough inquiry, but the duke's eyes narrowed sharply.

"Yes, well, the area is a prime locale for the import and export of goods." Atholl made a show of fussing with a stack of papers on his desk. "I have purchased several properties which I plan to utilize in the future."

"Have you been to Sheerness?" Colin spied the portrait hanging behind the duke's chair: five young children—a boy and four girls—all with red hair of various shades, cuddled around a mop-haired hound. "My grandmama speaks of the vast coastline and scenic walks. Mayhap you've taken your children there?"

Colin was baiting the man. He, himself, had never ventured to Sheerness. His father, the Earl of Coventry, was determined to erase their family's past, and doing that meant expunging everything his grandmama held dear, everything the woman had taught him growing up, including the connection to Porter "Fair Wind" Parnell, a known smuggler.

The duke chuckled at Colin's mention of family travels to the far reaches of Kent.

Atholl shook his head. "No, no, the children are too old to enjoy time away from London. Heavens, where would my son continue his fencing lessons or my daughters secure an adequate musical instructor, let alone a dressmaker in Kent?"

In the portrait hung behind Atholl, the children appeared to vary from ages seven to possibly twelve summers. Still rather young, as families went, though at the duke's age—certainly as old as Colin's father—toting around a brimming family of seven would be a task only a brave man would undertake.

Colin did his best to smile and laugh along with the man. If he hoped to bring any useful information back to Molly, he needs must be at ease in Atholl's presence—playact he was only here due to their mutual interest in Sheerness, not because his family's most treasured—and hotly debated—item was likely in this very room.

CHAPTER 4

OPHELIA COULD NOT remove her narrowed gaze from the closed door of the study the stranger had been escorted into by the Atholl butler. Here to meet with her father—but for what purpose? The man's appearance in *her* home, of all places, was highly suspect. Especially after Mr. Oliver had been nonresponsive to Ophelia's questions upon first seeing him at the bookseller's.

And for a second time, he hadn't noticed Ophelia's presence where she and Lucianna had pressed themselves against the stairwell wall to remain unseen.

Ophelia waved over her shoulder to her friend. "I think I will remain home," she said. "Edith and Lord Torrington will be meeting you, correct?"

"Yes, but—"

"No one likes a fifth wheel, as they say." Especially Ophelia. After Tilda's death, she was always the third of their small group—and since Montrose and Torrington had joined and made them five, she was the unneeded extra wheel of their carriage. There if needed, but forgotten more often than not.

"Shall we be off?" Roderick asked. "I believe she is duly occupied, and we have a bridal trousseau to gather before we depart for Scotland."

Their chatter faded as Ophelia approached her father's study, quickly pulling a book from the small shelf outside the closed door before she leaned against the wall. No servant would question if Ophelia were seen standing in the corridor with her nose in a book.

Flipping open the cover, she settled on a page about halfway through the book…a title on…oh, bother, the history of English imports from the Turkish Isles. While her presence with a book would not be viewed as peculiar, seeing her enthusiastically reading a volume on commerce and trade certainly would.

Ah, well, she was committed.

Besides, it was not necessary for her to actually read anything in the tome, only use it as a ruse to keep her true intent a secret.

She side-stepped several inches until her shoulder rested against the doorframe of the study and then crossed her ankles as if she were merely enjoying a few moments of silence for reading. However, her head was tilted ever so slightly toward the closed door, and her breath was held as she attempted to catch any stray words that might make their way through the closed portal.

Blast it all, but her father had always been a quiet man, never raising his voice in anger nor in exuberant joy. Level-headed, calm, and cool—all the things Ophelia strived to be but never fully achieved.

Her father's light chuckle sounded, accompanied by that of the stranger.

Rarely did her father allow himself the luxury of a moment of fancy—he worked hard every day to make certain the Dukedom was enough, would always be enough, for the care of the many Fletcher children. With four siblings—Jacob, Sarah, Elizabeth, and Jennifer—Ophelia could only imagine the pressure upon her father to see them all wed with proper families of their own, all while keeping Jacob in line to continue running the Dukedom after Atholl no longer could.

The laughter died quickly, and with it the sounds from within. If Ophelia moved any closer, she'd be perched in the doorway of the study, and eavesdropping was certainly not a proper activity for a young woman of quality. Ophelia bit her lip, keeping her eyes trained on her open book as she pondered her next move.

The man she was now convinced was a lord, had appeared rather tense and irritated at Oliver's a fortnight ago; however, she heard no shouting or anger from the study at present.

Was it possible that her father knew the man?

The words blurred together on the page before her, though she did not focus enough to sort them out.

"My lady?"

Ophelia yelped and nearly dropped the book when the Atholl butler cleared his throat to gain her attention.

"May I help you with something?"

She glanced around the deserted hallway in search of any excuse to send the servant on his way. "I—well—I was—" Ophelia closed the book and held it up for the butler to see, as if that should answer his question, but the man only continued to stare at her expectantly. "I was reading this book…and awaiting an audience with Father. Do you know how long he will be?"

"I do not, my lady." The servant appeared vexed at his inability to give her the information she sought. "His Grace is meeting with Lord Hawke, and I am uncertain how long they will be."

"I see." Ophelia did her best to appear perplexed by the situation. "I was under the impression my father had requested my presence while Mother and the girls were otherwise occupied."

"I will inform His Grace as soon as his guest departs, my lady."

"Wonderful."

The pair stood, staring at one another, clearly waiting for the other to depart.

Blessedly, a commotion in the foyer had the servant hurrying back to his post. It was likely only Montrose or Luci, returned to collect something they'd forgotten.

Alone once more, Ophelia glanced about quickly before boldly pressing her ear to the door. Her pulse increased at her daring act—something her father would punish her severely for if she were discovered.

And her cunning paid off in spades as bits of the conversation floated through the door, though many words were muffled.

Sheerness…a coveted book…smuggling…

The stranger's words were cut short by her father. "No, no, exports and shipping via the area's dock are all that hold my interest, though I can tell you that talk of age-old smugglers and pirates from the area has always piqued my curiosity."

Her father had an interest in anything other than matters of legitimate business?

She was uncertain which surprised her more; her father's bout of laughter a few moments before, or his admittance of curiosity regarding anything historical and, dare she say, adventurous.

The butler's raised voice sounded from down the hall in the foyer.

Ophelia drew away from the study door in case her father came out to investigate the commotion. It was advantageous Luci would be departing soon for Scotland, for if she continued making a ruckus in the duke's home, he may very well bid her find accommodations elsewhere.

Ophelia's slippered feet made no sound as she strode down the hall and around the corner into the foyer, a sharp rebuff on the tip of her tongue for Luci. Not only because of her disruptive nature, but also because Ophelia had, for once, been on the cusp of something—a bit of mystery surrounding the strange lord—and now she'd learn nothing more.

Maybe she did not rightfully possess Edith's inquisitive nature or Luci's cunning and daring demeanor.

She skidded to a halt the moment she rounded the corner and the foyer came into view.

"...I am a bloody fancy lady, ye yellow-feathered buffoon!"

"Madam, please!" The butler ducked as he tried to push the front door closed.

The pointy end of a stick shot through the opening and whacked the servant soundly on the shoulder, causing his hold to falter and the door to inch open as a footman rushed to assist.

"My heavens," Ophelia huffed. "Step back and allow the woman entrance."

The Atholl butler and footman leapt to attention, their movements allowing the front door to swing open—and crash into the wall.

In the doorway stood a tiny, silver-haired woman...swinging not a stick but a cane, her eyes wide with fury as they darted around the foyer in search of heavens knew what.

Ophelia took a hesitant step forward, and the two men retreated, keeping a watchful eye on the situation.

"Madam, may I be of service?" The woman was clearly confused, her cane coming to rest where it should as she stepped back from the open door. "Are you lost?"

Ophelia advanced, her brow pulled together with concern.

The woman tapped her forehead, chest, and nose before dipping her chin to almost touch her chest as she backed away from the door and toward a waiting carriage.

The butler lunged forward and slammed the door shut, collapsing with a groan against the wood. "My many thanks, Lady Ophelia. Bless my mother's soul, but that woman was as mad as a milk maid without a proper pail."

"Who is she?" she hissed as the woman let out another round of obscenities outside. Ophelia's face reddened, and the butler looked away at the crass mention of what the servant could do with his fancy speech and insulting manners.

When the butler shrugged, Ophelia asked, "We should offer assistance, correct?"

His eyes widened, and she sensed the man would not prove to be an ally in this situation. If she meant to confront the mad woman again, it would be on her own.

Ophelia took a deep, fortifying breath and opened the front door to see the woman blindly swinging her cane at the gardenia bush bordering the walk. She couldn't help but wonder what the plant could have done to anger the woman. The sight was both laughable and perplexing at the same time.

Though Ophelia was sure the Atholl gardener would not feel the same.

When the petite woman saw Ophelia exit the door, she held the cane high, clutched something hanging around her neck, and spat.

She actually *spat* on the ground between them.

Ophelia glanced behind the woman to the carriage waiting in the drive. The coachman and footman stared at everything but what was happening fifteen feet from them. It was as if only she saw the mad woman with her cane held high, ready to do battle.

"Ye cannot pass," the woman hissed, nodding to the spittle before tapping her forehead, her chest, and nose. "Your mark of the devil will not be bewitch'n me. Don't ye be come'n any closer, ye fork-tongued beast." She punctuated her words by spitting once more and swinging her cane in the empty space between her and Ophelia.

"I am afraid I am uncertain of what you speak, madam." Ophelia held her hands before her, but did not dare take a step toward the woman.

"Ye, with your hair like the devil, that be exactly what I be expect'n you ta say."

"My hair?" Ophelia touched the long, wavy lock that hung over her shoulder. What did her hair color signify? "If you find exception with my hair, why are you trying to gain entrance to a home full to brimming with fair-skinned, auburn-haired people?"

"I knew me senses be correct, ye cursed sorcerer." She swung her cane once more to keep Ophelia back. "Me grandson be in there, and likely be'n hauled straight to Beelzebub himself."

Ophelia must have appeared as confused as she felt because the woman laughed, a high-pitched, uncontrollable cackle.

"Yes, most certainly the look of a witch confronted with ye own misdeeds."

"I assure you, Lord Hawke is perfectly safe within."

"Ye be a crone, a hag, disguised by the Prince of Darkness himself with yer fair skin and heavenly glow. An enchantress is what ye be."

"Why I never—"

The woman spat once more, cutting off Ophelia's words as the spittle landed close to the hem of Ophelia's morning gown.

"Do stop this dramatic display, madam." Ophelia cocked her hip, her hand settling there. "I demand to know your name."

The woman's eyes narrowed to slits. "So ye can put a hex on me? I not be stand'n for it."

"Do calm yourself before you suffer apoplexy."

"Is that what your curse be?" The woman faltered back a step, and Ophelia feared she had suffered a malady; however, she continued. "Release me Colin from your evil charms, give us the book, and we be on our way, sure as the day is long."

"Molly!" The stern voice had the older woman cocking her head to the side and her eyes widening as she glanced around Ophelia. "Put your cane down and return to the carriage this instant."

The woman's glare returned to Ophelia, and she spat again, her hand clutching her pendant once more as her cane lowered. However, she made no move to follow through with the last order.

"Now," the man seethed, and Ophelia recognized the desperation she'd heard in his voice when he was at Oliver's Book Shoppe. "Please, return to the carriage and cease with your superstitious ramblings."

Ophelia kept her eyes trained on the older woman as she placed one foot behind the other, slowly backing toward the waiting coach, the cane at her side. It wasn't until Ophelia backed up and bumped against something solid—and the elderly woman allowed another curse to slip out—Ophelia realized she stood pressed against the chest of Lord Hawke.

CHAPTER 5

COLIN STOOD RIGID as the woman's soft curves molded to him from his chest to his knees. Her crown of wildly unrestrained auburn hair created a halo above her head and partly blocked his view of Molly. Everything about her made him want to take a half step forward and press more soundly to her back, maybe slip his arm around her waist to hold her close. The scent of lavender mixed with a hint of vanilla drifted between them, distracting him for a brief moment from the spectacle happening before him—in the Duke of Atholl's drive, in the most fashionable part of London.

Bloody well fantastic.

He glanced over his shoulder to see several Atholl servants gawking from the open front door.

Blessedly, Molly reached the coach, and a footman assisted her in.

The woman pressed against him took a step forward with a sigh of relief.

"Colin, ye hurry along, lest this fork-tongued heathen with her devil's curse drag ye straight ta the fiery pits of—" Molly spat out the carriage window without finishing her words and tapped her forehead.

However, Colin couldn't continue watching as she perpetuated her usual ritual.

"Miss," he said, ducking his chin in shame at his grandmama's outrageous accusations. "I am truly sorry for Molly's—err, my grandmama's—behavior."

When the woman made no move to accept or acknowledge Colin's apology, he brought his eyes to her as she turned to face him.

The first thing he noticed was the sprinkling of freckles across the bridge of her nose. So delicately spaced, as if the hand of a great artist had placed each in the exact spot they would reside forevermore.

"It is you…" The girl from the framed painting behind Atholl's desk. She was older, more woman than girl, but he was certain it was the duke's eldest daughter. The painter had captured her cobalt eyes perfectly with their slight upturn at the corners, though he'd flawed unforgivingly at catching the plump curve of her smirk.

"Pardon, my lord?" She swallowed, and her clasped hands quivered.

A tingle of embarrassment swept up his spine at her nervous stare.

Colin cleared his throat and glanced over the woman's shoulder as renewed humiliation filled him.

"Me lad!" Molly slapped her cane against the side of the carriage as she hung out the open window. "Don't be fooled by her sinful smile. She is naught but a mermaid responsible for take'n ships ta watery graves at the bottom of the ocean."

"Your grandmother certainly has a vivid imagination, Lord Hawke."

The only thing he heard was his name from her lips, not Molly's continued harassing comments.

The only thing he *saw* was the slight upturn of her lips, not Molly attempting to depart the carriage again, all the while his footman and coachman kept her blocked.

Certainly, he was aware of everything, but he could not take his attention off the woman before him.

"You know my name?" his brow rose in question,

and her face flared the most attractive shade of pink.

"She be a siren if'n I ever saw one!" Molly yelled. "Let me depart this blasted coach, ye addlepate."

"My butler informed me my father was meeting with a 'Lord Hawke.' It only stands to reason that you are he." She glanced at the ground, her pink cheeks deepening to red.

"You look much like your portrait in the duke's study." Blast it all, but he hadn't meant to say anything regarding that, and neither should it have been uttered on a sigh. Colin straightened his shoulders and adjusted his neckcloth. "What I meant to say is that your father speaks highly of you."

The man hadn't said a word about any particular offspring, yet Colin would not admit to any such thing.

"That is kind of you to say, my lord; however—" Her chin rose, and he suspected the woman knew he lied. "I would not be surprised to hear my father entirely forgot about his children."

"Sometimes, I wish my family would fail to recall me," he replied.

Sure to form, Molly started her beating on the ducal carriage once again. His father would be enraged to find his prized landau battered. There was no avoiding it. Colin was loath to take his leave before finding out the woman's name.

"You cannot mean that." Her stare widened as she fidgeted with the seam of her gown.

How to explain to a perfect stranger he, in fact, *would* relish that exact thing?

The continuous war between Colin's parents and his grandmama was utterly draining. The trio never failed to place him in the middle, forced to choose between the woman who was far more than merely his grandmama and the pair who had given him life, a proper upbringing, and an adequate education.

"Don't be believe'n that witch's banbury tale of cock and bull. Don't be purblind, Colin."

He held up his finger to silence Molly; however, his grandmama had never been deft at listening to others—or remaining silent when bidden.

With a weak smile, he said, "Allow me a moment to calm her. Please, do not go anywhere, I will be back momentarily." When she only nodded, he continued, "And I swear on all I possess, she is not as addlebrained as she appears."

"We rarely are."

Colin wanted nothing more than to question her further on her peculiar comment, but Molly began howling his name again.

"One moment is all I need," he promised. "I will return."

"Of course." Her flushed cheeks had returned to their normal coloring, and her smile suggested she was just as interested in him and he was in her.

Colin hurried to the carriage, his frown deepening the closer he came to Molly. Perhaps his father was correct in his decree that the old woman was better off at Tintinhull Court in Somerset, surrounded by Coventry servants who were both loyal and discrete. At least there, she could practice whatever superstitions she fancied useful, and would not cause Colin embarrassment, especially before an utterly bewitching woman. And that was exactly the wording he should not use when describing Atholl's daughter, especially not in front of his grandmama, lest Molly redouble her accusations of witchcraft and sorcery.

"What in all that is holy are you doing?" he demanded.

His anger caused Molly to lean back into the carriage, her mouth gaping.

"Have ye gone mad, me lad?" she hissed. "What charm has that fiery-haired siren thrown at ye?"

"She has done nothing, Molly." Colin took a moment for his breathing to slow, and his pulse to stop racing. "You, on the other hand, are jeopardizing everything."

"Did that thief in duke's garb give ye the book?"

"No, he did not, and he is not a thief."

"Then he told ye where ta find it?" she prodded, her brow pulling together as her voice lifted with hope. "Let us be off ta collect Fair Wind's book."

"Duke Atholl has promised to look for the book amongst his collection"—he paused, pinching the bridge of his nose—"however, your treatment of his daughter might very well alter his cooperative nature."

Molly peeked around him, and Colin feared she'd begin yet another tirade. Thankfully, she kept her mouth closed and leaned back into her seat, crossing her arms. She appeared the sulking, petulant child, which suited Colin perfectly, at least until he could make his amends with the woman and seek his leave.

"Now, stay out of sight and remain silent until I can apologize for your outlandish behavior."

"I not be sorry for any of it..." she huffed.

"That I know well, Molly; however, I *am* sorry for the mortification you caused the woman—outside her own home, no less."

Molly waved her hand as if to dismiss him, but did not meet his eye. "Do as ye must, lad, but I caution ye against put'n any trust in a woman so clearly marked by the devil himself."

"Am I to believe you to be deranged, as Father would have me believe?"

"*Humphf.*"

"Very well, sulk all you want." He glanced over his shoulder to see the woman had inched forward a few feet and listened intently to his conversation, even though her stare was trained on a row of shrubs bordering the drive. "Besides, I have no need or want to trust this woman, only make certain she does not tell her father of your deplorable accusations."

When Molly didn't argue further, Colin returned to the woman to offer his apologies for Molly's words and also anything she may have overhead while he'd conversed with his grandmama.

Thankfully, the servants had gone about their chores and closed the front door.

He stopped before her, at a loss for what to say. He owed her an apology and needs must beg her forgiveness even though Molly showed no contrition.

"My grandmama has always been a bit rattle-pated," he tried his hand at explaining Molly's off-key nature.

"Rattle-pated?" she asked, tugging at her ear.

"Oh, it seems when I spend too much time in her company, I adopt her seafaring jargon." Colin shook his head. "She has always been a whimsical woman, taken by notions of fancy and steeped in superstition. It is the reason my grandpapa fell in love with her, if my father is to be believed. But that is neither here nor there. Her accusations were unfounded and uncalled for, and I owe you an apology, Lady…"

"Lady Ophelia Fletcher." She curtseyed, her hair falling over her shoulders when she bowed her head slightly. "And as we've established, you are Lord Hawke."

"Colin."

Her cheeks blossomed once more when she straightened.

"It is nice to make your acquaintance, Lord Hawke," she replied. "Do not let me keep you from your grandmother."

"I will depart only if you accept my remorseful apology, Lady Ophelia."

"If you insist." She smiled and pressed her gloved hand to her mouth to cover her toothy grin. "Now, I must return inside or risk displeasing my father."

"Farewell, Lady Ophelia." He gave a simple wave. With one last smile, she twirled and rushed back in the house, the door opening for her as she reached the landing. "Until we meet again…"

Colin had no doubt they would meet again, but under what circumstances, he was uncertain.

CHAPTER 6

OPHELIA GLANCED OVER her shoulder at her waiting carriage and back again through the murky front window of Oliver's Book Shoppe, all while people pushed past her on the crowded walk. The swoosh of skirts, the brush of a man's shoulder against hers, the idle chitchat buzzing in her ears…it was all too much.

Overwhelming.

Daunting.

It had her face heating, her breath coming in shallow, labored gulps, and every instinct telling her to flee. She should return to the safety of her home. Await Edith's and Luci's return from Gretna Green.

What had possessed her to journey to Bond Street with only her maid as a companion?

She pulled the note from her cloak pocket.

Luci's looping script, upon her newly arrived cream stationery with silver trim, glared at her. She didn't need to open the letter to know exactly what it said. Or, more appropriately, what it demanded of Ophelia during Luci's absence from London.

Sliding her finger over the thick paper, Ophelia's eyes drifted closed for a brief second.

Ophelia was not to write a piece for the *Mayfair Confidential.*

Ophelia was not to investigate, follow, or snoop around Abercorn.

Ophelia was not to put herself in harm's way.

Ophelia *was* to remain close to home and away from any harmful activities until Luci and Edith returned.

And her dear friends expected her to do just that.

Remain the timid, reserved, quiet girl she'd always been; happy to tag along on their adventures but never seeking any of her own. Overjoyed even, to remain in the shadows as Edith and Luci found love. And content to be their scribe for the *Mayfair Confidential*.

"M'lady?" her maid's concerned call came from the waiting carriage where Ophelia had insisted she remain while Ophelia questioned Oliver.

She gave the girl a quick smile and shoved the note back into her pocket.

The time had come to seek her own adventure— no more hanging on to the coattails of her friends nor simply reading about thrilling escapades in her books.

Her chin tilted up a notch, and she squared her shoulders, pasting a confident smile upon her lips.

Surely, if she presented confidence outwardly, it would also take hold within her.

For not the first time, Ophelia realized she was not the great poised beauty Luci was, nor the witty and intelligent woman Edith was.

But that did not make her any less capable.

She would find the book Lord Hawke sought and return it to him.

Despite the man's grandmother and her peculiar accusations, Ophelia was determined to help him.

That he was handsome, intelligent, and had kind eyes impacted nothing.

That she'd had a difficult time concentrating on anything since she met the man several days before also did not signify anything.

That every book she selected somehow had the

hero resembling Lord Hawke—Colin—with his fair hair and piercing green eyes was far more disconcerting. Every tale she read, whether it was swashbuckling pirates or Arabian princes took on the sun-kissed complexion of a certain baron.

Ophelia could not stall any longer. Her family would worry about her whereabouts if she did not return home before afternoon social calls began.

The bell sounded overhead as she pushed through the door. The familiar smell of grass with a hint of vanilla filled her nose, along with the overpowering stench of burning wax. Beeswax to be precise, not the far more affordable tallow used by many merchants. It spoke to Oliver's prestige as one of the finest booksellers in London proper. Perhaps that was where her next adventure lay—where does Oliver gain his funds for beeswax candles with proper wicks?

That was a mystery for another time. This day, Ophelia had one goal: find out what Oliver had told Lord Hawke, and how that corresponded with the man's visit with her father.

It was a simple enough inquiry.

Harmless on all accounts.

"My lady, it is good to see you!" Oliver's greeting usually never varied, but the thin, wiry man stared over Ophelia's shoulder as if he were expecting other clientele. "But where are your friends?"

Ophelia allowed a hesitant laugh to escape her. Of course. Ophelia normally shopped with at least one of her friends in tow. "I am afraid they are otherwise occupied today; however, there is something I have need to ask you, and I did not wish to wait for their return."

"Certainly, my lady. Though I do hope this has nothing to do with your last visit to my shop," he nodded with a grave smile. "May I help you locate a book, perchance? Might I recommend a new set of Colonial adventure novels I received just this morn?"

Any other time, Ophelia would have been thrilled at the opportunity to possess such a rare collection. "Unfortunately, I am not in the market to purchase any new books today."

The shopkeeper's brow rose. "Oh?"

Ophelia journeyed farther into the shop, stopping before the tall desk Oliver stood behind. "I am here about a book—"

"But I thought you said you were not here about purchasing a book."

"I am not. You see, I believe this book has already been purchased."

He tilted his head slightly and pursed his lips, tapping his cheek with his forefinger. "Then you are looking to hire me for an acquisition?"

"Not ex—"

"There is a man, Lord Cartwright, who does a fine job of locating books."

"No, no," Ophelia sighed. "I believe you were in possession of this book not long ago and know its current owner."

His eyes narrowed behind his wire-rimmed spectacles. "I cannot disclose personal information about my clients, my lady, as I told you before."

Once again, Ophelia was losing the man's willingness to assist her. Drat! She would not allow Luci's assertions to be proven correct.

"I am looking for a book. It is about smuggling in the area of Sheerness."

Recognition dawned quickly in the shopkeeper's eyes, and his welcoming smile returned. "Blast it all, but I do wish I knew what all the fuss was over this book. You are the third person in the past month requesting information on the whereabouts of Fair Wind's book on smuggling."

"So you *do* know of it?"

"Certainly. I sent information round to another lord only a few days past; however, what knowledge an outdated book could provide to anyone is beyond my comprehension." The man turned and retrieved an oversized, leather-bound ledger from the shelf behind him. "Let me give you the information I found on the book. That won't harm anyone, I don't think." His flipped several pages and ran his finger down a list.

A tingle of excitement rushed down Ophelia's back at the thought of what she sought being so easily obtained. Perhaps her detection skills were superior to Luci's and Edith's, after all.

"Ah, here it is," he said, lifting his gaze to her with a triumphant smile. "Written by Fair Wind Parnell during the Seven Years' War."

"That is it!" At least, Ophelia hoped it was. "Can you tell me who purchased the book…and when?"

He dragged his finger across the page before stopping and pointing at a name. "I shouldn't give you the name, but since it's your father, I think it will be fine. Atholl. That's all it says, and is exactly what I told the last man who came sniffing around."

"My fa—" Ophelia clamped her mouth shut.

"Are you certain you do not wish to purchase the Colonial adventure volumes?"

"Not today, Mr. Oliver, though if they are still here on my next visit, I shall be persuaded to make them mine."

"Very good, my lady!"

The shopkeeper closed the ledger with a thump and returned it to its shelf.

All the while, Ophelia's mind swirled.

Lord Hawke had spoken with her father because he had solid information leading him to the duke, but if what she'd heard spoken between Molly and Lord Hawke was correct, the duke had promised to preview his collection for it.

But certainly, her father must know where the book is. He was a meticulous man, a keeper of records, a treasurer of the unique. This would certainly be of distinctive historical significance.

"Good day, Oliver," Ophelia said, not bothering to suppress her excitement over her discovery. "Thank you again for the information."

"I still do not understand the import of…"

The man's voice trailed off when Ophelia pushed through the door into the bright afternoon sun, the bell overhead chiming once more. Her step was lighter than it had been since before Tilda's death. The shame of admitting she'd been so engrossed in her book that if someone *had* pushed her dear friend down the stairs, Ophelia had been too preoccupied to see the culprit was suffocating. It was nice to have some relief.

"GOOD DAY, ANDREW!" Ophelia chimed, removing her gloves as she came through the front door. "Is Father in his study?"

The entire carriage ride home, she'd debated how to address the situation. There were no grounds for assuming her father had done anything wrong or had come into ownership of the book in any unsavory way.

"No, my lady." The butler took her gloves and helped her with her cloak. "He is out for the afternoon with the duchess and your siblings.

Odd, her father rarely traveled around London with his horde of children and wife, and surely not during what he considered *prime business hours*.

"However, you have guests."

"Guests?" Ophelia didn't get many visitors, unless you counted those who came to see her mother and were polite enough to request an audience with her, as well. And Lucianna and Edith had long ago stopped being considered guests in the Atholl household; besides, they were safely on their way to Gretna Green at present. "They are in Mother's salon?"

"Yes, Lady Ophelia." Andrew gave a low bow.

"They were served refreshments a few moments ago."

Tea, already? "How long have they been waiting?"

He glanced at the tall clock before wincing. "Going on an hour, my lady."

"I best see to them," she replied with a quick smile. Heavens, but who would wait that long to meet with Ophelia? She hurried to the salon, the door cracked enough to hear giggling from within. She'd know that laughter anywhere. "Lady Prudence and Lady Chastity!"

Ophelia entered the room with a genuine smile.

"Lady Ophelia," both called in unison, popping off the lounge, causing the pastry Lady Chastity held aloft to bounce to the floor.

"Oh, dear, I have soiled your rug." Chastity's face flamed with embarrassment, and she scrambled to her knees to retrieve the sweet treat. "I will make certain—"

"Do not fret," Ophelia said with a light laugh. Lord Torrington's younger sisters were quite persistent when they set their minds to something, and they'd settled on making Ophelia and Lucianna their bosom friends. Edith had escaped the girls' tireless pursuit, for when she wed Torrington, they'd be more than mere friends, they would be sisters. "I shall tell no one."

Chastity regained her seat with a grateful nod.

"To what do I owe this visit?" Ophelia couldn't help but ask. She'd arrived home with a plan; however, until Chastity and Prudence took their leave, she could not see it through.

The pair exchanged a quick glance before Prudence, the dominant of the pair, turned a pitying look on Ophelia. "We presumed since the trio of us were not included in Lady Lucianna and Lord Montrose's trip, we would take the opportunity to keep you company."

Keep her company, or had Edith requested the girls keep watch on her?

It galled Ophelia to think her friends thought she needed someone to keep an eye on her in their absence.

"What Pru means is that with Lady Lucianna away, you must be in need of a friend—or two."

She was hard-pressed to deny a friend would be appreciated, especially with everything circling Lord Hawke and her father. The time to think through everything and gather her thoughts hadn't presented itself. Perhaps, Lady Pru and Chastity were willing to lend an ear.

They may not be as versed in observation as Luci and Edith, but they looked willing as they sat on the edge of the lounge across the table from her.

"Well, there has been a bit of excitement to be had since Luci and Montrose left town—"

"Oh!" they chimed at once. These were the type of females she aimed her *Mayfair Confidential* columns toward—young, innocent women who were susceptible to influence. Both girls perched their chins on her hands, their elbows balanced on their knees. "Do tell us."

With Luci and Edith, Ophelia wouldn't hesitant to share what she'd discovered. She trusted them implicitly. However, sharing Lord Hawke's family tale seemed a breach of some unspoken pact between Ophelia and the handsome lord. Perhaps she could share a bit about the man without breaking his confidence.

"I met a lord." Ophelia paused as both women's eyes widened. Did they think her incapable of meeting a man, or were they only sharing in her excitement? It didn't matter. Ophelia hadn't anyone to confide in when she'd first spotted Lord Hawke at the bookseller's. "He is very dashing with hair the color of sunshine and eyes as green as Sherwood Forest."

When Prudence's brow furrowed, Ophelia realized she hadn't thought to consider if they'd read the tales of Robin Hood.

They recovered quickly and nodded, their wide-eyed stares begging Ophelia to continue.

"I first saw him at Oliver's Book Shoppe—a

bookseller I frequent often—" she clarified before continuing. "He was there demanding a book that belonged to his family."

She was close to crossing a line, but she could not help herself.

"He did not notice me then, but he appeared at my home several days later to meet with my father." Lady Chastity's mouth hung open, and Pru clutched her sister's hand in anticipation. "His name is Lord Hawke. Very fitting, I dare say."

"Very fitting, indeed," Chastity murmured. She retrieved her tea from the table and took a cautious sip, never taking her eyes off Ophelia. "What did he come to Atholl Townhouse for?"

"The same book." The words were out of her mouth before she could stop herself. "I mean, I do not know much about it, only that it is old and has to do with Sheerness in Kent. But, you came to visit me, and here I am, prattling on and on about nothing."

Ophelia sat a bit straighter when the clock chimed the top of the hour. Her father, with the rest of the Atholl clan in tow, would be home shortly. It would effectively cut her off from any further searching, at least until the morrow.

The women must have noticed that she made no move to pour herself tea, nor did she offer to freshen theirs because Chastity took one last sip and set her cup and saucer back on the serving tray at the same time Lady Prudence cleared her throat.

"We very much enjoyed our visit, Lady Ophelia." The pair stood, issuing the proper curtseys. "We do hope you will visit us when you are about on social calls."

A measure of guilt ran through Ophelia at her unladylike manners. These poor girls had been through much in the last several months, losing their stepmother to an illness of the mind and now their brother wedding Lady Edith in a few short months. They were looking for a friend, and Ophelia desperately wanted to be that to them; however, this moment was inopportune to further their kinship.

"Father is taking us for a ride in Hyde Park this afternoon," Pru ventured to say. "Mayhap we will see you there?"

"I'm afraid I have several prior engagements today; however, I will call on you shortly." Ophelia gave the pair a reassuring smile as they all stood. "Do give my best to your father."

"Of course." Lady Prudence nodded.

"I shall walk you to the door." Ophelia ushered the ladies back to the foyer, attempting to keep her pace leisurely and not rushed. "Again, it was lovely to see the pair of you. I do hope your time at Hyde Park is pleasurable."

The Atholl butler opened the foyer door, and the women hurried out to their waiting carriage. Glancing beyond, Ophelia saw no other conveyances in the drive. There was still time.

"Father is still not home?" She smiled, determined not to let this delay set her back in any way or diminish her buoyant countenance.

"No, my lady." Andrew closed the door behind Lady Prudence and Lady Chastity. "Is there something I can assist you with?"

"No, Andrew. I was going to query father about a…" She needed to keep her wits about her and devise a new plan if she hoped to locate and return Lord Hawke's book. "About a new collection of Colonial volumes at Oliver's Book Shoppe; however, it is not so important that it cannot wait until supper."

The servant eyed her, his gaze narrowing. "I can inform him of the matter when he arrives home."

That would be too late, certainly, and it worked best for her if he never found out what she was about to do.

"No, thank you, Andrew." Ophelia did not trust

her father to be completely honest with her anyways, as he hadn't been with Lord Hawke. "I believe I will retire to Mother's sitting room to read."

"I will have Ms. Paulson prepare fresh tea."

"That is kind," Ophelia said, touching the servant's arm before turning back toward her mother's sitting room, which was directly across the hall from her father's study.

She was in search of her own adventures, and while snooping in her father's study was not the most exciting of activities, it was something she'd never dreamt of doing before.

And, if she were being honest, her pulse increased at the mere thought of doing something so outlandish.

Ophelia paused outside her mother's blessedly empty sitting room and glanced toward her father's closed study. No one would question her if she were found in his private room as she'd regularly gained access to collect a new book or debate a subject with her father.

But the duke could arrive home at any moment, putting an end to the opportunity. Ophelia darted across the hall. The latch released without a sound, and the door swung open on well-oiled hinges, revealing her father's most private domain.

It likely appeared cluttered and disorganized to those who did not know the Duke of Atholl, but to Ophelia, it epitomized her father. Every nook and cranny was filled with objects of worth, though some appeared to be little more than rubbish to an outsider.

The sheer size of the collection seemed daunting.

It could take her weeks to search each shelf, open the many drawers, and examine the cupboards lining the far wall.

Ophelia could only assume her father was aware of the book's location and had been taken by surprise by the baron's appearance. The duke prided himself on cataloguing every item in his study…

Scrutinizing the room as a whole, Ophelia looked for any item out of place, but everything appeared as it should be—exactly as she'd witnessed since her childhood.

Ophelia tapped her chin, debating the wisest place to begin her search.

Certainly, the only logical place was her father's desk.

It was where Ophelia kept *her* most prized possessions—in her writing desk. At least it had been before Luci had invaded her personal chambers and displaced all of Ophelia's things.

Hurrying behind the desk, she began pulling drawers open. Riffling through each with an eye for only what she sought before re-organizing the contents. There were no books, only folders with paperwork, maps, quills and ink, and her father's seal.

Next, Ophelia pulled on a knob to a small cupboard below the desk drawers. When the door did not open easily, her fingers slipped from the knob, her nail digging into the dark wood.

Locked!

If Ophelia had something she wanted to hide, she would surely place it in a locked cabinet.

Using her fingernails, she pried at the edge of the door, hoping to shift the lock out of place, but the thing would not budge. She leaned close, trying to ascertain what exactly held the door closed. Blast it all, but Edith would know how to fuss with the lock and have it open in no time, or Luci would simply slam the thing with her elbow and it would give way out of fear.

But it was only Ophelia here. She needed to figure out a way to open the door on her own without assistance from her friends.

"I need something flat." Ophelia popped to her feet and surveyed her father's desk, her eyes alighting on the sharp, short blade of her father's penknife. It would fit perfectly between the door and the side of the desk—and with any luck, it would be sturdy enough to pop the latch holding the door closed. Returning to her kneeling position, Ophelia slipped the knife into the slot and lifted.

Sure enough, the latch opened, and she pulled the door wide as she stared into the deep, cavernous cabinet. Reaching inside, she retrieved a stack of books; one on trade winds off the Kent coast, another detailing the journey past Denmark to Prussia, a small pocket volume detailing the landscape of Russia, and finally, the book Lord Hawke had come looking for.

Smuggling: A Journey from Kent to Denmark by Fair Wind Parnell.

She turned the book over in her hands, running her finger down the worn, brown leather binding. Someone had spent much time with this tome, judging from the deep creases in the cover. Leaning down, Ophelia took in the scent of a fresh ocean breeze, as if the book had never left its place at sea. The pages were yellowed by many years in the elements.

The sound of a door closing echoed down the hall and through the study's open door, followed by the clomp of booted feet as her siblings hurried up the stairs.

Her father was home!

Ophelia haphazardly placed the books back in the cabinet, minus Lord Hawke's book, and closed the door. There was no way for her to re-latch the cabinet without the key, which she most certainly could not locate before her father caught her in his study. There was naught she could do but pray that her father did not remember locking the door.

She leapt to her feet, clutching the book, and placed the penknife back on the desk before jetting around to the front. Her skirt caught on a drawer she'd absentmindedly left ajar. Pivoting, she tugged at the fabric with her free hand and was rewarded with the telltale sound of her seam ripping.

"Bollocks," she hissed, grasping her skirt tighter and giving it one final pull as her mother's voice floated down the hall on her way to her sitting room.

The fabric tore completely to the hem, but at least Ophelia was free.

She dashed to the room's entrance and peeked out, just as Lady Atholl closed the door to her sitting room, giving Ophelia the opportunity to slip from the study and make her way to the servants' stairs. Her breath left her on a loud exhale as she fled to safety.

CHAPTER 7

LADY SISSY CASSEL glared at her brother across the table as he speared a boiled egg and popped it into his mouth. His jaw worked to chew the large bite, pieces falling from his parted lips as he swallowed. It was a fact that Franny, or Lord Abercorn as he was rightfully addressed by the *ton*, was most agreeable and pliable—with his belly full. She'd learned this when he was a young child—and she already near adulthood.

"My dear brother," she cooed, setting her knife aside. "Have you heard from that bookseller as yet?"

His stare snapped from his meal of roasted pheasant, his utensil scratching against the delicate silver plate. Sissy knew the importance of being subtle with the man. A woman—especially an unwed, older, spinster sister of a duke—was not free to speak her mind or question their brother's handling of their estate and title; however, she was used to taking such liberties with Franny. At least when they were in a private setting.

"No, I have not, dear sister." He returned his focus to his meal as if the subject at hand were nothing more important than discussing the weather. "Do collect me another plate of eggs."

At her brother's demand, a servant set a small dish

containing three boiled eggs at his elbow.

"Do you know who I saw again today?" Sissy asked.

"I must say, I haven't the faintest notion." He cut one egg in half, speared it and a piece of meat before bringing it to his mouth. "However, I am certain you will tell me," he mumbled around his mouthful of food.

She had absolutely no desire to correct his manners while dining—if it kept away other money-hungry maidens and black-haired sirens, it was all the more pleasing to Sissy.

"The Dowager Lady Coventry," Sissy seethed. There was no tamping down her fury at seeing the woman again. "Can you believe she thinks to return to London as if she *belongs* among the *ton*? She is naught more than a status seeker—born at the docks, no less. The wife of a—"

"Sissy, watch yourself," her brother warned, but his words lacked any backbone. "She is a widow, and your quarrel with her was decades ago. I am certain the entire family has long forgotten what transpired between the pair of you—I think it best you do the same."

"My...quarrel... Forget?" Sissy's blood boiled as she stammered. "You know well and true what that family stole from me—from us! And it is all that woman's fault."

Franny shook his head but kept his stare trained on his plate as he spoke. "I know only that the king did what was in his right to do. Besides, I have little use for what Coventry now possesses."

Sissy pushed her chair back to stand. "You are infuriating, Francis."

"So you've told me day in and day out since I was old enough to know the meaning of the words."

"You know that land was to be my dowry. They took it from me."

"It was at least thirty years ago, not too many years after my birth," he argued. "It had nothing to do with me."

"Yes, but you have not followed through with your promise."

"I am searching for the bloody book, Sissy!" He slammed his knife down and stood, glaring across the table at her. His anger fled quickly as it always did when it concerned his only living family member. "Leave us." He motioned to the footman to depart.

When the door closed silently, and they were alone, Sissy said, "Franny, you promised me I'd have my inheritance back; however, you have not been doing enough to see it done."

"Did I not agree to entertain your fancy and look for this book that is only fabled to exist?"

"It *does* exist," Sissy whined.

"Yes, yes, but now you ask that we scurry off to the coast of Kent in search of this or that." He pinched the bridge of his nose. "And, of course, my love for my only sister is great enough to have me leaving London during the height of the Season just to make you happy. I should remain here, in search of a wife, or have you forgotten the Abercorn name could very well pass to some distant, far-removed cousin if I do not produce an heir?"

"That is why this is far more important."

"Returning your dowry?" he sighed. "That helps me in no way whatsoever."

"At least you will not have to worry about me if something should happen to you." She spoke softly, knowing this was always the one thing that solidified his cooperation. "This distant cousin would have no qualms about casting an old spinster out. I would have no recourse but to seek employment in a workhouse."

Abercorn chuckled. "As if they'd keep you for long, Sissy."

"But you do not deny I could have no home to speak of if we do not find a way to gain back the estate we lost to that shrew of a woman?"

Her brother sighed and sank back into his chair. "No, sister. I do not deny that fact. I agreed to assist you. That is all I can do."

"Then I suggest you pack your things," she commanded. "We have a long journey ahead of us."

Without another word, Sissy turned and exited the room. It may be a fool's errand, but she had to see if the dowager's childhood home held anything that could help her gain back her long-lost legacy—and put the bloody Scrooge in her place for good.

COLIN INSPECTED THE report from his steward at Hawke Manor, his small holding near his father's country estate in Somerset. The crops were thriving this year, no doubt due to the rotation schedule he'd devised two summers prior, which allowed the soil's nutrients to naturally replenish themselves by the growing of dissimilar crops. His three-field rotation system, while seen as a fool's waste of viable land by some, was already reaping its benefits, his land's farmers seeing more food than they had in decades.

Most assuredly, leaving an entire field fallow for a season was unconventional, but it was proving successful, even as the winter wheat field thrived and the lentils in field two were producing adequately for the spring weather they'd had thus far.

Bloody hell, he longed to rush into his father's office and shove the report in the earl's face. He'd been Colin's number one naysayer since he'd spoke of the plan nearly three years ago. It was a success. If only Colin could convince his father to allow him to make similar changes at Tintinhull. If he did, both Colin's Barony and his father's Earldom would fill their coffers ten-fold in the coming years.

Colin chuckled. Even with the proof right under his nose, the earl would refuse the plan solely on principle. He knew best…and Colin's "whimsical project" at his own estate, no matter the proof of success, would not sway his father.

Not that the Coventry Earldom was in need of funds…no, the first earl—Colin's grandfather—had made certain his son and grandson would want for nothing in the years after his death.

Colin ran his hand through his hair and massaged the back of his head.

This was astounding news, yet it would mean less than nothing to his father.

A muffled shout followed by stomping sounded through the closed door of the room Colin had converted into his study while in London.

His workspace was next to his father's private office.

A door slammed, and the shouting began once more.

"What in the blazes?" Colin mumbled, pushing to his feet and dropping the report back to his desk. Now was not the time to show his father the latest yield reports if he was already angry.

Colin strode from behind his desk and pulled his door open.

His mother stood in the hall, her arms crossed, and her head shaking from side to side.

"What is it, Mother?" he asked.

Her pinched expression made her normally pale, smooth skin appear wrinkled and aged, and it should have been Colin's first clue as to what had infuriated his father.

She threw her arms wide, in her usual helpless gesture. "Molly, of course. What else could have your father so up in arms?"

Molly.

Colin had gone a full four hours without thinking of his grandmama and the promise he'd made to her.

"You best join them. It is you they are arguing

over."

"Me?" Colin asked.

His mother turned to leave but paused, glancing over her shoulder. "Yes, he discovered you and Molly have been asking about London in search of a certain book."

"How is he aware?"

"Does it matter?" She shrugged and moved down the hall toward the stairs.

His mother was correct. It didn't matter how the earl had learned of their activities over the past week. Molly had been warned, hell, even Colin had been warned, but they'd both ignored his father demands.

With heavy footsteps, Colin moved to the office door. His cold fingers clenched into a fist, and he knocked.

The irate voices inside immediately halted, and his father shouted for him to enter.

How the earl knew it was Colin, he didn't know.

Colin pushed the door wide to see his father and grandmama standing before the hearth, each with hands on their hips, feet planted wide, and scowls on their faces.

Except for their varying heights, the pair was identical...and not only in their appearances, but also their stubbornness, determination, and sense of righteousness.

The most peculiar thing was, neither realized it.

They'd been at odds for so many years, each on their own side of this argument, they'd forgotten their bond—a connection that had started at his father's birth, or likely, before.

"What do the pair of you think to accomplish with this scheme of yours?" his father hissed, clearly demanding Colin's response but never taking his glare off Molly.

"Ye damn well know—"

"Watch your words!" the earl shouted, cutting

Molly's retort short. "Colin?"

"Molly asked a favor, and I was merely appeasing an infirmed woman." The answer was rubbish, and everyone in the room knew it.

"Are you even sick and in need of a London physician?"

Molly's shoulders stiffened, as much as a woman with her hunched stature could. "Ramsey, ye know damned—no, do not interrupt me," she seethed when the earl opened his mouth to chastise her once more about her language. "Ye know I'm ill. I not be have'n much time left."

"Then why are you spending it on this lark?" his father questioned. "You know as well as I that Porter sold that book. He wanted it gone. Why do you want it returned so badly?"

"Because ye be determined ta prove that your father was an unsavory, dishonorable man!"

"He was a common smuggler, a free trader with no respect for the laws governing this great country! He wanted the book gone. If he'd wanted any of us to possess it, he wouldn't have sold it for a mere few shillings."

It was the same argument, the same hurtful words hurled back and forth, and the same subject that never found a resolution or a truce between the mother and son. Colin's heart ached for the pair, who should be spending their time loving one another, but only fought every opportunity they got.

"Enough," Colin said, slashing his hand through the air and moving closer to the pair. "Father, you believe grandpapa was a no-good thieving smuggler?" His father nodded. "And Molly, you are determined to prove he was not only a smuggler but also a valuable ally of King George II?"

"Ye know exactly what I be say'n all these years." She turned her pleading stare on her only grandson. "I won't be go'n ta me grave with anyone think'n otherwise."

"Father." Colin turned his own pleading look on the earl. "What is the harm of asking about London for Fair Wind's book?"

"His name is Porter Parnell, the first Earl of Coventry, not *Fair Wind*." The earl shook his head, running his hand through his soft brown hair. "I have no intention of reminding all of England of our less than noble past, and you should not either. You will need a wife before long, and the grandson of a smuggler is not an attribute most London misses want in a husband."

"Your pretty, senseless wife did not mind wed'n the son of a bar wench," Molly retorted. "If'n me and my Porter's past in Sheerness makes ye feel less of a nobleman, then I have other concerns for ye. It be because of Fair Wind that ye have this fancy house, your hoity-toity society friends, and the title ye use."

The earl sighed and turned to stare into the hearth. "I have worked tirelessly to ensure that my Earldom— Colin's legacy, might I remind you—is not tarnished by our family's scandalous past."

The mention of Colin's future was the one thing that softened Molly's determination—every time— however, his future did not negate Molly's history and ensuring that her dear, beloved husband was not shrouded in dishonor for all eternity. While Colin was still unsure what to believe, he believed *in* his grandmama.

"Father, if we are discreet and draw no attention, what is the harm of searching for the book?"

The earl twisted around to face Colin, Molly now at his side.

His face was a mixture of unease and anguish. "What if you find exactly as I've proclaimed for years?"

"Then that is what we find," Colin conceded. "However, I think we owe it to Porter to at least try and prove what Molly asserts is correct. Imagine how the

Coventry Earldom will rise if it is proven Porter *was* an ally to the king."

The earl glared between his son and his mother, obviously torn. No matter how much they argued and fussed, Ramsey loved his mother—and his son. "You have seven days—and Mother remains close to home in case she is in need of a physician."

Colin and Molly nodded their agreement to the terms.

"And when Mother's treatment is complete and the doctor gives her a clean health record, she returns to Tintinhull—no more debating, and no more sneaking behind my back."

His father's brow rose when neither Colin nor Molly answered.

Molly clutched at Colin's arm. "We have seven days?"

"Yes."

"And you will not stand in our way?" Colin confirmed.

"As long as you are discreet, I will allow you your foolish quest."

"Thank you, Father." It was more than the earl had ever compromised on before, and Colin damn well didn't plan to squander the time. "We will keep to your terms."

"See that you do." The earl strode to his desk and sat heavily in his chair. "Now, if you will both excuse me, I have actual work to accomplish today."

Molly's back stiffened, and Colin feared she would lash out and ruin what little truce they'd agreed to only moments before.

"We will not keep you any longer." Colin tugged at Molly's arm, signaling it was their time to depart. "Also, I received word from my steward in regards to the crop rotation plan. I will have the report brought to you."

The earl had already begun riffling through the many files on his desk, his attention elsewhere. "Fine,

fine."

Colin had little hope his father would actually read the reports, but at least the earl hadn't outright refused him.

Molly took up her cane that leaned by the door as they departed.

He pulled the door shut behind him and paused, his lips turning up in a satisfied grin.

"We did it, Molly."

"We ain't done nothin' yet, me lad," she clucked, shaking her head. "We still need ta find that blasted book."

"I will visit the Duke of Atholl again. See if he remembers anything further about the tome and its whereabouts."

"See that ye do, but stay clear of that fiery-haired sorceress."

Colin chuckled as Molly tapped her forehead, chin, chest, and back to her nose.

He swore her superstitious ritual was becoming more and more complex by the day; luckily, she made no move to spit on the rug-covered floor.

CHAPTER 8

TO SAY THAT Ophelia was pleased with herself, at least thus far today, would be an understatement. She'd located the information she sought, found Lord Hawke's book, and escaped her family's townhouse without notice. After fleeing up the servant's stairs, she'd located her maid, and they'd slipped out the front door to find the Atholl coach still in the drive.

It had all been simple.

On any other day, Ophelia would have been convinced it was *too* easy.

But she hadn't time to dwell on the subject.

Perhaps she could convince Edith and Luci to allow her to take a more active role in the *Mayfair Confidential*, more than simply taking the information they gave her and writing the posts.

Even her friends would admit she'd done a marvelous job in their absence. She needs must dampen her jovial mood before exiting her carriage, though, lest the man suspect she'd gone to nefarious lengths to return his book and thus cast Ophelia in a less than proper light.

She glanced out the coach window at the massive townhouse. A plaque mounted to the stone exterior proclaimed the house *Knightsbridge*. A noble property situated across from Hyde Park in a most elite area.

Lord Hawke, while only a baron, must have a wealthy, prestigious family, indeed.

Even her father, a duke in a long line of Atholl dukes, did not possess the sheer wealth needed to obtain such a grand residence in London proper.

"I will remain here, my lady?" her lady's maid inquired.

"Yes." Ophelia gave her a confident smile. "I should be but a moment. I need return something that belongs to Lord Hawke."

"Very well." The girl didn't question her further, and Ophelia was happy for it.

Daring to arrive at a gentleman's home unannounced was highly inappropriate. However, besides having the book delivered by a servant, there was no other way.

…and this was the only way she'd be able to see the handsome man again. Maybe then he would be banished from her dreams, thus casting her back into reality.

Her footman opened the carriage door, set down the steps, and assisted her departure.

She hid the book in the folds of her skirts. The last thing she wanted was to make it necessary for the servants to lie for her if her father discovered the book missing—or, Heaven help her, he found out she'd called on a gentleman without his consent or her mother's accompaniment.

There was little chance Ophelia would allow such a trivial detail to stop her.

However, that did not stop her pulse from racing or her face from flushing as she walked toward the door. Blast it all, but she'd forgotten her fan in her haste to depart, and there was little she could do as her skin reddened to a shade similar to a ripe tomato.

Taking a calming breath, Ophelia raised her gloved hand to knock, making certain the book was still hidden in the folds of her skirts.

Her knuckles hadn't even rapped against the door when it swung open, causing Ophelia to yelp in surprise and hop backwards.

Likewise, the butler stared back at her with rounded eyes, his mouth gaping. He hadn't expected to see her standing on the stoop any more than she had predicted the door to open with such gusto.

"Miss," he said, his manners righting themselves quickly. "I do apologize. Lady Coventry is not receiving guests. Would you like to leave your card?"

Bollocks!

She'd forgotten her fan…and her calling card.

Her pride from a few moments before dimmed quickly.

Ophelia was not giving up, no matter if she made a cake of herself before Lord Hawke. "Actually, I am here to see Lord Hawke, and…Molly," she said, pasting her most sincere smile on her face. At the butler's furrowed brow, she continued, "If Lord Hawke is not at home, I can return at another time…"

"The dowager and Lord Hawke are in residence."

It was good news, but the butler still appeared puzzled by her request to see the pair. He did not show her in, nor turn her away, but stood staring as if she certainly must have more to say.

"Ah, yes, the dowager, please forgive my informal request." Her smile faltered slightly when the man continued to glare. "When I met the dowager, she was…"

Ophelia clamped her mouth shut. She was rambling, and just about announced Molly's harebrained antics in the Atholl drive. It would not do to inform the butler that the first time she'd met the older woman had been with her cane aimed at Ophelia's head.

Swallowing hard, Ophelia kept her stare on the servant, refusing to look away or show any weakness. "…she was waiting in Lord Hawke's coach." It would have been wise to refrain from mentioning Molly at all, but it was too late for that now.

"May I inform Lord Hawke and the dowager who is calling?"

A name…her name. Her missteps were adding up too fast for Ophelia to keep track of; no fan, no calling card, and utterly dismal manners.

"Lady Ophelia Fletcher, daughter of the Duke of Atholl," she added as an afterthought, in case the man did not remember her name.

Finally, the butler stepped aside, opening the door wide enough for Ophelia to enter. "Do come in, my lady."

She stepped into the foyer and was instantly surprised by the grandness. A silver chandelier hung from the vaulted ceiling, holding what must be over a hundred tiny candles. Matching sconces adorned the walls in every direction. Three shelves stood proudly, each arranged precisely with trinkets, books, and objects Ophelia could only assume were of great historical value, though she recognized none of them. The floor beneath her shone as if it had been polished only moments before she arrived, and the balustrade was crafted of the darkest wood she'd ever beheld. A rug covered the floor in the center of the foyer and was certainly worth more than all of the carpeting in the Atholl Townhouse combined.

Lord Hawke lived a life of luxury Ophelia could only dream of.

But then why was he desperately searching for an old book on smuggling in Kent?

Footfalls sounded, drawing her attention to a corridor leading to the left of the stairs, though the hallway was too dim to see anyone.

The butler gestured in the opposite direction. "My lady, this way to the dowager's receiving room. I will inform my lady of your arrival."

"Actually, it is Lord Hawke I am here to see," she

replied. It would not do to have Molly causing a scene the likes of which her servants would be unable to stop. It had been one thing to raise her cane at Ophelia in her own driveway with Lord Hawke coming to her rescue, but who would prevent the old woman from bashing her over the head at Knightsbridge? "I have something that belongs to him."

"Lady Ophelia?" She glanced over the butler's arm to see Lord Hawke striding her way. "What in heaven's name are you doing here?"

She glanced at the floor as a heaviness settled in her arms. Had it been unwise to come?

Belatedly, Ophelia remembered she had proper business here, she hadn't come out of some foolish fancy or on a whim.

Ophelia turned to face the lord, her chin notching up and a grin overtaking her lips. "I found the book you were searching for." With the volume, about the size of her adventure novels, proudly displayed before her, she took a step in his direction.

Her sense of accomplishment soared once more when he hurried toward her and snatched the tome from her hand then grabbed her arm with the other before pulling her toward a room off the foyer.

Lord Hawke pushed into the room, all but dragging Ophelia behind him, then kicked the door shut.

He released his hold on her at the same moment, and Ophelia stumbled a few steps before he reached out and steadied her.

Lord Hawke turned the book over and over in his hands, touching the binding, running his finger along the embossed cover, and he even bent forward to smell the thing. She wondered if he caught the scent of the ocean in its leather-bound exterior, too.

"Where did you get this?" His glare refocused on her. The words were a breathless whisper as if she'd presented him with a map of Atlantis or the fabled Trojan horse. "Your father said…"

Ophelia clasped her hands behind her back and rocked on her heels. "I went and saw Oliver. He told me my father had purchased the book. With that information, it was easy enough to locate the book in my father's study."

Lord Hawke glanced down at the book once more and shook his head, returning his narrow-eyed stare to her. "But Atholl said he hadn't any—"

"Yes, I thought that was odd, too, especially after I inquired as to what you'd visited Oliver's Book Shoppe for and learned my father was the last known person to be in possession of the book."

"Oliver's?" Lord Hawke stammered, his hand dropping to his side, the book forgotten. "How did you know I sought out the bookseller?"

"I—well—" Ophelia hadn't thought about how to explain her presence at Oliver's Book Shoppe, but a measure of honesty could be shared without mentioning Abercorn. "My father and I went there several times when I was growing up. I still frequent the shop. I was there when you came in and demanded the book. I did not think anything of it that day, but when you appeared at my home several days later, I decided to lend my help."

"Even after Molly nearly clubbed you with her cane?" He pinched the bridge of his nose and lifted the book once more. "It doesn't matter. Molly and I thought this book gone forever. It disappeared shortly after my grandfather passed and my father took his place as the Earl of Coventry."

The man's shoulders sagged as if a long-time weight had fallen away. His brow smoothed, and if Ophelia weren't mistaken, a slight grin settled on his face as he began once more to turn the book over and over in his hands.

"Where did you find it?" he asked, finally opening the cover.

"In a locked cabinet in my father's desk." She

couldn't help her triumph smile.

"I am surprised he handed it over to you so easily."

"Oh, he did not," she replied, gaining a sharp look from him. "I searched his office until I found the locked cabinet then I sprang the lock with a penknife and found your book." She took a deep breath before continuing. "I brought it straight here."

"You stole it from your father's study?"

His eyes narrowed on her, and his shoulders stiffened much like they had at both Oliver's and her family townhouse when he'd come searching. However, he had the book back. She'd returned it. Why did he appear so...irritated?

"Do remove your frown, or I will assume you are unhappy I returned the book."

"You took this from your father's study...without his knowledge. You must return it immediately before he discovers it missing."

"I will do nothing of the sort, my lord."

"Yes, you will!" he demanded.

CHAPTER 9

COLIN GLARED AT the woman, who despite his evident fury, did not back down or admit any wrongdoing. Lady Ophelia Fletcher was maddening, brazen, and in complete denial about the trouble she was in—and the discord she'd unwittingly brought to his doorstep. He need convince her to return the book immediately, or Colin would have little choice but to return it himself.

It was far too much of a coincidence for him to have come around inquiring about the book only to have it disappear from Atholl's study only days later. Plus, he'd gained information from Oliver... And now this?

If Lord Atholl discovered his desk had been tampered with, the magistrate would be at Colin's father's doorstep before Colin could get the woman out.

"Lady Ophelia, while I am overjoyed to see this book, it was not wise of you to steal it from your father." He gave her his most pointed glare, and her eyes brimmed with tears. Bloody bollocks, but he couldn't have the woman running from his home in tears, that would cause a scandal just as easily as the stolen book being found in Colin's possession. "Please, do not cry."

Her lower lip trembled, and a single tear escaped.

"I am a cad, my lady." He brushed the tear from her cheek before it could make its way down her face and off her chin. When she glanced up at him, her blue eyes were as clear as a cloudless London sky, as fresh as the air after a solid rainstorm, and as injured as a rabbit in a snare. "I did not intend to sound so gruff."

And it was all Colin's doing.

She glanced around the room, a most innocent blossom staining her cheeks, but her tears dried. "I guess I should have thought things through a bit more before…"

It would be ungentlemanly to allow her to take all the blame. "Truly, I thank you for your bravery and cunning in locating and returning my family's book; however, I cannot allow you to suffer any adverse consequences on my behalf."

She pressed her fist to her mouth, and her shoulders fell.

"Perhaps I can have a tiny look before you return it."

Her gaze snapped to his, and he felt rather than saw her spirits rise.

Colin turned his attention to the book once more. *Smuggling: A Journey from Kent to Denmark* by Fair Wind Parnell. He traced his grandfather's name, hardly able to believe the book actually existed—or, more accurately, *still* existed. He and Molly had spoken of it for so many years, it was like a mythological object, always spoken of in lore but never presenting itself in actuality. It was smaller than he'd imagined it to be—less than fifty pages. The binding, several decades old, should be tattered and cracking, yet it appeared unblemished.

That alone spoke to the book's worth.

Not a value in shillings or pounds, much like his father assumed was the measure of a man, a title, or an estate, but a worth measured in honor, integrity, and bravery. It was what Fair Wind said made a man, or at least that is what Molly had told Colin on hundreds of occasions. Property, possessions, and the extent of a man's coffers meant little if a man did not hold honor, loyalty, and love in his heart.

This was everything Molly proclaimed would elevate the first Earl of Coventry, Porter "Fair Wind" Parnell, from a known Sheerness smuggler to an ally and confidante of King George II. Within these pages, Colin could find indisputable proof his grandpapa was one of England's most trusted men during the Seven Years' War, taking missives between George and his nephew, Frederick II, in Prussia.

Colin could hardly draw breath.

His airway was constricted, and his body laced with tension.

Here, now, Molly would find her vindication.

Colin would be allowed to celebrate his grandpapa openly without his father's naysaying condemnation.

All he need do was open the book and read the pages added after Fair Wind's time serving the king was done, those that detailed his harrowing journeys from Sheerness to Prussia. Not from Kent to Denmark as the cover displayed.

Bloody hell, but excitement should be coursing through him, demanding he call for Molly, his parents…and anyone who'd disparaged his grandpapa in the past.

Yet Colin was unable to open the book, though he demanded his fingers do exactly that.

Instead, he brought the small volume to his nose and breathed in deeply. It was almost as if he could smell Fair Wind's many adventures at sea; the scent of a salty breeze cascading over the white caps of the open ocean.

Would it be in his power to give the book back once he opened it, or would he forever claim possession of his great family legacy?

He had to risk it, to know for certain whether all Molly had said throughout his life was true. That all the hate and unsavory comments his father hurled at both Colin and his grandmama over their belief in Fair Wind and his accounting of the past could be thrown to the wayside and forgotten.

Their family could be mended.

Their future one of solidarity, not strife.

It was almost too much to hope for, but it was exactly what he'd wished for his entire adult life.

He held within his hands the means to solve every problem the Coventry family had, debunk every revolting story about his heritage, and solidify his family name for generations to come.

"My lord?" Lady Ophelia laid her hand on his arm. The warmth of her touch quickly seeped through her gloved fingers, down through his coat sleeve, and heated his skin. "Is all as it should be?"

"It is, thank you," he choked out, his head swimming from lack of breath.

"Are you not going to open it?" she asked, her voice that of a melodic temptress. Undoubtedly, she was the siren Molly had accused her of being because with her question came the irrevocable need to do as she said. "I know I am quite interested to see what is so special about this particular book."

He glanced at her, inwardly praying she would take the volume from him and run—hide it where it would never tempt him again. But instead, her cerulean crystal eyes begged him to open the cover and show her what secrets the book held.

Colin was helpless to let the book go, just as he was powerless to look away from Lady Ophelia.

"Go ahead," she coaxed.

Reluctantly, and with a sense of great loss that burrowed deep within him, Colin removed his stare from her and focused on the book. He flipped the cover open to see his grandpapa's handwriting for the very first time. It was heavy on the page, the quill tip obviously having placed far more pressure to the paper than necessary—strong, bold, and unwavering, just as Colin envisioned Fair Wind to be.

He turned the next page…

And was greeted by the torn edges of several missing sheets.

His heart beat frantically, and he flipped several more pages only to find an accounting for Fair Wind's first journey out of the Sheerness port and the wilds of the North Sea.

Erratically, he turned page after page, determined to find what his grandmama claimed should be written within. But no detailed explanation of Fair Wind's true purpose at sea appeared.

Not even a scrap of evidence or a mere sentence to contradict his father's assertion that Porter Parnell was anything but a no-good, unscrupulous smuggler.

"How can this be?" he groaned. "Is this the condition in which you found the book?"

His penetrating stare landed on Lady Ophelia, and she shrank back in fright at the venom that could be heard in his words.

"Y-y-yes," she stammered. Her eyes showed nothing but innocence, not an ounce of guilt to be found. "I opened the cabinet and took the book, that is all. I brought it directly here."

"There were no other papers with it? Possibly a small stack of torn pages?"

She shook her head, her auburn curls falling over her shoulder. "The drawer held no papers, only a few other books on trade winds and the landscape of other lands, some assorted writing instruments, and an ink pot…oh, and an old accounting ledger."

"I think it best you return the book with all due haste." He worked hard to hide his disappointment from Lady Ophelia. It was no good to him, and would only serve to harm Molly further. Without Fair Wind's personal accounts of his travels for the king, the book was worth more as kindling in the Coventry hearth. Colin would not cause his grandmama any more pain.

"But you went to great lengths to find it." She refused to take the book even as he attempted to place it back in her hands. "You must need it far more than my father."

"It belongs to the duke. He purchased it from Oliver's Book Shoppe." Colin shook his head as she tried to hand the book back to him. "I think it is time you depart, Lady Ophelia. Your family must certainly be worried about your whereabouts."

Her brow furrowed, and she frowned. It was something that normally transformed a person's face into a less inviting version of their usual expression, but with Lady Ophelia, he found himself longing to smooth her brow, turn her frown into a smile once more, and tell her everything about…everything. His family, their strife, their scandalous past, and even his promise to Molly. Colin refused to admit his failure…especially to the divine creature before him. She was a lady, the daughter of a duke, and there was little chance she'd ever witnessed a scandal or had ever been touched by the less savory aspects of the human nature.

No, Lady Ophelia, with her fiery hair, fair skin, and eyes the color of a clear sea did not deserve to be drawn into his flawed and broken family.

"I suppose you are correct, my lord," she sighed, crossing her arms, the book clutched tightly to her chest. "The book belongs to my father. I will simply return it since you are no longer interested in it, and we shall continue as if this never occurred. Unless…"

Unease settled on Colin. "Unless?"

"Unless you are willing to tell me what this is all about and who Fair Wind Parnell is."

To tell her anything would lead to telling her everything. One certainly could not leave the conversation at: Fair Wind was my grandpapa and a famed smuggler.

There would be further questions, and the wanderings of Lady Ophelia's mind would likely end far worse than the actual circumstances behind it all.

"I guess I will be going." She paused for a brief moment, giving Colin the opportunity to speak, but he remained close-lipped. "Very well. It was a pleasure meeting you. I will see myself out."

She pivoted to quit the room, and Colin's chest tightened.

If she left without any further explanation, he suspected he'd never set eyes upon her again.

He should be satisfied to see her go, taking the blasted, no-good volume with her.

Neither she nor the book would bring him anything but trouble.

Then why did he feel a hollowness overtake him the more she moved toward the door—and out of his life?

LORD HAWKE WAS insufferable. Did he think her dim enough not to notice the light in his eyes when he spied the book? The way he'd held it with such reverence as he smoothed his hands over the binding. The innate rightness she'd felt when the book was in his possession.

Only to have him shove the thing back at her and demand she return it to her father's desk as if it weren't of great import to him.

Well, Ophelia would show the man. She would return the title to her father and make certain Lord Hawke never set eyes upon the book again. As far as she was concerned, the lord could jump into the Thames, and she would not bat an eye or assist him.

She placed her hand on the door latch, prepared to open it and flee. He had been correct, at least in part, her family would be worrying over her whereabouts at any moment.

"Lady Ophelia," he groaned. "Wait."

She froze, her hand on the handle, and waited for him to continue. After the embarrassment he'd caused her, Ophelia would not *wait* around for more. She'd risked much taking the book and journeying to Hyde Park in her father's carriage to see the title returned to its rightful owner.

"Fair Wind is a relation of mine," he said. "My family is originally from Sheerness, Kent, or at least my father's family is."

Ophelia turned back to face Lord Hawke. "Why is the book so important to you?"

His jaw was clamped shut, and she feared he'd said all he planned to say on the matter. Rubbing his hand across his face, Lord Hawke visibly relaxed.

"Fair Wind was my grandpapa."

Ophelia attempted to hide her shock at this information, but when he shook his head, his frame stiffening once more, she knew she'd done a poor job of it.

"If Fair Wind is your grandfather, then he was Molly's husband?"

Behind Ophelia, the door slammed against its hinges, sending a draft of wind billowing her skirts about her ankles.

"Ye better believe it!" Molly cackled, thumping her cane heavily into the bare wooden floor as she entered the room. "Fair Wind was the best bloody seamen there ever was—and an even finer husband."

"Molly!" Lord Hawke stalked past Ophelia and Molly, closing the door soundlessly before rounding to glare at the older woman. "Have you been listening to my private conversation with Lady Ophelia?"

"Sure have, ye foolish lad. Seems a boon I was, too, or ye woulda let Fair Wind's book leave this house without me have'n a look." The woman took a step toward her grandson, her skirts pressing against his legs. They would have been nose-to-nose had the woman been two feet taller. "You thought ta keep this from me, Colin, me boy?"

Her voice cracked, and Ophelia momentarily felt an immense amount of compassion. "Lady Coventry—"

The woman rounded on her, pointing her cane straight at Ophelia's heart. "Me name be Molly, none of this Lady Coventry nonsense."

"I was only going to say…" Ophelia gulped when the woman slammed her cane back to the ground and turned back to face Lord Hawke. Colin. "Molly, please—"

Suddenly, the room grew uncomfortably warm, and Ophelia's head began to swim. She cursed her forgetfulness once more and settled for fanning her heated face with her gloved hand.

"Don't just stand there, Colin," Molly chastised. But the woman's voice sounded far away. "The lady be about ta faint dead away."

Just as swiftly as it had started, her face cooled as a breeze cascaded over her scorching skin and her eyes refocused. Colin was waving his handkerchief before her as Molly dragged a straight-back chair in her direction.

"I don't mind if the devil-haired woman faints, but not in me receive'n room. Imagine the horrors if she conked her head soundly and bled out on me freshly polished floor."

Ophelia sat heavily in the chair with a mumbled thank you and leaned forward, hoping it would help her to breathe.

"Pull her hair forward."

"Great idea, Molly." Hands ran across the back of her neck, pushing her hair forward. "This should cool her quickly."

"Let me have a look."

Another set of hands touched her skin, these were

rougher with callouses, as Ophelia breathed in deeply. She hadn't succumbed to a case of the vapors in ages—since they'd rescued Lady Edith from the evil clutches of Lady Downshire.

"What are you looking for?" Colin said close to her ear.

"The mark of the devil. Ye be certain I'll find it, too."

"The what?" Ophelia squeaked, throwing her head back, at the same time Colin pulled Molly's hands away from her.

As Ophelia stood, Colin had hold of Molly and was slowly inching her away from Ophelia.

The old woman grabbed her pendant with one hand and tapped her forehead, chin, and chest before turning her head to the side.

"Don't you dare!" Colin warned. "You know mother does not favor having the rugs cleaned and the floors scrubbed due to your spittle."

"A pox on your mum," Molly grumbled, but allowed Colin to lead her to the chaise lounge closest to the hearth. "Don't see the harm in have'n a peek at the chit's neck—just ta confirm one way or the other."

"Confirm what?" Ophelia asked.

"If'n ye be in cahoots with the devil."

"That is preposterous, Molly," Colin sighed, giving Ophelia an apologetic smile. "If she were working with the devil—as you claim—why would she risk so much to bring us Fair Wind's book?"

Molly appeared to mull over her grandson's question as she rested her chin on the head of her cane. "I s'pose it could all be a ploy ta snare a husband…"

"My lady!" Ophelia glanced between Molly and Lord Hawke. He could not believe she'd done all this in a vain hope that Colin would be so grateful he'd pursue a courtship with her. "That is more preposterous than your assertion I am marked by the devil because of my red hair."

"Oh, is it now?" Molly's gaze narrowed on her, and Ophelia wondered for a quick second if she could be a carrier for the devil before shaking her head in denial. "Well, I had ta be certain. If'n ye aren't here on the devil's errand ta lay a curse on me grandson, then what be your reason?"

"Enough." Lord Hawke slashed his hand through the air, silencing Molly and bringing all attention to him. "Molly, she brought us the title we sought, there is no reason to question her motives."

"If'n ye say so, me lad." Molly let out an unladylike snort. "Now, hand over me damned book."

Both Molly and Lord Hawke turned their attention to her once more, and Ophelia noticed she still clutched the volume to her chest. She hadn't so much as dropped it during her near faint.

"I wasn't going to bother you with it because the pages are missing."

Ophelia handed the book to Molly and stepped back, hoping Lord Hawke would keep talking and she would remain unnoticed, lest he demand she return home again.

"Pages...miss'n? That cannot be."

"Are you certain that Fair Wind added the pages and had the book rebound after the king's death?"

Molly vigorously nodded, her tightly coiled hair at risk of toppling into her face. "Oiled the leather meself and watched him scribe late inta the night ta make certain he wrote everythin' down."

Opening the book, Molly ran her finger down the inside of the spine, and Ophelia could not help moving closer. Indeed, there were at least a dozen pages ripped from their place, leaving only the jagged edges where the paper had attempted to hold its place.

A great sob filled the room as the tears began slipping down Molly's cheeks to land on the open book, her shoulders shaking with each outcry.

"There is no way I'll prove me Porter an honorable

man," Molly choked out as her sobs turned to ragged sniffles.

Colin knelt before her, taking the older woman's hands into his, his thumbs gently rubbing the backs of her ungloved fingers.

Ophelia abruptly stepped back, fearing she was partaking in a private moment between the pair. One she had no right to witness. However, she could not wrench her stare away as Colin embraced his grandmama, pulling her close and murmuring in her ear. The older woman nodded, so slightly Ophelia nearly missed it, before Colin pulled back and stood.

Pushing off her cane, Molly gained her feet as Colin placed a hand under her elbow for support. Molly shook off his assistance and moved toward Ophelia, her cane in one hand and her late husband's book in the other.

Her eyes still brimmed with tears but they no longer fell.

"This book, it belongs ta your father," Molly sighed, holding it out for Ophelia to take. "Thank ye for bring'n it ta me—us—but, sadly, it is of no use ta us now."

"But Fair Wind still wrote it," Ophelia challenged. "Would you not like to keep it?"

"Not if'n it means bring'n trouble down on your head, foolish girl." Molly thrust the book at Ophelia once more, and she had no option but to take it or watch it fall to the floor. "Now, the pair of ye, be gone. I'm need'n some privacy."

Molly's shoulders stooped more than Ophelia had noted before as the woman shuffled back to the lounge.

"I will return, grandmama," Colin said, nodding at Ophelia as he moved toward the door. "I will send Beth in with tea."

Ophelia followed, unsure what else to do. Any offer of condolence might push the older woman into hysterics, yet if she said nothing and simply departed the room, it would be a blemish to Ophelia's place as a lady. One did not run away when another was hurting.

She paused at the threshold as the woman collapsed onto the lounge, her cane falling to the floor with a clatter. "Molly," Ophelia said. "I am abundantly sorry for causing you any pain. If I had known, I wouldn't have—"

Colin grasped her elbow and steered her from the room.

"My lord." She tugged at his hold. "I owe your grandmother at least a few words of…" A few words of what? Condolences, positive thinking, hope?

"She is not listening," he whispered as he once again urged her forward and they made their way to the front door. "I have known her all my life—many say I know her best, besides her dearly departed—and I can assure you, she is hearing nothing at this moment."

"I should have left when you bid me take my leave," Ophelia huffed. "Or better yet, I should not have come at all."

"But I am happy you did."

"Truly?" she asked, her chest fluttering at his overly kind—yet impossible—words.

He nodded as they entered the deserted foyer.

"But I upset her terribly." She'd given the woman the worst news possible, besides never locating the book in the first place. The volume was so light in her hands, ever so unassuming. How could it cause so much heartache? "It is not right to leave her wallowing in such sorrow."

"I will walk you to your carriage, see you safely on your way, and be back at her side in a few moments. You have my promise."

His word should not fill her with such faith, but it did.

The same servant who'd shown her in stepped into the foyer and opened the door, allowing Colin and Ophelia to make their way outside. Her carriage waited only thirty paces away, but he pulled her to a stop, and the door closed not far behind them.

No one could be listening from the house, and they were too far from her coach to be overheard by her maid or driver. They were alone in every sense but the visible one. The thought sent a shiver of expectation down Ophelia's spine. Colin placed his hand on the small of her back, causing her stomach to flutter with nervousness. Certainly, this was not normal—for Ophelia had never known the touch or kindness of a man beyond the normal interaction with her father and brothers.

"Lady Ophelia?"

At his soft words, she turned toward him, not caring that the front door could open at any time or that her maid was likely watching her. They stood so close she had to crane her neck back to see his face properly or be forced to stare at his muscular chest. The mere thought of his chest sent a rush of heat through her that pooled between her legs.

There was little doubt something was wrong with her. Could it be she was coming down with a sudden illness? Overheating, shivers, a fluttering belly—these were not at all common things to her.

He was waiting for her to speak, and Ophelia was mortified to realize she hadn't a coherent thought in her mind beyond the splendor of his form, the wayward fall of his pale hair, and the depth of his moss-green eyes. If he sought to discuss his physical attributes, she might well find her tongue. Beyond that, Ophelia only wanted to feel his hand on her lower back once more, hear her name whispered on his gravely exhale.

Bollocks, but she had the overwhelming urge to call him "Prince Amir," as if he were a character from one of her treasured adventure novels.

"Yes, Lord Hawke?" The words were spoken nearly too low for even her to hear.

But then, he smiled. "Thank you for bringing the

book. You did not need take such a risk, but I am happy you did."

"But, what now?"

"What do you mean, what now?"

"How will you prove your grandfather an honorable man?" Ophelia suspected the story of Fair Wind was not over yet, there was still much to tell—or in this case, discover—about the famed smuggler and his purported association with royalty. If this had all been a book, she would be helpless to put it down until she finished it. Certainly, Lord Hawke realized this was not over. "There must be another way."

A sorrowful note lit his eyes. "What is next is something I do not know, nor will I wager to guess at this moment." He sighed, and Ophelia couldn't help but wonder if he were giving up. "For now, I will console my grandmama and pray this does not further break her heart."

She stared up at him, her eyes silently begging him—for what, she did not know.

Lord Hawke took a step back, putting distance between them, and grasped her free hand. "With that, I will bid you ado." He leaned forward and placed a kiss on her glove-covered hand.

Just as quickly, he released her, turned back toward his front door, and disappeared inside.

Her coachman cleared his throat behind Ophelia, and she turned to see the steps down and the carriage door open, awaiting her.

The flutter, much like a horde of butterfly wings, in her stomach did not recede with Lord Hawke out of sight—neither did the tingle traveling through her ebb as she made her way to her waiting conveyance.

Peculiar, indeed.

CHAPTER 10

WHERE WAS THE blasted man?

Sissy paced back and forth in Francis's study. She'd been waiting for nearly two hours for him to arrive home from his afternoon social calls and for them to be on their way. There were important matters to be dealt with, yet, it seemed her brother was far more interested in finding his next ladylove than keeping his word to his sister.

Picking up the small bookend from Franny's desk, Sissy tossed the weighted object shaped like a goose from one hand to the other. The distraction did nothing to reduce her ire at her brother, nor her all-consuming need to be on their way. Time was running short...not for her, but for Francis. It would only be so long before he found another woman who caught his eye and Sissy would be relegated to the shadows once again.

If there was one thing Sissy despised, it was the men in her life—the males who ruled her very existence—putting her second to their whims. First, her father had gambled away her dowry. Then her betrothed had absconded with another when it'd become common knowledge she held not a farthing to her name. And lastly, and possibly the most enraging, was when her dear brother promised her he'd right the situation but could not keep his shaft in his trousers for long enough to secure Sissy's future and ensure her legacy returned. Oh, Francis never admitted it was lust that led him astray time and time again. No, the silly imbecile actually believed himself in love—on five separate occasions.

Yet, his actions made it impossible for Sissy to find love even once.

There was little need to address Franny's assertions that one did not need money, land, or title to find love. They both knew that was the biggest lie of all. One only need explore Sissy's past to know the folly of that thought. Without a dowry, men of the *ton* had passed Sissy up at every turn. Even the daughter—and then sister—of a duke could not find a suitable match without a certain amount of financial assurance.

Not that Sissy would ever find love now, especially at her advanced age—no, it was more about taking from that shrew, causing her family the embarrassment she'd caused Sissy in their youth, and taking back something that rightfully belonged to her.

She would have it back—at any cost.

Not that the stakes hadn't increased as the years passed.

Sissy had found it increasingly difficult to keep her brother focused on the matter. Did he not see that once Sissy had what she wanted, he would be free to pursue his own wants and needs?

"Mrs. Carnes!" Sissy shouted, setting the bookend back on Francis's desk.

The study door opened on well-oiled hinges, and the Abercorn housekeeper curtseyed to Sissy. "Yes, m'lady?"

"Have the coach readied," she instructed. "If my brother thinks to keep me waiting all day, he is sadly mistaken. Have my things loaded for the journey."

"M'lady, I will send word to the stables."

Sissy waved her hand in dismissal, and the housekeeper closed the door as quietly as she had opened it.

Franny may think her single-minded focus was out of place and misguided, but Sissy knew better than most what was due her.

She placed her hands on the smooth, wooden surface of her father's desk—the same one Francis had taken over after the duke's death all those years ago. Their father could have rested peacefully had Sissy been born a man and the Abercorn heir. Never would she have allowed such shameful acts heaped upon her family's name to continue unresolved.

The fact of the matter was: the Dowager Lady Coventry had taken something from her, and Sissy would have it back.

The door opened behind her. "Is the carriage ready, Mrs. Carnes?"

"Sissy." Abercorn huffed. "I made it very clear I would accompany you to Sheerness, but I had things to attend to first. I am a busy lord, sister. I cannot drop things every time you fancy a trip to the coast."

That the man still believed himself in command— in control of *her*—was comical. Francis was oblivious to many things happening around him…and Sissy had no urge to correct him.

"Oh, brother, I am so thankful you are home." She turned and hurried across the room to wrap him in a tight embrace. "I desperately wanted to make certain everything was handled and ready. I certainly know you are in much demand, and I owe you greatly for agreeing to accompany me to Sheerness."

It only took a few words and a tight hug for Francis's irritation to subside.

He pulled from her embrace and straightened his coat. "Well, I am pleased to know you understand the magnitude of calling me away from London at such a time."

"I promise, we will be gone but two days, at most."

He glanced about the room and moved to his desk,

straightening the bookend Sissy had handled a few minutes prior. "Do speak with Mrs. Carnes about the servants moving my belongings."

"Yes, Franny, I certainly will."

"Very well, let us be off," he replied with a nod. "If we hurry, we can be to the coast by nightfall."

…and be back in London by midday tomorrow with all the proof Sissy needed to take back what rightfully belonged to her.

With a confident smile, she followed her brother from the room.

COLIN STOOD IN the empty foyer, fighting the urge to turn and watch Lady Ophelia's carriage pull from the drive onto Hyde Street. There was naught for him to do but let both Lady Ophelia and his grandpapa's book go and return to Molly with all due haste.

It was better this way.

His father would never suspect the proof of Porter's past was forever lost.

Nor would Molly have him continue on this fool's errand.

He only prayed Lady Ophelia was skilled enough to slip the book back in its place before Atholl noticed it had gone missing.

Taking a deep breath, Colin shook off the feeling he had somehow disappointed Lady Ophelia. Which was a ludicrous thought. If anyone should be disappointed in him, it was Molly. He'd made her a promise to find the book and show his father proof of Fair Wind's true activities at sea.

He'd failed, and now he dreaded facing his grandmama.

However, there was naught to do but get on with it.

Perhaps with this concluded, Molly would take the

time to rest, see the physician, and then return to the country. She was happier there. She must be. Away from the watchful, doubting eyes of her son and daughter-in-law. Free to wander the country manor and its surrounding property.

In a way, Colin envied her freedom there.

He needs must put that thought from his mind. Colin belonged in London, learning all he could from his father in preparation for taking over the Coventry Earldom in the future. His days of frolicking about the country with his grandmama were a thing of the past.

Colin strode back to Molly's salon, fearing he'd find the older woman a sobbing, hunched form when he returned. No wails of sorrow or deep cries of misery greeted him as he approached the room, its door open as he'd left it.

Hurrying into the space, he found Molly not on the lounge where he'd left her but standing close to the hearth, her side profile facing him.

A smile played upon his grandmama's lips, creating creases of joy along her cheeks and at the corners of her eyes.

"Molly, how are you getting on?" He stepped fully into the room, and she turned toward him with more pluck than she'd exhibit in years. Her smiled faded to a frown. "I am sorry for the disappointment."

"It cannot be helped, me lad."

"That does not mean I do not believe every word you've ever told me about Fair Wind."

Colin moved to her side, and she raised her wrinkled, age-spotted hand to his cheek, patting it softly. "That I know well, Colin. It only be a burden ta know others do not have faith in Porter."

"Others do not matter, Grandmama."

"Tsk-tsk." She patted his cheek with more force. "Don't I wish that be true."

"I can continue searching for the missing pages." Colin hadn't any notion what made him volunteer to forge on with their quest; however, he knew for certain that it would break his heart if his grandmama didn't see her final wish to fruition. "There are more places I can look. Revisit Atholl and see if he was the one responsible for removing the pages…"

Molly laughed, which quickly turned into a ragged cough as she clutched her pendant and attempted to catch her breath. It happened more and more frequently in recent years, and it worried Colin to no end. The physicians were helpless to find what ailed her, the apothecary could not concoct a remedy to keep the hacking coughs at bay for longer than a few hours, and with it all, Molly became increasingly exhausted from the sudden fits.

"No, me lad, it is simply another bit of me beloved that will remain out of reach—much like this wasteful pendant he be give'n me when we journeyed ta Eton the first time ta secure your father a place at University." She flipped the jewel-encrusted necklace over in her hand to show Colin the back engraving, though they both had committed the inscription to memory long ago.

If'n it be answers ye seek, look ta where it all began, and ye shall be rewarded.

"I will keep Sheerness and our time there in me heart forever," she sighed, a rattle in her chest making it hard for her to inhale again. "Just as ye cannot allow your father's wicked thoughts ta invade and take root in your mind. Never will ye forget the work'n men who gave their all for ye ta live in this fancy house."

"Yes, yes," he reassured her. "I will never allow Ramsey's beliefs to corrupt my sensible mind."

"He was such a nob, your father. Still is." She lowered herself to the lounge once more. "Always go'n on and on about his da, the unscrupulous smuggler who sailed the seas, all while pose'n as a right fancy bloke and use'n my Porter's hard-earned coin to pay for everythin'."

"What…when did Grandpapa give you the necklace?"

Her brow furrowed at his question as she thought, rubbing the pendant between her fingers as she did. "Well, it be that time we sent Ramsey off ta school. He'd become a rebellious lad who sought ta lash out with harsh words at every turn. Porter and I came ta London for our first—and only—proper town stay— think'n it be benefit'n Ramsey when he graduated if we be accustomed ta town life and could introduce him ta society all proper like. Your grandpapa went out after, deposit'n me in this monstrosity of a house, and was gone for what seemed like days but was only mere hours. When he returned, he gave me this. Said for me ta hold it when all hope seemed lost."

But all hope was not gone, Colin would not allow it.

"Mayhap we should do exactly as Fair Wind bid?" he suggested.

"Whatever do ye mean, lad?" Molly sat forward on the lounge, her brow rising.

"We are looking for answers, and it only seems reasonable that we must go back to 'where it all began'." The thought was clear despite its impulsiveness. It was a wonder neither of them had thought of it before this moment; however, until a short while ago, they'd been convinced the proof lay in London, not along the rocky coast of Kent. "Grandpapa must have left some evidence of his work for the king in Sheerness. That is what this is all about, reminding not only us but also Father of our family's past."

She tapped her chin. "And that be in Sheerness," Molly said with agonizing slowness.

"Exactly, though I am uncertain if it is his writings on the travels for the king he wants us to find. Or something else." Colin's heart lifted, and then soared when he saw the light return to his grandmama's gaze. "We should leave today. Now, even. I will have the carriage summoned, and our bags readied." He paced toward the hearth and flipped around, moving back in Molly's direction. His sure, solid steps were muffled by the rug underfoot. "We will arrive after supper, but I am certain we can find lodging. They would never turn away the famed widow of Fair Wind Parnell. Oh, but you worked as a barkeep in your youth. They will know you as surely as they knew Grandpapa."

Molly stared at the head of her cane as Colin rambled. She seemed as overwhelmed by it all as he. Which meant, there was still hope.

Colin chuckled and started for the door. "You wait here while I make the arrangements."

"Me lad, ye know I can't be go'n with ye."

Nothing could have halted him in his tracks faster than those words. "What?"

"I am old, Colin…and sick."

"But the journey is only six hours, at most, and I will have Father's well-sprung traveling coach prepared. It will be as if you are here or in your private chambers." This was a task they'd begun together, and bloody hell, Colin was determined to finish it with Molly by his side. "We will be away from London for only a short time, and your next appointment with the physician isn't for several days."

Molly only shook her head. "I can't be travel'n ta Sheerness, lad, though I'd much enjoy see'n me old home—the first Porter and I shared after wed'n. Or that old tavern I earned me keep at before meet'n your grandpapa." Her gaze darted out the windows to the garden below, but Colin sensed she saw none of it. "If'n I ever make it back home, it not be today. Take the fiery-haired devil with ye."

"What?" Colin's entire body tensed as he attempted to hide his shock at her declaration. "Absolutely not. That is an absurd notion."

The time had come…Molly had lost all common sense.

"She possesses the book." Molly glared across the room at him from her seat on the lounge.

"We no longer need the book," he retorted.

"Well, the people of Sheerness are a loyal bunch." Molly nodded with pride. "They'll not be help'n ye, if'n ye trample into their town ask'n pointed questions. You will learn noth'n. But with the book and the woman at your side, the townsfolk might be more forthright with their information."

"One moment, you think the woman possessed by the devil—"

"I did not say I do not still think she—"

"And the next, you tell me to take the woman to Sheerness." He groaned at the severe consequences of such a thing. "How do you expect me to travel out of London with an innocent, unmarried woman and not find myself either shackled to her or at the end of her father's dueling pistol?"

Molly only shrugged in response.

His grandmama *shrugged*. The beat of his heart thrashed in his ears as his mind swirled around the possibilities…

No, there was no chance in hell that he would take Lady Ophelia with him.

"The book belongs ta her."

"It belongs to her *father*," Colin huffed. "I will simply call on her and say we have changed our minds. That we wish to keep the book. If I am in possession of the volume—and with my striking resemblance to Fair Wind—I should have no issues gaining the townspeople's cooperation."

"It seems ye have everythin' figured out," Molly sighed. It was the same sound she'd made when Colin had built his own boat to sail across the pond at his family's country estate. She'd said it would not hold for the time it would take him to paddle across, but in Colin's ten-year-old mind it was sturdy enough to cross the English Channel. Of course, he'd been only twenty feet out when the raft began taking on water. He'd ended up swimming to shore—and there Molly was, a feline-like grin upon her face. "Ye are a wise lad."

In other words, Molly was sure he had nothing figured out and that he was as unwise as he'd been in his youth.

"I am certain you know more than an old wench like me," Molly mumbled. "I am noth'n but a weak, frail woman with a mind not as solid as it was."

Frail? Weak?

Two words Colin would never dream of using when talking about or *to* his grandmama. Proof of her strength had been witnessed by his coachman, footman, and the duke's butler as Molly had swung her cane at Lady Ophelia in the Atholl drive.

"You are positive it is Lady Ophelia I should take with me?"

"I see no other choice, me lad."

Bloody hell. It seemed he was taking Lady Ophelia to Sheerness with him, he only need convince the auburn-haired beauty to make the journey.

But hadn't she already offered to help him continue his search for the truth?

CHAPTER 11

OPHELIA TILTED HER head back against the wicker chair, allowing the midday breeze to push her long tresses from her face, and the warm sun to kiss her lips. Pulling the blanket tighter about her shoulders, she sighed. The day had grown breezy after she left Lord Hawke's townhouse and returned to Mayfair—to an empty home.

Normally, especially since Lucianna had taken up residence with her family, Ophelia would enjoy the blissful silence of a deserted townhouse; her father meeting with his man of business, her mother paying social calls with Sarah, Elizabeth, and Jennifer in tow, and her brother, Jacob, at his weekly fencing lesson. Today, however, the silence only carried the weight of loneliness.

Luci and Edith were safely on their way to Gretna Green with the fine men they loved.

And she was left in London, alone.

Perhaps that was why Ophelia hadn't returned the book to her father's cabinet as planned but instead retired to the garden outside her mother's salon to read it.

At first, she'd hesitated, thinking she was crossing the line of propriety in some fashion, reading the private writings of Lord Hawke's grandpapa. When she'd stared at the book in her lap, her resistance hadn't lasted long as her interest grew and anticipation built.

Without a doubt, Ophelia knew the book held an adventure, even with the missing pages.

And so, she'd nestled herself in a wool blanket, perched on her mother's favored wicker chair, and read.

Page after handwritten page was filled with harrowing days at sea, stops at foreign and exotic ports, and logs of exports loaded upon the ship. And in between all that—a rare, shining light—were tales of Molly, written by the man who'd loved her above all else.

It was these brief asides that captured Ophelia's attention and kept her reading. Much like the one she'd just finished:

M'love, m'life, m'lady
It is for she and she alone I be at sea.
It is ta prove me love and devotion ta she that I continue.
Me Molly girl, ye be all I need.
Yur pretty curling hair, yer cunning, yer kind eyes.
They all bring me ta heel, but it be the way ye
smile that keeps me head above water.

These passages were utterly enchanting, powerfully moving, and made Ophelia long to find a man who would feel such immense feelings of love for her.

She'd read such novels for years—possibly longer—but they'd never affected her, reached to her very core, and left her wanting for things she'd never thought to be hers as this did. A love similar to that which Edith shared with Torrington and Luci had found with Montrose.

But that love had been denied, or rather cut short, for Tilda. How was Ophelia more deserving of a happy, content future filled with love and companionship than her dear friend?

Her eyes drifted shut, and she allowed her mind to

wander to things they had no business envisioning; a small cottage in the middle of a meadow, the bright, warm sun blazing above, the slight wind carrying the scent of lavender from the flowers that had been planted with love along the a small, fenced-in yard. And a small child, a boy with fair hair and tanned skin, playing with a set of brightly painted blocks. He stacked them high, toddled back to admire his handiwork, and then giggled as he knocked his tower down and began anew. In her mind, Ophelia laughed along with the boy, not at his purposeful action of destroying what he'd so painstakingly built, but at the merriment in the child's blue eyes when he waved her over to help.

Blue eyes…

They were mirror images of Ophelia's, but no other trace of her existed in the child, yet the boy was familiar to her in every way. From the fall of his tawny hair that covered his brow to the determined glint in his eyes when he set about constructing a tower taller than the last.

Yes, in her daydream, she was content and happy, wanting for nothing.

A chuckle sounded behind her, and Ophelia took her careful watch off the boy to see where the sound had come from. It was also particularly familiar and comforting; however, the laugh must have reached her on the breeze because no one stood there.

A deep hollowness filled her, taking over her lovely dream and causing the clouds overhead to roll in, threatening rain.

Ophelia glanced about, but the boy had also disappeared.

She was utterly, terrifyingly, unmistakably alone.

Her chest felt empty, a great hollow void.

She inhaled air, but nothing seemed to appease her lungs as they burned, demanding but never satisfied by the warm, lavender-scented air she drew in.

Her body weakened and crumbled as she

suffocated.

"Lady Ophelia?"

That voice…

Swiftly, she drew in a deep breath, and the emptiness grew less daunting. The panic of a moment before subsided as the clouds overhead drifted to the horizon to reveal the welcoming sun once more.

A hand brushed her cheek, and her eyes snapped open.

The blanket had fallen from her shoulder to rest on the arm of chair. A quick glance up told Ophelia no more than an hour had passed since she'd allowed her eyes to close and her mind to wander.

Squinting, Ophelia sat up straight and glanced around her. Someone had said her name—touched her cheek?—but the bright sun kept her momentarily blinded. Her panic returned, and Ophelia leapt up, the book sliding from her lap to the dirt at her feet.

"My lady," Lord Hawke said, as if mere inches from her ear. "It is only I."

"How, I mean, when…" she stammered, her stare finally coming into focus to see Lord Hawke leaning unflappably against the garden gate, his boots crossed at the ankles, and not close to her at all.

"My apologies for frightening you." He pushed away and strode toward her, a lock of hair falling to cover one eye…so familiar. "I arrived in the drive"—he gestured behind him to his waiting coach—"and saw you sitting here, so peaceful I almost didn't have the heart to wake you."

"I—well—" She shook her head, attempting to collect her thoughts and banish her daydream. Her cheeks heated at the thought, and Ophelia ducked to collect the book to hide her embarrassment. "I was reading, and I must have closed my eyes for a brief moment."

"I've been watching you in slumber for nearly an hour."

"You have?" The shrill edge to her voice was nearly as mortifying as her blush from being caught in her silly daydream.

He nodded solemnly, and his brow pulled low. "I must say, you have a snore men three times your size would envy." Her mouth gaped open, and he chuckled, just as he'd laughed in her dream. "Come, Lady Ophelia, I am a man most noble."

"Certainly," she sighed. "You would never do something so wicked as watch a woman sleep without alerting her to your presence."

"Errr, no," he said. "I would never be so dense as to mention a woman's snoring in polite company."

Lord Hawke was utterly perplexing. Had he been watching her but didn't witness her snore, or had he just walked up and did?

He laughed again, the sound breaking through her unease. "I arrived only a moment ago, and you were completely silent—so quiet I stilled myself from checking for your breath."

Quiet was good. That meant she hadn't spoken aloud in her dream.

"Well, thank you for waking me." She smiled, hoping to change the topic. "If you hadn't, I fear to think how I might have become burnt by the noonday sun…my complexion ruined and my freckles spreading from my nose to my cheeks and forehead."

"What are you reading—"

"Why are you here—"

Ophelia dipped her chin and grinned as they both spoke at the same time.

He cleared his throat. "I came because Molly and I had an idea for finding confirmation of my grandpapa's true intentions at sea."

"And I was reading your grandpapa's book." She held it out to him.

His brow rose. "I do hope it is a compelling read."

"You haven't read it?" she asked.

"I saw it for the first—and only—time when you arrived with it earlier."

"Well, while I highly recommend you at least skim the book, it is a lot about daily life at sea and more than a dozen logs and lists of imports he brought back to England—oh, and the occasional verse about Molly." The blasted shiver traveled down her back once more, and Ophelia adjusted the blanket she held around her shoulders. "He also wrote of Sheerness. It sounds like a lovely town. It's a shame the book lacked the adventure I normally favor in a read."

"Real life is rarely as grand as Robinson Crusoe."

"You know Crusoe?" Her breath hitched.

"Certainly." He cocked his head and shook it. "I may not be as worldly as Fair Wind, but I have read a novel or two."

"I did not think—" His chuckle halted her words, and they both smiled. "Besides, I know life is not always a grand adventure; however, it does not harm the soul to escape into fantasy every now and again."

Ophelia feared she'd said something wrong when he glanced around the small garden, crossing his arms. "I am happy to hear you think Sheerness a lovely town because," he paused, his stare narrowing on her as if his next words and her response meant much, "that is where I—we—are headed. Molly and I believe answers reside in the town she and my grandpapa both loved so much."

"Thank you for letting me know. I truly cannot wait to hear what you find—"

"No." He held up his hand to stop her.

He hadn't come to say goodbye or inform her of their change in direction. "Oh, you came for the book!"

She pushed his family heirloom toward him, once again feeling she'd stepped over some invisible boundary when she'd chosen to open and read Fair Wind's writings. How could she have ever been so foolish to think the baron had come to see her?

Lord Hawke had come for his family's legacy, that was all. Not out of any lasting responsibility to her.

"I suppose it is a good thing I haven't returned the book to my father as yet."

She gave him no choice but to take the title from her or leave her looking ridiculous with her arm outstretched, holding it toward him, her other hand clutching the blanket about her shoulders.

"There was actually something else I came to ask you." His stare focused on something over her left shoulder, clearly avoiding eye contact with her. "It is…ah…"

"Yes, my lord?" They shared no other entanglements or associations. Would he request she ask her father about the missing pages, see if he was aware that they'd been torn out?

Lord Hawke rubbed the back of his neck and swallowed. "Molly thinks it best you accompany me to Sheerness."

"Me?" There was no way to mask her surprise. "But she thinks me a marriage-hungry maiden with the mark of the devil."

It was nearly impossible not to laugh at the woman's assertions, though Ophelia feared it would make her appear all the more deranged if she broke out in unbridled mirth.

"Yes, but, as she wisely pointed out, the book belongs to you." They both glanced down at it, firmly in his grasp. "And beyond that, she believes we will be better received and locate the information we seek far easier together."

It sounded as if he still endeavored to convince himself of her usefulness.

"I cannot simply collect my bag and disappear with you to Sheerness." She pressed her hand to her chest, concentrating on slowing her erratic heartbeat—and the notion of adventure set before her. "What would I tell my parents? What would society think of a proper lady gallivanting about England alone…with a man?"

CHAPTER 12

HE SIGHED; THE weight that had settled earlier lifting from his shoulders. "This was the exact concern I spoke to Molly of. It is not proper at all. It is imposs—"

She tapped her chin in thought. "Though, if I collected my things quickly and we left now, no one would be the wiser, and we would be long out of London before anyone even came searching for me."

Every instinct in him flared with alarm. "You are actually considering this?"

"When did you plan to depart for Kent?" she answered with her own question.

"Today, actually," he stammered. "Now, in fact. I have my traveling coach at the ready in your drive."

"Then I request but a few moments—ten at the very most—and I will be ready."

"But—but—I only came to request the book, not convince you to risk your reputation only to prove correct my grandmama's long-held belief about Fair Wind."

"It is clearly important to you—and Molly," Ophelia said, her chin notching higher. "And if Molly thinks I can be of assistance, it would be unkind of me to refuse."

It was absurd of her to agree. Possibly the most

foolish errand his grandmama had ever requested of him—and she had sent him with her pendant, as well. This was important to the old woman, more than Colin had ever suspected, and deep down, it was just as vital to him. Once this mess was behind him, Colin would either have the proof necessary to convince his father, or he would be relegated to asking for his father's forgiveness for the years spent arguing over their family past. Either way, Molly would be banished back to the country, and Colin would continue as Lord Hawke, heir apparent to the Coventry Earldom.

"You will wait for me?" she inquired, her voice so melodic and...innocent, as if she were asking him to wait for her to hand her glass off at a ball so they could dance, not climb into his coach and travel hours from her family with no protection but that which Colin provided.

He hadn't thought about leaving without her. "Of course, my lady."

The brilliant smile she turned on him was worth the risk they were taking.

"Oh, thank you for taking me with you on this adventure! I will meet you at the coach." She turned quickly, the blanket falling forgotten to the ground as she raced toward the house, entering through a side door that opened into the small garden in which he stood. "I will only be a moment."

The door closed behind Lady Ophelia, and despite the rock that had settled in the pit of his stomach, he was smiling on the inside and certainly looking forward to their carriage ride. If for no other reason than to find out why a lady would jeopardize her reputation and future to help a man she barely knew.

Colin made his way back to the coach, nodding to his driver as he held the book at his side.

An adventure?

He snorted and mumbled, "Not bloody likely."

This trip would be more of a disaster—of epic

proportions—than an adventure. At the very least, Colin was seriously compromising Lady Ophelia's reputation, even if no one found out that they journeyed alone together to Sheerness.

His head pounded, and he massaged his temples. He could only image the story she'd concoct to keep the magistrate from chasing them down. It would be Colin's blasted luck that he'd find himself in trouble for this entire debacle. And this was all due to Molly's whim— well, that and his insistence that information could be found in Sheerness. But there was no reason he couldn't have outright refused to even consider including Lady Ophelia in this adventure...far more aptly called a *misadventure*. The book was not explicitly necessary for the journey. She was not integral to discovering the information he needed. Nor should he be listening to a woman who truly lived by the superstition red hair was a mark of the devil.

Yet, here he was.

And here came Lady Ophelia around the side of the house, a satchel held securely under her arm and a thick woolen cloak over her shoulder. The wide brim of her bonnet did not hide her feverish grin as she rounded the corner and glanced to make certain the front door was closed before hurrying to the coach, tossing her traveling bag inside, and leaping in after it.

He peeked in the conveyance as Lady Ophelia climbed onto the rear-facing seat and began arranging her skirts after her mad dash.

"Shall we be off, my lord?" she called, a bit too excitedly for Colin. "It would not suit either of us to have my father stumble upon us in the drive."

"We would not want anything of the sort to happen, especially not before we've even begun our journey." He slowly climbed into the carriage, and his footman lifted the steps and shut the door, the only light within from a single pulled drape casting a shadow across Lady Ophelia's face. "Ready?"

"More than ready, my lord," she said, arranging her cloak and satchel on the seat next to her.

For the first time, Colin noticed her change in attire. She had switched from a sage-green walking gown to a deep blue riding habit, the neckline cut daringly low and offering him an ample view of her heaving bosom as she continued to breathe hard from her run to the coach.

She riffled through her bag, giving Colin a moment to inspect her further without alerting her to his task. The traveling habit highlighted her fair complexion and complemented her already crystal eyes. The sleeves were tight about her arms, the bodice stretched tightly in a most alluring manner, and the skirts flowed to the carriage floor where they pooled, hiding her boots. She'd also pinned her hair at the back of her neck in a prim knot suitable for traveling, yet her hat was far grander than was needed in an enclosed conveyance.

A knot lodged at the back of his throat as his stare landed on her low neckline once more. He'd only met the woman on three occasions, this being the third, but in their short acquaintance, she'd always favored gowns of a far more modest cut and color. There was little chance they'd successfully travel to Sheerness and back without notice with her dressed in such a captivating habit; even now, Colin was incapable of taking his stare off her.

"My lord?" She waved a small paper-wrapped parcel in front of him. "I asked if you were hungry."

Blinking several times, Colin hoped his smile was not as sheepish as he felt being caught lavishing over her bosom. "My apologies. I was pondering our plan once we arrive in Kent."

"Oh?" Lady Ophelia set the parcel in her lap and untied the twine holding the paper closed to reveal a loaf of flat bread and a wedge of cheese—and even a large portion of plump, purple grapes.

"When did you have time to collect a meal?" The

woman was full of surprises—though this was a welcome one, as he hadn't eaten since early that morning. "You were not inside for more than ten minutes."

She unhurriedly retrieved a cloth napkin from her bag and smoothed it over her lap before answering. Her chin lifted as she spoke. "I find the best way to accomplish something with all due haste is to enlist the help of a trusted servant. In this case,"—she paused to arrange the food on the cloth and presented the feast to him—"it was my maid, who was more than willing to pack our meal while I collected my things and changed."

"Are you not worried she will tell your father where you've run off to?"

She waved her hand before popping a grape into her mouth, the translucent juice marring her lips as she chewed. "Heavens no," she commented around her food.

Colin shrugged as he accepted a portion of the bread and a sliver of cheese as they hurried through the crowded afternoon streets of London toward the country.

"Where did you tell your maid you were going?" He could not believe she'd speak the truth of the matter, or risk them being stopped long before they reached Kent.

"To Gretna Green." She placed a hunk of bread between her lips, her eyes drifting closed as a sigh escaped her. "Have you ever tasted anything as heavenly as fresh bread, Lord Hawke?"

"Gretna Green?" he groaned.

Her eyes opened, and her stare narrowed on his look of shock. "Of course," she sighed heavily. "They wouldn't believe if I said I was running off to any other destination, and they would worry. It was the only way to assure they would not send someone after me."

Her satisfied grin only confused him more. "How is the Scottish border meant to keep them from coming after you? I would think it would be all the more reason to stop you from doing anything foolish." Perhaps Lady Ophelia *was* looking to ensnare a husband, though he'd be loath to admit that Molly was correct.

"Foolish, my lord?" Her brow rose, and her cheeks blossomed with pink. "I can assure you, I have never done anything even the slightest bit foolish, with the exception of this trip to Sheerness."

"There is traditionally only one reason a woman travels to Gretna Green…"

"I am aware. To wed."

"And this would not concern Lord and Lady Atholl?"

"Well, they very pointedly forbid me from going; however, they will know I am not in harm's way." She spoke slowly as if he were the one dull of mind and not the other way around. "How long did you say the trip to Kent would be?"

"Ummm, well…" Everything about the woman threw him off course. Perhaps Molly had actually spotted a kindred spirit in Lady Ophelia but had misinterpreted her has a crux. "Six hours at most, with a stop for fresh horses in Dartford. But can we not return to the topic of Gretna Green?"

She handed the remaining foodstuffs to him and returned to her bag, ignoring his question. "Six hours…in a carriage…with naught to occupy my time— " She pulled a small red leather-bound book from her pack and held it aloft. "I suppose I will get much reading done. You do not mind turning up the lamp, do you? Reading without proper light is known to cause significant harm to a person's eyes."

Colin could do nothing but stare, wide-eyed, as she reached over and increased the wick on the lamp and settled her book in her hands. She flipped it open, her mouth moving as she read silently, leaving Colin to finish the meal she'd brought.

The bread was tasteless, and the cheese unsatisfying

as he watched Lady Ophelia settle in across from him; her posture at ease and her brow furrowing as she read.

Her complete repose and ease with their inappropriate situation did nothing to diminish his apprehension.

TO COLIN'S GREAT surprise, Lady Ophelia did let slip a slight wheeze as she slept, many would call it a deep, labored breath, though it was entirely at odds with her soft, angelic beauty. It hadn't taken long for her lids to droop and the book to slip to her lap as her chest rose and fell in peaceful slumber.

It was not so easy for him. He'd inspected the road behind them on more than a dozen occasions, fearful that Atholl had sent someone to chase them down, but the road behind them remained deserted. They stopped in Dartford for a fresh pair of matching greys and continued their journey, all without waking the woman across from him.

He marveled at her serene nature, unlike the tortured slumber he'd interrupted in the garden earlier. When he'd happened upon her in Atholl's yard, she'd appeared restless; her brow pulled low, her jaw clenched shut, and her fists balled tightly. It was perhaps the reason he'd started their conversation off lightly and had, against his better judgment, asked her to accompany him.

It had been Molly's doing—all of it.

If his grandmama hadn't raised her cane at Lady Ophelia and created such a spectacle, would Colin even remember the woman?

Yes, he would remember her. There was no chance he'd forget the woman before him.

Her long hair had escaped from its knot sometime during their travels and fell down around her shoulders, nearly reaching the seat beneath her. He wondered if it would slip like silk through his fingers or perhaps have a sturdier, thicker texture.

Shortly after they'd departed Dartford, the sun had set, and Colin had turned the lamp to low to avoid disrupting Ophelia's sleep. The gentle sway of the carriage had nearly tempted him into slumber, as well, but he needed to remain vigilant during their journey. With only his footman and driver, they were an optimal target for highwaymen. His father's lavish traveling coach spoke of immense wealth, though Colin's barony barely brought him enough funds to make repairs in the village and maintain the small manor house, which was truly little more than a cottage.

Lady Ophelia was his responsibility as long as she was in his care.

And he would bloody well not allow any harm to come to her.

A sharp rap from his driver signaled that they'd arrived in Sheerness.

Ophelia shifted on her seat, her eyelids fluttering as she woke. Her back arched, and her boots poked out from beneath her gown, much like a feline stirring from a long slumber in the stables. The hint of a smile touched her lips, as if she remembered a dream from her hours of rest, but it disappeared quickly when her eyes fully opened.

"Have we arrived in Sheerness?" she asked, her voice rough with sleep.

"Yes." He pulled the drape back to reveal an empty yet well-kept inn yard. The thatched-roof building bordering the property must be the inn. Proving his suspicions accurate, a young lad ran out and spoke with his driver before hurrying back into the building. "It is late, but I will request a meal be sent to your room as soon as you are settled."

"That is not necessary, I can—" But her stomach betrayed her with a loud growl. "Well, very well, a meal would be welcome, however..." She grasped her satchel and slipped her hand into each pocket, feeling around before moving to the large main pouch.

"What is it?" he asked when her gaze darted to the discarded paper from the meal they'd shared earlier, and her shoulders slumped.

Concern knitted her brow, and a sheen appeared in her eyes. "I—I—forgot my pin money."

Bloody, rotting bollocks but the woman was going to cry.

Her bottom lip trembled as his footman swung the door open.

In an instant, and before thinking better of his actions, he knelt before her, his hands on the seat cushion on either side of her legs. "Do not fret," he soothed. "I will handle the room fee and your meals. You are on this harebrained journey because of me, after all."

"But—but—but—that is far too much, my lord!"

"Come now, it is the least I can do, especially if we are found out and your reputation is compromised."

She released a huge breath, and her clenched hands stopped trembling in her lap.

"That is better," he coaxed. "Gather your things, and we will inquire about rooms and a meal. Tomorrow, the true adventure begins." He almost choked on the word *adventure*, though he suspected it was what she needed to hear to collect herself.

Colin grasped her satchel and held it out for her to fill with the few possessions she'd removed in her frantic search.

With her bag in hand, he assisted her from the coach, and they made their way into the inn.

As he'd feared, the ale room was vacant and closed for the evening; however, the proprietor stood at the ready when they followed the hall down to the main staircase.

Short, with tufts of uneven grey hair and a rounded belly, the innkeeper looked upon them with a welcoming smile and a greeting to match. "Welcome ta Sheerness, m'lord." He bobbed his head. "And welcome ta ye, m'lady. I be Caruthers. Will ye be need'n a room?"

"Two rooms, kind sir." Colin glanced at Ophelia from the corner of his eye as the innkeeper scrutinized them. "And a hot meal, if that is not too much trouble. We have been travelling for many hours and are famished."

Caruthers turned away with a grimace. "We don't be have'n two rooms, m'lord," he curtly replied. "Only inn around, and this be a busy night, a busy night indeed."

"One room will do, I suppose." Ophelia tensed on his arm at his words. "How about a hot meal?"

"Will a warm one do?" He came around the desk and took Ophelia's satchel from Colin's shoulder. "Me wife already gone ta bed."

"One room and a warm meal sounds heavenly, Mr. Caruthers," Ophelia said with a wary laugh. "Thank you for accommodating us this late into the night."

"'Tis me job, lass," he huffed and started up the stairs.

Colin gestured for Ophelia to start up before him as he took his bag from his footman and followed Ophelia and the innkeeper up the stairs—to their single room. Now was not the time to ponder how he'd gone from searching for a fabled book to sharing bedchambers with Lady Ophelia.

One thing he knew for certain, Molly would find endless amusement from her grandson's predicament.

Would his grandmama have sent him on this quest if she'd known he would be forced to sleep in the stables with his footman or share a bedchamber with the fiery-haired sorceress?

CHAPTER 13

THEY'D ARRIVED IN Sheerness a couple of hours before the sun set after a quiet journey across the breathtaking English countryside. While Kent was a lovely enough part of England, Sissy much preferred the Southwest shire of Somerset—her true home. Her quaint dwelling, a mere manor house compared to many country estates she'd visited, had been named for her after her birth, Sissiela Hall. Her father, the previous Duke of Abercorn, had been so proud of his first child that he'd purchased the land and manor home to bequeath to her and her bridegroom when she wed.

She'd visited the home, not far from Tintinhull, many times in her youth. It was absolutely perfect.

Yet, Sissy's piece of happiness had been stolen from her before her fifteenth birthday.

Heavy in debt, her father had lost the property and the land surrounding it. She'd even heard the Earl of Coventry had renamed her home, Hawke Manor.

But she was very close to having it returned to her.

And Sissy would relish Sissiela Hall being hers once more.

Currently, she pushed around her evening meal at the only Inn in Sheerness; a drab establishment not suited for noble guests. They'd spent an hour questioning shop owners and residents to find the best place to search for what she sought. She'd allowed Francis to do most of the talking as she played the innocent female relation. It had been unnerving to stand by and allow her brother to blunder through his half-hearted inquiries. However, she bit her tongue and permitted him to speak for her.

"Are you not satisfied with your sole?" Francis asked, his own plate emptied of the savory fish. "London severely lacks fresh sea fare."

Sissy kept her eyes trained on the room around them. Any of the customers—or even the servants—could be a relation of Molly or Porter Parnell. They need be careful what they spoke of and who they spoke to.

"Do stop sulking, dear sister." He pushed his plate away, waving to a servant to remove the dish. "You pleaded for me to bring you to Sheerness, and we are here. We will continue our search tomorrow, though it baffles me what you think to find after all these years."

Of course, he had no clue as to what resided in Sheerness. The bloody man did not realize the many things that occurred under his *own* roof—the acts Sissy had undertaken to keep her brother safe from his own bleeding heart. And if all worked as she'd planned, he'd never have need to know.

"I am only anxious for the morrow, Franny." She looked up at him from beneath lowered lashes to gauge his mood. "My entire life may very well change drastically with our return to London."

"And if all remains as it has been my whole life, we will not be the worse for it. You will always have me, by your side, to protect and take care of you." His tenor was calm and reassuring. It was the voice of the brother who'd pledge to Sissy that he would seek vengeance from all those who'd harmed her. Yet, that promise had been made by a fifteen-year-old boy…and forgotten not long after the words were spoken. "You trust me to care for you, right, Sissy?"

She eyed him from across the table. He'd aged in the last year since his wife's death, his hair had greyed, and his face had wrinkled from strain. His once smooth, golden skin was now marred by age spots—matching her own. His eyes, once alight with mischief and excitement, were now dulled by loss. She wondered if hers mirrored his…

"Of course, I trust you, Franny," she insisted.

However, Sissy saw nothing wrong with working herself to ensure her future—and the downfall of the Dowager Lady Coventry.

OPHELIA GRASPED HER travel bag where it sat upon the single bed as Colin moved into the hallway to settle the account for the room. The bed was barely large enough for one person but was neatly made with a light green coverlet. The chamber was sparsely furnished with a washstand, armoire, and two straight-back chairs with a small round table between them. Only a glimpse of Sheerness could be seen through the tiny window set high in the wall above the table.

Unfortunately, it was black outside, which halted her from climbing upon a chair to gain a view of the seafront town.

What the room lacked in furniture, it made up for in charm; the coverlet was hand-sewn with a landscape of the coastline about the edges, a glass vase full to brimming with sea shells on a side table, and a ceramic washbowl with ships sailing from port painted inside on the washstand.

Tiny but spotless, the room would do for one night.

She exhaled softly. The journey had been tiring, made even more exhausting as she'd feigned sleep for nearly the last three hours. Her neck ached from the impossible angle she'd held it, with her head against the side of the carriage. She hadn't taken a decent breath since she'd slipped—rather, tugged, squirmed, and shimmied—into Luci's daringly low-cut traveling habit. She glanced down at the swell of her breasts over the top of the bodice, and a flush overtook her. The sight of her was utterly indecent. It was a wonder Lord Hawke had agreed to bring her along with her dressed in such a provocative manner; however, Ophelia had reveled in his gaze upon her the entire journey.

It had been her belief that he'd have settled on the ride and read Fair Wind's journal, but he hadn't taken his eyes off her except to glance out the window every hour or so. He'd thought they'd be followed—and hadn't she been responsible for giving him that exact impression?

She'd known full well what she was doing when she told him that she'd left word that she was off to Gretna Green. What she'd kept to herself was that her two dear friends were headed there.

It had been great fun to see him twist with worry. For those scarce moments, Ophelia knew what if felt like to possess Luci's and Edith's great beauty and wit. It had been an exhilarating start to their adventure together.

Until she'd misguidedly agreed to share a room with Lord Hawke.

She'd sought adventure, not complete ruination.

She inhaled as deeply as her gown would allow and placed her hand on her lower back where a twinge of pain had started when she alighted from the traveling coach. If there were any night she needed a restful, rejuvenating sleep, it was this one.

The thought of sleeping in the same room as Lord Hawke banished all thoughts of deep slumber from her mind.

"Well, Lady Ophelia," he said, entering the room behind her. "Caruthers promised our meal would be brought up shortly. I will dine with you—if that is agreeable—and then find lodging in the stables with my men."

His decision should have brought her relief. "You cannot sleep in the stables, my lord." She turned to face him, the door open at his back.

"It is only one night," he replied. "Tomorrow, we will set out early to find what we came for and, with any luck, be on our way back toward London by midday."

"As you said, it is only one night." Why was she arguing with his decision to keep her reputation intact? "There are plenty of blankets. I shall sleep on the floor, and you may have the bed."

"I would never allow a lady to sleep upon the ground," he scoffed, shaking his head.

"All right, I will sleep in the bed, and you can take the floor. Is that more agreeable?"

"Certainly, but—"

"Then it is settled." Ophelia gave him a curt nod. She hadn't given him the opportunity to renew his efforts to sleep in the stables. "Besides, we may very well have a tiring day tomorrow, and we need to be rested with our minds ready. Otherwise, we may be forced to spend another night in Sheerness."

He avoided her stare as he looked about the room, and she knew she'd won this battle.

They would share the room.

Why did Ophelia suspect this was the first step to her losing the war?

A light tap at the door signaled their meal had arrived. "Good evening, m'lady, m'lord." The maid, a young woman, likely a relation of the proprietor, hurried into the room, balancing a tray with two covered plates. "The cook here be one of the finest for miles. We be have'n fish caught this morn with plum rice and bread."

She quickly set the meal out on their tiny table and bobbed a slight curtsey before she departed the room, closing the door behind her.

The click of the latch and the girl's footfalls down the hallway echoed through the space.

Ophelia had never been alone in a room with a man. Why did the mere presence of a bed make this seem bolder than the previous six hours in the coach together?

"The table does not appear large enough for us both to dine," he said, as if the size of the table were the only thing to focus on—and not the fact that Ophelia had made a huge mistake by thinking they could share the room without lasting consequences. "I will remove my plate and eat on the bed."

"Then I will join you." Ophelia collected both plates and returned to the small circular rug between the door and the bed. She eyed the neatly made cot as Lord Hawke took his seat. "Besides, we have yet to discuss how we plan to go about finding information on your grandpapa."

She sat beside him on the bed, each of them perched on the edge with their plates nestled on their laps. The fish, a translucent white piece of meat, smelled divine, and the rice appeared well seasoned. The bread was not as fresh as the chunk her maid had packed for her, but neither was it stale.

They sat in silence, picking at their meals, and Ophelia feared she'd set out on this adventure with him without so much as questioning their actual course of action. She was unfamiliar with the area, she hadn't the slightest clue where to begin looking, nor did she know what Lord Hawke and Molly thought to find in Sheerness.

Her positive outlook thus far became somewhat diminished. If Edith were here, she'd know what to do and where to look for answers. Lucianna could question someone without them even suspecting they were being questioned.

"Lady Ophelia," Colin said, looking up from his plate. "I realized I do not know much about you. Why did you so readily agree to come with me? Do you seek to anger your father? If we are discovered, you would be compromised."

This was the exact topic Ophelia had tried her best to not think about since she'd hurried into her townhouse and gathered her belongings. She hadn't thought of the consequences if they were caught alone together, nor had she meant to incite her father's wrath. If she admitted any of this to Lord Hawke, she'd appear the senseless girl everyone thought her to be.

However, if she avoided acknowledging at least a bit of the truth to him, she would be abandoning her own integrity. Perhaps a compromise—just enough to satisfy his question without baring her soul about her friends leaving her behind when they traveled to the Scottish border. Odd that she hadn't thought of Tilda or the muddled, unresolved mess with Abercorn all afternoon. She had lived with the events of that night, they'd weighed upon her every day since her friend died; however, a few hours with Lord Hawke had drawn her thoughts in a completely different direction.

"I truly did not consider my father or my reputation when I agreed to accompany you," she admitted. "It seems I am always the woman to wait around for directions, to be present but still go unnoticed, always part of another's exciting moment but never feeling like I fully belong. So, I saw an opportunity and grasped at the chance to embark on my own adventure."

"You left word that you were departing for Gretna Green?" When she nodded, he continued. "How did you expect to get there?"

"Stagecoach." Her tone held too much bite. It wasn't Lord Hawke's fault that while Ophelia craved adventure and excitement, she hadn't taken any time to think though…well, anything.

But he nodded politely as if silently agreeing to overlook her less than ingenious plot or his earlier mention of the most common reason for traveling to Gretna Green.

"Well, it appears your adventure has turned into a misadventure of sorts."

"How so?" Ophelia knew exactly how but was unaware why he'd think things had gone awry.

"Well, you speak of wanting your own adventure, but alas, we have departed London on an excursion that has little—or nothing—to do with you." His brow rose in challenge.

"Not so. Not so at all." Bother! Lord Hawke was correct, but Ophelia would rather stuff her entire rice portion into her mouth and swallow than admit it. "The book you need belongs to me."

"What do you think of Fair Wind and his past as a smuggler?" At any other time, she would have felt the question was offensive and insensitive.

Lord Hawke's lips pressed into a straight line as he pondered the question. "He died before I was born, and since my father insists on acting like grandpapa never existed, I have only heard tales from Molly." He paused to take a bite of bread, and swallowed before continuing. "As you can assume, her stories of Fair Wind's heroics have only become grander as the years passed, but I do believe there is a measure of truth hidden within each story. The fact that my father rebuffs everything, tells me Molly's stories are far closer to the truth than the current earl would ever want to admit."

"But if your grandfather *had* assisted the king, it would be a great honor for your family."

Lord Hawke nodded. "Yes, that has always been my view, as well, but my father believes the harm to our family name would be irreparable if it were determined Fair Wind had been nothing more than a smuggler who'd been granted a title and lands for no purpose."

They fell into a companionable silence as they finished their meal, and she pondered what he'd said.

Ophelia was aware of the risks involved, better than most young women. She, Luci, and Edith had been tarnished by their accusations against Abercorn the year before, and even now, with both her friends betrothed and in love, there were scarce invitations bestowed upon the trio.

Her family had been like Luci's and blamed Ophelia for speaking out against Abercorn, yet she knew they all suffered. Ophelia had four siblings whose futures were affected, and she hadn't considered that at all.

Much as she had impulsively absconded from London with Lord Hawke.

"Lady Ophelia," he whispered, taking her empty plate with his and returning them to the table. He stood tall and glanced out the high window. He stared for so long, she wondered what could have captured his notice no fully that he seemed almost in a different place entirely. "We do not know much about one another, do we?"

His inquiry took her by surprise.

"I suppose we do not." Yet, his loyalty to Molly showed him to be a man brimming with heart. His defense of Ophelia, despite Molly's claims to the contrary, showed he was a champion of the unjustly accused. He was above reproach, and not a speck of her felt the least bit hesitant in his company. What more did she need to know? "What will you do if we find no proof of Fair Wind's honorable dealings?"

The mettle of a man was not found in their successes but in their failures.

Ophelia had never understood the deep-rooted meaning of that until now, though her father used the phrase often.

Many men, her father explained, gave up, or worse yet, they pushed their failures off on others. They blamed everyone and anything besides themselves.

"I will keep searching," Lord Hawke sighed as he

turned to face her. Sorrow was etched on his downcast expression. "If it gives Molly any measure of happiness and continues to be important to her, I will search until the end of my days."

"That is a long time."

"Not so long as an eternity endured with a shadow cast over oneself." He returned to sit next to Ophelia on the bed. "What will you do if we return to London and our adventure together is exposed?"

She shrugged, clenching her hands in her lap to stop herself from reaching out for him. "It will not matter overmuch."

"A woman who so easily disregards her reputation." It was Lord Hawke who reached out first, laying his hand upon hers. "I would be most aggrieved if our adventures caused you any hardship."

CHAPTER 14

HE STROKED HER clasped hands lightly, afraid his slight movements might frighten her. The way she leaned toward him, her head bowed a fraction of an inch, spoke volumes. He'd been wrong about her—wholly incorrect. She was not the innocent debutante he'd believed her to be since their first meeting, nor was she worldly. Her nature hinted at something darker, however—more than the modest and demure figure he'd known thus far.

It had struck him as a whimsical flight of fancy when she'd so readily agreed to accompany him to Sheerness.

But now, he wondered if she sought more than just adventure.

Or, more accurately, if she ran from something.

"As the daughter of a duke, I would think your reputation would matter greatly—especially to you." There must be something he was unaware of, some information that, had he been one to dabble in societal gossip, he would know. "Has your marriage been arranged already?"

Her stare finally left her lap and settled on his as he held his breath, not at all prepared for her answer. He would be a thousand times a scoundrel if he'd been fool enough to not only leave London with an innocent woman but also another man's betrothed.

She had spoken of Gretna Green earlier. Would her parents assume she'd run off with another man?

Colin cursed Molly's outlandish demand that Ophelia—*Lady* Ophelia—accompany him. He should have dismissed the entire thing completely in that moment.

"Of course, I am not betrothed." She pulled her hands out of reach. "It is just that not all debutantes, even the daughters of dukes, are vigorously sought after. And you, the son of an earl and a baron in your own right, why are you not wed?"

Her face flushed, and Colin chuckled when she covered her mouth.

"Do not be embarrassed," he said. "That is by far the easiest question to answer."

She looked up at him from under lowered lashes, and he was reminded how angelic she'd appeared in the carriage. Even now, with the candle on the washstand behind her, a soft glow surrounded her. The pale expanse of skin revealed by her low-cut gown was not as enchanting as the guarded look in her eyes, or the way she clutched her skirt with nervousness.

He was uncertain why, but he needed her to understand the severe consequences if he returned to London empty-handed. "My family has been in turmoil for years—longer than years, decades." Colin sighed. He'd never spoken of his family's discord with anyone, least of all a woman he barely knew. "Once he was old enough to know not all families came from small sea towns and accumulated their wealth by means other than inheritance and savvy business investments, my father only spoke ill of Fair Wind. When Molly and my grandpapa decided to send their son for a proper education, he became exactly what my grandparents had fought against becoming when they were bestowed the Earldom by King George."

Thankfully, Lady Ophelia remained quiet, allowing him to speak.

"My father became entitled and condemned Molly and Fair Wind for their less than noble past. He grew bitter and angry when reminded of his own meager upbringing in Kent. Ramsey, my father, erased all traces of the Parnell family past as soon as Fair Wind died. He expelled Molly to the country, banishing her from his home in London."

"Poor Molly," Ophelia whispered. "Your father does not sound like a kind man."

"You misunderstand, he is not an *unkind* man, he is just a lord who embraced his arrogance and his right to his title." Colin shook his head at his father's folly. "He thinks of what's to come but forgets the past. One has no future when there is no history to build on."

"And you plan to show him the error of his ways?"

He couldn't tell if she meant the question as a jest or asked with seriousness. "No, above all else, I want to end the war within my family." The struggle seemed insurmountable in that moment. "I want the strife over. Whether Fair Wind was an ally of the king or a mere common smuggler from Kent, I want the truth known. Either way, I am not ashamed."

"I think that is most noble of you, Lord Hawke."

"Colin. Lord Hawke is too formal," he said with a smile. He'd never truly realized how alone he felt wedged between his father's disapproval and Molly's adamant, never-ending insistence. "And I do not do this thing out of any noble intent, I assure you. It is quite unbearable being placed in the middle of my father and Molly. They are so very similar in many ways: stubborn, determined, and neither is ever wrong."

They both laughed at his unplanned jest.

Colin sober quickly, though. "Molly adores me because I am a mirror image of Fair Wind, and I think my father remains detached from me for the same reason."

"That must be hard." She sighed, picking at the seam of her gown. "However, if people are willing to fight, then does that not mean they care enough about the other to put forth the effort to quarrel?"

"You are a wise woman, Ophelia." Her eyes dipped to her lap once more when he used her given name. "Has no one ever praised your intellect?"

"It is hard for one to notice most of the time."

"How so?" he asked. "Every time we speak, I am reminded yet again how brilliantly insightful you are."

"My lord. Colin"—she corrected quickly—"that is very kind of you to say."

"It is also true."

She was still, in many ways, a mystery to him. There was something about her that spoke of heartache and loss, yet she blushed like the innocent debutante she was. She shared astute perspectives on issues a woman of her standing should know naught about.

The glow from the single candle behind her cast a shadow across her face at the same time her hair surrounded her much like a fiery halo. She appeared the temptress Molly suspected her to be; however, if Lady Ophelia were casting a spell on him, Colin was glad of it.

Her cerulean eyes lifted to meet his. It was more of a collision than any innocent meeting.

She pulled him in, and he was desperate to follow wherever she led.

Straight to Hell? Colin was prepared for the burn.

To the deep depths of the ocean? Water had never felt so welcoming.

As high as the clouds above? He would revel in the fall back to solid ground.

Colin was incapable of moving away, standing, or departing the room—as he bloody well knew he should.

Walking away was no longer an option. Every instinct told Colin he should run...away from Lady Ophelia, back to London, hell, he should flee to Hawke

Manor.

Instead, he closed the distance between them, bringing their lips within a breath of one another…and he waited. She need only move a fraction of an inch, and their mouths would meet.

Ophelia had the choice to pull away. Seconds passed, but she didn't move, her breaths fanning against his heated face as their eyes held. Holding himself back from wrapping her in his arms nearly broke Colin.

As time continued, and their breathing slowed, something far more intense traveled between them— filling the inch separating them and decreasing the abyss unraveling them. He could almost feel her warm, soft lips against his—their touch, their texture. Could imagine how she'd settle against him in his arms—all womanly curves against his solid body. Colin committed to memory the scent of her—like spring blossoms on a rainy London morning.

Lady Ophelia was greater than any woman he'd had the pleasure of meeting. She was Heaven on Earth, a beacon of light in a dark fog, and a woman Colin could never hope to make his.

Just as the night with the coming morn, he would be powerless to grasp hold of her and keep her near.

Thud. Thud. Thud.

They leapt apart when a barrage of fist falls hit their door.

"Water for ye, m'lord!" a man called.

She stood, glancing at the dwindling candle on the washstand and then back to him. The blush he expected to see did not creep up her neck, nor did she shrink from him in shame.

"Enter," she commanded, her voice raspy, unlike her usual light, melodic tone.

The inn servant bustled into the room with a large, copper basin. The water steamed and sloshed over the edge onto the wooden floor as he set it close to the washstand.

Colin barely took his stare off Ophelia to thank the servant as he departed the room.

"You must be exhausted." Colin leapt from the bed, his gaze darting about the room. "I will bid you good night, my lady."

Her brow pulled low. "Where are you going?"

"To sleep."

"Where?"

Could it be that she did not want him to leave?

"I will find my rest in the stables with my men as mentioned." There was only so far Colin would push the boundaries of propriety. Many would say he already crossed the line when asking Lady Ophelia to travel to Sheerness—alone—with him. However, Colin suspected he'd traversed across long before that…when he'd agreed to Molly's outlandish plan. Now that they were here, Colin could not, in good conscience, stay in such close proximity to her, especially after what had transpired between them only moments before. He shuddered to think what might have happened had the servant not interrupted them. "It is improper for me to stay here." *With you*, he added silently.

The increased rise and fall of her bosom as she inhaled and exhaled made Colin think Ophelia was also pondering what could have transpired if they hadn't been disturbed.

He shook his head, refusing to let the notion gain purchase in his mind.

Lady Ophelia, while openly seeking an adventure, had not agreed to be ruined.

Nor did Colin seek to take advantage of her.

"The room is large enough for us both." She spread her arms wide as if to convince him that remaining, overnight, in the same private room was in any way a sensible idea. "Please. The journey was long for the both of us. At least stay here where it is warm."

He frowned, scrutinizing the room.

Ophelia took a step toward him. "Come now," she

said, gesturing to the bed. "There are sufficient enough pillows and bedding for you to make a proper sleeping area close to the hearth."

He released his held breath in a loud exhale, relieved she hadn't suggested the actual bed to be large enough for the pair of them.

"Please." She clasped her hands before her, turning her widened, imploring stare on him, freezing him in place. "I would never forgive myself if you were made to sleep in the stables, especially knowing you funded the coin for this room."

Colin looked from the bed, to the floor, to the closed door.

No one would know, except for them.

And he would never breathe a word to anyone.

"Fine," he grumbled. "Under one condition…"

Her lips turned up in a victorious grin. "Anything."

"I will only use one blanket from the bed." His brow rose as he begged her to argue or deny his condition. It would make everything simpler; however, she nodded with all seriousness. "I will use my coat under my head."

"If you wish." She turned and removed her satchel from the end of the bed, depositing it on the floor before collecting the thickest blanket. "Here you are, my lord."

"Good night, Lady Ophelia."

"Sleep tight, Lord Hawke."

Why did Colin suspect he'd lost some greater battle that had been going on without him noticing?

With a sigh, he turned his back to her and spread his blanket on the floor—the cold, hard floor.

The rustle of fabric sounded behind him, and Colin imagined her undressing, slipping into a nightshift before crawling into bed.

However, when he turned, she was merely removing her cloak and gloves. He hadn't even noticed she'd worn them throughout their meal and conversation.

"I will step outside so you can change in private."

Her cheeks did blossom with color at that, giving Colin the urge to step close and continue what they'd started earlier.

"There is no need," she replied. His breath hitched at her meaning. "I will sleep in my gown for warmth"— they both glanced to the paltry fire in the hearth—"and change into a fresh dress on the morrow."

After one final, searching stare, Ophelia looked away and blew out the candle. She pulled the covers down before crawling onto the bed. She snuggled in deep and shifted to face the wall.

Had he mistaken the longing in her eyes? It was far more likely that it was regret he saw in their blue depths, a churning turmoil that was a result of their combined making.

It was difficult to ignore the interest she'd taken in him—and his family. And she hadn't latched on to his words because of their sordid nature or his family's unsavory past.

Certainly not. Lady Ophelia had been genuinely concerned and had gone so far as to offer her own words of wisdom on the situation.

Colin moved his coat and lay on his makeshift bed, the hard, wooden floorboards pressed into his hip. The pain would be worth it to remain close to Ophelia. If he'd retired to the stables, he would have fretted so much over her being alone in the inn he'd have journeyed back and slept outside her door to make certain she remained safe.

Listening, her breathing became slow and shallow as she found sleep.

Something Colin envied greatly.

No measure of relaxation would bring him rest with the fiery-haired temptress so close at hand. Molly held her beliefs that Ophelia's auburn hair marked her as a sorceress—luring men to their demise—however, the woman asleep in the bed behind him was pure light and goodness, with a caring, compassionate side he'd never seen in another.

Colin shifted to his back to relieve the ache in his shoulder and hip from the floor, entwining his fingers and placing his hands under his head as he focused on the ceiling. His gaze traced along the planks of wood above him. If he listened intently, another inn guest could be heard snoring from the room next to theirs. He wondered how that man had come to be in Sheerness, and if he sensed the immense change happening so close to where he slept.

The soft breathing continued, and Colin's own inhales and exhales aligned with Ophelia's until they breathed as one.

Turning, Colin saw she'd also moved to her back, her closed eyes facing the ceiling.

A lump in his coat pocket pushed at the tender area behind his ear when he removed his hands from behind his head. He slipped his fingers into his jumbled coat and pulled out Molly's treasured pendant—her one piece of jewelry, and the only item she'd kept on her person as far back as Colin could remember. As a young boy, he remembered toying with the jewel-encrusted piece as Molly read to him at night. When they'd been out by the lake at Tintinhull, the sun had gleamed off the pendant, and Molly had spoken of the keepsake as his grandpapa's remaining eye on earth.

Colin held the thing above his head, the chain hanging down inches from his face, but it appeared like any other necklace worn by a woman. His grandmama had told him many times that the power of the piece came from the person who wore it, not the object itself—and perhaps that was true. The thing did not glow or sparkle as it did when it was about Molly's neck. The stone did not hold the depth of color he'd beheld all these years.

The treasured pendant had come with Colin as an

omen of good luck to be had.

There was much riding on his journey to Sheerness, and that was without even factoring in the impact it would have on his entire family. Molly would either be vindicated or heartbroken by the information he returned to London with. His father would be forced to make amends with Molly or banish her to Tintinhull in Somerset for as long as she took breath.

Colin clutched the pendant to his chest as his eyes fluttered shut, heavy with sleep.

As he drifted into a restless slumber, his mind conjured the most startling image—Lady Ophelia, with his grandmama's treasured stone securely fastened about her neck.

CHAPTER 15

OPHELIA WOKE WITH a start—everything wasn't as it should be. The bed she lay upon was lumpy, the coverlet was coarse where it was gathered by her cheek, and her entire body ached. Unable to move, she raised her head slightly to note that the bedding and her gown had become unbearably tangled during her fitful rest.

Breathing…someone was breathing soundly very close by.

The labored inhale and exhale was rhythmic and deep. Part of her prayed the noise would lull her back to sleep.

Unfortunately, the scent of stale air, smoke, and meat cooking made escape impossible.

Ophelia pushed the coverlet down and struggled to sit up—blast it all, but she'd been foolish enough to sleep in her riding habit. Not even her dress, but Luci's low-cut, curve-clinging traveling outfit. No wonder she couldn't move her legs. The skirting was sturdy and thick to keep her protected from traveling dirt and grime. She hadn't dreamed it could also be used as a solid means of restraint.

Glancing over the side of the bed, she saw Colin lying sprawled on the floor, also in his clothes from the day before, his coat securely tucked under his head.

The high window only allowed a fraction of early morning light to touch her, but it was enough to see the room was as it had been when she'd rolled toward the wall and concentrated on slumber.

She'd been a fool not to change into her nightshift when he'd offered her privacy the evening before, but she'd been afraid he'd change his mind and not return, departing in favor of a night in the stables. Added to that, Ophelia would not have been able to unfasten and shimmy from Luci's constricting gown without assistance—and so, she'd spent nearly a day now in a dress that prevented her from gaining a deep breath. She'd more than noticed the way Colin had observed her in the carriage.

Again, she was in the same precarious position as the evening before.

How was she to unfasten Luci's gown without her maid to change into a new one?

She could request Lord Hawke's help, but after last night, Ophelia did not trust herself to keep him at arm's length. She'd barely been able to keep him a breath away the previous night…and she'd had all her clothes firmly fastened, including the buttons on her cloak.

Would she be able to resist leaning into him if the promise was much more than a kiss?

Ophelia had fallen asleep with dreams of his lips against hers—demanding, yet tender. He'd guide her as to how to execute a proper kiss, and she would allow him to teach her all. Willingly, she would have accepted his gift without rebuff. Yet, something had held her back as they'd sat on the bed, knees nearly touching with his mouth so close she could almost taste the meal they'd shared.

If Colin had been disappointed that she hadn't leaned the final inch toward him to bring their lips together, he hadn't shown it.

Ophelia wondered if they'd been given a few more moments, if the servant hadn't interrupted them, would she have pressed her lips to his?

She'd been so befuddled by it all, she'd forgotten to wash up with the water the servant had delivered. A quick look at the full water bowl on the washstand confirmed that Colin hadn't cleaned up after their long day of travel either.

Could it be that he'd been as taken aback by their moment of intimacy as she? Certainly not. He was a man of wealth and title; surely such things would not affect him. It was more likely he was shocked by her forthright nature and thought her a woman of low morals and no decorum. Add this to her preposterous and imprudent decision to accompany him to Sheerness, and Colin had every right to think poorly of her.

Even more damning, she'd all but begged him to sleep in the same room as she.

What had she been thinking?

She hadn't been, at least not with her normal, rational mind.

Luci had been justified in warning Ophelia against looking into Abercorn in her absence. Neither of her friends would be shocked by the muck she'd gotten herself into since they left for the Scottish border.

Colin shifted, his foot kicking out and knocking against the leg of the small, round table, rattling their dinner dishes.

She held her breath, waiting for him to rouse.

When his breathing continued, unperturbed, she relaxed once more, taking advantage of the time to inspect him without his notice as he'd done when he thought her asleep in the carriage.

It should strike her as an invasion of his privacy; however, this seemed less personal than reading Fair Wind's book. She wasn't merely an outsider delving into his past any longer.

In a way, Ophelia was now part of Fair Wind's legacy, be it good or bad.

Colin had said he resembled his grandfather with

his fair hair and sun-kissed complexion. This morning, a lock of silky blond hair lay across his face, tousled from sleep. One hand was balled into a tight fist at his chest, and the other was at his side. She could imagine him at the helm of a ship, the waves crashing against the portside bow as he commanded his men. He was reserved, though she suspected he took charge when the time called for it.

Lord Hawke's compassion and caring for Molly and her wishes spoke volumes about the man he was. He was not concerned about tarnishing his family name if he did find proof that Fair Wind was merely a smuggler with a jaded past.

Even now, he seemed at ease sprawled on the floor, a confidence about him Ophelia was hard-pressed to understand. It wasn't arrogance or entitlement, but more of an understanding of one's self and an acceptance that was far more than just skin-deep.

She trusted him enough to flee London by his side without knowing so much as a single detail about their plan, except the town they were headed to. She'd never been one to blindly follow another without cause. Certainly, her faith in Luci and Edith was grounded in years of unconditional friendship, only solidified by Tilda's tragic death, but what had Colin done to gain such unquestioned trust?

Ophelia had no answer for that.

Far more startling was why *he'd* trusted her on this journey.

There was no doubt that Ophelia knew far more about Colin than he did about her—and still, he hadn't hesitated, beyond a brief moment, to include her in everything. His excuse—her being the rightful owner of Fair Wind's book—had been a ruse. One only need half a brain to see that much. She'd offered to return the book, but he'd turned her away.

The heady aroma of frying meat, fresh bread, and coffee filtered into the room from the tavern below.

Boots sounded in the hallway as other guests roused and went in search of a meal to break their fast. Voices floating up from the gathering crowd below finally had Colin stirring.

"Good morn," she called from above as his eyes opened, and he smiled. "Sleep well?"

He pushed to sit as something tumbled from his chest into his lap. The small amount of sun entering the room gleamed off the object, reflecting an array of dancing colors and light across the far wall.

"Is that Molly's pendant?"

Colin cleared his throat and grasped the necklace, holding it high for her to see. "Good morning, and yes, it is." His voice was deep and raspy from sleep, but he rubbed his eyes with his free hand and slipped the pendant into the pocket of his wrinkled coat. "Have you been awake long?"

At least an hour, she thought, but her words betrayed her with a fib. "Only a few moments, my lord."

"Very well." He pushed to his bare feet and stretched, his hands nearly touching the low ceiling. "I am famished. Shall we dress and break our fast?"

Ophelia was hungry, that much was true, but a meal was not the most prevalent thing on her mind at the moment. There was little doubt she could have attained all the nourishment she'd need if only she were allowed to observe the confident, handsome Lord Hawke for another hour or so.

CHAPTER 16

COLIN PACED AT the bottom of the stairs, awaiting Lady Ophelia so they could find their meal and be on their way. He looked into the tavern once more to see the crowd had further thinned as guests ate and departed. The room had been teeming with people when he'd first arrived downstairs.

What was taking her so dreadfully long?

He'd given her privacy to dress, but now he wondered if that had been a mistake and something had gone wrong above stairs. Colin wasn't versed in women's attire; however, it should not take this bloody long to change one's gown.

Convinced there was something keeping her, Colin started up the steps toward their shared room. The hairs on the back of his neck stood on end in warning. He passed an older couple as he hurried down the hall toward their closed door.

"Good day," he said by way of greeting as he slipped past them.

Coming to a halt outside their room, he raised his hand to open the door but thought better of it. She could possibly be indecent on the other side. Instead of reaching for the latch, he knocked.

"Lady Ophelia?" he called, but no answer came.

He placed his ear to the door, hoping to block out the sound of the people in the tavern below. He heard the rustling of fabric and a low curse. She was inside, but then why not answer his knock?

"Lady Ophelia, it is Lord Hawke—" Bloody hell, she knew damn well who he was. "May I come in?"

There was a flurry of sounds; more footfalls, the scraping of the chair, and finally, the sagging of the bed ties.

"Do answer me, or I will be forced to enter in fear you are in danger, my lady."

"Come in," she said in a trembling voice that barely penetrated the wood.

Colin took hold of the handle, uncertain what he'd find on the other side of the door when he entered.

He pushed the portal wide, the interior of the room lit only by the light coming in through the small window and the single candle from the night before. Their empty dishes still sat on the table, and the blanket he'd used was folded neatly on the end of the bed with Lady Ophelia's satchel on top.

She sat beside her traveling bag, her head in her hands, partially gowned in a dark blue dress with one side hanging loosely down her arm. Her shoulders shook, and she did not look up when he entered, closing the door behind him.

"Ophelia?" He took the three steps to her and kneeled, lightly pulling her hands from her face. "What is wrong?"

She glanced up at that moment, and his heart plummeted from his chest as tears pooled in her eyes and streamed down her cheeks. The blue was no longer the color of the ocean several feet off shore, but the deep cobalt of a growing storm.

A quiet sob escaped her on a hiccup.

"Shhhh," Colin murmured. His leg weakened beneath him as he continued to crouch. "Do not cry."

Never would anyone consider Molly a woman

prone to fits of tears—and not on one occasion had Colin witnessed his mother in any state as vulnerable as Ophelia appeared at present.

"Please, allow me to fix whatever has upset you." His attempt to soothe her was met by yet another sob, this one not as quiet. "Do you wish to return to London? We can leave now, this very moment." When she only shook her head in refusal, he continued, "Did someone come to your door after I left?"

He shouldn't have left her alone, no matter how secure and protected the inn had felt to him.

"No, no one," she stammered. "I—I—I—"

"What, Lady Ophelia?" he demanded softly. "Tell me what has upset you, and I will do my best to fix it."

Her lower lip trembled as he searched her face for any sort of answer as to what could have possible transpired while he'd waited at the bottom of the main stairs.

"I—I cannot—I cannot fasten my gown." Though her words were shaky, Ophelia lifted her chin and stared him directly in the eyes as if she were imparting her only grave flaw or admitting a serious transgression. "Can you assist me, my lord?"

Colin pushed to his feet and held his hand out to her. "Come, my lady. I would be honored to offer my skills as a lady's maid."

Her chin tilted up as she met his stare, a small smile touched her lips, and she placed her hand in his…her blessedly bare hand. Wrapping his fingers around hers tightly, he helped her to her feet, and she turned to face away from him. Her corset was still tied and her undergarments in place—it was only the back of her gown that remained unfastened, a long row of pearl beads serving as buttons.

"Do not chastise me if I am not overly adept at fastenings, Lady Ophelia." He reached forward, starting with the bottom button and began the arduous task. It was little wonder women were in need of maids. Colin was able to adequately dress himself and tie a cravat without his valet's assistance, but these…these tiny, nearly ungraspable buttons would prove him worthless if he were not a determined man. She shifted slightly, her hands wringing before her. "I am nearly halfway done. I promise not to miss a single one."

"Thank you, Colin."

His aching fingers faltered, stumbling over the next button before he could focus and continue.

An eternity later, that also struck him as only a few hurried moments, he pushed the final pearl button into the top hole, allowing his hand to graze the back of her neck where her hair was already secured in place with several metal pins.

"Finished." He stepped back and admired the long row of pearls, each slipped into the correct slot. There must have been fifty of them in total. "Are you ready to depart? The public room was nearly empty below. We should be able to eat quickly and be on our way."

"I will collect my things." Taking hold of her satchel, Ophelia turned.

No longer were her eyes moist with tears, nor did her chin tremble.

He now faced the woman who'd climbed into his carriage the day before; reserved, poised, and with an almost undetectable glow in her stare.

The midnight blue gown hugged her body in a more modest fit than the low-cut habit from the previous day—and Colin had to admit, at least to himself, it suited her far better. This was the woman he'd saved from Molly's uplifted cane. This was the proper miss who'd thought to do him a kindness by returning his grandpapa's book. It was this demure, serene female nervously worrying her hands and standing before him who he'd happened upon in the Atholl gardens the day before.

She needn't attire herself in risqué gowns to capture Colin's unwavering attention.

No, Lady Ophelia need only concentrate on presenting herself to others.

They left the room and made their way down to the public area; all the while, Colin kept her pulled close to his side.

Several stares turned in their direction when they entered the room and selected an empty table. There was little doubt every eye was focused on Ophelia, and not Colin with his rumpled coat and unpolished Hessians.

Bloody hell if Colin didn't stand a bit taller as he escorted her to their table. A servant hurried over, pulled their chairs, and assisted Lady Ophelia to her seat.

"The meal be boiled eggs, bread, cheese, and ham…coffee or ale ta drink." The servant didn't waste any time scurrying back toward the kitchen and returning with heaping plates.

Their meal was eaten in silence, giving Colin time to think through where they'd begin their search. Molly had been kind enough to send him with a list of places she thought they'd find things left by his grandpapa. He'd nearly forgotten that he'd slipped the envelope into his coat's inside pocket for safekeeping.

He retrieved the paper and broke the seal while Ophelia's head remained lowered over her plate. She ate slowly, her table manners everything he'd expect from a woman of elevated refinement. Her movements as she sliced an egg in half, speared a section, and brought it to her lips fascinated him in an unfamiliar way. He dined across the table from many people—beautiful, intelligent, and witty women included—but something about Ophelia's delicate nature had him disregarding their purpose in Sheerness and the limited time they possessed to achieve it before departing for the return trip to London.

"What have you there?" she asked, wiping the corners of her mouth with her napkin.

Glancing down, he realized he'd been clutching the slip of paper in his hand.

Colin pushed his plate to the side and smoothed the letter on the table between them, reading it for the first time. "It is a list of places Molly suggested we visit for information."

Ophelia's brow rose in question, but she made no move to ask anything further as she took her last bite, giving Colin a moment to inspect the list. The places appeared easy enough to find if he spoke with the innkeeper and collected directions. Sheerness was not a large town and was inhabited by mostly seafaring men and their families. If Fair Wind had chosen to call the town home, even decades after taking his place in London, then the people here must be as kind as he.

A man chuckled at a nearby table, and Colin looked over to see it was the lord and lady from upstairs, also having their morning meal. The gentleman appeared oddly familiar, but there was little chance Colin would be acqualnted with another person in Sheerness.

Colin turned back to the note before him, folding it to slip it back into the envelope as Ophelia continued watching the pair at the next table. When he made to return the paper to the envelope, it caught on something and would not slip farther in. Turning the envelope upside down, Colin shook it and another paper fell out, as small as a calling card, but with his grandmama's hurried script across the front. He flipped the page over, and the back was blank.

Strangely peculiar.

It must be something that hadn't fit on the other paper—or perhaps an afterthought Molly had added after jotting down her list.

Colin, me dear lad.
I had no option but ta send ye where it all began for
Porter and meself. I hope ye find what ye seek, just as we
did.

Take care of Lady Ophelia.
Molly

He blinked a few times, thinking he must have read the note incorrectly before glancing around the room. Colin sensed that all eyes were on him—that Molly had somehow tricked him and would, at any moment, leap from her hiding spot with her cane held high and a thunderous laugh.

But no one paid him any mind, even Lady Ophelia continued to scrutinize the older pair at the table across the room.

Molly was no doubt up to something, and it had naught to do with Fair Wind.

Hastily, he returned her note to the envelope, but kept Molly's list at the ready. He would ask the innkeeper where they could find their first location.

If they hurried, they could be on their way before the sun crested.

Colin remained silent when he noted Ophelia's lips pressed into a grimace and her frozen appearance. She hadn't moved, but still kept watch on the couple.

"Are you acquainted with the pair?" he asked. A chill ran down his back at the thought that Lady Ophelia would be ruined long before they returned to London if they encountered someone she knew.

Instead of answering, she pushed back her chair and stood. "Shall we be off? An adventure awaits, my lord."

Her posture was straight, and her chin held high, but her smile wavered slightly, belying her eagerness. For not the first time since they had departed London, he wondered what she hid from him. Though, if Colin pushed her for answers, she'd likely ask him questions he was uncomfortable with answering, as well.

Tucking the envelope with Molly's note into his pocket beside the pendant, he stood. "I think it is time our day began. I have Molly's list ready and thought the best place to start would be to ask the proprietor for directions."

He searched the dim, public room, but the innkeeper was nowhere in sight. The space was nearly vacant at this hour, most travelers having departed with the rising sun and the fare more than the local community could afford.

"If you will wait here, I will find directions and have my driver prepare the carriage."

She hurried around the table, setting her hand at his arm. "I think I will join you. Sheerness cannot be so large that we will need the carriage."

"I think you are correct, my lady." Colin scanned Molly's list once more. "Shall we start at the beginning?"

Stepping into the open inn yard, the sun cast a shadow, and the cool ocean breeze blew about them, ruffling Colin's neckcloth and billowing Ophelia's skirts about her ankles. Two carriages pulled from the inn yard, one heavy with trunks, and the other a well-adorned traveling coach, its wheels throwing dust into the air.

A stable boy trotted up to them, a lopsided grin on his face, his clothes a size too big but clean. "Can I fetch ye coach, m'lord?"

"That will not be necessary." He glanced at Ophelia to confirm their decision, and she nodded. "We will take in Sheerness on foot."

"Fine notion, m'lord." The boy's head bobbed up and down.

"You would not happen to know where we can find a tree where people carve their names?" Colin held the list high, reading Molly's words. "The Tower Tree."

The servant's jovial, helpful nature subsided, and he shook his head from side to side.

"You do not know that place?" Ophelia asked. "Mayhap we should—"

"No, m'lady. I be remember'n that tree. Me pa used Ma's fish knife ta cut their names."

"Can you tell us where to find it?"

"Well, in the inn." The boy pointed toward the public room they'd just exited. "Ol' Bosworth cut the tree down and made tables for the tap room."

They cut down the tree?

Colin swallowed hard, his shoulders slumping as the news sank in.

There was no hallowed tree for them to search. Molly's carefully collected places had been reduced from four to three, and they hadn't so much as left the inn yard.

Lady Ophelia placed her hand on his shoulder and gave a comforting squeeze before plucking the list from his hand. She shielded her eyes and inspected the next place.

"Oh, this should be simple enough to find," she mumbled. "Thank you—"

"I be Owen, m'lady," the boy chimed in when Ophelia paused.

"Well, Owen." She shook the paper before her. "Thank you for your assistance. We are off to the docks."

Colin couldn't help but admire her optimism as they set off toward the water's edge, which could be seen down a long, wide lane from the inn. They passed dock workers and a lady pushing a cart filled with fresh sea fare for the market. The salty sea odor increased the closer they journeyed to the water lapping against the wooden docks and the tiny fishing vessels dotting the coast. It appeared any merchant ships were either not in the port at present or had taken their business elsewhere.

The wind increased as they walked, teasing Lady Ophelia's locks from their pins to dance about her shoulders.

She stared out at the water, not noticing—or at least not commenting on—his stolen sideways glances.

"Have you been to the ocean, Lady Ophelia?"

Colin knew many Londoners who'd never been near open water except when they traveled near the river Thames. He, on the other hand, had grown up on stories told to Molly by Fair Wind and his father's occasional tales of his youthful visits to Sheerness before they'd permanently settled inland.

"Only a few months ago, when Luci and I went to Southend in Essex to rescue—errr, *collect* Edith; however, the trip was not a long one, nor traveled for pleasure." Her hands clasped his arm tighter the more she said. "I fear I was not able to enjoy the sea breeze or the sound of the waves."

Rescue? Yes, he'd heard the word before she'd corrected herself.

"Tell me more about your friends. It sounds like a trip to Essex—no matter the hurried nature—counts as an adventure of sorts."

Her stare fell away from the water in the distance to the ground before them.

She gave her head a soft shake. If he hadn't been watching her from the corner of his eye, he would have missed the subtle gesture.

"Come now, Sheerness hasn't been your only adventure outside London," he prodded, knowing there was more on the topic of Southend he needed to hear. "Tell me, Lady Ophelia."

"Southend was not my adventure, my lord," she sighed. "While I will not deny the daring and exciting aspects of the journey—a trip that would have seen us returning without Edith in tow—I was merely there to aid my friends."

"So, you crave your own quest?" He didn't expect a response, for the answer was obvious. It was a subject Colin could understand. So much of his own life had been written by his father or commanded by Molly, much like the reason they were in Sheerness now. It wasn't one of his choosing, but an obligation of sorts. "My arrival with plans to travel to Sheerness seemed the perfect opportunity, then."

She laughed, a light chuckle captured by the wind and blown inland. "Yes, I am happy to see you agree with my decision."

"I cannot say I agree with your choice to flee London without leaving any true note as to our destination—putting your reputation in jeopardy—and all for my grandmama and a family tale that may not be grounded in fact." He did not add the more preposterous part about being accompanied by a man and insisting on sharing sleeping quarters. Neither of them need be reminded of what had almost occurred during their private hours at the inn. "However, I do fully understand your need for something to call your own."

At least Colin had his small estate, Hawke Manor, near Tintinhull Court in Somerset. It wasn't anything grand, but it belonged solely to him as Baron Hawke. No one could take it from him. Though, women rarely owned land, lived in a home not of their father's or husband's choosing, or traveled unaccompanied.

Freedom, what little he possessed, had always been something he'd taken for granted.

Lady Ophelia—and other society maidens—lived under a staunch set of pre-determined rules of conduct. Any infraction would see the woman publicly shamed— or worse, cast from society altogether.

Would this adventure cause Lady Ophelia lasting ruination and shame?

Colin shuddered to think of the consequences their actions could cause. The mere notion of Lady Ophelia suffering due to him was unthinkable.

"My friends, Lady Lucianna and Lady Edith, are on their way to Gretna Green at the moment," she shared, bringing her stare back to the ocean. "Luci is to wed the Duke of Montrose."

She'd left word with her lady's maid that she was departing for the Scottish border, and now it made sense as to why her parents would not fret overmuch. They would assume she was safely with her friends—and not alone with a stranger on the coast of Kent.

"But you were not invited on their adventure?" he asked.

"It is not so much that I was not invited as I was forbidden to accompany them by my father."

"It is a long journey, especially for a woman not in her family's presence," he mused aloud.

"My father's reasoning exactly, my lord."

"Why do I think you were not all that upset at his refusal to allow you to accompany your friends?"

"You are very perceptive." She glanced at him, the hint of mischief he'd noted in her bearing as they'd left London returned. "While I do so wish to be at Lady Lucianna's side when her vows are spoken, it is always a bit tiresome being surrounded by two couples who openly adore one another. I sometimes gain the impression that I am utterly invisible and useless to the foursome. They have a carriage with four wheels…and a fifth simply has no place."

Every driver was aware that a spare, fifth wheel was always wise to have on hand, but Colin kept that knowledge to himself. "That cannot be the extent of their feelings toward you."

"Oh, heavens no, the girls are so very much in love with Torrington and Montrose I am certain they do not notice my melancholy in the slightest."

Colin had lost track of their progress as he'd been listening so intently to Lady Ophelia. She'd afforded him a glimpse into her world—one Colin was unfamiliar with. While his parents were cordial with one another, he would not label the wedded couple *in love*. He would, however, describe them as indifferent to Colin's comings and goings except how they affected the Coventry Earldom. Molly had been the only person concerned with Colin's upbringing, and mostly she'd remained at Tintinhull Court for his entire life.

To have family—or even close friends—who cared about his well-being and took an interest in his life seemed foreign.

"Why did you not disregard your father's edict and journey with them?" he asked as they turned around a large warehouse building and began walking parallel to the water, making their way toward the docks—and the tiny ale house Molly had written was situated between the fish market and the Sheerness office that kept track of all ingoing and outgoing ships and their cargo. "It seemed easy enough for you to slip away."

"Perhaps I did not truly wish to accompany them. We have spent much time together since our dear friend, Tilda, died. Mayhap it was time for me to find a measure of independence." She halted and looked straight ahead, giving him no opportunity to comment further. "It seems we have arrived…"

Her voice trailed off as her hand slipped into his and their fingers intertwined. The warmth of her skin through her gloved hand warded off the morning ocean breeze—but did nothing to keep the foreboding feeling from settling around him.

"It appears we will not be finding what we seek here."

CHAPTER 17

OPHELIA STOOD BESIDE Colin, their fingers interlocking as they both took in the sight before them. The fish market was a buzz of activity as fishermen brought in their morning catches. The records office, only noted by a wooden shingle hanging above the door, was yet to open for the day.

And between the two businesses—a shell of a building, its burned and decaying walls falling in on themselves with a sign to ward off anyone who might trespass. The single window on the front had been smashed out, no glass remaining.

She squeezed Colin's hand, a silent plea to not lose hope.

To her surprise, he didn't pull his hand back, but held hers tighter.

"Where to next?" she sighed, glancing up at him standing at her side, but he remained staring straight ahead. "We have two more places on the list, correct?"

Colin closed his eyes for a moment, and his chin fell.

She could not imagine the bleakness coursing through him at yet another setback.

"Yes." With his free hand, he retrieved the list from his pocket, unfolding it with one hand and keeping his grip on hers. "My grandpapa's old ship may still be at the dock. Molly says he kept all his important maps and notes aboard."

That the vessel would still be at port after all these years seemed difficult to believe—the notion of his possessions being on board was downright preposterous.

However, Ophelia held her tongue, she was hesitant to further dampen his mood. "Then we should be off to the dock."

"I do not know how to identify the boat if it is there," he said with an exasperated sigh, releasing her to run his hand through his hair. His light locks reflected the sun as they fell to cover one eye. The disheveled look suited him well, and Ophelia thought for not the first time that he would appear at home on a vessel on the open water. "I should have forced Molly to travel with me."

Her stomach clenched. It was absurd, but Ophelia felt as if she'd disappointed him in some way. It wasn't even conceivable she could assist him beyond giving him Fair Wind's book, though that did not halt the feelings of failure and dejection. Luci and Edith would know exactly what to do if they were here. They wouldn't allow defeat to stop them from finding what they sought.

Straightening her shoulders, Ophelia smiled broadly and turned toward Colin, determined to show him she could be useful. She wasn't merely the odd woman out this time, nor the one taking directions from those who "knew better."

"I think we should ask at the records office." She pointed to the building bordering the burned-down ale house. "They will have logs that make note of all the ships coming and going from Sheerness—and, hopefully, have record of Fair Wind's vessel."

She was hard-pressed to tamp down her confidence at finally taking a measure of control in their adventure.

"Very well," he said with a nod. "Let us begin there."

He held his arm out, and she slipped her hand into place. It was as if they'd strolled together for many years, their pace was evenly matched, and his hold on her felt right. She wondered for a brief moment what it would be like to dance with Colin, perhaps a waltz or a lively reel, with an entire ballroom bearing witness. Would other debutantes cast envious stares her way? It was more likely they wouldn't even notice Ophelia in Colin's arms as his handsomeness would certainly be the only thing attracting anyone's notice.

It was odd, this journey with Lord Hawke. She'd never been away from her family—or her friends—for such an extended period of time. It was freeing in a peculiar way. The fact that she hadn't given a second thought to what her parents might think was unsettling—and a bit selfish—but blast it all, Ophelia rarely stood on her own two feet without someone there to support her.

Along those lines, it had been nearly an entire day since she'd thought of Tilda and everything that had happened with her friend. She hadn't been plagued by night terrors as she'd slept, Colin on the floor close by.

The records office appeared closed from afar, but as they moved closer, a light could be seen through the open window, along with a man sitting behind a desk, quill in hand. As they entered, the clerk glanced up, his eyes widening in shock. His chair scraped against the scarred, wooden floor when he stood, glancing about as if they'd entered his private domain and he was uncertain how to proceed.

"Good morn, sir," Ophelia said. "Do you hold the records for Sheerness?"

His head bobbed, and he hurried across the room, his hands clutched before him. "Certainly. Certainly, miss. Births, deaths, land, and sea. I'm Mr. Ackerson."

"Lovely to meet you, Mr. Ackerson." Ophelia remained close to the door. The business office was piled high with crates, trunks, papers, and files, making navigating any farther an unwise decision lest she risk being crushed by falling boxes. "We are looking for a boat."

Ackerson's eyes narrowed, and he glanced over his shoulder to the area at the back of the office. "Sea it is. I keep everything in the back. Come along."

Ophelia glanced at Colin and shrugged before he stepped in front of her and led the way toward Ackerson. The man hurried ahead of them, clearly familiar with the safest and most expedited route to the sea records. Despite the clutter, not a speck of dust had settled on anything. She could not imagine that many people visited the record's office, but everything appeared clean, if not orderly.

Slipping by an upright pile of rolled maps, Ophelia decided her father would greatly enjoy a visit to Sheerness, if only to spend an entire fortnight exploring this room. Maybe she would speak with him about it when she returned home.

"Almost there," Colin whispered over his shoulder. "I do not see how the man can find anything in this mess."

Ophelia crossed her fingers and held them high for him to see, and they both laughed, though she noticed his chuckle was more hesitant than hers. Yet, she was determined to think positively. They needs must find some information to take back to London—and this ship was only one of two leads left. Mr. Ackerson and his impractical sorting methods was possibly their best—maybe their only—option.

"What are you looking for?" Ackerson asked, his hands on his hips as he surveyed the pile of folders and papers haphazardly stacked. "Shipment manifest? Export log? Injury details?"

"Er, we are looking for a ship."

"Name?" he queried.

"Sadly, I do not know," Colin admitted.

Ackerson turned sharply toward them, his stare narrowing as he brushed his palms down the front of his trousers. "No name." He scratched his head. "Type of vessel?"

"I am afraid we do not know that either," Ophelia answered when Colin's shoulders fell. "But we know approximately the year it came and went."

Ackerson pursed his lips and returned his gaze to his files. "That may help. What is the date?"

Ophelia looked to Colin, a bit of hope returning.

"A little over fifty years ago. During the Seven Years' War…"

The man exhaled heavily and shook his head. "That was a busy time for Sheerness to be certain. We had ships coming and going nearly every day for four years. Exports, imports, and even a few ships belonging to the king. Are there any other details you can share? If not, the three of us will be here searching long into next month."

It was a difficult topic, but Ophelia suspected Colin would have to name Fair Wind as the captain they were here about. Was Colin's grandpapa a well-known man in Sheerness, or had his memory faded and disappeared with time?

Certainly, even the tales of a smuggler's adventures would be passed down with the town folklore. Ackerson must be the town historian, as well.

"Would the captain's name help?" Ophelia asked.

"Depends," Ackerson mumbled. "Again, lots of boats coming and going…most not from around here, so I won't have record of them all."

Colin paused, and Ophelia nodded in support. "This man was from Sheerness."

"From Sheerness, you say?"

"Yes," Colin said, clearing his throat, and Ophelia feared it would be all he'd say. "He was born here, wed my grandmama here, and only moved away because he had no other choice."

The man slipped his hands into his trouser pockets and rolled back on his heels. "Not many folks leave Sheerness," he mused. "Suppose I'd have some record of him, or my pa might remember him."

"Porter Parnell," Colin said in a rush, it was as if he waited another moment, he'd lose the nerve to speak his grandpapa's name. "He wed Molly Kirkwise."

Ackerson tilted his head to the side and hummed, narrowing his intense stare on Colin. "Porter Parnell— married to ol' Kirkland Kirkwise's eldest gal?"

Ophelia wasn't certain if Ackerson knew whom he spoke of, or was only stringing together the oddest name he could think of, but Colin nodded confirmation and smiled.

"You're looking for Fair Wind?" Ackerson asked.

"Not Fair Wind, his vessel," Ophelia corrected, but the man didn't take his stare off Colin.

"Afraid you won't have any luck finding his ship in these parts." Ackerson took a step toward Colin, and Lord Hawke moved away until the back of his legs collided with a large trunk. "Well, I must say I am surprised I didn't notice right when you walked in."

Ophelia had the odd urge to step between the men and block Colin from Ackerson's intense scrutiny.

However, Colin spoke before she could move. "Do I look so much like him?"

"I never met him in person, but his portrait hung in the ale house next door until it burned to the ground." Ackerson tapped his forehead, chin, and chest in the same way Ophelia had witnessed Molly doing during one of her tirades. "You must be his son?"

Colin chuckled, and the tension in the room fled. "Grandson, actually. Colin Parnell, Lord Hawke when I'm feeling particularly formal."

"It is a pleasure to meet you, and it is a swell thing that we aren't high in the instep here in Sheerness."

"You said I would not be finding Fair Wind's vessel at the dock?"

"'Fraid not." Ackerson shook his head in apology. "Boat was nearly sinking. Merchant company, some businessman from London, came through a few years ago and bought the ancient thing from Molly's cousin, Jedidiah. I can see what other logs I have, though if I remember my father's tales correctly, Fair Wind kept meticulous notes of his journeys…did not favor leaving them here with the records office."

It was another false trail. Certainly, there would be no proof of Fair Wind's true purposes at sea in such a public office where anyone could request information. Without the boat and what could be hidden within, they had nothing. Colin's grandpapa, whether smuggling goods into England or running missives for the king, would not value his personal information spreading to the townsfolk.

Ophelia could not imagine the time and effort Fair Wind had put into hiding his missions for the king. There was no other explanation than he was a loyal, dedicated servant during his time at sea. It was either that or Colin's father was correct in proclaiming the man a no-good smuggler.

There was no chance she would allow Colin to depart Sheerness without proof, one way or the other.

It meant a great deal to him—and, surprisingly, to Ophelia, too.

"Thank you, Mr. Ackerson," Colin said curtly. "We will not monopolize any more of your time this day."

The man smiled, raising his ink-stained hand and taking hold of Colin's, giving it a healthy shake. Next, he turned to Ophelia and bowed low.

"It was an honor to meet Fair Wind's grandson and wife, I assure you." He nodded, sending his hair back into his eyes. "It was lovely to make your acquaintance, Lady Hawke."

"Oh, no—"

"That is not—"

Ophelia and Colin spoke at the same time, but both laughed at Ackerson's mistake.

She took a step closer to Colin and set her hand on his arm. "It was a pleasure meeting you, Mr. Ackerson. Do have a lovely day."

Tugging lightly on his arm, Ophelia turned Colin toward the door and proceeded back into the morning sun.

They walked only a few steps before Colin pulled her to a halt.

"Why did you allow him to think us wed?" he asked, his brow furrowed.

She couldn't admit that she thought the title "Lady Hawke" sounded appealing, nor would she admit she'd dreamed of just that thing the previous night, though Ophelia hadn't remembered it until a moment before.

Colin stepped in front of her, and she lifted her chin to look him straight in the eyes. Before leaving London, she would have been reduced to a mumbling mess with pink-stained cheeks at such a misspoken comment. But not now, not in Sheerness...and not with Colin.

Something had altered her in the last day or so— truly, she'd noticed it begin the day she eavesdropped on Lord Hawke in Oliver's Book Shoppe.

Ophelia leaned up on her tiptoes, and before she could change her mind, placed her lips against his. He remained still, likely in shock, for only the span of two heartbeats. They were Ophelia's rapid heartbeats, but two nonetheless, before his lips softened and parted, beginning to move against hers.

It was not the private moment from the previous night. It was not the chaste kiss she'd thought to give him to stop his line of questioning or rampant thoughts. And it certainly was not the harmless gesture of a friend.

Before she knew what was happening, her hands clutched his shoulders, and his arms encircled her, pulling her against his muscular chest. The midsection of a man who toiled and knew the hard work of the sea—or perhaps gained his daily exercise in the stables or working the land.

It was the most peculiar thought at such a grand moment.

Her first kiss.

Ophelia's fingers released their grip on his shoulders, and her palms slowly drifted down to his chest, and the mere inch separating them.

She allowed him to set the pace of their kiss, their lips moving together in a slow, sedate rhythm, his hands kneading her lower back in the same movements. It was then that Ophelia remembered Luci's first kiss with Montrose—if one could call it that—and she slipped her tongue across Colin's lower lip.

She was rewarded with a deep moan.

Yes, if she remembered correctly, Montrose had been so lost in pleasure he hadn't realized Luci was about to bite him for his impertinence.

But Ophelia had no such plans.

Actually, she had no plans at all.

Beyond this moment.

Beyond this embrace.

Beyond this kiss.

She did not worry about her parents' wrath at her fleeing London. She was no longer disheartened by her friends leaving for Scotland without her. She was beyond fretting about where they'd next look for Fair Wind's past. And neither did she believe all men were like Lord Abercorn, a danger to women. Colin was most assuredly not a scoundrel or a rake—as her friends had learned about Montrose and Torrington.

Ophelia sighed, pressing herself closer to him and reaching her arms up and around his neck.

In this moment, Tilda was not gone, her first London Season was not shrouded in mourning, and everything about being in Colin's arms was right. She didn't long to expose dangerous men of the *ton*. She felt no urge to be the champion of all young women. She was not living on the outside of Luci's and Edith's friendship.

No, she was with Colin…and he was holding her close, their lips meeting and moving together as if they'd been born for this moment. As long as he was with her, nothing else mattered.

CHAPTER 18

WITH THE SUN beaming on his back and the ocean breeze playing with his hair, Colin pulled Ophelia ever closer. Her petite size melded perfectly against him, her bosom pressing into his chest as his hands explored her backside. He was helpless to do anything else as her tongue slowly slid across his lower lip once more, his moan deeper than the last.

The woman was a temptress, a sorceress, a bewitching nymph in ladies' clothing.

And Colin wanted her enchantments focused solely on him.

Today. Tomorrow. And every day thereafter.

How had he ever lived without this?

Bloody hell, he didn't even know what *this* was.

Without thinking, he reached up and uncoiled her arms from around his neck and stepped back. But he knew it was a mistake when he looked down at her plump, kiss-bruised lips and her wide-eyed stare of desire. At some point, long tendrils of auburn hair had escaped her coiffure and hung about her face and shoulders. Everything about the woman screamed heat…and passion…and utter oblivion.

Her large, blue eyes turned blank, the fire dying quickly as her chin fell to her chest before she looked away from him toward the ocean beyond in the harbor.

He placed his finger under her chin and tried to bring her gaze back to his, but she pulled away and cleared her throat.

"I believe we have one final place to search." Her tone was raspy, as if she'd just woken from a deep slumber—or barely escaped the throes of passion without getting burned. "Shall we request directions?"

Had she been unaffected by it all, or was she hiding pain he'd unwittingly caused?

Bloody hell, but they were only several hundred feet from the fish market where people came and went. Anyone could have seen them. In fact, Mr. Ackerson had a perfect view from his front window. The man would think nothing of a couple kissing, especially since he was under the mistaken impression that they were wed.

Colin glanced around them, rubbing the back of his neck to relieve the sudden tension threatening to take over. No one paid them any mind, no one halted and gawked at the pair of them in a scandalous embrace.

"Mayhap it is best we start back for London," he sighed. It was past time he returned her to her home before he caused her any further harm. If they remained any longer in Sheerness, they might be forced into another night away from London. After their kiss, Colin doubted he'd be able to turn her away—or remain in command of his own longings—for another long night. "It is unlikely we will find anything, or worse, prove Fair Wind merely a common smuggler. Going back without any new information could be a mercy for Molly."

Ophelia swung back toward him, her glare meeting his, and he swore he saw sparks of outrage in their deep blue depths. "Molly would not give up. *We* cannot give up. We, at the very least, need to venture to the final place on Molly's list. If we find nothing there, we return to Mr. Ackerson and request to speak with his father...or mayhap Molly's cousin who sold Fair Wind's ship. This is not over."

He didn't want it to be over, either; although, he was now uncertain of his motivations. Did he still seek answers for Molly and his father, or was he being selfish and only thinking of keeping Ophelia close for as long as possible?

"Lord Hawke," she sighed, taking a step closer. Colin had the urge to recoil at her return to formality, but he held his ground. "Life is not about conquering every problem and obstacle set before you, it is about what you do when the problem is unsolvable or the obstacle seemingly insurmountable. Are you prepared to return to London and tell Molly that we gave up when things became difficult?"

Colin remained stunned, staring at the woman before him. She should be unrecognizable, so at odds with the woman he thought he knew, but for some unexplainable reason, it was as if he were seeing her true self for the first time. She was giving him a gift, one she held close and allowed few others to witness.

Finally, she cast her gaze back toward the sea. "I, for one, will not return to London without something—anything. Molly disapproves of me as it is, and I will give her no other reasons to doubt my steadfast nature."

Her words were said with an edge of steel behind them.

Ophelia believed everything she said.

Colin's hand slipped into his pocket to retrieve the list and find their final stop. He would continue on, if not for Molly, then for Ophelia.

As much as this was his responsibility, a journey he had agreed to venture out on…this was Ophelia's adventure. There was little doubt she needed to solve the mystery surrounding Fair Wind's past, possibly more than even Colin did.

His fingers did not find the notes from Molly but her pendant. The familiar hunk of stone, set in silver with a long chain, was warm in the palm of his hand.

He'd grown up believing his grandmama's favored necklace held powers not of this world but of another altogether. It was pure fancy, and something Colin still believed in no matter that he'd dispelled his youth a long time back.

Colin pulled the pendant from his pocket and held it between them. It dangled in the breeze, the sun casting rays of light off its many facets.

Undoing the clasp, he stepped toward Ophelia and refastened the chain at her nape. The pendant hung low, settling between her breasts. Colin had never noticed how the red hue matched Ophelia's hair perfectly. If he didn't know the pendant had been specifically crafted for his grandmama by the man who loved and cherished her, Colin would believe the stone was cut and placed in its silver setting just for Ophelia.

She glanced down at the necklace. "This is Molly's treasured pendant. I cannot…she would not approve…this is not meant for me."

In that instant, Colin didn't care if they were standing alone in their private chamber at the inn or the middle of a crowded London ballroom.

As she reached up to remove the necklace, Colin stilled her hands, taking them within his. "Upon reflection, I think Molly suspected this would one day belong to you."

"But, I cannot, this is—" she stammered, glancing from him to the pendant and back again.

"I have always been told, by both Molly and my father, that I am similar to Fair Wind in many aspects. My father thought I'd inherited his less than savory ways. My grandmama held close that I was the loyal and undaunted man Fair Wind was." He paused, collecting his thoughts—choosing his words correctly. "Today, I wholeheartedly want to be the man who would have this precious stone cut and set for the woman he loved. I want to be the man who gave up all he loved in life to make a better future for his family—and those yet to come. With that being said, this belongs to you, Ophelia. Another thing I am most certain of is that if it hadn't been for Molly, my grandpapa would not have been the man he was on that day he commissioned this necklace."

Colin was terrified to look too closely at her. Would she be repelled by his words? Would she demand they return to London? Would she think him addlebrained like Molly?

He needs must get it over with, confront her without reservations; good or bad.

When he returned his stare to her, he saw both everything and nothing he'd thought to see. Her eyes were moist with gathering tears. Her cheeks were glowing, but not with embarrassment over his proclamation. The most noteworthy was that she leaned toward him, not away.

"Ophelia!" a female voice shouted over the sound of carriage wheels on the wooden planks underfoot.

"There you are! I thought we'd never find you!" another woman called.

They turned as a carriage, pulled by four large greys, halted beside them. The door flung open, and two women exited, followed closely by a pair of men dressed as if they should be in London making social rounds and only happened upon him and Ophelia while out and about.

Ophelia hurried to embrace the women; one with hair the color of night and the other with pale hair the color of spun sunlight.

Colin fought against the feeling of abandonment that crept through him.

The pair of men, completely at odds with one another in appearance much like the trio of women now exchanging hugs, pinned him with intense stares.

He wanted to demand to know who the foursome was and how in the bloody hell they had found him and Ophelia all the way in Sheerness.

It was only Ophelia's joy at seeing the two women that kept Colin from pulling her back to his side and demanding answers from the group at large. Another pang of what could only be jealousy sparked within him as Ophelia embraced both men. The one as large as a small house slipped his arm around her and squeezed gently as she laughed. Next, the man at his side patted her shoulder before hugging her with one arm, as the tall, midnight-haired woman returned to his side.

Mercifully, Ophelia turned back to him and hurried to his side, grasping his hand and pulling him toward the group. She lifted her chin, and he nodded at her beaming smile. His irritation receded as he took in the utter transformation in her. Certainly, she was nearly always optimistic and happy, but there was something new here now, something that had been missing during their acquaintance thus far. He couldn't look away from her as he noted the new light in her blue eyes. No longer did they appear a shrouded ocean but rather a clear, blue sky on a warm day. Anyone who could bring such sparkle to Ophelia's eyes was worth his notice.

"Lord Hawke, Colin,"—her tone deepened with his name—"may I introduce Lady Lucianna and the Duke of Montrose?" Colin nodded to the couple. "And Lady Edith and Lord Torrington."

"These are the friends you spoke of?" he asked, not realizing he'd said the words aloud. "Lady Lucianna, Lady Edith—it is a pleasure to meet you both."

Colin couldn't be certain, but he thought he heard the large man, Torrington, growl at the word *pleasure* used in conjunction with Lady Edith's name. He was fine with that as he'd been ready to do battle with the two men when they'd embraced Ophelia.

"My lords." Colin bowed stiffly to the pair. "It is also a pleasure"—he paused on the word with a smirk—"to meet you both."

"What are you doing here?" Ophelia breathed. "You should be solidly on your way to Gretna Green."

"We traveled as far as Northampton before Luci realized she could not wed Montrose."

"What?" Ophelia exclaimed.

"…without you present," Lady Edith said with a smirk. "However, when we arrived at Atholl Townhouse, your maid said you'd followed us to Scotland."

Colin couldn't help but allow the good cheer and banter to surround him. This type of easy, close friendship was a thing he'd been denied most of his life.

"Thank the bloody stars for Pru and Chastity." Torrington leaned over and placed a kiss to Lady Edith's forehead. "If they've learned anything from the trio of you women, it is to listen not only to what's being said, but also what's being avoided."

"And that led you here?" Ophelia asked.

"No, it led us to Oliver's Book Shoppe during the dead of night…and then here," Montrose grumbled. "We traveled all night to reach Sheerness only an hour ago."

"Come now, Monty," Torrington slapped the man on the back. "It isn't as if traveling the dark England roads at night is something new."

"Speaking for yourself?" Montrose snapped back. "And do not call me Monty again, or you'll find yourself harnessed to the carriage and pulling us back to London."

"I may be as large as a bison—as you've so kindly called me on occasion—but I can still outrun you if needed."

All three women giggled at the exchange, even though Colin tensed with concern. The men did not appear to get along well enough to travel all the way to the Scottish border without injuring one another—either with words or fists.

"Do not mind them, Lord Hawke," Lady Edith said, turning her kind smile on him. "We feared Ophelia might be in trouble, so we came with all due haste."

Ophelia tensed at his side, her fingers digging into his arm.

"I am afraid it was I who was in trouble and in desperate need of help, which Lady Ophelia so kindly offered to give." He ignored the startled looks from the two women and continued. "She has been instrumental in helping me locate information about my grandpapa's past."

CHAPTER 19

TRIUMPH COURSED THROUGH Sissy as she held the pages securely in her hands. She had the sensation of being young again, the thought of everything that would be hers once more making her entire body hum with anticipation. There was no need to suppress her glee at the discovery so easily found nestled in plain sight. They'd been in the room only a short time before Sissy spotted what she was looking for—and after their near disaster at the inn that morning, she'd almost thought they'd be the ones exposed. Yet, Lady Ophelia had barely given her a moment's glance. The girl's eyes had settled on Sissy with a quick look of possible recognition, but quickly returned to her companion. Sissy had held her breath for what seemed like hours as the auburn-haired woman once again focused on her meal and the man before her.

Thankfully, Franny preferred his back to the room and indulged Sissy in her love for remaining in the shadows—or they would have surely been discovered.

It had taken every ounce of calm she possessed to hurriedly finish her food and spirit herself and Franny from the tavern before the auburn-haired woman made the connection in her mind. Sissy had seen the silly chit in Lady Lucianna's wake only a month prior when they'd come to confront Francis about his offer of marriage.

But still, Sissy would recognize the woman anywhere.

What had surprised her was the gentleman Ophelia was seated across from.

Lord Hawke, Colin Parnell—the dowager's grandson.

Had he found the location of his grandfather's private belongings, too?

She'd rushed poor Franny out the side door of the establishment, convincing him it would cut down on the walking distance to the building she'd learned belonged to Porter Parnell—which, in turn, would have Francis back in London in time to attend a ball or some such other societal engagement.

"Do tell me again what these papers have to do with gaining back my property in Somerset," Francis inquired, still huffing from climbing the flight of stairs to locate the small living quarters.

My property, Sissy thought.

"...and I must insist again, no one will care a whit about the Coventry family's past. We had a notorious gambler and rakehell for a father—certainly, a free trader is not all that scandalous."

But there was so much more—oh, so much more!—to the matter. Things the dowager's son, Ramsey Parnell, didn't want those in London to discover.

"Don't you fret about anything, Franny," Sissy crowed. Coventry was unworthy, even her own brother could use a proper dressing down for his part in Sissy being made to wait so many years to reclaim her home. "With these"—she waved the pages in the air between them nearly swiping at his nose—"I have what I need to return what is mine to our family."

"It only seemed a grand hassle for something so insignificant." He meandered about the dusty room, a bleak expression overtaking his normally jovial demeanor. "And if what you plan to do when we return to London is any indication, the disturbance to our lives will only increase."

It irritated her that Francis thought securing his sister's future was so burdensome—an unnecessary disruption to his daily life. "I am doing this for us. This is our family's due, and it is our responsibility to see it returned to us."

"The land—and the manor house—are likely worth little after all these years." He scoffed. "Why go to such lengths to see it returned to us when we have our townhouse in London, home in Bath, and our country estate?"

He had a London townhouse, a home in Bath, and a country estate—Sissy did not.

And when Francis wed again, all of it would belong to the new Duchess of Abercorn. And the woman would very likely label Sissy an irritation, a relation not worth supporting…and then where would Sissy go?

Sissy was growing older, and she was tired of fighting every day to have something to call hers. The day was fast approaching when she might not be able to handle the next possessive woman who entered her brother's life with her sights set on being a duchess.

"This is something that is all mine and cannot be taken from me." Sissy stuffed the pages into her handbag and pushed past Franny toward the exit. "Now, can we be away from here? This filth is likely to ruin the hem of my gown."

With a smirk of satisfaction, Sissy listened as her brother's footsteps treaded behind her as he was forced into the position of following *her* from the room and down the staircase.

A SHIVER OF anticipation traveled down Ophelia's

back as she watched Edith's and Luci's mirrored expressions of shock transform into knowing sideways glances as they noticed the large necklace nestled between Ophelia's breasts and the way she held Colin's arm as if she'd cease to exist if she let him go. Her chest filled with pride—in herself and the man at her side. Edith and Lucianna hadn't thought Ophelia had been in any real danger, but had needed to feign concern to gain Torrington and Montrose's support in following her to Sheerness. Essentially, they'd duped their betrotheds into making the mad dash to Kent.

Ophelia's only question was: why.

"How can we help?" Montrose asked, glancing at Luci. "I assume we will not be journeying back to London until Lady Ophelia and Lord Hawke have found what they came for."

"You assume right, my love," Luci chimed in. "I don't care what Torrington says about you...you are the brightest man I know."

Montrose threw a narrowed glare at Torrington, who only laughed and slammed him on the back again.

At first, Ophelia had the urge to turn away their help and send them back to London; however, both Edith and Luci turned expectant stares on her. They were her friends. They loved Ophelia, and their journeying all the way to Sheerness only convinced her that she'd been too hard on them. Especially Luci during her stay with Ophelia after her father had cast her out.

"We have discovered nothing of great significance as yet," Colin said, making the decision to accept their help. "We have one last place to visit, and then we will be reduced to questioning the townsfolk about a man who hasn't lived in Sheerness for many years."

"Lead the way." Montrose motioned for Colin to take the lead.

"My grandpapa and Molly rented rooms above the blacksmith's shop," Colin said.

"Oh, we passed the place when we drove through town." Edith smiled, always one to make note of certain things that did not appear important but nevertheless always seemed to be useful. "It was only three doors down from the inn we stopped at."

"You stopped at the inn?" Ophelia gulped.

Luci winked, letting Ophelia know they'd discovered that she and Colin had shared quarters the previous night. "The proprietor pointed us in the direction of the docks. It appears an auburn-haired beauty is difficult to miss in such a small town."

Ophelia's cheeks heated as a blush crept up her neck. She looked up at Colin, but he appeared unaware of her embarrassment or the fact that her friends had discovered their scandalous sleeping arrangements.

Instead, he started off, everyone following behind her and Colin as they made their way back toward the inn and the blacksmith's shop beyond.

It should be an invasion of her privacy, the act of her friends swooping in to take over her adventure, except they trailed her—they didn't push her aside or demand she follow their lead. Colin, with her on his arm, was in charge. The ladies were here because they genuinely wanted to help, and were desperate to learn more about the man Ophelia had fled London with. There had been a time, not many months ago, that Ophelia had been similarly curious about Torrington and Montrose.

They reached the inn quickly, the duke's carriage following them at a distance, and hurried on toward the blacksmith's shop.

"Molly says this building still belongs to her family and no one has lived up top since she and my grandpapa moved to London after accepting his Earldom from the king." Colin spoke aloud, even though Ophelia assumed he was working everything out in his mind. "If there is anything to be found here, it will be the room they shared for the first five years of their marriage."

Ophelia glanced over her shoulder, and Edith's brow rose in question. They hadn't the time to explain everything now. It was a long story, one that could be imparted on their journey back to London.

The blacksmith's shop was deserted, the doors wide open, and the forge lit with various tools lying discarded about the large room. Whoever worked within mustn't be far.

"Hello?" Ophelia called into the dim interior. They all waited just outside the doors, not wanting to shock the blacksmith if he were inside. "Anyone here?"

"Doesn't appear to be anyone about." Colin stepped back, releasing her arm to survey the stairs leading up the side of the building to a landing above. "That must be their rooms up there."

He started to climb the steps, and Ophelia leapt into action behind him, keeping close pace as they climbed. She held her skirt high to avoid tripping and tumbling back down the steep steps. They appeared clean of dirt and well swept.

A pounding in her chest had her placing a hand over the area as she fought to catch her breath as she climbed. It was not her heart beating erratically, but the pendant swinging and thumping her bosom. Ophelia wrapped the precious stone in her hand and was immediately filled with a sense of comfort. Was it Porter "Fair Wind" Parnell reaching out to her from somewhere beyond her meager existence? The question needed more pondering...but now wasn't the time, nor the place. Or maybe it was the exact place for such consideration.

Making the landing, Colin paused and waited for her to reach his side before he grasped the latch and pushed the door open.

Ophelia sucked in a breath. She'd imagined the door would be locked to avoid trespassers, but they stepped over the threshold without anyone coming to stop them. The room was empty except for two cloth-covered pieces of furniture; one being a table, and the other a large shelf. The hearth was also bare and swept clean of debris.

Colin walked farther into the room, his footsteps kicking up dust from the floor and causing Ophelia to sneeze.

No one followed them, and no footfalls sounded on the stairs outside.

Lady Edith and the others must have remained below.

The windows were shrouded in heavy, brown fabric, reducing the light in the room to a hazy, patchy glow, casting shadows into the far corners not reached by the light streaming in from the open door.

"There doesn't appear to be anyone living here," she mumbled, needing to say something to break the silence. "There is an inch of dust on every surface."

Colin's stare scanned the room once more and settled on the mantel above the open hearth.

A tiny wooden box rested there, devoid of the years of dirt and grime covering the rest of the room. The pieces of a broken lock had been placed atop it, and the latch was sprung.

"Someone has been here"—he paused, scanning the room once more—"and very recently."

"But who?"

He didn't answer, and she hadn't expected him to. As everything else surrounding Fair Wind and his past, it would likely remain a mystery.

Colin approached the hearth—and the tiny box—with caution.

Ophelia could not blame him for his hesitation. Whatever the box held, it was certain to change his life—for good or bad. If it was empty, they'd accomplished nothing in Sheerness. If it held the missing pages, Colin would be forced to return to them Molly and cause more friction between his father and grandmama. Ophelia suspected it would not be so simple to cast aside all his father had believed for his entire life.

Setting the broken lock aside, Colin picked up the tiny wooden box and returned to her side.

"My great-grandpapa, Fair Wind's father, was a master carver." Colin smiled, and Ophelia knew he was in another time, another place. "He lived here, in Sheerness, crafting trunks, boxes, and even furniture for the many sailing vessels."

Colin turned the box over in his hands and held it out for her to see.

In perfect script on the underside of the box was *Parnell*.

"The box could have been crafted yesterday." Ophelia reached out and traced the word with her fingertip. "It is beautiful. Your family has much to be proud of."

"And many secrets to keep hidden, it appears."

She set her hand on his shoulder in comfort but he winced, stepping away from her.

"Shall I wait outside?" she asked. This should be a private moment for him. If it were Ophelia on such a cusp of discovery, she'd need space and time to process everything. "I will join the others downstairs."

She made to turn, but Colin reached out, grasped her gloved hand, and tugged her back to face him. He said not a word, only raised her hand to his lips and placed a light kiss on her open palm. It was an invitation—no, a demand—that she stay.

Here. With him.

No matter what they discovered about his family's past, they would return to London together. She wanted to tell him that she'd be at his side through it all. Whether they returned with good news or no news, she'd be there.

For him.

"Go on, open it," she coaxed in a whisper. "Let us

see what adventure lies in such a tiny box."

He released her hand and focused on the box once more.

For the first time since leaving London, Ophelia was overwhelmed. Her head spun, her vision blurring. Closing her eyes, she took a deep, calming breath, and begged her mind to remain in control of her body. She would not faint…not here, not now. She gulped down another deep inhale and allowed her eyes to flutter open.

"You are beautiful," Colin breathed, taking a step closer to her, the box between them. "Have I told you that today?"

"You've…you've…you've never told me that," she stammered, unable to collect her thoughts with him so close.

"Ah, rest assured, I've been thinking it since the moment I rescued you from Molly's wrath in the Atholl drive."

"Perhaps it is my sorceress spell," she teased. "Beelzebub come to drag you to the Underworld."

"Or, perhaps"—he leaned in so close their lips nearly met—"it is only you and your inner light that has captured me so completely."

"My lord, I must say that sounds far more likely than Molly's accusations of the devil's mark."

This time, it was Colin who moved the final inch and captured her mouth.

Unlike their previous kiss, this time, their mouths met and danced in a light, undemanding cadence. Neither deepening the kiss nor parting their lips. It was a promise of intimate times to come, the assurance that no matter what they found in the box, they'd still have one another. Their time together would not cease once they returned to London. Ophelia wholeheartedly believed that.

She would never be able to walk away from him and not look back.

He'd been burned into her mind. His composed confidence and determination etched there.

Colin was not the arrogant and domineering gentleman Torrington and Montrose appeared to be. He was not the shrewd businessman Luci's father was. He was not the cunning, manipulative lord Abercorn certainly was.

He was something altogether different...and that fact made him all the more special to Ophelia. He'd allowed her this journey, this adventure, never questioning her motives yet believing in her ability to assist him.

"Are you ready?" he said on a soft exhale. She could only nod, not trusting herself to speak.

Clutching the box in one hand, Colin lifted the lid with the other, and they both peeked inside.

Nestled in the emerald green fabric lining the box was an envelope with one simple word written on it.

Molly.

The sure, solid print was unmistakable to Ophelia. She'd read nearly all of Fair Wind's travel log and his bits about Molly and his home. Porter Parnell had addressed the envelope to his wife, the woman he'd loved above all else.

Whoever had broken the lock hadn't taken the letter. She wondered if something else had been housed in the box at some time.

The envelope was too thin to hold all the torn pages from Fair Wind's book.

Ophelia glanced up at Colin to see a single tear slide down his cheek. He'd been so strong and unaffected since their arrival in Sheerness, despite their many setbacks, but it appeared the letter was too much.

She reached in and grasped the envelope. The paper had yellowed with age, and the ink had faded with time.

"It is addressed to your grandmother. Should we take it back to London?"

Colin shook his head firmly, his lips pressed into a frown. "No, we open it here. There is perhaps information we need inside."

Handing the note to him, Ophelia collected the box and returned it to the mantel while Colin studied the letter, pacing from one end of the room to the other. He stared at the note with all seriousness, and Ophelia noticed for the first time how exhausted he appeared. His strong posture had receded, and his eyes were glazed over with fatigue. He'd never given up; however, it was as if he needed a month's worth of rest now that he held something concrete in his hands.

If Ophelia could make this all easier for him, she would. She'd do anything to lessen the burden on Colin's shoulders.

This was where her adventure ended, and Colin's real-life struggles took over.

CHAPTER 20

COLIN HAD IN his hand the one thing he'd been searching for, and he wanted nothing more than to return it to its box on the mantel and run—return to London, tell Molly they'd found nothing, and continue as he had since childhood. Forever in the middle of his family's strife. Would that be preferable to knowing the truth of his family's past? At present, Colin was seriously pondering that exact question.

Until he glanced up at Ophelia.

Going back and forgetting all that had transpired in Sheerness would also mean erasing Ophelia from his life. Forgetting the feel of her soft lips. Putting from his mind the long, silky, auburn locks that even now hung with wild abandon about her shoulders. Most of all, erasing her tenacity and determination to help him in such a selfless manner. She'd risked everything to accompany him—at first, he'd believed she was bored and in need of distraction, but it was so much more than that. Over the last day, he'd discovered a deep-seated, undaunted determination within the woman that he'd come to admire greatly.

Bloody hell, but he more than *admired* her.

He couldn't imagine returning to London, and his life, without her.

Molly had been correct. Ophelia had cast a spell over him, and he never wanted it lifted.

But he needed—*they* needed—to finish here in Sheerness before talks of the future were possible.

Colin smiled, knowing it did not reach his eyes and slipped his finger under the seal holding the letter closed.

When the flap opened, he removed the single sheet of paper and was instantly reminded of the note Molly had sent with her list. Had she known Colin would find himself so enamored with Ophelia? Had she foreseen that the adventure would bring Colin close to Ophelia, closer than he'd ever been to another person?

He shook his head to banish the thought.

Unfolding the note, he read:

My dearest Molly ~

Me love for ye has no bounds—it is not restrained by land, sea, time, or distance. Yet, I find meself here, in Sheerness, and ye in London with Ramsey. Neither of us could'a imagined what the king had planned for me; not the journeys ta Prussia nor the title and land. It was not what we planned, and never what I wanted. But ye believed in a better future for us. London is not me home. I am ever pulled to the sea, but ye draw on me is far stronger than the sea. Me home is where ye are. If'n I destroy all the records of me service ta the king, we can return to Sheerness, live the life we always dreamed'a. Ye with yer family close and me close ta the two things I love: ye and the sea. I am a coward, my dearest Molly. Here I be, where I believe I—we—belong—and I cannot do it. The sea is a dangerous place. Ye be worthy of a good husband, not a man too long at sea, or worse, lost ta the murky depths of the unforgiving waters. Ramsey deserves better—a title without scandal and gossip of times long past attached. Not a scoundrel of a pa. And so, I be leave'n the pages here along with me past and me need for the water—and return ta London the gent me king made me...but I promise ye, we shall return. One day...

With all me heart, Porter, Lord Coventry

Colin reached out and took Ophelia's hand in his as he read the letter several more times before handing it to her. He assumed it had been written not long after his father finished his studies and was taking his place in society as the son of the Earl of Coventry. The letter said so much, yet so little all at the same time.

Porter "Fair Wind" Parnell had been an ally and trusted courier for King George II. That much was certain, but the box did not contain the missing pages. The proof.

His grandpapa had sacrificed his own happiness for that of his son, Ramsey.

He'd remained in London, played the lord, all to secure a better future for Ramsey, and in turn, Colin when he inherited the Earldom. To expose his position as the king's loyal servant, Fair Wind would have been forced to also uncover his jaded past as a smuggler.

Had Molly known all this?

Fair Wind must have spoken of it during the years after his final trip to Sheerness before his passing.

Both Colin's father and Molly had been correct. However, the truth lay far deeper than the surface. Yes, Fair Wind had worked for the king, but he'd been a smuggler, a seaman at heart. He'd given up his life's blood for the two people he loved above all else—including the sea.

The letter was significant proof of Porter's past, yet it had been written during the critical time when Ramsey and his father were feuding. Their family's past hadn't been important until Ramsey discovered other men of the *ton* had long lines of lineage, spanning hundreds of years and a dozen titled ancestors before them.

Ramsey was the grandson of a wood carver and an ale house proprietor from a small fishing town—no more than a village during those times. Even his mother, Molly, had served as a wench in her family's tavern while Porter earned his coin by unsavory dealings at sea.

Society was not particularly forgiving of such dubious past indiscretions.

His grandpapa knew that, and was still willing to all but erase any word to the contrary.

"This is beautiful," Ophelia sighed. "So different from his earlier writings but still very much his words."

Leave it to Ophelia to notice the eloquent nature of the letter, beyond the poignant message given. His grandpapa hadn't wanted anyone to find proof of his past. Without solid evidence, no one could refute Ramsey's right to the Earldom, despite it being awarded by the king. For all intents and purposes, the Parnell family were country folk blessed by a king who needed no explanation for his royal decrees. It had been an intelligent move on his grandpapa's part, and one not appreciated by Colin's father.

"I think we are done here in Sheerness." He turned a weak smile on Ophelia.

"But we have not found the pages." She folded the letter and returned it to its envelope. "They must be here somewhere."

He glanced at the box and back to Ophelia, his excitement over finding the box diminishing. "The lock was broken, and the latch opened. Someone found the pages before us, but I believe the letter will confirm everything for Molly—and my father will have little choice but to end their feud."

She shrugged and toyed with the pendant he'd placed around her neck.

"We will collect our carriage from the inn and return to London by nightfall." His words left him with more force than intended, but he offered no apologies. They'd done as Molly asked and would return home. They should both be satisfied with their discoveries and take a measure of pride in the knowledge they'd be responsible for bringing Molly peace. "I will meet you downstairs."

He glanced at her in time to see her chin lift before

she turned and rushed from the room. Her walking boots barely made a sound as she descended the stairs, leaving him alone in the place Molly and Fair Wind had once called home.

In no way did Colin feel satisfied with the information they'd found, nor pride in the discovery they'd return to Molly.

CHAPTER 21

"I AM COMING with you," Ophelia said with a stomp of her foot, ignoring the audience watching them. "I have had the last several hours to ponder everything, and I have made the decision to be at your side when you speak with Molly."

The evening breeze whipped her hood from her head as she stared Colin straight in the eyes, his carriage horses stamping their hooves with impatience. She'd ridden in Colin's carriage, with Luci and Edith, all the way back to London. The men taking up residence in Montrose's conveyance. Propriety had been maintained, and Ophelia had been able to share the entire story with her friends.

Ophelia suspected her determined demand had much to do with the way Colin had cast aside her words in the room above the blacksmith's shop. She'd thought there was more to find in Sheerness, and he'd dismissed her out of turn, treated her as if she had no say in anything pertaining to their journey.

"My father clearly has a guest," he said, gesturing to the carriage parked farther down the drive. "It is not the best time to discuss this."

Bloody bollocks, she thought, commandeering Edith's most prized expletive.

She narrowed her stare on him, and his nostrils flared ever so slightly with his irritation at her continued insistence. Why had she thought Colin lacked the arrogance and domineering nature so present in Torrington and Montrose? He could be bloody stubborn when the need presented itself. However, Ophelia found herself in possession of a doggedly persistent character, as well.

The Coventry butler held Colin's townhouse door wide, awaiting his entrance, and her friends—with Montrose and Torrington in tow—had all gathered in Montrose's carriage, waiting to deliver Ophelia home.

However, *she* was not leaving.

Not until she and Colin had spoken with Molly and passed on the letter from Fair Wind.

Besides, Ophelia needed to return the older woman's pendant.

It was the least she was owed for agreeing to throw caution—and her reputation—to the wind to embark on the adventure with Colin.

"I said I would call on you in the morning and inform you of how Molly took the news, as well as my father's reaction." His Hessian-clad feet were placed wide apart, his stance unyielding. His voice firm and filled with conviction.

But the man did not know Ophelia well at all if he thought her daunted by his seemingly unwavering determination to see her removed from the final portion of their duty. She would see everything through to completion.

"While that is very kind of you, my lord," she seethed, her hands settling on her hips as she leaned in close, lowering her voice. "I insist on being with you when you speak with Molly."

He sighed, and the tension drained from his shoulders.

With a satisfied smile, Ophelia turned to her waiting friends and shouted, "I will be out shortly."

Luci and Edith waved from the carriage before sitting back in their seats to wait.

"Shall we, my lord?" Ophelia's brow rose in question as she attempted to mask her grin with a serene smile. There was little need to anger him further. She'd gotten her way, and there was no need to rub the victory in his face. Nor do anything that would have him changing his mind before they were securely in the house. "I do look forward to seeing Molly's reaction when she sees the letter."

He reluctantly held out his arm, and she placed her gloved hand into the crook of his elbow. Holding her chin high, they entered the Coventry townhouse.

"I have warned you, Lady Ophelia," he leaned close and whispered in her ear. "My father can be a particularly ill-tempered man if he's interrupted while entertaining."

"As cross as you are now, Lord Hawke?" she asked with a smirk.

"Cross? Heavens, no," he said with a chuckle. "I believe *furious* better describes his nature."

Ophelia swallowed past the lump that had settled in her throat, blocking her airway. She refused to back down or cower. They'd been so close during their time in Sheerness, but it had all changed swiftly after finding Fair Wind's letter—no, correction, after Colin had read the letter, and she'd insisted on searching the town for more information.

If she could take it back, she would. Anything to banish the shadow that had settled on Colin. It was a cloud of unidentifiable darkness. Sorrow? Anguish? Confusion? Disappointment?

Perhaps a mix of all four.

Ophelia's own confusion had taken over during the long ride back to London. She'd meant to support him, be by his side the entire way, but unwittingly, she'd pushed him away. When he'd requested to ride with Montrose and Torrington, Ophelia had been hurt and conflicted. Certainly, she'd wanted some time with her dear friends—to explain everything—but more than anything, she'd longed for a few private moments to speak with Colin. Discuss what they'd found and make some attempt to sort through everything before they arrived back in London.

But she'd been denied that.

"Lord Hawke," the Coventry butler greeted him with a nod. "Lady Ophelia."

He'd remembered her name from her single visit to the Coventry townhouse. Ophelia ignored the servant's startled expression as he caught sight of Molly's pendant around her neck.

"Can you tell me where I might find Molly?" Colin asked.

"The physician departed an hour ago," the servant said, pointing down the hall. "She requested her meal be served in the salon."

"Does she have guests?"

"No, my lord." The butler cleared his throat and glanced down the hall to his father's personal study.

"Matheson?" Colin asked. "Is there something you are not telling me?"

"Well, my lord...it seems... Your grandmother does not have a guest; however, your father has two guests, and I've been instructed to keep the dowager away from his study," he said in a rush. "My lord, your father says I am to use force—if necessary. Force is always necessary with Lady Coventry."

The man worried his hands before him as if he were a debutante attending his first musicale and was fretting over hitting a wrong note. A bit of Ophelia's ire dissipated at the man's unease. She'd been in his position herself but had been on the receiving end of Molly's cane at the time—though, in all honesty, the woman's words wounded far deeper than her walking stick.

"And who, exactly, is my father meeting with?"

Matheson cast a quick look down another corridor before whispering, "Lord Abercorn and his sister, Lady Sissy."

Ophelia and Colin gasped at the same time.

Ophelia rounded on Colin, pushing him slightly when she withdrew her hand from his elbow. "You know Abercorn? Why did you not say?"

"Because I do *not* know Lord Abercorn," he retorted, his eyes narrowing on her.

"How convenient that a man you do not know is even now meeting with your father." Ophelia crossed her arms, her anger returning swiftly. How many things had he failed to tell her?

"How do you know Lady Sissy?" He took a step toward her, lowering his voice.

"I do not *know* Lady Sissy beyond her kinship— and resemblance—to Lord Abercorn."

"Why are you perturbed by Abercorn's presence here?"

"I am far more than perturbed, Lord Hawke," she seethed. "I am—" Ophelia's voice broke, and an uncontrollable shiver ran down her spine. "I am shocked such a heinous man would be allowed within your father's home."

"Then we are much in agreement, although I cannot fathom why Lord Abercorn would put his sister at such risk after what happened." Colin pinched the bridge of his nose before taking a calming breath. "Why do you despise Abercorn?"

"Why would Lady Sissy be at risk?" she demanded.

Ophelia pushed her shoulders back and watched him closely. He could keep his secrets about why he'd rushed back to London from Sheerness and why his demeanor and treatment of her had altered so drastically in a span of only a couple of minutes, but Abercorn was responsible for Tilda's death. If the man were now involved in yet another aspect of Ophelia, Luci, and Edith's lives, then she would bloody well find out how.

"I will ask one more time, my lord." Her pulse thrummed through her, resulting in a deafening echo in her head. "Why would Lady Sissy be at risk?" When he only stared at her, she continued, "Perhaps I should join them in the study and find out for myself."

"My lord, my lady," Matheson squeaked. "Can we not continue this conversation in another, more private room, or better still, on the morrow?"

"You are correct, sir," Ophelia said with a smile, but from the servant's sudden recoil, she could only assume she'd given him a sneer. "I find I wish to join Lord Coventry and his guests. I am acquainted with Abercorn, though we have had a rather tumultuous relationship. Shall I announce myself?"

She only managed two steps toward the study when Colin grabbed her arm, halting her.

"Lady Ophelia, you cannot—"

"I most certainly can." She had little clue what had come over her. The last time she'd knowingly been in Abercorn's company, she'd nearly succumbed to a case of the vapors, but at present, she only felt outrage and venom. She couldn't count spying on the man at Oliver's Book Shoppe because Abercorn hadn't suspected she watched him; therefore, she'd been in no danger. "Step aside, Colin."

He released her, and she started for the study once more, her footsteps sure as she worked through the coming confrontation in her mind.

"Stop, Ophelia," Colin pleaded at her treating back. "Molly and Lady Sissy were involved in a skirmish at a ball many, many, many years ago. It resulted in Molly's final banishment to Tintinhull Court, and Lady Sissy's—along with her brother, the duke's—lifelong dislike for my father."

Her steps faltered and she stumbled, but Matheson caught her arm and righted her quickly. In her fury, she hadn't noticed the servant hurrying to announce her.

"Then why is Lady Sissy here now?" Ophelia asked

without turning.

"That lie'n, slimy, dicked in the nob woman be in this house?"

"My lady!" Matheson yelped as all three turned to face Molly. "May I bring you tea in the salon?"

"Lady Sissy hadn't an ounce of steel in her then, and she sure as the morn'n sun don't have it now." Molly shuffled into the foyer, making a show of looking in every direction for the offending woman before spitting on the floor. "What Banbury stories is that vile bit of muslin spread'n now?" She narrowed her eyes on Ophelia before turning to Colin. "And when did the pair of ye arrive?"

"Only a few moments ago," Ophelia said. She was certain she appeared as frightened at the Coventry butler. "We were coming to find you."

"Did this beetle-browed knave think ta keep me unawares of an enemy in me own home?" Molly lifted her cane and pointed it at Matheson's chest for emphasis. "Ye be dismissed."

With a curt nod for Colin and a low bow for the women, Matheson disappeared toward the kitchens, likely in search of a drink—if he were smart.

"Now—" Molly leaned her cane against the wall and slipped her arm through Colin's before hobbling over and doing the same with Ophelia. "What be the plan ta get this buck fitch and his doxy outta this house?"

Ophelia and Colin shared an uneasy glance over Molly's head.

"I am right pleased ta have the pair of ye home," the older woman said as they reached the door to Colin's father's study. "Not a soul I can trust but ye two."

Ophelia couldn't barge into the room and confront Abercorn without knowing more about the feud between Molly and Lady Sissy. "What happened between you and Lady Sissy?"

"That no-good trollop came at me, right after me Fair Wind went ta the hereafter, accuse'n me family of steal'n her land." Molly glanced up at Ophelia, a crooked, satisfied grin on her face. "So, I shoved her, and she fell over a refreshment table and inta the crowded dance floor. Last time I heard her say anythin' about me family."

"Do you know why she is here now?" Colin asked.

"Ta claim ye Hawke Manor be me guess," Molly shrugged as if Lady Sissy's claim was unfounded and of no consequence. "But I plan ta send her on her way again, ye wait and see."

The door to the study pulled open, slamming upon its hinges into the wall behind it.

Ophelia, Molly, and Colin stood in the path of a very angry, red-faced Lord Abercorn and Lady Sissy.

"Sissy," Molly hissed.

"Molly," Sissy jeered. "So, you have returned to London."

"Lord Abercorn, Lady Sissy," Lord Coventry called from the study. "Please return so we can attempt a compromise."

"We do not compromise with the likes of Satan." Molly released Colin and Ophelia, pushing her way into the room.

Abercorn and Lady Sissy were given no opportunity to flee before Colin entered the study and turned to Ophelia.

"Go back to your friends, have them return you home safely." His stare pleaded with her to understand, but every part of her knew she needed to be in that room, she'd just been given the opportunity to question Abercorn about Tilda. "This is a private family matter. You understand, do you not?"

Ophelia felt her head nodding, but truly, she didn't understand at all.

Lord Coventry's voice rose as he commanded everyone to take a seat.

"Please, go home. I will call on you tomorrow." With one final look, he closed the door, shutting her out for a second time in the same day.

She wanted to slam her fist against the door. Scream that she be allowed entrance. Demand Abercorn answer her questions about the night of Tilda's murder.

She was uncertain how long she stood outside the study door, or when Matheson had appeared at her elbow, but instead of doing what she longed to do, she allowed the butler to escort her to the front door.

What was happening in the Coventry study was a family matter, and Ophelia, despite how close she and Colin had become during their travels, was not his family.

CHAPTER 22

COLIN LEANED HIS forehead against the closed study door, wishing with every breath he took that Ophelia could be by his side in the study. No part of him had wanted to shut her out and close the door in her face. He exhaled sharply, waiting to hear her receding footsteps as she fled his family's home.

But he heard nothing.

Not so much as an inhale—and mercifully, not a sob.

If he had, Colin would have ripped the door from its hinges and taken her into his arms, his family and their dubious past be damned.

He no longer wanted her by his side, safe and protected—he *needed* her there.

This, his family's sordid past now coming back to haunt them, was something she shouldn't have to bear witness to. She deserved a man who was above reproach, a gentleman who'd never cast a shadow over her reputation, and a love that would not tarnish her future.

Colin could guarantee her none of that.

His character was forever blemished by his family's past.

While Ophelia was nothing but goodness,

compassion, and caring. She'd sacrificed her future to accompany him to Sheerness, and why? Because Molly, his sometimes addlebrained grandmama, had demanded it?

Colin was more to blame than anyone. He'd allowed it all to happen; their journey, their shared private quarters, and their kiss.

Bloody hell, but he would never regret that.

The feeling of Ophelia wrapped in his arms, held tightly against him…his body surged with heat at the thought.

"Colin?" his father barked. "You may go."

He pushed away from the door, and his shoulders stiffened. "This matter has as much to do with me as it does you, Father. I will stay."

"Bollock and toads!" Molly slapped her knee as Colin moved into the room and took the seat next to his grandmama and across the low table from Abercorn and Lady Sissy. "Lad, these filthy scavengers think ta steal your land—twist'n your father's arm the entire time. I not be let'n 'em get the best of me then, and I sure as a rainstorm on a breezy Somerset night won't be consent'n ta them have'n what belongs ta ye now."

"What is all this about?" Colin looked at his father, who paced before the hearth. "And why is my estate involved?"

"That was my dowry, young man," Lady Sissy seethed, leaning across the table toward Molly. Abercorn cast a restraining arm between the women and pushed Sissy back. "Because of your grandfather— that common free trader—it was taken from my family and given to yours."

"You were stripped of your family lands?" Colin felt a measure of sorrow for the woman.

"That is not exactly how everything happened," the earl grumbled. "The owner was heavily in debt, and a note had been placed on the property with three different gaming hells. The king confiscated the land when the men brought legal action against Abercorn's father. It ended the dispute. He gifted the property, with the title, to the first Earl of Coventry for his unborn son—me. The letters from King George II cannot be disputed."

Lady Sissy shot to her feet. "They can be, and I am!"

"Oh, stuff a roast bird in ye mouth and pipe down, ye—"

"Molly!" Lord Coventry warned. "Lord Abercorn came to talk, nothing more."

Colin eyed the man, remembering all that Ophelia had said—and all she hadn't said. The duke was responsible for Miss Tilda Guthton's death. He had wed the young woman, and she'd faced a tragic fall on what should have been the first night of her wedded life. Ophelia hadn't shared Abercorn's name the night she'd told him of her friend's passing, but there was no doubt this was the man whom she'd spoken of.

"I want my land, or"—Lady Sissy held her handbag before her and riffled around before pulling out a handful of paper—"I will take these directly to the *Gazette* or *The Post* and have them published in tomorrow's edition."

Colin didn't need to see the script on the pages to know they were the missing pages from Porter's book. They'd been stored for safekeeping in his and Molly's rooms above the blacksmith's shop in Sheerness.

His father rubbed the back of his neck. "It will not lead to the return of Hawke Manor, I can assure you, Lady Sissy."

The woman sneered, her lips rising to reveal uneven, yellowed teeth. "Perhaps not, but the truth of your family's past will be revealed. The lot of you are nothing but the descendants of a bar wench and a smuggler."

"My father and his vessel were commissioned by the king himself, and Porter Parnell was ultimately

awarded the title of earl and given land and fortune."
Coventry halted and turned his penetrating stare on
Lady Sissy. "I am proud of my heritage and the
sacrifices my father made to assure his family's future."

Colin shook his head softly, making certain he'd
heard his father correctly. Ramsey Parnell, the second
Earl of Coventry, was *proud* of his father? After all these
years of denial, arguments, and ill will toward Molly and
Porter, his father admitted this?

"Now, I think it best if the pair of you depart
before I collect Molly's cane and allow her at you!"

"Whack 'em both over their empty, pea-shaped
heads, I will," Molly said with a triumphant smile.

"Lord Coventry, I do believe this has all been a
misunderstanding—"

"There has been no misunderstanding." Coventry
stepped around the lounge, closer to Abercorn with
each word. "You will leave this house and never, ever
threaten my family again."

Lady Sissy waved the pages in the air before her.
"I'm taking these directly to *The Post*, I assure you."

"You will do what you must, Lady Sissy." The earl
waved his hand in dismissal. "I have faith that my family
will survive—no, better yet, we shall *thrive*."

Lady Sissy shoved the pages back into her handbag
and clutched it to her chest as if she feared Molly would
rip them from her grasp, yet Molly hadn't so much as
moved a muscle since Ramsey's proclamation.

"Matheson!" The butler opened the door a breath
after the earl's summons. "See Lord Abercorn and Lady
Sissy out, please. Do make certain the entire staff knows
they are not welcome on Coventry property—*any*
Coventry property, including Colin's estate."

"Yes, my lord," Matheson said, gesturing with his
arm for the pair to proceed him out of the study. "This
way, please."

Abercorn bustled from the room with Lady Sissy
following a bit more hesitantly, keeping a close eye on

Molly until she'd crossed the threshold into the hall.

Colin watched his father all but collapse onto the lounge next to Molly.

"Father, I—"

"Close the door, Colin," he commanded, though his voice held none of the steel from a few moments before. When he did as instructed, his father continued. "Sit."

He took the seat across from his father and grandmama in the chair Abercorn had vacated.

His father rested his arm around Molly's shoulders, pulling her in tight. It was the first time Colin had ever witnessed any sense of physical love between mother and son. Colin was struck again by how similar the pair looked, in complexion and demeanor.

"Damn it all, but that felt good," the earl whispered.

"Admitting your pride in Fair Wind?" Colin asked.

"No." His father shook his head. "Finally putting that woman in her place. She's been holding our family's past over my head since I inherited the title. Threatening to expose us to the *ton*—all these years. I should have dealt with her ages ago, but I did not want you growing up under a shadow of sordid gossip and scandal."

"You did this for me?" Colin asked, his eyes round in surprise.

"And your mother," Ramsey admitted. "She wed me not knowing our family's past. I couldn't allow her to be ridiculed by society because I was too much of a coward to admit and embrace the Parnell family history."

Colin looked to his side, reaching out, but his hand met with only empty space. Ophelia should be next to him. She'd had a right to witness the culmination of their adventure—or misadventure, as it were—but he'd thrown her from the room.

"Why were you so against us finding the book?"

"Because then I'd be forced to admit everything—

and I was uncertain I could protect you, Molly, and your mother from society's anger."

"Never cared a whit about those insufferable nobs anyhow," Molly grumbled.

"I know, Mother." Ramsey leaned over and placed a kiss to Molly's forehead. "But I spent so many years denying everything, that I was uncertain how to go about fixing things."

"You could have trusted me with the information." Colin had been a fool, gallivanting about England in search of something his father had never needed. Something his father was very aware existed. The one thing his sire had hoped would never be found. "I could have helped you sort through it all."

"Yes, well, when your grandmama came to me and begged me to allow you to search in Sheerness, I could not deny her request."

"Wait. You knew—" Colin looked between the pair. "You knew I went to Sheerness?"

"Of course. Molly said the trip was important and would very likely determine the future of the Coventry line."

Colin returned his focus to Molly, noting the grin she made no attempt to hide...the same smile she'd had just before begging him to travel to Sheerness with Lady Ophelia as she'd entrusted him with her pendant for good luck.

"Molly?"

"Yes, lad." The satisfied smirk only intensified.

"What do you know of this?" He wanted to know, but at the same time, he didn't want to hear her say the words.

"How else was I ta get ye and that fiery-haired siren alone?" She cocked her head to one side.

"Why would you want us alone in the first place?"

She laughed until she doubled over in a coughing fit. "Why? You think'n I didn't see the way ye stepped between us in the drive that day? Ye wanted ta protect her, even if that meant me cane bash'n your skull, lad."

"I would have done the same for anyone," he insisted.

She shook her head vehemently. "Oh no, Colin, you were protect'n her. Any other time, ye woulda stepped in ta protect me."

Colin clamped his mouth shut, stalling his retort as he pondered her accusation. He'd spent his entire life defending and protecting Molly—from anything and everything that would harm her. He'd spent months each year with her at Tintinhull Court so she wouldn't succumb to loneliness and sorrow. Since her arrival in London, he'd barely left her side—except to travel to Sheerness, which he hadn't thought twice about doing.

"See, Ramsey, the lad is in love, sure as the fish swim in the dark." Molly swatted at his father's arm. "Where did she run off ta?"

"I sent Lady Ophelia home," Colin mumbled.

"Oh, ye foolish lad, ye best be goin' after her before she finds—"

Colin didn't wait for Molly to finish as he sprang from the chair and fled the room. His grandmama was correct, as always. Colin had been wrong to send Ophelia away. His boots thundered down the corridor as he shouted for Matheson to have the stable lad bring around his horse. He only hoped that when he found Ophelia, she'd forgive him.

"Lord Hawke?"

Colin slowed his pace, turning toward the voice coming from an alcove nestled below the grand stairs— the Duke of Abercorn sat on the single bench seat. He didn't appear the sturdy, haughty lord from his father's study, but rather a man who'd lived a long life and was…exhausted.

His chin dipped toward his chest, and at some point, he'd untied his cravat as it hung loosely down the front of his jacket.

"May I have a word with you before my sister and I

depart?"

OPHELIA STALKED IN the shadows outside Colin's family townhouse, avoiding the torches lighting the driveway. It would be highly satisfying to hear the stomp of her kid boots; unfortunately, they made barely any sound. She didn't want Luci and Edith to notice her and demand they deliver her home. Colin was in there, and she needed to secure a way to see him—or she'd wait here in the darkness all night long if she had to.

She settled on biding her time until Abercorn and Lady Sissy departed before demanding to speak with Colin. Truly, she had no urge to remain in a room with Abercorn, to sit across from him and act as if her blood did not boil every time she caught sight of the man. Even surrounded by Colin and his family, she'd be vulnerable.

No, Ophelia would bide her time, and then demand answers from Colin.

Why had he all but ignored her after finding Fair Wind's letter?

Why had he insisted on riding with Montrose and Torrington back to London?

And most importantly, why had he pushed her from the study and closed the door in her face as if she meant nothing to him, and him nothing to her?

If their intimate conversation at the inn and their kiss at the docks had meant nothing to him, then he should have said as much, and she would not pester him again. He owed her nothing. Nothing but the truth behind his actions. After that, they could return to their normal lives; she to the London ballrooms, and he to…whatever he did on a usual day.

Her steps faltered, the toe of her boot catching on a slightly elevated cobblestone, and she nearly tumbled to the ground. Pacing in the dark was far too risky. Thankfully, Ophelia caught herself and settled for tapping the toe of her boot, her arms crossed. She kept her narrowed stare on the door, pushing the many colliding thoughts from her mind. They created a din of noise louder than the racket from a hundred carriages. This might very well be her last chance to speak with Colin—she needs must have her wits about her if she meant to gain the many answers she sought.

There wasn't even time to think about Abercorn and his connection to Colin and his family.

Since when was exposing Abercorn not her main priority?

A jolt of guilt coursed through her. Tilda, and bringing down the man responsible for her death, had been Ophelia's main focus since that tragic night. It should *still* be of the utmost import to her—yet, standing here, in the Coventry drive, she longed only to speak with Colin.

Perhaps she should risk it all and knock on the door. Matheson was a kind enough butler, and would certainly not turn her away. If she could only implore him to fetch Colin for her—they would speak, and she could return home, knowing she'd done all in her power to help him, even if her assistance was no longer required or wanted.

Closure. It was about seeing their situation through to the end.

She and her friends had yet to gain closure with regards to Tilda's death, but Ophelia's situation with Colin was not completely out of her control. Yes, she had been curtly dismissed and escorted from his home, but she would not believe it was what he wanted. Not until he looked her in the eyes and told her to go, to leave and never return.

Ophelia yelped when the door opened, and Lady Sissy exited—alone.

The older woman glanced at her carriage parked close to the end of the circular drive. Molly obviously hadn't gotten to the woman with her cane as her hair was still perfectly pinned, and her gown without so much as a wrinkle. The torches positioned on either side of the front door cast enough light to see the woman clearly. She was certainly older than Abercorn by many years, but the resemblance was unmistakable. Her hair had turned from brown to coarse grey, and her skin was sallow. Except for at Oliver's Book Shoppe, Ophelia had never seen the woman in public. She didn't remember noticing Lady Sissy at Tilda's wedding or the following celebrations. If she'd been present, she'd kept to herself and away from the guests.

Yet, she was the daughter of a duke, just as Ophelia was. Why hadn't she wed in her youth, started a family, and created her own home?

As if sensing Ophelia's scrutiny, Lady Sissy turned toward her, spotting her in the shadows.

"Lady Ophelia Fletcher." Her lip turned up in a sneer as she joined Ophelia in the shadows. Unease drained every ounce of anger from her as Ophelia watched the woman move slowly toward her as if she viewed Ophelia as her prey. "I thought you'd hurried home after being dismissed by Lord Hawke." When Ophelia didn't immediately respond, Lady Sissy's brow rose. "Oh, has a cat escaped with your tongue? I had heard you were prone to fainting."

Ophelia suppressed the tightening in her chest. The woman was only baiting her, trying to stir up a reaction because she had pent-up rage.

"Lady Sissy. I can assure you, I am not on the cusp of fain—"

"Pity…" She pressed her finger to her chin and looked Ophelia over from head to toe.

"What are you doing here?"

"I could ask you the same thing," Lady Sissy sneered, taking a step closer to Ophelia. "You and your *friends* seem to pop up and stick your nose in business that doesn't concern you."

Ophelia glanced over Lady Sissy's shoulder as Luci

and Edith exited their carriage that had been waiting on the opposite side of the circular drive from the Abercorn town coach. Satisfaction coursed through Ophelia knowing that Lady Sissy would be irked all the more to see the full trio of women popping up yet again.

"I find it quite peculiar that the more I try to be rid of you all, the more you seem to be underfoot." Lady Sissy pivoted toward the front door and continued pacing. "I thought I'd be rid of the lot of you after that chit was taken care of, but no, then Franny thought himself *in love* with the gangly, raven-haired hellion. Unacceptable."

"Tilda?" Ophelia's voice rose sharply. "What do you know of Tilda?"

Lady Sissy turned back toward Ophelia. The twin pools of light from the torches surrounding her. Her eyes were aglow with—pleasure? Her chin notched up, and her sneer transformed into a genuine smile, yet nothing but apprehension filled Ophelia.

"My brother—may the good Lord forgive me for saying—is a forlorn, senseless, disappointment of a man. He makes promises, only to break them when another light skirt catches his fancy." She shook her head as if what she'd just shared were truly tragic. "Instead of gaining back what belonged to our family— what belonged to *me*—he focused on this chit or that chit."

"Tilda was an innocent, intelligent, kind spirit, not a light skirt."

Lady Sissy waved her hand. "That is of no consequence, now is it? She is gone, and once again, my dear brother—heartbroken and desperate for attention—is devoted to me."

Ophelia blinked rapidly, trying to understand what Lady Sissy meant by all this.

"But then that raven-haired harlot caught his notice," Lady Sissy scoffed. "I thought her safe enough because she was wed, but no, the woman took Franny from me—and again, his promises to me went by the wayside."

Lady Downshire? She must be speaking of Lord Torrington's stepmother who had been Abercorn's mistress.

"Thankfully, the woman disappeared, making it far easier for me." Lady Sissy's demeanor once again shifted, her eyes widening. "But imagine my surprise when yet another dark-haired hoyden cast a wicked spell on my Franny."

A spot of movement caught Ophelia's notice behind Lady Sissy. Luci and Edith crept up the drive, coming ever closer to Lady Sissy, who was so consumed with her own ranting and raving that she didn't notice the women approaching her from behind.

"Do you know what happened to Tilda?" Ophelia needed to keep the woman talking. If there was any hope of finding out the truth—that Abercorn had pushed Tilda to her death—it seemed Lady Sissy might have it. "Please, tell me what happened to my friend."

Lady Sissy cackled, throwing her head back, the disturbing sound echoing in the night. "Did you know Franny was planning an entire year traveling the Continent with his latest bride? It was then I realized the chit had to go. Wedding and bedding Miss Tilda Guthton would not satisfy my brother. No, he wanted a wife and a family. Where would that leave me? What would I have after he produced a horde of heirs and spares with that broodmare?"

Her glare snapped to Ophelia.

"Alone," she seethed. "I would be alone, forever, with no home of my own. All because of the Earl of Coventry."

"But I thought you blamed your brother?"

Ophelia realized her mistake when the woman took a hurried step toward her, her hand rising as if to strike Ophelia, but she halted.

"Francis is a weak, sniveling man." Her hand

lowered back to her side. "If I had been born a man, I would have returned our family's property immediately. However, it is never too late."

"What do you mean?" Ophelia kept her eyes trained on Sissy—and not Edith and Luci, who motioned for her to keep the older woman talking. "Hawke Manor has belonged to the Coventry Earldom for two generations now."

The conversation was moving swiftly between topics, but Ophelia needed to steer it back to Tilda.

"While Franny did not agree with my methods, I have provided the earl with enough reasons to return the property to me—or risk ruination for his family."

That could mean only one thing. "You stole Fair Wind's pages from the box in Sheerness?"

Sissy clutched her handbag close to her side. "Yes, but they will not be with me long, as I am on my way to *The Post*. They will be giddy with pleasure to have such scandalous knowledge of Coventry's past. He—and his family—will never be welcome in polite society again."

"How does that lead to the return of your family's land?"

She shrugged, allowing her bag to fall to her side. "It is of little import. Lord Coventry, the dowager countess—as well as Lord Hawke—will be tarnished. The baron will never find a suitable bride. I suppose our families will be even then."

"Abercorn will find another bride," Ophelia said, hoping to bring their conversation back to Tilda. "It will only be a matter of time before he falls in love once more, and you are cast aside like you feared when he wed my friend."

Lady Sissy shook her head, "Tsk-tsk, Lady Ophelia. When will you learn I am a very resourceful woman? Determined, much like you and your dear friends. I will handle the woman much like I did Miss Tilda."

"You killed Tilda?" Ophelia asked on a shocked exhale.

"I cannot say I killed her, but the fall certainly did. I only helped her along."

"How?" Ophelia noticed Luci clutching Edith's arm several paces behind Sissy as they listened in abject horror. "Luci saw Abercorn flee at the top of the stairs."

"My brother could not harm a fly, I assure you," Lady Sissy spit out. She clamped her mouth shut, as if realizing she'd said too much. But with a nonchalant shrug, Sissy scrutinized Ophelia once more, obviously coming to the conclusion she posed no threat to the woman. "You and your friends were all cozy in my mother's library, talking as senseless chits do. It was not hard to hurry up the stairs, donned in my robe, slip my dear brother a sleeping tonic, and return to have a private conversation with the new Duchess of Abercorn before she joined my brother in his chambers. But the woman would not listen to reason. In fact, she outright refused my request to discourage Franny from leaving England on their trip. The chit thought I had no say in my brother's life. She was wrong...and it was very advantageous on my part that my brother still owned the matching robe I bought him during the previous Christmastide."

"Sissy! What have you done?"

Ophelia turned toward the front door, now thrown open with a gaping Lord Abercorn exiting the threshold and Colin close behind.

CHAPTER 23

"...BUT THE WOMAN would not listen to reason. In fact, she outright refused my request to discourage Franny from leaving England on their trip. The chit thought I had no say in my brother's life. She was wrong...and it was very advantageous on my part that my brother still owned the matching robe I bought him during the previous Christmastide."

Abercorn's entire body tensed where he stood before Colin, and he rushed over the threshold.

The older man stumbled to a halt only a few feet from his sister. "Sissy! What have you done?"

Ophelia and Lady Sissy turned to face them as Abercorn took the final steps and grasped Sissy's arms.

Colin stumbled himself when he took in Ophelia's terrified stare, her hands clutching her throat.

The gravity of the situation sank in, and a void opened in his chest. He'd sent her from his home, only to further put her in jeopardy when Lady Sissy sank her venomous claws into her. Colin should have departed the study with her, delivered her home safely, and returned to his father's townhouse. Instead, he'd been too consumed with his own troubles, his own need to discover what his family had kept from him all these years.

He'd failed Lady Ophelia again.

Colin stood helplessly by as Lady Edith and Lady Lucianna rushed to Ophelia's side, the trio wrapping their arms securely around one another. These were the people who were worthy of a woman like Ophelia. They cared about her, thought of her above all else—they deserved her, and Ophelia deserved them.

What Lady Ophelia didn't deserve was a man like Colin—a man willing to push her aside for things that were nowhere near as important as she was. Trivial details that, in the larger scheme of life, meant nothing to Colin. Yes, they had a jaded past, but that did not determine his future or how he chose to live it.

Ophelia did…or at least, Colin longed to make her such.

"Sissy," Lord Abercorn demanded, putting his finger under his sister's chin and raising her eyes to meet his. "Did you push Tilda, my dearest love, down the stairs?"

"I—well—"

"Do not lie to me!" His hand still held her arm firmly, and he shook her. The woman's teeth clacked together. "Tell me what you did!"

"She was not right for you," Sissy stammered. "I am the only woman you need."

Abercorn released his hold, then pushed her away and turned to Lady Ophelia and her friends, still clinging to one another. "Lady Edith, Lady Lucianna, Lady Ophelia…you must believe I loved Tilda with all my heart. I know there were many years between us, but that did not diminish our capacity to love one another. She was to be my duchess"—his voice broke on the word and his eyes pooled with tears—"was to give me the family I always longed for—"

"I am your family, Franny," Sissy called. "I love you…it has always been you and me."

"I begged you for years to let your anger and resentment go, to find a husband who would make you happy, but you refused my advice at every turn." He turned sharply toward his sister, pinning her with a steely glare. "You are nothing to me," he sighed, his shoulders caving in. "I loved Tilda, and you took her from me, just as you've taken everything from me over the years. I have nothing more to say to you." Next, he addressed Colin. "Send for the magistrate. I will have my wife's murderer sent to the Tower."

"Franny, no!" Sissy fell to her knees, her scream ripping through the cold night air as her handbag tumbled to the ground, forgotten.

Without a second look for his sister, Abercorn nodded to Ophelia and her friends and started for his waiting carriage. He didn't pause or hesitate for even a second before climbing inside and taking off.

Colin envied the man, to be able to rub his hands together and, just like that, walk away from the situation.

"You...you did this!" Sissy pointed her finger in Colin's direction. "If it weren't for you, I would have kept my Franny close and had my land returned."

He glanced over his shoulder to see Molly and his father had arrived to witness Abercorn's departure.

Colin stepped toward Sissy, but Molly sprang from the steps before his father could stop her.

"Me?" Molly strode forth, barely using her cane as she navigated the dim drive toward Sissy. "Ye killed a woman—and for what? A crumble'n estate manor and cropland? You could not convince me then ta return the land, and ye shan't convince me now. My grandson—Colin—he is a fine lad, an honorable lord, and he deserves all that's been given ta him, just as me Fair Wind earned his Earldom and fortune by serve'n the king."

His father set his hand on Colin's shoulder, stopping him from stepping between the women. "Son, allow Mother her say," Coventry sighed. "She's been quieted for too many years."

Instead of interfering with the older women, Colin

moved to Lady Ophelia's side where she and her friends huddled close. He'd thought them terrified a moment before, but when he stepped closer, it was relief he noticed from them all. They weren't huddled close to protect one another, they were supporting each other.

"I should'a thumped ye over the head years ago when I had the chance, mighta given ye an ounce of sense in that addled brain of yours." Molly lifted her cane high. "I suppose it ain't too late."

His father signaled for the two waiting footmen, and they sprang into action, taking Lady Sissy under the arms and guiding her back into the house. He collected his mother and followed, leaving Colin alone with the trio of young women. Holding one another tightly, they murmured softly to each other. In that moment, Colin was the outsider, listening in on a conversation he had no right to hear. But he was helpless to walk away and give them privacy to reconcile the loss of their friend. He was a part of this. As much as he felt otherwise, Colin was inexplicitly linked to Ophelia and her friends. He too had suffered at Lady Sissy's hands. The years of family strife were solely due to that woman, not because Colin's father despised his grandpapa.

In a way, the earl had spent years sacrificing for his family, just as Fair Wind had sacrificed before him.

None of this would have been resolved without Ophelia. There would be no shining light after a lifetime of doubt had it not been for her courageous nature. Even now, Ophelia appeared to be the one consoling her friends. If Colin possessed even a tiny portion of her dauntless daring, he would have set out years before to mend his family's conflict. Instead, it had taken a woman like Ophelia to show him how to accomplish what needed to be done.

Bloody hell, but he could not imagine a day without her by his side.

It was hard to believe it had only been that morning they'd awoken at the inn in Sheerness and went in search of his family's truths. She had utterly taken over his life, and Colin was uncertain he could go on without her. When they'd set out on *her* adventure, she'd been lost and searching for something of her own. Now, she was *his* compass.

OPHELIA BREATHED IN deeply, the scent of Luci's lavender soap and Edith's choice lemon perfume mingling to fill her with a deep sense of rightness. She was exactly where she belonged, with her friends there to support her. She thought she could do everything on her own, break away from Luci and Edith, prove she was more than the sum of her parts, a woman independent of her friends.

But she'd been wrong. They needn't conquer things on their own to prove their worth. They were friends, first and foremost. Their friendship was based on love, understanding, and loyalty. Luci and Edith had come back for her, and when they'd not found her where she should have been, they'd set out to locate her. Not to bring her back or take over his adventure, but to offer their assistance. Ophelia had done everything on her own, she'd been responsible for luring the information from Sissy.

She held Luci and Edith close, each confused and conflicted by Sissy's confession. Ophelia had little doubt they'd each be reeling for days to come. They'd been wrong, so inexplicably wrong in their belief that Abercorn was responsible for Tilda's death. They'd targeted an innocent man.

Lifting her head from Luci's midnight hair, Ophelia noted Colin standing a few feet away, his hands tucked deep into his trouser pockets as he attempted to give them a moment together. Her heart tugged, and she pulled away from her friends. They willingly let her go, and she hurried to Colin, wrapping her arms around his neck and lifting up on her tiptoes to place a gentle kiss to his lips. His hands encircled her waist and held her close.

Ophelia pulled back and stared into his dark green eyes, shrouded in fear. But what had he to be fearful of?

"Thank you," she mumbled.

"For what?" His brow furrowed, and his hold on her loosened. "Lady Sissy could have hurt you, and it would have been all my fault."

In response, Ophelia did the only thing she could think to do, she tightened her arms around his neck and pulled him down toward her, pushing her body close to him. "No." She shook her head, uncertain what she was saying no to. This moment—this was the *moment*—and she needed him to hear her. "You showed me I could do things on my own. I did not need to follow others, remain in the shadows while everyone around me lived. You asked me to accompany you to Sheerness because Molly demanded it, but I think you had other reasons for bringing me."

She released him and scooped up Lady Sissy's forgotten handbag and held it out to him.

"I think this, or at least what's inside, belongs to you." Ophelia gave him a nod, pushing him to take the bag. "Go on, take it."

His eyes searched hers, and Ophelia only hoped he saw what she did. She felt whole, fulfilled, and invincible when she had him by her side. It was those exact things she wanted him to feel, as well, even if it wasn't because of her.

"Lady Ophelia," he said before pausing to clear his throat. "Ophelia, since the moment I saw you stand up to Molly, even with her cane held high above your head, I knew I needed you—by my side and in life."

Tears welled in her eyes. She blinked to hold them back, but one escaped and trailed down her cheek.

Colin leaned forward and kissed along its path, stopping the drop from falling from her chin.

"My lady, I think it best I tell you something. Now, before any further surprises present themselves."

She couldn't help but laugh, a quiet teasing sound that filled her with such contentment and ease. There was little guessing what Colin would say next, but Ophelia knew, deep down, it would alter her life far more than what they'd experienced thus far.

"What is it, my lord?" She kept him close, refusing to give him any opportunity to pull away from her. "Colin…"

"I fear I am in love with you."

"You fear?"

"Yes, I fear. Because my love for you puts me at a severe disadvantage, my lady."

"And why is that?"

He took a deep breath and leaned close, their lips all but touching. "I will do anything, agree to anything, to have you close. You can see how that might—"

"You think I aim to take advantage of your love for me?" she asked. When he only nodded, she continued. "It is a sorry state we find ourselves in then, Colin, for my circumstances may be far more dire."

"How is that?" His breath cascaded along her cheek, and he tensed. "Tell me what I need do to—"

"Because I love you, too," she confessed.

His brow rose in shock, and he pulled from her hold, pushing her to arm's length as he searched her face for any sign she was jesting.

But Ophelia wasn't joking in the slightest. She'd held and hugged her friends, but she longed to have Colin's arms around her. She'd needed his comforting embrace when she learned of Sissy's part in Tilda's death.

It had been only Colin she'd wanted in that moment.

Ophelia did not fight to bring him close once more, but took the opportunity to take in all of him—and sure enough, her love was mirrored in his eyes.

She couldn't help but wonder if Luci and Edith had experienced this same life-changing moment with Montrose and Torrington.

Could it be that she'd found her forever love, too?

"Ophelia?" Luci called.

She'd forgotten Luci and Edith still stood in the drive behind them.

With a smile bright enough to light the dark evening, she turned to face her friends, her hand finding Colin's in the space that separated them.

The cold night air blew against her face as she and Colin, hand-in-hand, stood before Luci and Edith.

"I think it best Edith and I return home now," Luci said, her stare remaining on Colin. "What shall I tell your parents? I am certain they will be worried when I arrive home without you."

Ophelia hadn't thought about how worried they'd be—and probably had been since that morning. "I will be home shortly, and I will explain everything, Luci. Will you tell them that?"

"*We* will be there shortly," Colin corrected at her side.

"I can trust you to see her home safely?" Edith asked.

"Of course," Colin issued a curt bow. "It is best you both hurry out of the cold. I am certain Torrington and Montrose would have me strung up in Hyde Park if either of you were to become ill."

Ophelia released Colin's hand and stepped forward, giving both women a quick hug to reassure them that she'd be fine and would be home soon.

"I think it best we visit Tilda's parents on the morrow and let them know what we found." Luci's return to her no-nonsense ways should have been expected. "They deserve to know before all of London finds out."

"I agree." Ophelia nodded, returning to Colin. "But for tonight, we deserve a few hours to allow Sissy's confession and Abercorn's declaration of love to sink in. We've thought for over a year—lived in fear of something similar happening to each of us—that every man we encountered had the opportunity to harm us or another young woman. Abercorn loved Tilda, and if her words on her wedding night were true, she loved him, as well. Tonight, I will sleep soundly knowing this."

Edith stepped forward and wrapped her arms around Ophelia. The woman's blond curls blocked Ophelia's sight, but she was certain she saw Luci brush a tear from her eye.

"Now, hurry home, the both of you," Ophelia said sternly.

The women hurried to their waiting carriage and set off, Ophelia giving them a small wave as they pulled out of sight.

"My lord, my lady?" the butler called behind them. "The dowager and Lord Coventry have requested your presences inside."

"Shall we?" she asked, looking up at Colin. Her heart stumbled as his tongue darted out to moisten his lower lip.

He ran his hand through his hair as his gaze settled on her. "Ophelia, may I—"

"There will be time later to talk privately, Colin." In truth, she was scared to hear what he had to say. Would he take back his confession of love? Would their mutual love not be enough? If there were other factors that would make their relationship impossible, Ophelia didn't want to think about them until tomorrow—or the day after. "Let us not keep your grandmother waiting."

She didn't allow him time for a response as she slipped her hand into the crook of his elbow and started for the front door. It seemed as if hours had passed since he'd pushed her from the study and closed the door in her face, causing her to flee to the driveway. It had probably only been minutes, but more than a lifetime of changes had occurred.

The truth surrounding Tilda's death had been learned. Lord Coventry had exited the townhouse with Molly on his arm. Her friends had whispered their words of praise for her courage. Colin had told her he loved her.

And, possibly the most important occurrence, she'd confessed her love in return.

The stark truth was that she'd felt the blossoms of love since he happened upon her napping in the Atholl gardens with Fair Wind's book open on her lap and dreams of fair-haired, tanned, swashbuckling adventurers clouding her thoughts.

The butler showed them into the study, the same room Colin had denied her entrance to earlier, but now he escorted her by his side across the threshold to face his father and grandmother. Lady Sissy was nowhere to be seen.

The dowager and Lord Coventry made an unnerving pair.

What they probably didn't realize, was that Ophelia had faced far more daunting people—and situations—in her short life.

These past events had thrown her life into chaos and uncertainty.

But this situation, these people, did nothing to deter Ophelia. For once, she was completely confident in her choices, her feelings, and what she wanted for the future.

And he stood at her side.

Ophelia straightened her shoulders when Molly set her hands on her hips and scrutinized her from head to toe. She would not allow the older woman to intimidate her, even though she sensed her cheeks reddening and her heartbeat increasing. Collapsing under the woman's stare was not an option, especially if Ophelia sought a future with Colin.

"I see the lad gave ye me pendant," she said.

Ophelia grabbed the necklace with her free hand,

its warmth infusing her with a feeling she'd never known before. All the while, she knew the time to return the necklace was now. It belonged to Molly, a gift from her true love, encapsulating all that he'd sacrificed for his family.

Colin placed his hand on hers at his elbow, halting her from removing the pendant.

Molly paced toward them, and Lord Coventry stood from his place in a chair before the hearth, uncertain what the woman's course of action was.

In response to Molly's continued perusal, Ophelia's chin lifted.

"I have one question." Her eyes sparked with each word as she moved her intense stare to Colin. Ophelia released a sigh, as it seemed Molly now focused on her grandson, but too soon, her stare swung back to her. "Lady Ophelia Fletcher…"

"Yes, Lady Coventry." It was her proper name as the dowager countess, but it didn't fit the formidable, stoop-shouldered woman before her.

"What, may I ask, are your intentions with me grandson?"

Her intentions…with Colin?

Ophelia fought the smile that threatened to overtake her as the woman's stare softened and she gathered her thoughts.

"Well, my lady," Ophelia started with poise. "My intentions are to make an honest man of your grandson, Lord Hawke. Bare him a horde of fiery-haired hellion daughters, and a perhaps one or two fair-haired, broad-shouldered sons. Love him until my last breath. And make certain he never wants for anything."

Colin tensed beside her. They hadn't spoken of marriage—let alone children.

Lord Coventry chuckled as he moved to the sideboard and poured three tumblers of amber-colored liquid.

But it was Molly who Ophelia kept coming back to.

She hadn't moved, hadn't uttered a word, and Ophelia feared she'd said the wrong thing. Likely, she'd crossed the line when she mentioned fiery-haired hellions.

Ophelia cared not a whit.

The woman had asked, and Ophelia had spoken the truth.

Her truth.

Her vision for their future.

CHAPTER 24

COLIN HELD OPHELIA close to his side, as Molly stood stock-still, allowing the words to sink in. Hell, he'd need a month of Sundays to truly understand everything Ophelia had proclaimed. She not only loved him, but she wanted to be at his side forevermore. She'd spoken the exact words he'd been thinking and had prepared to say himself—yet she'd proclaimed them first.

"My love for him has naught to do with the devil nor any sorceress enchantment I've cast over him. If anything, Molly, he has ensnared me in *his* spell."

Even if she were proven the sinister being Molly had accused her of during their first meeting, he would thank the devil himself for bringing Ophelia into his life.

If it hadn't been for her, Lady Sissy might have torn his family completely apart as his father tried to keep their family's past hidden, and Molly sought to prove her husband's honor. Without Ophelia, he would have given up hope, and never would have traveled to Sheerness because the book would have never been found.

"Molly," Colin said, his voice gravelly as he fought to keep his own emotions under control. "If it weren't for Ophelia—her wit and many sacrifices—I would have given up hope. So many times, I was prepared to return from Sheerness with nothing, but it was Ophelia who reminded me that all hope was not lost and that we needed to keep searching."

His father returned to the group, handing each a tumbler. Ophelia released his arm and took her glass, eyeing the liquid suspiciously.

Lord Coventry held his glass high, smiling at Colin, Ophelia, and lastly, Molly. "To the woman who put our family demons to rest, brought us all together as we should have been from the start, and put a hex on the most formidable dowager countess."

"She did what?" Molly screeched, her stare darting between Colin and Ophelia. "She cannot—"

"To the woman who taught me how to live—one misadventure at a time," Colin said, raising his own glass. "May our next adventure prove fruitful."

"Next adventure?" Ophelia stared up at him with rounded eyes, her confidence from a moment before slipping slightly. No one else in the room would notice, but Colin did.

"My dear." Colin handed his glass back to his father before plucking Ophelia's tumbler from her trembling fingers. Coventry gladly took the glass from Colin. "It was you who asked for my hand in marriage…and I will not allow you to forget it. You promised to make an honest man of me. There is paperwork to be drawn up, arrangements to be discussed, and my dowry to be settled on."

Ophelia laughed, her eyes lighting with a look of love he was certain she saw in his, as well.

Molly cackled before doubling over in a coughing fit.

Straightening, the older woman held her glass high, clinked his father's tumbler, and they both drank. "Should'a known it would take a siren ta capture Colin's heart." Molly shook her head. "He is far too much like your father, Ramsey."

"How so, Mother?"

"He needs a strong woman ta guide him," Molly said. "Make him the man he was always destined ta be."

Colin pulled Ophelia into his arms, ignoring his father and grandmama as they departed the room. The door closed behind them, and the latch clicked into place.

He didn't know what the future held, where they would go from here, or how they would convince Lord Atholl of their love. However, there was one thing Colin had no doubt of—Ophelia would be his. And he would be hers.

He didn't care where his destiny lay, as long as Ophelia was next to him.

If society found out about the Coventry family's past, Colin knew, without asking, Ophelia would stand by him. She was not the follower she'd always thought herself to be. No, she just hadn't found the situation—or person—worth standing up for.

Ophelia would stand up for him, speak up to protect him, and never allow anyone to speak ill of his family.

And he would dedicate the rest of his life to doing the same for her—starting with convincing her father to allow them to wed.

If there were an emotion deeper than love, adoration, and unwavering commitment; it would be how he felt for Lady Ophelia.

THE WAS ONLY she and Colin in the room—if anyone else lingered, Ophelia did not notice or care. She looked up into Colin's green eyes and smiling face. Had he ever appeared so happy and…at ease? In all the time she'd known him, he'd always had an invisible weight of sorts on his shoulders. It weighed him down far more than he realized, and Ophelia only understood the magnitude of it now that it was gone. He'd lived his life under the burden of his feuding family, always at a loss for where he fit in and searching for ways to stifle the fighting.

Finally, the war between his grandmother and father had come to an end.

It was time for Colin to find out who he was and what he wanted in life.

...and he wanted her.

His finger lifted her chin when she made to look away, bringing her stare back to him. "Ophelia?"

The mere sight of him, his hair disheveled, his shirt wrinkled from their travels, and his satisfied grin had her heart racing. She could end every day looking up at him, just like this.

"Yes," she said with a breathless sigh.

"You are brave." He paused to place a kiss on her forehead. "You are fearless." He placed a kiss on the tip of her nose, and Ophelia stifled a giggle. "You are smart." He kissed her chin. "You are beautiful." He dipped low and pressed a kiss to her chest, just above her beating heart and Molly's pendant nestled against her bosom. "And you are utterly enchanting."

Her chin shook, and her breath caught in her chest. They were words she'd never believed would be spoken to her—about her. Especially by a man she'd come to love and cherish beyond anything. Love and happiness had found Edith and Luci—and Ophelia did not hold their contentment against them, even though she'd never suspected it would one day be hers.

Ophelia longed to tell him it was *because* of him she was all those things. Only a fortnight ago, she would have kept that to herself, never uttered the words, but she could not allow this moment to pass without saying all she had to.

"It is because of your trust and belief in me that I am brave, that I squashed the fear that resided in me and overcame the doubt that plagued me my entire life.

Before you, I did not shine, I was trapped within myself, living a life and following a path that others set for me." She paused, determined to say everything. "But not anymore. My destiny is mine to grasp"—she took hold of his arms above the elbow—"and I choose you, Colin."

There were a million little things she'd wanted to tell him a thousand times during their short acquaintance, like that he made her feel like more than she'd ever longed to be. It was odd that most of their time together had happened away from London and everything that was familiar to her. She'd defined herself as Luci's and Edith's friend, Tilda's champion through her writing for the *Mayfair Confidential*, a duke's perfect, demure daughter, and a confirmed bookworm, but she was far more than those things. She was Ophelia, with or without being all the things she'd thought herself to be, and what others expected of her.

"You've shown me that adventure does not lie solely between the pages of a book. Passion is not reserved for the fanciful tales of old. And love is not meant only for Lucianna and Edith, but for me, as well, if only I am courageous enough to accept it—and remain steadfast in my determination to hold on to it."

Her grip tightened, proving her point that she was never letting him go. Not today, certainly not tomorrow, and most definitely not years from that moment.

"No matter the misadventures to come—and I can assure you, there will be many if I have anything to say on the matter"—he paused, his laugh unforced and relaxed—"you will be at my side. There is no other woman I'd rather be deserted in the Sahara with. No other lady who could lead me safely through the viper pits that are most London soirées. And no other woman I'd trust if faced by a panther in the Amazon rainforest."

Ophelia had to laugh along with him. "I can assure you, there is quite a difference between a ballroom and the wilds of the Amazon. I do not think the two are comparable, my lord."

"Have you ever been to the Amazon?"

"No, but—"

"Well, I have been to my share of London balls, and I can assure you, they are quite daunting indeed."

"Then it is very beneficial that you have selected such an undaunted debutante to have at your side."

"Debutante?" His brow rose in question. "Certainly not, my lady, before long, you will be Lady Hawke."

"We have yet to—"

The door crashed open behind them, slamming against its hinges, causing both Ophelia and Colin to whip around toward the door. For a brief moment, she feared Lady Sissy had escaped the footman and come back, but the thump of her cane against the polished wood floor announced Molly's arrival.

"Enough with the bloody details or the pair of ye will still be yap'n inta next year," she shouted, tapping her cane with each word. "You love me lad, and me lad loves ye. There be nothin' else ta speak of. Kiss the damned woman, Colin!"

"Yes, Grandmama," Colin said, turning back to face Ophelia and gathering her into his arms. "With pleasure."

And kiss her he did.

EPILOGUE

One last word for young women of the ton: *Hold tight to*
your determination.
Remain undaunted and steadfast, no matter what life
presents you with.
Life is not about becoming what others want you to be, but
about trusting your worth, finding your true self, and taking
chances—even with a perfect stranger.
Lastly, pay close heed to things you are naturally drawn to;
be it person or possession.
Here, you will find your path, passion, and purpose.
Fare thee well, good readers of the Gazette.
-Mayfair Confidential, London Daily Gazette

EVERY EYE IN the dining hall was on Ophelia as she
slowly walked down the length of table as she greeted
guests and accepted their words of good tidings. It
would only last a few short minutes—though it was a
time when all attention was on her. She'd never believed
she longed for a time when she was the center of
everyone's thoughts.

Glancing down the table, he nodded to her, giving
her the courage to continue on.

She paused by Lucianna, Ophelia clutched Molly's

pendant close and leaned down to whisper in her ear, "It is lovely to see your mother and family."

Lucianna turned to look up at Ophelia—and she was taken aback by the happiness and warmth in Luci's smile. "Yes, well, my mother and siblings will be staying with Montrose—for the time being."

Or until Lucianna's father relents and approves of her betrothal to Montrose, Ophelia added silently to herself. Not that his disapproval would stop Montrose from taking Luci as wife. They'd agreed on a Christmas wedding, and all hoped Lord Camden would have a change of heart by that time and reunite with his family.

"Ophelia," Edith called from across the table. "I do hope you can spare a few moments after our meal."

"Of course," she conceded with a laugh. "My father's library?"

When Edith nodded and Lucianna laughed, Montrose and Torrington shared a look of question; however, Ophelia and her friends only ignored the men's inquiries. It was a tradition they would continue until each was happily, safely, unequivocally wed—in honor of Tilda, in a way. They would disappear into the library to speak in hushed tones and laugh about the night to come. This will be Ophelia's first wedded night. At Christmas, it would be Luci's.

They'd even invited Lady Prudence and Lady Chastity to join them.

Torrington would certainly not relish his younger sisters being part of such an intimate conversation; however, friends were friends.

And Ophelia was honored to call Chastity and Pru friend.

"I can hardly contain myself and finish our meal." Edith giggled, giving her betrothed a sideways glance. "I most assuredly have things to speak of."

For once, it wasn't Ophelia's face that flushed scarlet, but Edith's.

It would be an utter lie if she didn't admit she was

looking forward to hearing the scandalous tidbits Edith had to share about the marriage bed—though the woman was no more wedded than Lucianna at that moment.

With a wink, Ophelia continued down the table and nestled close to Colin's side, resuming her seat at the banquet table.

Her husband.

Colin Parnell, Lord Hawke, heir to the Coventry Earldom.

The mere thought that they'd met and wed with such haste still had her mind swirling, but Colin was always there to make certain she remained upright with the frenzy surrounding them.

She glanced around the crowded room; row after row of finely dressed men and women ate, drank, and laughed together as course after exquisite course of delicate dishes were set before them.

Ophelia and Colin, flanked by Edith and Lord Torrington on one side, and Lucianna and Montrose on the other, sampled the savory and sweet plates placed before them as all in attendance celebrated the blessed joining of Baron Hawke to Lady Ophelia Fletcher in wedded bliss.

Lady Hawke.

It was quite simply the only decision she'd made in recent months that no one could dare call a misadventure.

No, everything about their whirlwind betrothal and morning wedding in her family's gardens behind the Atholl townhouse was exactly as it was fated to be.

Even Molly had given her blessing—by way of some obscure and intimidating dance ritual that could have as easily been her placing a hex on Ophelia and Colin's entire bloodline. Yet, that did not matter. If Ophelia were cursed, as Colin's grandmother had once thought, then there was no other person she'd rather share a life of misadventure with than the man at her side.

"You are smiling again, dear wife," Colin whispered close to her ear. "If you keep this up, everyone will think you deliriously happy and satisfied in love."

"And if that is exactly what I want everyone in this room—and all of England—to think?" She looked up at him from under lowered lashes with a hint of a smirk caressing her lips. "Is that so awful?"

He placed a kiss to her forehead. "Certainly not; however, we cannot allow all these people to assume we have wedded life figured out. They will demand to know our secrets."

"We will never share our secrets to finding wedded bliss." Ophelia shook her head gravely. "Not unless they hold a burning candle to my toes."

His brow knitted and his tone turned serious. "That is all it would take?"

"Well, that and the promise of plum pudding!"

"Sweets for my sweet?" he said with a chuckle.

Their intimate conversation was interrupted when someone cleared their throat, drawing his and her attention away from one another to the man standing before their table. Ophelia had been so consumed with her new husband that she hadn't noticed Lord Abercorn approach them.

The older man bowed deeply. "May I offer my sincere congratulations on your union, Lord and Lady Hawke. I am ever so pleased to be included in such an intimate gathering."

Ophelia smiled at the man, his cheeks blossoming pink at her attention. Her friends, Edith and Luci, had been as surprised as Abercorn at the invitation extended to the duke, who they'd thought only a few short weeks ago was responsible for Tilda's death. But much had changed with Lady Sissy's confession that night outside Colin's father's townhouse—not only had the woman confessed to pushing Tilda down the stairs, but also to poisoning Lord Abercorn's two other wives.

They were all victims of Lady Sissy's need to control and exert power over all who surrounded her.

"It is an honor to have you among us, my lord." Ophelia spoke each word with a deep-seated conviction and new appreciation for the man. He'd loved Tilda, as they all had, and she'd been taken all too soon. But Ophelia and her friends hadn't been the only ones to grieve her passing. "I do hope your sister is settling in at The Retreat."

Colin placed his hand on the small of Ophelia's back as if to show his support.

Abercorn nodded several times. "She is adjusting to life in York—and the restrictions she must now live within—as well as can be expected. I plan to visit her as soon as the physicians assure me she is stable and that my attendance will not upset her."

"I commend your dedication, Abercorn," Colin chimed in.

"And I very much appreciate your understanding and compassion for my sister's situation." Abercorn gave them both a curt bow and made his way back to his seat.

"Are you certain we did the right thing?" Colin asked as they both scrutinized the man when he regained his seat next to—of all people—Lucianna's mother. "Sometimes, I wonder."

"We must have faith that we did." They'd had the right to see Sissy locked away in the Tower—never to see the light of day again; however, Abercorn was a victim, too and if they'd allowed Sissy to be prosecuted, then Abercorn would have had no chance at a decent marriage or a family. "She will remain in York, unable to harm another person until her last day. Condemning Lord Abercorn to a future outrunning the scandal would only punish him."

"You, my love"—Colin placed a kiss to her forehead—"are a compassionate"—he lightly brushed his lips along her cheek—"understanding"—he lifted her chin when she blushed and tried to hide her embarrassment over his attention—"giving woman. Whom, I might add, I am proud to call my wife."

"I did what I thought was right." Even if Luci hadn't been completely satisfied or in agreement that Lady Sissy had received a punishment worthy of the crimes she committed. Ophelia knew, without a doubt, that Sissy would not have lasted long in the Tower or Bedlam. The harsh conditions prisoners lived under were trying, even on the hardiest of men.

Ophelia looked into Colin's green eyes, the depth of caring for her she saw there never waning, even after they'd been forced to explain to her parents where she'd gone during her absence from London. Even in his wedding day finery with his golden hair trimmed well above his collar, he was still the man who'd protected her from his own grandmother, not that Ophelia thought Molly would have harmed her if Colin hadn't arrived when he did.

"I love you," she sighed.

"And I, you, Ophelia," he declared loud enough for Montrose and Torrington to overhear and give an appreciative celebratory shout.

"Everyone seems to be enjoying themselves," she replied, bringing her sherry goblet to her lips to hide her insanely happy smile. "Do you think every day will be as perfect as this?"

"As long as we are together, not a thing can tarnish the perfection we've created for ourselves."

"Attention, attention!" The Earl of Coventry stood, calling for everyone's notice. When the crowd quieted, and all guests turned their full attention to Colin's father, the man held an envelope high for all to see. "It is with great pleasure that I share with my son—and his exquisite bride—a letter that arrived only yesterday from King George III."

Applause filled the room, nearly as loud as the moment she and Colin had been announced husband

and wife—Lord and Lady Hawke.

Coventry shushed the room before making a grand show of opening the letter. "As you all know, my father, Colin's grandpapa, served our king's father, King George II, as the royal courier between Sheerness, Kent, and Prussia."

Ophelia noticed Colin's chest puff up with pride as his father spoke of Porter Parnell, the first Earl of Coventry. Love swelled within her to see how far Colin's family had come to mending their ties to one another. It had only taken Colin's father admitting that he'd known the truth all along. Once that happened, it was as if the chains holding Colin down vanished.

The earl unfolded a single slip of paper and held it high for everyone to see the royal crest at the top of the page. "He sends his good tidings and blessed wishes for Lord and Lady Hawke's future." Colin's father quieted as he read farther down the paper, his brow rising in surprise as his breath hitched. "This cannot be," he muttered.

"What is it, Father?" Colin sat forward, waiting for the earl to finish reading.

Even Ophelia's own father stood, alarmed at what else a royal letter from the king could hold.

"Well, this is quite interesting."

"Don't be such a tease, Ramsey," Molly huffed, slamming the tip of her cane into the floor of Ophelia's parent's ballroom. Atholl cast a glare in the older woman's direction but had the good sense to hold his tongue. "Is Georgie think'n ta give me Colin a proper wed'n gift?"

"Ummm, no, it is more that the king wishes something *from* Colin and Ophelia," the earl mused.

"What is it, Coventry?" Atholl demanded, drawing back toward his seat. "What can the king want from my daughter?"

Ophelia's heart stopped for a brief moment, her stare moving from her father to Colin's sire.

The Earl of Coventry winked at her, a mischievous grin overtaking his face.

How had she not noticed the elder man's resemblance to Colin?

"As stated here, the king so decrees that Lord and Lady Hawke's first child born with hair the color of pure, red-hot fire is to be named George—after him. If the child is female, she will be called Georgina!"

The silence that had settled on the entire room as they waited in stunned shock to hear what their king demanded of the new couple broke as a shriek echoed through the space.

Molly shot to her feet, lifting her cane and thumping it on the long, wooden table before her. The crystal glasses, now drained of sherry, shook with her forceful strikes, and the other guests at the table—Lady Prudence and Lady Chastity—pushed their chairs back to avoid being caught in the woman's snare.

"That bloody, yellow-tailed, sniveling weasel!" Molly faced reddened deeper than Ophelia's auburn hair. "The contemptible, lick-spittle imp!"

"Mother!" Coventry shouted over Molly's tirade. "I am—"

"The man thinks ta have me great-grandbabe named for him?" she seethed. "Ye bet on everything I possess, no Parnell babe ever be named George—or Georgina!"

Ophelia burst out in laughter, doubling over as the sound filled the room, only to have other sounds of merriment join her own.

"What is so bloody amusing, Ophelia?" Molly demanded.

She sobered enough to notice her new grandmama's injured expression and rushed to soothe the woman's ruffled feelings. "It is only that I am surprised it is a *name* you find unsuitable and not the thought of being the great-grandmama of a red-haired babe."

Molly slumped into her seat with a chuckle of her own, folding her arms. "Don't be think'n the child be escape'n me search for evil marks."

"Evil marks?" Ophelia's father's glare flipped between Coventry, Molly, and Colin before settling on Ophelia, who laughed again—the other guests seeming to enjoy the banter between the newly joined families.

"Do take your seats." Colin stood, resting his hand lightly on Ophelia's shoulder. "Lady Hawke and I thank everyone for bearing witness to our joining on this day. However, I think it long past time my bride and I retire."

Ophelia stood quickly, smoothing the wrinkles from her light blue gown. "Before we go…" She didn't dare glance in Colin's direction. There was much she longed to say, though she'd planned to say nothing. "I have something to share."

All eyes were on her, and Ophelia took several deep breaths to calm her rising nerves. She'd never had the urge to put herself in a place of great attention; however, for the man next to her, she'd live every waking moment in the spotlight of the *ton* if that continued to make him happy and content.

"While many of you were not acquainted with my husband prior to our betrothal, I can attest to his kind heart and giving nature. He loves his family and friends—both new and old," she said, gesturing to everyone in the room. Edith nodded encouragingly when Ophelia fell silent. "I know he will cherish me and our family as much as he does others in his life." She risked a glance at Colin then, her mouth going dry, and her words sticking in her throat. She coughed, gaining a few precious moments to gain her composure. "I am so very thankful that similar to my two dearest friends, Lady Edith and Lady Lucianna, I have found my true path in life. I have been blessed far beyond what I deserve, and though many may consider our meeting a misadventure of sorts, I have come to realize it was far more than a mere adventure—or misadventure—but the first step toward the grandest accomplishment of my life…finding love."

"Hear! Hear!" the guests chanted in unison.

Ophelia made no attempt to hide her tears of joy as they slid unabated down her cheeks.

She was happy—and utterly in love with the man next to her.

She'd feared for so long that love was not something in her future, and even if it were, that there was the chance her life would mirror Tilda's tragic one.

But that was not the only course available to Ophelia and Colin.

No. They were free to love one another without fear or reservation.

Colin leaned down and pulled her body against his, capturing her lips in a searing kiss. One that conveyed the way he felt about her—and her words.

He released her mouth, the same mischievous smile lighting his face as had his father's only moments before. "Lady Hawke, I dare say you have a marvelous way with words. I can only wonder why you have not taken pencil to paper as yet. You would make a fine storyteller—or perhaps, a columnist for the *London Daily Gazette*."

Edith and Lucianna burst into laughter, mingled with the more reserved chuckles from their betrotheds.

Colin waited not a moment longer before bringing his lips to hers—masking her stunned expression.

The cheers that erupted reverberated off the walls and high ceiling, causing a nearly deafening commotion as Colin slipped his arm beneath Ophelia's knees and carried her from the room.

AUTHOR'S NOTES

Thank you for reading *The Undaunted Debutantes Series!*

If you enjoyed the series,
be sure to write a brief review at any retailer.

I'd love to hear from you!

You can contact me at:
Christina@christinamcknight.com

Or write me at:
P.O. Box 1017
Patterson, CA 95363

www.ChristinaMcKnight.com
Check out my website for giveaways, book reviews, and
information on my upcoming projects,
or connect with me through social media at:

Twitter: @CMcKnightWriter
Facebook: www.facebook.com/christinamcknightwriter
Goodreads: www.goodreads.com/ChristinaMcKnight

Sign up for my newsletter here:
http://eepurl.com/VP1rP

ABOUT THE AUTHOR

USA TODAY Bestselling Author Christina McKnight writes emotional and intricate Regency Romance with strong women and maverick heroes.

Her books combine romance and mystery, exploring themes of redemption and forgiveness. When she's not writing, Christina enjoys trying new coffeehouses, visiting wine bars, traveling the world, and watching television.

Email: Christina@ChristinaMcKnight.com
Follow her on Twitter: @CMcKnightWriter
Keep up to date on her releases:
www.christinamcknight.com
Like Christina's FB Author page:
ChristinaMcKnightWriter